DELIVERANCE

A DEFIANCE NOVEL

ALSO BY C. J. REDWINE

DEFIANCE

DECEPTION

DELIVERANCE

A DEFIANCE NOVEL

C. J. REDWINE

BALZER + BRAY

An Imprint of HarperCollins*Publishers*

Balzer + Bray is an imprint of HarperCollins Publishers.

Library of Congress Cataloging-in-Publication Data
Redwine, C. J.
Deliverance : a Defiance novel / C. J. Redwine. — First edition.
    pages cm
Sequel to: Deception.
Summary: "Rachel Adams has been kidnapped by enemy
forces and is being taken to Rowansmark while her love,
Logan McEntire, is imprisoned and awaiting trial, unable to
leave Lankenshire. As uneasy alliances are tested and their
enemies plot against them, will the two manage to find a way
to rid their world of the tyrannical Commander and destroy
the tech that controls the deadly Cursed One once and for
all?"— Provided by publisher.
    ISBN 978-0-06-211723-6 (hardback)
    ISBN 978-0-06-235950-6 (int.)
    [1. Fantasy. 2. Prisoners—Fiction. 3. Kidnapping—Fiction.
4. Survival—Fiction. 5. Love—Fiction.] I. Title.
PZ7.R2456Dl 2014   2014010011
[Fic]—dc23   CIP
                                                        AC

Typography by Alison Klapthor
14 15 16 17 18   LP/RRDH   10 9 8 7 6 5 4 3 2 1
❖
First Edition

For Hilmer Palmquist: sticky bun baker, tree swing maker, and the best grandpa in the world. I still miss you.

CHAPTER ONE

LOGAN

"Five minutes." The soldier guarding Lankenshire's dungeon raps sharply against the bars of the cell I've been in for the past three hours.

Three hours since the Commander showed up outside Lankenshire with an army and a demand that I be released to him by dawn or he'll attack the city. Three hours since the Rowansmark trackers inside Lankenshire demanded that I give them the device Willow hid in the Wasteland or they'll call the Cursed One—the *tanniyn*—to destroy Lankenshire. I'm assuming the gray metal boxes I saw mounted to buildings throughout the city while I was being marched from the gate to the dungeon—boxes that match the one Ian pointed out to me in the square—all contain a signal capable of summoning the beast. Maybe capable of summoning more than one beast, if Ian's claim about multiple *tanniyn* roaming the earth is correct.

Three hours since Ian took Rachel and disappeared.

"Five minutes until what?" Willow asks from the cell beside

mine. "Until you let us go? Why wait? Open our cells now, and we'll be gone before you can finish locking the doors behind us."

The soldier doesn't look amused. "Five minutes until I escort you to your trial, where the triumvirate will try to figure out a way to appease both the Rowansmark trackers you've managed to upset and the army waiting at our gates."

"It'll be fine." Willow sounds far more confident than I feel. "Logan has a plan. Right, Logan?" When I don't answer, Willow's voice sharpens. "*Right*, Logan?"

"Do you?" the soldier asks softly, his eyes locked on mine.

I open my mouth. Close it. Swallow against the lump of fear that wants to close the back of my throat and say, "I'm working on it."

"You're *working* on it?" The man steps closer to the iron bars that separate us. "You listen to me. This is my city. My *home*. I have family here, and I don't want to lose them because some refugee from Baalboden brought trouble down on our heads." He shoves his green cloak off his shoulders and points to the row of gold bars that line up neatly over his heart. "I'm a ranking officer in Lankenshire's army. I haven't pulled dungeon duty in years, but I'm here today because the triumvirate thinks you merit special treatment. They think you've got a way out of this impossible situation. So don't tell me you're working on it. Figure it out before all of us die. You have five minutes."

He turns on his heel and stalks toward the entrance of the dungeon, his boots slapping against the stone floor as he goes.

"That was dramatic," Willow says as she leans against the bars of her cell and looks at me.

"That was accurate." I close my eyes against the terrible image of Rachel, badly injured, traveling to Rowansmark at the mercy of my murderous brother Ian while I sit in a dungeon, faced with the impossible task of appeasing both the Commander and the trackers, unable to save her. "Every worst case scenario running through my head has come true."

"Oh, please," Willow says. "Knowing the way your brain works, I'm sure there are at least five scenarios worse than this one that you've spent useless hours worrying over. Besides, this isn't *that* bad."

"Not that bad? Willow, the Commander is sitting outside the gate with the Carrington army and what's left of Baalboden's guards and he's promised to attack the city at dawn if I don't give him the device by then. He's a man who keeps his word. And the trackers are going to call the *tanniyn* to destroy Lankenshire the same way Baalboden was destroyed if I don't give the device to *them* instead. But I can't give the tech to either of them, because if I do, I have nothing to use for ransom when I arrive in Rowansmark to barter for Rachel's life." I rub my eyes and try to think my way around the impossibility of it all.

There has to be a way out of this. Too many lives depend on it.

Willow's voice is steady. "If you give the tech to the trackers, it's the same as giving it to Rowansmark itself. That should satisfy the ransom for Rachel. Then we just have to deal with the old man and his stupid army."

I'm already shaking my head. "The second I give up the device, I've lost my leverage over both the Commander and Rowansmark. Plus, I doubt Ian's pain atonement vendetta against me will be satisfied by hearing that the device made its way back to

Rowansmark. He wants to hurt *me*, and what better way to hurt me than to hurt Rachel?"

My throat closes over her name, and I can't push away the fear that pounds through me, taunting me with images of Rachel hurt. Bleeding.

Dead.

"So the trackers, the Commander, and rescuing Rachel—those are all of your worst case scenarios?" Willow asks. "Because you forgot to mention that my brother, the bastion of self-sacrifice, went missing too. Presumably to track down Rachel, since no one would be crazy enough to kidnap Quinn. Of course, Ian is a lunatic who wouldn't recognize sanity if it slapped him in the face, so there's that."

"Thank you for summing that up. I feel so much better about the whole situation now."

"I thought we were just listing our problems. Nobody told me I was supposed to provide sympathy." Willow sounds irritated.

The fear pulsing through me makes it impossible to stand still, so I start pacing the small confines of my cell. "I don't need sympathy. I need a plan. My people are trapped. The clock is ticking. And I'm stuck inside a Lankenshire prison cell without a weapon or a shred of tech within reach."

I'm also stuck in an endless loop of thoughts that have nothing to do with my present circumstances and everything to do with the secrets I recently uncovered about my past. I was born in Rowansmark. Fine, I can adjust to that. I was kidnapped by the Commander as a newborn and kept in Baalboden to coerce my father into turning over his invention for calling and controlling the *tanniyn* once he completed it. I can adjust to that, too.

But knowing that the woman who called herself my mother was lying to me, knowing that Rachel's father, Jared, brought regular reports about me to my father in Rowansmark and never respected me enough to tell me the truth, and wondering if Oliver, the closest thing I ever had to a father in Baalboden, knew my secrets all along and only looked after me to protect the Commander's investment—I can't adjust to that. I can barely stand to look it in the eye.

The foundation on which I built my life is lying in pieces around me, but I can't stop to put it back together. I have a prison break to engineer, an innocent city to protect, a murderer to track down, and two power-hungry leaders who need to be stopped. Personal reflection will have to wait.

"I wouldn't say that we don't have any weapons," Willow says.

I jerk to a stop and whip my head toward Willow's cell. By leaning against my cell door, I can just see her. She's crouched against the front corner of her cell, her back pressing against the iron bars that lock her in. With deft movements, she unties the leather strap that binds her long, dark braid and slowly pulls it free. My eyes widen. A length of thin silver wire is attached to the end of the strap and is woven into her braid. She holds her braid secure and tugs until nearly half a yard of wire slides out of her hair and lies in her lap.

"Brilliant," I breathe.

"Agreed." Willow coils the wire around her left wrist and secures the loose end against the leather tie. It looks like she's wearing a simple silver bracelet, but I have no trouble imagining the kind of havoc Willow can wreak with that length of wire.

Picking locks.

Jabbing eyes.

Slitting throats.

"Have I told you recently that I'm grateful you and Quinn decided to stay with our group instead of trying to find another Tree Village to join? I don't know what I'd do without you."

Willow flashes me a smug little smile, and I make myself smile back, but inside, my desperation is growing. One weapon alone won't help us fix this. I need tech, supplies, people . . . a *plan*.

And I don't have a single workable idea.

The soldier picks up two lengths of chain and strides down the corridor toward our cells. Our five minutes are up.

"If you're going to make a plan, you'd better think fast," Willow says as the soldier stops before my cell, a heavy iron key in his hand.

"I'm *trying*."

I run through my options as the man opens my door, wraps chains around my wrists, and then puts a matching set on Willow while she gives him a look that would drop a lesser man to his knees. He doesn't give the silver "bracelet" on her wrist a second glance.

Best Case Scenario: I think of a way out of this before we reach the courtroom, and no one dies.

Worst Case Scenario: Everything else.

My stomach cramps as Willow and I, flanked by another pair of Lankenshire soldiers, follow the man through the long stone hallways that lead from the dungeon to the courtroom.

Short of cutting myself and the device in half and giving a piece to both Rowansmark and the Commander, I can't think of a single way to keep this city and the Baalboden survivors who followed me across the Wasteland—survivors who are family to me now—safe.

"What's the plan?" Willow whispers as we turn a corner and begin climbing a set of steep steps carved into the stone. The torches that bracket the stairway are lit, their golden light gleaming against her dark hair as she looks at me.

"Um . . ."

"You don't have one, do you?"

I shake my head and force myself to think smarter. Faster. Rowansmark needs to believe that Lankenshire is turning me over to them, or they'll use the beacons. The Commander needs to believe that I'll be in his custody by dawn, or he'll attack the city.

And I need to be out in the Wasteland, free of them both, so that I can track down Rachel and Quinn.

"Do you have a plan yet?" Willow asks as we leave the stairs behind and enter a spacious corridor with white marble floors that sparkle beneath bronze gas lamps. A bank of wide windows to the right lets in the brilliant light of the setting sun.

Rachel has been missing for three hours now. Three hours is a decent head start in the Wasteland, but I know I can catch up.

I *will* catch up.

"Logan!" Willow shakes her bound hands in front of my face, the iron chain links slapping together harshly. When I meet her eyes, she leans close and says through gritted teeth, "We're about to walk into that courtroom. What. Is. The. Plan?"

Panic shoots through my stomach and somehow lands in my chest, where it feels like a vise is slowly crushing me.

I don't have a plan. I don't have a single viable scenario. All I have is desperation and the terrible fear that I'm about to fail everyone I love.

The soldier leading us stops abruptly and motions to a narrow door situated between two bronze gas lamps. "You two wait in here until it's time for the trial to start." His eyes meet mine, and he lowers his voice. "And I certainly hope that in the time since you told me you were 'working on it,' you've come up with something, because in about two minutes, you're going to need to explain it to the one person who can make it happen."

Without another word, he motions us inside the cramped little box of a room, leaves the pair of Lankenshire soldiers to stand guard outside the door, and locks us in.

"The one person who can make it happen . . . we must be meeting with Clarissa before the trial starts," I say.

Clarissa Vaughn—leader of Lankenshire's triumvirate and quite possibly the most formidable woman I've ever met. Enduring the soldier's frustration at my lack of a plan will be nothing compared to facing her.

Willow paces the room, scanning the plain white walls and the knotted pine ceiling like she thinks she can find a secret exit that will dump us straight into the Wasteland. I'm scanning the walls too, for all the good it will do me. We need a plan. A real one. And I've got no ideas and no more time to figure it out.

As if she can read my mind, Willow asks, "Still got nothing?"

I meet her eyes for a second, letting her see the sheer desperation churning through me, and then turn to the door. I have to tell Clarissa something. Maybe if I look at this from a different angle. If I examine ways we can neutralize the beacons to take the teeth out of the trackers' threats. If I talk to Coleman Pritchard, head of Lankenshire's security, about methods to defend the city against the Commander . . .

Who am I kidding? I know nothing about defending a city against an army, and I can't tell Clarissa how to neutralize the Rowansmark beacons without seeing one for myself, and even then . . . what if I can't figure it out? What if—

"Hey!" Willow smacks my shoulder lightly. "Stop disappearing into your head and listen. I know what to do."

I blink and stare at her. "You do?"

"Don't act so surprised. I just figured the fastest way to get out of here and into the Wasteland is to remove the obstacles in our way. We'll start with the trackers and then move on to the army—"

"You want to take out an entire contingent of Rowansmark trackers—"

"I don't see why not."

"—and then go after an *army*—"

"Don't be an idiot. Not the *whole* army. Just the leader. Cut off the head and the rest of the body just sort of flops around uselessly."

"You want the two of us, who are currently weaponless . . ." I pause as she wriggles her wrist at me. The silver wire she took from her braid shimmers. "Fine, you want the two of us who are *mostly* weaponless, and who are chained up like criminals, to take out a group of Rowansmark trackers. What are we supposed to use against them? We need a bigger weapon than chains and attitude."

"That's a very negative way to look at this."

A bigger weapon than chains and attitude.

I stare at Willow, but I don't see her. I finally see possibilities. Scenarios.

Plans.

The pain in my stomach eases.

"We can't kill all of the Rowansmark trackers," I say.

"Speak for yourself." She glares at me.

"We need to leave a few alive to testify that Lankenshire had nothing to do with our escape in case other trackers come to the city," I say slowly as a risk-filled plan for how we can break out of prison without endangering either Lankenshire or the Baal-boden survivors takes shape inside my head.

"And how are we going to escape?"

"I have a plan." I can't believe what I'm about to suggest. "It's stupid and bold and could fail in a hundred ways before we even get fifteen yards."

She grins. "You cover stupid. I'll take care of bold. Now, what's the plan?"

"We're going to get the Commander to break us out of prison."

CHAPTER TWO

LOGAN

The air inside the little room grows stale while I pace the floor, talking through the details of the riskiest plan I've ever conceived and waiting for Clarissa Vaughn to tell me I'm crazy and that I've just cost her people their lives.

When I've finished, I meet Clarissa's gaze. Her expression tells me nothing. Beside her stands a girl who looks like a younger version of her—right down to the proud tilt of her chin and the air of power wrapping around her like she was born to it. Clarissa introduced her as Cassidy when they arrived. Cassidy's shoulders are ramrod straight beneath her white tunic and dark-green cloak. A black scarf is pinned to the right shoulder of her cloak by a gold medallion with a scale etched onto its surface. Books lie on one side of the scale. A dragon's head lies on the other. The books weigh more.

She's a courier for Lankenshire. An official emissary charged with handling state business with other city-states. For a moment, I imagine that if Rachel had been born in Lankenshire instead of Baalboden, she might've been an emissary for a city-state that valued her brains and her skill without worrying about her gender. Or she might be in the army. Or, eventually, in the triumvirate.

A small part of me wishes that had been her path. The rest of me holds fast to the girl with the fiery hair who defended me when schoolboys caught me scrounging for food in a trash heap, who challenged my ideas and my sparring skills, and who kissed me like I was the air she desperately needed to breathe.

Clarissa and Cassidy are still watching me in silence, and I clear my throat.

"That's it," I say. "That's the plan."

"Let me get this straight," Clarissa says. "You want me to send an emissary to the army outside my gates, tell the Commander that you will give him the device in exchange for freeing you from our dungeon, and then have that emissary lead him to the dungeon through the underground tunnels at midnight to break you out of prison."

"Yes." I try to sound like the prospect doesn't fill me with dread.

"In the meantime, you're going to plead guilty at your trial, and you expect me to hand you over to the Rowansmark trackers while somehow still keeping you in our custody until the Commander can come for you." Clarissa's eyes narrow as she studies me.

I resist the urge to break eye contact with her and say, "Yes, let the trackers have control of the dungeon, but keep them from leaving until dawn by telling them you have to sort out last-minute details like . . . I don't know . . . having me sign a confession to send to the Commander so that he knows to take up his cause against me with James Rowan? Think of something so that when the Commander comes for me—and he will—the Rowansmark trackers won't suspect that you were involved."

"It's not a bad plan," Willow says as she leans against the wall closest to the door.

"It's a terrible plan," Cassidy says, her dark eyes flashing. "We're deceiving the people who can press a button and call the *tanniyn* to destroy us while simultaneously allowing the army who is threatening our city to access our secret tunnel system. What part of that sounds like a good idea to you?"

"The part where you realize it's the only plan you've got," Willow shoots back, somehow managing to look menacing despite the chains that bind her wrists.

"This afternoon, before the trackers attacked you and the army surrounded my city, you told me you could build a replica of Rowansmark's tech in exchange for me offering asylum to your people." Clarissa's voice cuts through the room like a knife, silencing both Cassidy and Willow.

I hold her gaze. "I did. But I won't have time now."

"You'll have until midnight," she says.

"It's not just time. I need supplies. Sixteen-gauge braided copper wire, several high-voltage batteries, thin sheets of silver, and a transmitter capable of sending a signal for at least five hundred yards. And I'd need to be able to work without having trackers looking over my shoulder, which will be difficult given the fact that after the trial, I'll be in their custody." I meet Clarissa's gaze. "I'm sorry. I meant to keep my word. The best I can do now is deflect Rowansmark's suspicion so that they have no reason to call the *tanniyn*."

"I'm not interested in apologies." She waves her hand through the air, a gesture at once regal and commanding. "I'm interested in results. Your plan might work, but it's hardly a guarantee of safety for my people or yours."

"I realize that. I don't know how to—"

"Cassidy, the beacon, please." Seeing my raised brows, Clarissa says, "I had one removed from one of the western outposts since the trackers are distracted by your presence in the dungeon and by the Commander outside the gate. It isn't likely to be missed, but I want to put it back in place as quickly as possible."

Cassidy pulls a dark-gray metallic box from the inside of her cloak and hands it to Clarissa. The beacon is about two hand-spans wide and as thick as the sole of my boot. When Clarissa pops the back off, revealing the powerful tech inside, I run my fingers over the intricate silver mechanisms and then examine a transmitter that's twice as powerful as the one inside the device Willow hid in the Wasteland. I'm surprised—and impressed— at the difference between the two. This piece of tech makes the device look like a harmless toy. I have to wonder why Rowansmark is expending so much effort to recover something so inferior to the tech they now possess.

Maybe it really is a matter of restoring honor, as Ian claimed.

Or maybe James Rowan knows the only way he can gain control over the rest of the city-states is by keeping them from copying and then improving on his tech. That would also explain why my father's pain atonement sentence alone wasn't enough to rectify the crime of letting tech like this out of Rowansmark hands. I'm guessing from James Rowan's perspective, Ian's mission has nothing to do with honor and everything to do with removing a threat to Rowansmark's plan to subjugate the rest of the city-states.

"Can you use any of these parts to make something we can use to protect ourselves?" Clarissa asks.

The transmitter may be more powerful, but unlike the device's ability to send the creature in any direction, this one has only two frequencies. One to call the beast and one to keep it away. I smile grimly as I realize what this means. I can keep my promise. I can keep Lankenshire safe.

"I can do better than that." I tap the transmitter. "This has two active components. One component generates an ultrasonic sound wave, and the other produces an infrasonic wave. The infrasonic—the sound set low enough to cause the ground to rumble if there's enough power behind the transmitter—calls the *tanniyn*. If you disable the infrasonic in each of these beacons, the trackers won't be able to destroy your city unless one of them has the tech skills it takes to rebuild a transmitter and set it to an exact frequency."

"And if one of them does know how to fix it?" Clarissa asks.

I reach inside the beacon and gently disengage the transmitter from its position. "I assume you or one of the other members of the triumvirate has a necklace set to a sonic frequency that repels the beasts, right?"

From beneath her tunic Clarissa pulls a flat disk hanging on a thin silver chain.

"Good. Attach it to the transmitter like this." I show her how to splice the transmitter's wire on to one inside the tech she wears. "Now it will amplify your ultrasonic emission—the sonic frequency that repels the *tanniyn*—by at least three hundred percent."

She tucks the necklace and the transmitter away, and says, "Do we need to remove the transmitters from every beacon to disable them?"

I shake my head and show them how to disable the infrasonic component inside the tech.

Clarissa taps three times on the door and then studies me while Cassidy hides the now-useless beacon inside her cloak again. "You upheld your end of our bargain. I'll do the same. I will send an emissary to the Commander with the terms of your deal. And your people will be offered asylum within our city as long as they agree to be governed by our laws."

"Drake is leader in my place." Something tight wraps itself around my chest as I realize I'm leaving the rest of the survivors behind, and I might not be coming back. I can't guarantee that I'll survive my encounter with the Commander, much less my attempts to rescue Rachel and bring down Rowansmark.

One of the soldiers guarding the room's entrance taps once before opening the door. "All clear, ma'am."

Clarissa nods but makes no move to leave the room. Instead, she continues to watch me. "What will you do?" she asks. "Once you give the device to the Commander—provided you survive that encounter—what will you do next?"

I meet her gaze. "I'm going to Rowansmark."

The tiny creases around her eyes deepen. "If voluntarily giving yourself over to the Commander isn't suicide, heading to Rowansmark certainly is. Why not just go to the other city-states and show them how to disable the beacons?"

"Because Ian—the tracker who was disguised as one of us—took my . . ." The words to describe what Rachel is to me won't come. "He took Rachel. And he's going to kill her if I don't show up at Rowansmark with the device to ransom her back."

"The device you're supposed to give to the Commander?" Clarissa frowns. "I don't want him to blame me for a double cross, Logan."

"He'll be dead before he has a chance to blame anyone for anything," Willow says as the soldier in the hall pokes his head in again.

"Ma'am, the proceedings are ready to start. Hallway remains clear of trackers."

"Thank you, Paul." Clarissa leans closer to me. "I hope your plan for ransoming Rachel is stronger than your plan for getting out of Lankenshire, because you're going to need a miracle to survive Rowansmark."

"I understand that it's a trap, but—"

"Yes, a *death trap*," Cassidy says, holding her cloak close. "Clearly you haven't heard the news that Schoensville and Thorenburg, formerly allies of the Commander, have committed their entire armies to the defense of Rowansmark in anticipation of the Commander and Carrington marching south. The word is that it was either protect Rowansmark or have their cities burned to the ground just like Baalboden and Carrington."

"Carrington is gone?" My mouth is dry, my heart racing. How can I possibly ransom Rachel and destroy the tech inside Rowansmark when I'll have not one but three armies waiting for me there?

"It is," Clarissa says, her voice crisp, though her eyes are shadowed.

"You can't show up at Rowansmark with just the two of you and expect to win." Cassidy moves toward the door.

"I count for at least ten," Willow says.

Cassidy rolls her eyes. "Maybe you do, but still. Ten against three armies? You don't have a chance."

She's right. I close my eyes and play through the scenarios. Any way I look at it, there are no clear-cut paths. No easy solutions. I promised to find Rachel. I also promised to destroy both the Commander and Ian for the pain they've caused so many people. And I can't imagine finding any peace until the threat of Rowansmark's tech has been put to rest. Since Ian, Rachel, and the tech will be in the same location, I can't keep one promise without finding a way to deliver on the others.

But how can I reach Rachel, kill Ian, and obliterate Rowansmark's threat all by myself? Especially when Rowansmark is already expecting me? Even if Willow counts for ten, the odds are nearly insurmountable.

"Logan?" Clarissa's voice compels me to open my eyes, but I don't see her. I see the army outside the gates. The city-states up north who don't realize that they can alter the transmitters in their beacons and break the yoke of Rowansmark's tyranny. The leaders who might recognize the need to sacrifice now for the sake of lasting peace later.

Leaders who might not listen to me, but who *would* listen to the one man who has always held more sway over the other leaders than anyone else: the Commander.

As long as I can convince him that it's in our best interests to work together.

My hand shakes as I raise my fingers to touch the scarred brand on the side of my neck—a brand the Commander burned into my flesh while I was in his dungeon. I can't think of the man without seeing my mother dying on the streets of Baalboden, flogged for daring to leave her home without a Protector. Oliver bleeding to death in a wagon, killed by his leader's sword for the crime of being important to Rachel. Jared committing treason because he could find no other way to protect others against the monster who ruled his city.

The thought of being allied, even temporarily, with the Commander makes me sick. I want to hurt him. I want to light him on fire and watch him burn, but I can't. Not if I want to keep my promise to stop Rowansmark, deliver justice to Ian, and protect Rachel. An alliance with the enemy of my enemies might feel like walking barefoot over shattered glass, but it's the only logical course of action. Emotion isn't going to help me reach my agenda. I can swallow the rage and the bitterness long enough to keep my promises.

The very second those promises are kept, the Commander is dead.

"Mom, we need to leave. The trial starts soon," Cassidy says.

"Wait." I reach my manacled hands toward Clarissa before she can turn to follow her daughter into the hall. "I have to go to Rowansmark. I refuse to leave Rachel behind. And we both know that the tech Rowansmark is using to leverage control over the other city-states has to be destroyed. I can't do that on my own, and I won't have to."

Clarissa raises a brow. "Who is going to help you?"

"The Commander."

Willow makes a strangled noise in the back of her throat, and I hurry on. "He already has the combined might of Carrington's army plus what's left of Baalboden's guards behind him. He understands military strategy—better than that, he understands James Rowan. And if there is anyone who wants Rowansmark stopped more than I do, it's Commander Jason Chase."

"So now you're going to try to create an alliance with him?" Clarissa asks. I can't tell what she's thinking.

"I have to."

"What bargaining power will you bring to the table?" she asks.

I straighten my shoulders. "Troops from the other northern city-states. I'll visit them—"

"Logan!" Willow sounds angrier than I've ever heard her.

"Willow, what choice do we have? We can't take down three armies on our own. We need help. I can show the city-states how to destroy the beacons in exchange for a commitment of troops to march south under the Commander." I look at Clarissa, and I see she understands what I haven't yet asked.

"And you want to start with troops from Lankenshire?"

"Yes."

The silence that stretches between us is filled with tension so thick it seems like I could reach out and touch it. Finally, she says, "I will send an emissary with you to the closest northern city-state. To Hodenswald. If you can convince Lyle Hoden to give you troops, I will convince the other members of the triumvirate to give you one-fourth of our army."

"One-fourth!" Willow's laugh is scornful.

Clarissa's expression feels like a stone settling across my shoulders. "Understand this. If we commit troops to you, Rowansmark will know it. If the trackers within our city don't realize it, the ones guarding Rowansmark will surely recognize the uniforms, the fighting style, and the weaponry. If you fail, my city is next in line for destruction."

She steps closer, and I catch a whiff of perfume, crisp and powerful just like the woman who wears it. "Don't fail us, Logan."

"I won't," I say. Another promise to add to the list I'm already struggling to keep. Another responsibility to keep me up at night chasing worst case scenarios.

Clarissa turns on her heel and leaves the room, and I look away from Willow as I think through what I can possibly say to the Commander that will convince him he wants me as an ally instead of as a corpse.

CHAPTER THREE

RACHEL

I'm dreaming again. I know I am, but I can't make it stop. The landscape billows around me like a sheet caught in the wind: streaks of green, smudges of brown, and a river of red that seems to follow my feet as I run. A yellow house wavers in the distance, its familiar rooftop beckoning me home where Dad is waiting. Where Oliver is baking. Where Logan is sitting at the table, pretending not to stare at me while he eats.

I run past the streaks of green, the smudges of brown, with the bright-red river nipping at my heels. I run, but the yellow house remains just out of reach, like the sun hovering against the corner of the sky. Close enough to feel the warmth. Close enough that if I squint, I think I can touch it. But always too far away, no matter how fast I run.

A voice cuts through the river.

"Rachel."

I run faster, my bare feet slapping against the ground, but the house is too far away. I strain to see Dad on the porch, waiting for me, but the porch is empty. The chimney is cold.

"Rachel, wake up."

The river snaps at my heels, and a bright streak of pain shoots through me.

I run and run, my breath sobbing in my chest, tiny daggers piercing my lungs. The house shimmers and grows pale, the color slowly draining from it until I can see through the walls into the rooms inside.

Dad isn't there. Neither are Logan and Oliver. The emptiness presses against the walls like a living thing, and I fall to my knees as cracks spread across the plaster, raining ash.

"Get out of that wagon now, or you don't eat."

White-hot agony tears through me, dissolving the house and jerking me awake. My right arm lies beneath me, the blackened burn that stretches along my forearm rubbing against the rough wagon bed and sending spikes of pain from my fingertips to my jaw. I crane my neck to see one of the Rowansmark trackers who kidnapped me—a tall man with graying black hair, dark skin, and a thin frame—leaning against the wagon's entrance.

Gritting my teeth against the pain, I carefully sit up. I've been traveling inside this wagon ever since Ian and his tracker friends forced me to leave Quinn behind in a clearing outside Lankenshire earlier today. A thread of weary triumph snakes through me as I remember Quinn's eyes closed as if he was dead while his heart beat strong beneath the lightweight armored vest he was wearing under his tunic.

Ian stands a few yards away, watching me as I slowly climb out of the wagon. His dark-blue eyes sharpen as he notices the way I cradle my injured arm to my chest. I remember that he promised me a lesson in pain on this journey and lift my chin to meet his gaze head-on. If he's waiting for me to break, he's going to be disappointed.

I broke when the Commander killed Oliver in front of me. Lost myself when I found my father's grave in the Wasteland. Slipped into a silence that cut me off from the grief and misery I couldn't stand to face after I killed Melkin. And shattered completely when my best friend, Sylph, died of the poison Ian injected in her bloodstream as part of his pain atonement vendetta against Logan.

It wasn't until Quinn found me trying to feel something— *anything*—by ripping apart the wound in my arm that I understood what it would take to heal. Quinn told me that healing takes the courage to face the things that hurt me. I still have a lot of grief inside of me, but I'm no longer the mess Ian seems to think he can destroy so easily.

I'm a survivor. If Ian thinks the burn on my arm—something *he* caused when he lit white phosphorous fires around our campsite outside Lankenshire—is going to break me, he's as stupid as he is crazy.

Turning away from Ian, I take a second to get my bearings as shadows swim in front of my eyes. I can't afford to pass out from pain and exhaustion. It's one thing to sleep on my own inside the wagon. It's another to be unconscious while the trackers might search me and find that I have a knife hidden in my boot. A knife Quinn risked his life to give me.

"We're stopping for the night," Ian says. "Make yourself useful, or you don't eat."

"Going to be kind of hard keeping me alive all the way to

Rowansmark if you don't feed me," I say. The tracker who awakened me pulls me away from the wagon before Ian can reply.

"Best not to antagonize," the tracker says in a soft, controlled voice that reminds me a little of Quinn. I look into his dark eyes and find no malice. No murderous rage. Just steady confidence that he can face anything and survive to tell the story.

"I'm not very good at not antagonizing people."

"Learn." He helps me step over a fallen log, and though I want to shake off his hand on principle, I don't. It's been less than twenty-four hours since I woke up in Lankenshire from a three-day coma thanks to Ian's nasty white phosphorous firebombs. My chest burns when I breathe. My arm aches in sharp throbs. And my head feels only distantly connected to my body. Without the tracker's support, there's a very good chance I'll fall on my face and be unable to get back up.

I cradle my injured arm against my stomach and scan my surroundings. A faint road carves a path through slender tree trunks and clumps of ferns. Moss clings to the base of the trees, and glossy green leaves block out most of the sky. The light that filters through looks more orange than gold.

Sunset.

The crumbled gray rock and beaten-down grass that make up the road slice through the forest east to west, and the wagon is facing the fiery orange light bathing the canopy above us.

We're heading west.

I frown as the tracker nudges a slender stick my way and says, "We're gathering firewood."

Rowansmark is south. Why are we moving west? Even knowing that Ian obviously needs a way to move a wagon through the

Wasteland, it makes no sense. There are roads that lead north to south. Surely in the few hours that I spent dozing in the back of the wagon he could've found one.

I bend to pick up the stick, and my head spins as my pulse pounds painfully against my skull. I need sleep, but I'm not going to get it. Not when Ian wants to use me as his personal punching bag in place of Logan.

And not when I have my own secrets to protect.

The knife hidden inside my boot presses against my leg as I lean forward to grab another stick. The tracker squats beside me and scoops up a few thick branches that lie beneath the trees.

"Why are we heading west?" I ask quietly.

He casts an appraising glance at me. "How did you know that?"

"The sun is setting in the same direction we've been traveling." Does he think I'm an idiot? Anyone could figure that out. "Rowansmark is south. Why are we going west?"

"Oh, we'll go south soon enough," the tracker says as he places another handful of twigs in my arms, careful to avoid my wound.

I try to stand, and the forest lurches sideways. Gasping, I reach for something solid to lean on and find the tracker already there, his hand cupping my elbow as he holds me steady.

"You should just sit and tend the fire," he says. "And keep quiet. You're in no shape to take more punishment tonight."

I blink away the brilliant lights that dart at the edge of my vision, and take a deep breath. "Thank you."

Three months ago, I could never have dreamed of a situation where I would not only willingly lean against a Rowansmark tracker as he helped me navigate the forest floor, but thank him for his trouble.

Of course, three months ago my family was still alive, my city was intact, and I was still confident that my first impression of anyone was absolutely right. Now I know that sometimes, for better or for worse, people aren't who they seem to be. Sometimes the thing you think will fix everything ruins it instead. And sometimes what hurts you has to tear you apart before it makes you stronger.

I've also learned that a little deception goes a long way toward lulling your enemies into a false sense of security. Ian taught me that lesson, and I don't plan to forget it.

I let my shoulders slump and make sure to stumble twice as the tracker helps me back toward the wagon.

"I'm not sure I'm up to eating." I make my voice as small as I possibly can.

"You'll never heal if you don't eat," he says. There isn't an ounce of concern in his voice, but I don't care. He's talking to me. Trying to take care of me. That counts for something.

I need the pair of trackers who are with Ian to believe I'm not a threat. It's the only chance I have of catching them off guard.

"I'm Rachel," I say as we reach the wagon. The other tracker, a short, muscular woman with bright red cheeks, is already skinning a brace of small game. Ian is nowhere in sight.

Beside me, the tracker's cool expression doesn't change. "I'm Samuel." He eases me down onto a half-rotten tree stump at the side of the road. "And we aren't friends, little girl. Remember that."

Samuel moves away to build a fire, and I make sure to look

frail and nonthreatening in case he looks my way again. He's old enough to be my father. I swallow the stab of hurt that thought brings and focus on the goal—appearing weak enough to make the trackers overlook me.

The second they give me an opportunity, I'm going to make Ian wish he'd never set eyes on me or the citizens of Baalboden.

CHAPTER FOUR

RACHEL

It's dark inside the wagon where Ian told me I had to spend the night. I huddle on the floor, my back against the bench, and shiver though it isn't cold. Now that I'm not falling down with exhaustion like I was earlier, I find it impossible to sit inside the wagon without being flooded with memories that cut into me like daggers.

The rough, splintery floor reminds me of lying beside Sylph, clutching her hand and whispering that I loved her as her life slowly drained away. Of watching Oliver's blood pour from his throat while I tried to stop it even though I already knew it was too late. The canvas above me is a prison door locking me inside with memories I can't stand to face.

My throat feels like I've swallowed a rock, and I pull sharply at the neckline of my tunic. I can't get enough air. My fingers tremble, and there's a faint ringing in my ears as I force myself to breathe slowly. In through my nose. Out through my mouth. Just the way Dad taught me when I needed to force my body past paralyzing fear and into a fight.

It isn't working.

My heart races, a thick jerky rhythm that pounds against my chest. Somehow I'm convinced that I can smell blood—a metallic sweetness that fills my mind and sinks into my tongue until I gag with the effort to keep from swallowing it.

I can't stay inside this wagon for another minute.

Telling myself that I'm not running away from something I know I need to face, I get to my knees and move toward the exit, pausing every few seconds to listen for Ian and his tracker friends. If I'm outside, I can observe my captors and maybe learn something useful. I can look for weaknesses that I can use to my advantage.

I can breathe.

And I can be on the lookout for Quinn.

I don't know how fast he can track us. Between the smoke inhalation he suffered while rescuing me from the fire and the head injury he got fighting Ian in Lankenshire, he's in bad shape. Still, I know he's coming for me. He didn't follow Ian out of Lankenshire just to pretend to die so that he could give me a knife. He followed me because he's committed to protecting me. So is Logan. Probably Willow as well. There's no way she wouldn't follow her brother. I just hope she doesn't blame me for the fact that, once again, Quinn is in harm's way because he chose to help me. I begged him to leave. To save himself. He refused.

Even Willow can't blame me for Quinn's stubbornness.

The knife Quinn gave me is a thin piece of comfort against my ankle as I crawl the rest of the distance to the wagon's entrance. Quinn has sacrificed himself on my behalf time and again. Part of me feels humiliated—I was trained better than to lose my head in a battle. The rest of me is grateful that Quinn's protection bought me enough time to start climbing out of the pit of misery, guilt, and fear I've been living in. I don't intend to let his sacrifices go to waste.

Slowly, I slide the canvas flap away from the wagon's entrance and peer out. The stars are woven through the sky in a tapestry of silver that bathes our campsite in cold, clear light. Samuel, the tracker who helped me gather firewood, is seated on a log at least twenty yards from the ashes of the campfire, his back to the wagon. He sits straight and still, his hand resting comfortably on the hilt of his sword as he keeps the first watch.

The other tracker, Heidi, lies asleep beside the fire's ashes, wrapped in her bedroll. Her sword rests beside her, where she can grab it the second she awakens. I give the idea of stealing her sword about two seconds of consideration before admitting that trying to sneak up on a sleeping tracker to take a sword that looks too heavy for me is suicide. Especially when Samuel is alert, and Ian might be awake as well.

Besides, I need to look fragile and weak if I want to trick them into overlooking me.

Quietly, I lean out of the wagon, holding on with my left hand while I press my injured right arm against my stomach. Turning my body to the side, I feel for the wagon step with my right leg.

"Going somewhere?" Ian asks behind me.

Startled, I lose my grip on the wagon, my foot grazing the edge of the wagon step as I tumble backward. Strong arms wrap around me and jerk me to my feet before I can hit the ground.

"Do you really think I'm stupid enough to let you just walk out of the wagon and into the Wasteland?" Ian sounds irritated. His arms tighten until my ribs ache.

"Let go of me." I drive my left elbow into his stomach before I remember that I'm supposed to be acting weak and nonthreatening.

It would be a lot easier to be nonthreatening if the boy who killed Sylph and burned down my city wasn't holding on to me as if he'd like to break me in half.

"You think you're stronger than me? Think your precious daddy taught you every technique you need to survive an encounter with a Rowansmark tracker?" Ian's laugh is ugly.

"You think your precious leader taught you everything you need to know to survive *me*?" I speak quietly, aware that Samuel is sitting a mere twenty yards away. Twisting and squirming in Ian's arms, I pretend I'm trying to break free. The second he adjusts his grip, I slam my head backward and hear a satisfying crunch as my skull connects with his face. Pain spreads along the base of my skull in sharp throbs. I hope the pain in his face is fifty times worse.

Ian swears viciously.

"Ian?" Samuel calls from his perch on the log. "Everything okay?"

I swallow the words I want to say and let the harsh rasp of my smoke-scarred lungs as they struggle for air speak for me. Ian will never believe I'm too injured to fight, but Samuel might.

Something dark and wet drips off of Ian's cheek and lands on my hand. I shudder and wipe my skin against my cloak before his blood can linger.

"Ian?" Samuel sounds like he's coming closer.

Ian shakes me, his fingers biting into my arms. Dizziness joins the pain in my head, and I bite down on the urge to slam my boot into his instep. Not when Samuel is near enough to see us clearly. Instead, I let out a little whimper. When no one reacts, I whimper a little louder and add a breathy sob to the end of it. It isn't hard. My body hurts in ways I never imagined possible.

"Stop that." Ian shakes me again. I go limp, letting my legs give out as if I'm about to faint. Ian drops me onto the forest floor. My knees hit first, and I roll to the left so that my good arm takes the brunt of the fall. Ian shoves me with his boot. "What are you doing? Get up and fight back."

"Enough," Samuel says. "We need her in one piece."

Ian kicks me in the hip, and I gasp even though what I really want to do is grab the knife from my boot and turn Ian into a eunuch. Samuel steps closer to Ian and puts a hand on his shoulder. Maybe I should cry. Most men can't stand the sight of a girl crying.

Or maybe that would oversell the damsel-in-distress image. Especially considering the fact that Samuel already witnessed me antagonizing Ian earlier in the afternoon.

"This is between me and Rachel." Ian sounds like he's speaking through clenched teeth.

"No, this is between James Rowan and Logan McEntire." Samuel's voice is calm. "If you injure her—"

"She deserves it."

My throat burns as I swallow the flood of bitter words I'd like to throw in Ian's face. I deserve a lot of things. I deserve to answer for killing Melkin. I deserve to share the responsibility for failing to stop the Commander while we had the chance. I deserve to ache with guilt because if I hadn't defied my leader, Oliver would still be alive.

But Ian deserves to die. And everything in me wants to be the one who kills him.

Samuel continues as if Ian had never interrupted him. "If you injure her too badly, her pain atonement will be considered paid in full." His voice becomes cold. "And if she dies under our watch, and we fail to return both Logan and the controller, we won't survive our punishments. I'm not willing to die because you hate this girl."

No wonder Samuel cares what happens to me. He wants to save his own skin. I can appreciate that.

Ian takes a single step away from me, though his eyes glitter in the starlight as if a silver-white flame burns within them.

"Get some sleep," Samuel says. "Both of you. We have a long day of travel tomorrow."

"Fine." Ian turns toward the wagon. "But I'm sleeping in here with her so she can't try to escape."

Oh yes, please. Please let Ian sleep in the wagon with me. The second he drifts off, I'll slice his throat the way he sliced Donny's while the boy stood guard over our camp in the Wasteland. My pulse pounds against my skin, and I press my lips together to keep from baring my teeth.

Samuel is quiet for a moment, and then he says, "She'll keep watch with me or sleep beside Heidi." The tracker looks at me.

"Get up and either join me or lie by the fire. And if you even think about trying to escape under my watch, I'll tie you to the wagon bench for the duration of the trip." Without waiting for a response from either of us, he turns and strides across the campsite toward his log.

Slowly, I climb to my feet. My head spins, and my arm throbs in never-ending spikes of pain. I want to lie down and let darkness claim me, but that's not an option.

"He's not protecting you," Ian says. For the first time since he revealed himself as the monster behind the death and destruction that followed the Baalboden survivors through the Wasteland, he sounds weary. "He's only protecting himself. That's all he's good at. He'll turn on you the second keeping you safe doesn't guarantee his own life." Bitterness seeps into his voice. "He won't even protect his closest friends. Not if it means he might miss his next promotion."

"He wouldn't have to protect me at all if you weren't trying so hard to hurt me."

Ian's chest heaves, and his fists clench at his sides. "Someone has to pay. Justice requires sacrifice. Blood and pain to wash away the crime." His voice rises. "Someone *has* to pay."

"Someone will." Drawing myself up straight, I ignore the dizziness in my head and step closer. Close enough to see the shine of starlight in his eyes. To see the cords of his neck stand out as he glares at me. "I'm not the one who needs Samuel's protection. You'd better watch your back, every second of every day, because you have crimes to answer for, and I'm not going to stop coming for you until you pay for them with your life."

"You can't kill me." He sounds insulted.

I smile. "We both know I can."

"Samuel and Heidi would punish you in ways you've never dreamed."

My smile grows. "No, they wouldn't. I have to arrive in Rowansmark alive and well or they'll pay the consequence for their failure. You, on the other hand, never have to arrive at all." I turn my back on him and walk away.

CHAPTER FIVE

LOGAN

I can't tell what time it is, but several hours have passed since I pled guilty before the triumvirate and was once again locked with Willow in Lankenshire's dungeon, this time with Rowansmark trackers as our guards. The dungeon creaks and a draft blows from the end of the corridor closest to us, making the light in the hanging oil lanterns outside our door flicker. The entire place smells of damp stone mixed with the harsh metallic tang of the iron bars that hold us here.

I pace the floor, swinging my arms in circles as I walk. I need to be limber. Loose. Ready.

Rescue could arrive at any minute.

We need to survive the ensuing fight. And then, once we're out in the Wasteland surrounded by the Commander's men, we need to survive yet again.

Willow stretches slowly, arching her back as she stands on her tiptoes. The silver wire she pulled from her braid gleams dully against her wrist.

It's the only weapon we've got.

The dungeon door creaks open, and voices drift down the corridor. Willow meets my eyes, and we both tense. Waiting for the sound of conflict. Swordplay.

Something.

Instead, the steady cadence of boot steps approaches our cell. Seconds later, the head tracker, the man with the shaved head who first confronted me in Lankenshire's square earlier today, comes into view, fully outfitted for travel. Two more trackers are at his back.

"Open it." The head tracker gestures toward our cell door, and then looks at me, his dark eyes fierce. "Fight us, and I'll start cutting off body parts."

"What's going on?" I ask as Willow and I back away from the door. The metal bars swing outward, and the two men step inside, leaving the head tracker in the corridor.

"Transfer to Rowansmark," one of the men says as he steps toward Willow.

The dungeon door clangs open again, and more voices fill the space. More trackers, all dressed for travel. More swords standing between us and freedom.

"I thought we weren't leaving before dawn," I say, but of course we are. I would've done the same thing. What better way to short-circuit any attempts at a double cross than to significantly alter the expected timeline? I kick myself for not anticipating this.

The tracker smiles, but it isn't friendly. "We're leaving now. Surely it doesn't matter to you one way or the other, does it?"

"Not at all," Willow says, her smile just as dangerous as his. "I've always wanted to travel the Wasteland with a full escort of uniformed idiots."

"Willow—"

"Let her run her mouth," the tracker says. "It will make punishing her for her part in your treachery all the sweeter."

Willow laughs as one of the men inside the cell grabs her upper arm and pulls her toward the door. "One of your kind already tried to kill me once. Three guesses where I left his body."

The tracker holding her spits on the floor. "You didn't best a tracker. You're nothing but a Tree Person."

Willow whips her body around and snaps a kick straight into the man's windpipe. He falls to his knees, clutching his throat while his face turns red as he gasps for air.

"Still think I'm nothing?" she asks. I shove past the tracker beside me as she wraps her fingers around the wire at her wrist.

"Willow."

She looks at me. I don't shake my head. I don't look at her wrist. I give nothing away as I beg her with my eyes to remember that her weapon might be the only leverage we have. If she reveals her secrets now, when we're surrounded by trackers and have absolutely no chance of escape, we'll be improvising with nothing but wishes and thin air.

Slowly, her fingers relax and move away from the wire. Seconds later, I'm grabbed roughly from behind and another two trackers rush into the cell to wrestle Willow into submission. The man she kicked lies on the floor, moaning and retching, but at least he's still breathing. The last thing we need is for the head tracker to decide that Willow deserves to give her life for the life of one of his men.

"Get them out here," the head tracker says as he pulls his sword and looks at Willow. "You're lying. Do you know how I know that? Because if you'd actually killed a tracker, you'd be dead as well."

She rolls her eyes. "You mean because of the little internal bomb you all have in case you get killed in the line of duty? Please." She nods toward me. "We saw that in action when we killed a tracker on our way back to Baalboden. You know an easy way to avoid getting hurt by flying body parts? Stand back and shoot an arrow. Also, you might want to rethink the whole if-you-kill-me-you-will-pay-dearly strategy, because the biggest danger is the mess. Kind of hard to injure someone when all that's left of you are scraps."

"Enough!" the tracker barks at Willow as the men holding her pull her to a stop right in front of him.

Panic surges through me at the way he studies her. He might not kill her, but he's going to punish her, and I don't think I can stop it.

"We're cooperating," I say, and walk faster, half dragging the tracker who grips my arms as I struggle to catch up to Willow. "We'll do whatever you say."

The head tracker doesn't look at me. The torchlight gleams against his shaved head as he bends his neck to stare at Willow. The men holding her shove her to her knees. She keeps her head held high and glares.

"I told you that if you fought me, I would start cutting off body parts." The head tracker's voice is cold.

"She didn't fight you." I try to move closer to Willow, to somehow put myself between her body and the sword that points steadily at her heart, but the man holding me jerks me to the side. My shoulder slams into the stone wall of the corridor. "She didn't. She's ready to show you where she hid the controller. She's ready to go to Rowansmark if you want her to."

I try to sound calm, but my words come out too fast. Too desperate.

I can't stop him from hurting Willow, and everyone in the dungeon knows it.

The head tracker glances at me. "She kicked Jefferson in the throat," he says.

"Jefferson deserved it." Willow's voice is as proud as the tilt of her chin. "It's one thing to take me into custody for simply obeying my leader. It's another to insult me and get away with it."

The man nods slowly, and I draw one shaky breath of relief before his next words rip that away from me. "He behaved dishonorably, but it was a small infraction. You admitted to killing a tracker—"

"I make it a habit to kill those who are trying to kill *me*."

"—and then you tried to kill Jefferson for merely insulting you." His sword wavers as he looks Willow over as if trying to choose where to make his first cut. "I'm a man of honor, and I am responsible for my people." His eyes flash to hers. "I pay my debts."

Her lips peel back from her teeth in a snarl. "So do I."

"Take me!" I blurt the words before the thought has finished forming. "Punish me instead. I'll pay her debt."

The head tracker frowns. "Only family members are allowed to assume the pain atonement for each other, and that's only when the offending member is either too young or too infirm to satisfy the debt owed."

Willow glares at me. "I can take whatever he gives me and then some."

"I know." I hold her gaze. "I know you can, but you shouldn't have to. You're only here because I asked you to hide the device. It's my fault. All of this. My fault." I look at the tracker again. "She's my family now. And I deserve to take her punishment."

"Don't be stupid, Logan," Willow snaps.

The door at the end of the corridor groans as more trackers enter the dungeon. At this point, there must be at least a dozen hovering near the exit, waiting for us. One of them, a tall woman with narrow shoulders and a pointy chin, calls out, "Sir? We're ready."

I push away from the wall and drop to my knees. The tracker holding me adjusts his grip but doesn't let go.

"We're wasting time," I say. "You want to get the controller and be on your way to Rowansmark before the army outside this city realizes you're gone, don't you? Then punish me."

"Logan, don't you dare—"

"Punish me!" I raise my voice to drown out Willow's protest, and the head tracker smiles slyly as if he's only been waiting for an excuse to hurt me.

"Grab his hand." One of the trackers holding Willow lets go to reach for me.

"Don't release her, you fool! Didn't you learn anything from watching Jefferson nearly get his throat crushed?" The head tracker steps closer to me while behind him, another man rushes toward me.

"Logan McEntire, if you do this, I will never forgive you." Willow's voice shakes. She twists against the men holding her but can't get any leverage.

Before the man can reach me, I lay my left hand on the rough, cold stone beneath me. If I have to lose a hand, better to make it the one I don't use to hold a sword. My mouth goes dry as the tracker grabs my wrist, anchors my palm to the floor, and spreads my fingers wide.

"Don't touch him!" Willow's voice echoes through the dungeon, silencing the trackers at the exit.

"It's okay, Willow." I meet her eyes and try to speak like it isn't taking every ounce of stubbornness I have to keep from trembling. "I'm responsible."

She curses, her eyes glistening in the torchlight as the head tracker raises his sword. Her voice is full of violent promise as she says, "I swear to you if you hurt him, nothing—not your stupid trackers, your precious technology, or your army—will be enough to keep you safe from me."

The head tracker swings his sword.

The blade slices through skin, muscle, and bone and slams into the stone floor. My little finger rolls away from my hand, and blood pours from the wound. For a second, I can't feel anything. I stare at my finger as if trying to force the sight of it lying separate from my body to somehow make sense to me. Then pain hits hard, searing my entire left arm with fire. Sweat beads along my skin, and I feel like throwing up. Passing out. Both.

I press my lips closed and swallow the cry of agony that

wants to escape. Some small, savage part of me welcomes the pain. The debt I owe isn't to Rowansmark, and it certainly isn't to this tracker, but I spoke the truth when I said I felt responsible for Willow, for Rachel, for every person in Baalboden who suffered because of who I am and what I chose to do. Losing a finger isn't nearly enough penance, but this wasn't about absolution. This was about assuming the full burden of leadership. Willow is mine to protect, and I'm through with failing those I love.

The pain subsides beneath a wave of shock that clouds my thoughts and makes me feel sleepy and faintly dizzy. I lean my face against the wall and try to draw in a breath while above me, the tracker says, "Cauterize it, and let's go."

"No," I say, my stomach pitching as I remember the unbelievable pain of being branded with white-hot metal in the Commander's dungeon.

The man who held down my hand stands, plunges a dagger into the flame of the nearest lantern, and looks at me.

"No," I say again, and struggle to sit up. My hand throbs in time with my heartbeat, and blood rushes out of me in a steady stream. I try to tuck my wounded arm against my chest, but the man holding the dagger crouches beside me, the edges of his blade glowing orange.

I gulp for air, and brace myself, but I can't contain my scream as he presses the hot metal against my bleeding flesh. For a moment, I'm back in the Commander's dungeon, lying on the filthy floor while a member of the Brute Squad sears the Commander's brand into the side of my neck. Nausea churns through me, and I choke as I try to move away from the source of my agony.

Dimly I realize that Willow is shrieking a nonstop litany of death threats so inventive, I'd admire her resourcefulness if I wasn't busy trying not to vomit.

"Be quiet," the head tracker says, "or I'll cut off his entire hand."

Willow's mouth snaps closed, but the look in her eyes promises that the very second he doesn't have her fully restrained, she's coming after him.

"Get them up. We're leaving." He turns on his heel and marches toward the exit. The trackers on either side of me haul me to my feet. My knees shake, but they hold me.

Beside me, Willow is dragged to her feet as well. She ignores the men holding on to her and looks at me. Her eyes are haunted and furious.

"Nobody stands in my place. Ever." Her voice is still shaky.

"Let's go!" the female tracker calls to us. The men assigned to us begin pushing us down the corridor.

My skin feels clammy, and I keep sucking in deep breaths of damp dungeon air as if the oxygen will somehow chase away the lingering pain and nausea that swamp me. I meet Willow's eyes.

"A true leader protects his people. More than that, family stands up for family."

Her expression softens for a second. Then she glances at my left hand, at the blackened stub that used to be a finger, and everything about her hardens.

"I protect my family too, Logan." Her eyes find the back of

the head tracker as he organizes his people into two lines on either side of the exit.

Before I can reply, the dungeon door flies open with a resounding crash, and all hell breaks loose.

CHAPTER SIX

LOGAN

Men dressed in the dark-blue uniform of Baalboden's guards, along with a few who wear the golden talon patch of the Commander's Brute Squad, pour into the dungeon, their swords already flashing. The trackers respond, moving like a synchronized unit as they pivot into position and engage the intruders. The harsh screech of metal against metal fills the air, and the head tracker yells for his people to defend the gap and keep Willow and me safe. The men holding Willow and me pull us backward until we're in front of our open cell again, a good thirty yards from the fighting.

Willow laughs as a man in a green-and-brown Rowansmark uniform falls to the floor, his eyes staring at nothing. Seconds later, his body explodes in a cloud of bloody mist that briefly obscures the others fighting there.

More of the Commander's men enter the dungeon, their faces set with purpose, but still they're dying faster than the trackers. The Baalboden guards rely on strength and force. The trackers use precision, strategy, and a lethal understanding of the fastest methods to destroy the human body. Sheer strength is intimidating, but strategy only requires an opponent to make a single mistake.

Willow struggles against the men who hold her, but they move in sync to keep her subdued. I tense my muscles, considering the best way to get free of my keepers, but nothing workable comes to mind. My hand throbs mercilessly, and my stomach feels like I could be sick at any moment.

I start calculating the odds and running scenarios just to have something besides the pain to think about. Baalboden guards are dying at a ratio of nearly two to one. Every time a tracker falls, the others pivot to keep a Baalboden man between themselves and the imminent explosion. Willow can say what she wants about the trackers being unable to cause much damage to others with this strategy, but it's clear that damage isn't the point. Distraction is, and it's working in Rowansmark's favor. If this keeps up, we're going to end up going to Rowansmark as prisoners with no leverage and no feasible way to defeat the armies that wait for us.

That scenario is unacceptable.

A few more guards rush through the doorway, but they're immediately fighting for their lives. The trackers, working back to back, have found their rhythm—slash, pivot, parry, kill—and the Commander's men have neither the expertise nor the space to maneuver into a better position. We need to give the trackers something else to worry about. Fast.

"Fight harder!" A cruel voice chops the words into sharp pieces as the Commander steps into the doorway, his dark eyes lit with a predatory gleam while the scar that bisects the left side of his face pulls his mouth into a lopsided grimace. "I want the boy."

Two more guards flank the Commander and rush into battle. There are so many fighting in the small confines of the corridor that it's impossible to see the action clearly. But even in the confusion, I can see that Rowansmark is winning.

The Commander sees it, too. With a roar of fury, he draws his sword and steps toward the closest tracker.

He's seventy-five if he's a day. There's no way he can best a tracker. Not for long. He'll die, killed by the certainty that no one is his equal, and without the Commander's credibility with the northern city-states, I'll be left with no way to convince them to commit troops against Rowansmark. No way to keep my promises.

No way to save Rachel.

This time the bile at the back of my throat has nothing to do with my injury. I want the Commander dead. I've wanted it since the moment my mother bled to death and left me to fend for myself on the streets of Baalboden. I used to warm myself on freezing winter nights with the fantasy of one day climbing the fence around the Commander's compound, sneaking into his bedroom, and driving a knife through his heart. The events of the last few months have only added fuel to the flames of my hatred. I want him *dead*, but if he dies, so does my chance to rescue Rachel.

I meet Willow's eyes for a split second, hoping she can read my expression, and then I moan and go limp like I'm losing consciousness. The tracker to my left loses his grip. I bend at the waist as if I'm about to be sick, then plant my feet and come up fast. My fist plows into the tracker gripping my right arm. His head snaps back, and our momentum carries us into the wall. I wrap my hands around his neck and use him for leverage as I slam my boots into the chest of the other man. He stumbles into the trackers who hold Willow. One of them goes down, and she bursts into action.

The tracker I'm holding brings his arms up fast, breaks my choke hold, and punches my kidney so hard I nearly double over from the pain. I pull my injured hand close to my body to minimize the tracker's opportunity to use my wound against me, and we trade blow for blow.

I don't have time for this. Even now, the Commander could be dead.

I also don't have the stamina. I'm woozy from blood loss, and one good hit to my left hand will incapacitate me with pain.

"Logan, down!"

I drop, landing hard on the dungeon floor, and Willow leaps over the top of me. The tracker I'm fighting braces himself, but instead of crashing into him, Willow lands in a forward roll, snatches his dagger from his boot, and drives it into his inner thigh as she stands.

The tracker goes on the offensive, but he's off-balance and losing blood. Willow lands a blow on his collarbone and then digs her thumb into the soft spot behind his ear. His eyes roll into the back of his head, and he drops.

I turn and find the other three trackers who were holding on to us sprawled on the dungeon floor, unconscious.

"Look at that. Four trackers taken down by a Tree Person,"

Willow says, a feral gleam in her eyes.

I get to my feet and see that the Commander is still standing. Still fighting. I suspect that has nothing to do with his prowess and everything to do with the fact that the surviving members of the Brute Squad have converged to stand like a shield between their leader and the remaining seven trackers.

What's left of the dead trackers is nothing but a mist of bone and blood smeared across the dungeon, all that remains after each body explodes once the heart stops beating. I can't tell how many of the Commander's men litter the dungeon floor, but only five remain standing. Seven trackers. Five Brute Squad guards. And us.

"We need to distract—"

My words die as an arrow flies past me and buries itself in the throat of the closest tracker. I turn to see Willow holding a bow while she tugs another arrow free of the quiver strapped to the back of an unconscious man. She grins.

"Nice of Rowansmark to come down here all weaponed up and ready to travel." The arrow zings past me, and another tracker goes down. The first man lies on the floor, his eyes staring at nothing. Seconds later, his body explodes, sending bone and blood flying. The head tracker, who'd been facing away from us as he engaged the Commander's men in battle, whips around.

Surveying the scene, the head tracker locks eyes with me. Anger coats his words as he shouts his orders. "Monroe, Thristan, and Ella to the door. Kill anyone who stands in your way. Lysford, with me. I want the prisoners alive, but I don't need them pretty."

I grab the dagger that still protrudes from the unconscious tracker's thigh and brace myself. Willow is still trying to pull another arrow free when Lysford and the head tracker reach us.

"Willow!"

She flips to her right, narrowly avoiding Lysford's sword. I lose sight of her then because the leader swings his blade at me. I leap back, and he attacks. He holds a dagger in one fist, his sword in the other, and he moves with efficient, lethal power. I block one blow with my right arm and am forced to use my left as well when he quickly parries.

He drops his sword and grabs my injured hand instead. Pain screams up my nerve endings, and brilliant sparks flash across my vision. He pins my left arm, effectively blocking my ability to retaliate, and crushes my charred flesh against his palm. I'd kick him, but my knees suddenly feel like they won't hold me.

I grit my teeth to keep from crying out, and he laughs.

"What a waste of time this was. You should know by now that you need your best and your brightest when you challenge Rowansmark, but what did you bring to the fight? An old man and some poorly trained soldiers. Pathetic." He leans closer, his hand still crushing mine.

Sweat beads along my forehead, and my breath comes in harsh bursts as I say, "That's not all I brought."

"That's right." Willow rises up behind him. "He brought me."

The tracker releases my injured hand and half turns as if to block her. She leaps onto his back, wraps her legs around his waist, and reaches her right arm across his throat to grab the spool of wire circling her other wrist.

He whirls around and slams her against the wall, but she

doesn't let go. I lunge forward, my dagger flashing, before he can flip his short blade around and plunge it into her. He parries my blow, leans forward, and throws himself against the wall again.

Willow grunts, but doesn't lose her grip. Digging her left hand into his shoulder, she wraps the loose end of the wire twice around her right wrist.

Whipping her right arm across his throat, she lays the thin silver wire against his skin. He stiffens and swings his fist toward her head, but she's already in motion. Pulling the wire taut, she uses it to balance herself as she lets go of his waist and moves her feet to the small of his back so that she's crouched against him with nothing but the pressure of the wire keeping her from falling. A line of blood wells up as the wire bites through his flesh.

He grabs the wire with both hands, but it's too late. I can see the desperate fear in his eyes as she twists them both away from the wall and pushes off from his back to launch herself toward the floor, the wire firmly wrapped around his neck.

He's dead by the time they hit the ground.

"Willow, move!" I shove the tracker off her as the anatomical trigger inside of him begins ticking down. She grabs my arms, and we roll behind the man with the wounded leg seconds before the head tracker's body bursts apart. A shard of bone embeds itself in the stomach of the man we're using as a shield. I stare at it as I get to my feet.

"So much for saying no one could get hurt with the scraps of a tracker," I say.

"I stand corrected."

Behind us, the dungeon is quiet. I glance at the doorway and find the Commander with three surviving Brute Squad guards watching us. Every tracker still alive lies on the floor unconscious or badly wounded. The Commander's eyes flicker between Willow and me as if trying to understand how a girl could beat one of Rowansmark's best. I turn my back on him and lean down to help Willow to her feet.

One of the trackers she knocked unconscious is starting to stir. She moves toward him, and I put my good hand on her arm.

"Leave him. Someone has to absolve Lankenshire of responsibility here."

"Fine. But I get his weapons." She wrestles a quiver of arrows off his back and picks up the bow she discarded earlier. I take a sword, a scabbard, and the dagger I used against the tracker. We turn toward the door and find the Commander, flanked by his three Brute Squad guards, standing a few yards behind us with their weapons pointed at our hearts.

"Kill the girl," he snaps.

"No!" I jump in front of Willow before she can finish whipping an arrow into her bow. A tall guard with squinty eyes stops just short of driving his sword through my stomach on his way to Willow.

"Get out of his way, or you die too." The Commander's voice is ruthless.

Willow tries to sidestep me, but I mirror her movements. I'm not worried that she can't defend herself. I'm trying to keep the Commander alive.

The irony is nearly unbearable.

Willow peeks around me and glares at the Commander. "You stupid fool. I'm the only one who knows where the device is hidden. If you *kill the girl*"—she mocks the Commander's choppy cadence—"you ruin everything you've worked for."

A muscle in the Commander's jaw jumps, and he levels his fierce glare on Willow. "You have a big mouth."

"I need a big mouth to keep up with my big brain."

The scar that bisects the Commander's face knots and prickles. His voice is soft as he says, "Watch yourself, girl. The very second you fail to be useful to me, you will die. Slowly."

Willow laughs, a dark sound that has the guard in front of me tightening his grip on his sword.

"We need to hurry before the trackers wake up or Lankenshire soldiers arrive," I say, trying hard to sound calm, though the pain in my hand and the stress of trying to keep Willow and the Commander from killing each other on the spot is making me wish for a dark corner to crawl into for the next twelve hours.

The Commander glances at me briefly, and then waves a hand at the skinny guard who still has his sword aimed at me. "Fine. If the girl is the one who knows where the device is, we'll take her with us. Kill Logan. Leave his body as a lesson about what happens to those who turn against me."

The guard lunges toward me, his sword flashing dully in the torchlight. I grab for the sword in my scabbard, already knowing that I can't get my weapon free in time. Something brushes past my hair, and an arrow slams into the guard's throat. He chokes, frothy blood bubbling from his lips, and drops his sword to wrap both hands around the arrow.

Willow notches another arrow before the guard's knees hit the dungeon floor.

"Who's next?" she asks.

"How *dare* you defy me?" The Commander's voice shakes as he reaches for his sword.

"Wait!" I say before Willow can loose her arrow. Before the Commander can charge her. Before the plan I scraped together falls apart and leaves me with absolutely no way to keep my promises.

"You need me alive," I say to the Commander.

"Why?" The Commander hurls the word at me.

"Because I know how the Rowansmark tech works. Because I can not only use it, I can improve it. And because I know the full extent of what waits for us at Rowansmark and how to use their mistakes to our advantage. You and I are the only ones who can convince the rest of the northern city-states to give us troops so that we can defeat James Rowan and break his hold over this continent."

"And how are you, an outcast traitor, supposed to help me gain troops from the other city-states?" he asks.

"I can disarm the beacons Rowansmark installed in every city-state. We offer them immediate protection and long-term results, provided we get the troops we need to mount an offensive on Rowansmark soil."

The Commander waves at his men to lower their weapons. Willow slowly relaxes her grip on the bow. The Commander and I stare at each other in silence for a moment. Finally, he nods. "Take him."

The Brute Squad guard on his left grabs a length of chain from the dungeon's wall and approaches me.

"What do you think you're doing?" Willow asks, her fingers tightening on her bow again.

"I'm locking up my investment before he can commit treason against me again." The Commander's scar pulls at his lip while his dark eyes bore into mine.

"It's okay, Willow," I say as I hold out my wrists.

"We really need to discuss your definition of *okay*." She lowers her weapon. Neither of the Brute Squad guards looks reassured.

I don't blame them. The metal chains are cold against my skin as the guard wraps my wrists tight. My left hand throbs, and my vision blurs when one of the chain links smacks against the stub that used to be my finger.

"Should we shackle the girl too?" a guard asks.

Willow whips her bow up and snarls, "Try it."

"We don't have time for this." The Commander sounds impatient. "If she so much as touches her bow, kill the boy. Now, let's go."

I take a few steps forward and pause in front of him. Straightening my shoulders, I look him in the eye. Let him see that I don't fear him. That I won't pretend to honor a coward. His eyes narrow as I meet his gaze, but then his lips curve into a predatory smile.

"I'm going to enjoy killing you someday," he says softly.

I swallow the words I want to spit at him, and give him a predatory smile of my own as Willow and I brush past my former leader and into the darkened hallway beyond.

CHAPTER SEVEN

RACHEL

"**H**ow long have you been a tracker?" My breath breaks up my words harshly, as if someone reached down my throat and scoured my lungs with sand. I sit on the ground, my back leaning against the log Samuel is using as his guard post, and hold my injured arm against my chest while my eyes continuously move over the dark expanse of the Wasteland, hoping to catch sight of Quinn.

Not that he'd let us see him until he was already on top of us. He's too well trained to make that kind of mistake. Still, I look for him, my body tensed. Quinn won't abandon me. I just hope he understands that I'm not going to return to Lankenshire until Ian is dead.

"Why do you care?" Samuel doesn't sound irritated, but he doesn't sound happy either.

"Just making conversation." I cough.

He waits for me to find my breath again and then clips his

words short. "Night shift guard duty isn't the time for making conversation."

I know that, but I also know that *if* Quinn catches up to us tonight, which is unlikely given his injuries and the fact that our wagon moved swiftly through the afternoon, the best help I can offer is to keep Samuel distracted.

I make my voice sound small as I say, "I'm sorry. It's just that . . . I'm hurt, and I'm a long way from anyone who actually cares about me, and I feel very alone." I have to blink my eyes against the sudden sting of tears as the truth of my words settles into me.

"I'm not your counselor," Samuel says.

"Who else am I supposed to talk to? Ian?" My laugh is bitter. "I can see how well that would go. 'Hey, Ian, let's forget about all the innocent people you killed because you assumed Logan knew where he was from! Let's forget about how you destroyed my city for a crime your own father committed against your leader!'" I cough again and then ask, "How fast do you think he'd stick his sword in my mouth just to shut me up?"

"I myself am wondering what it would take to shut you up."

I shift my weight and the rough, splintery bark behind me scrapes loudly against my leather cloak. Samuel sighs.

"Why don't you go lie near Heidi and get some sleep?"

"Not tired." I lie with all the conviction of the miracle-cure salesman Oliver once threatened to whip if he didn't stop giving the poverty-stricken people in South Edge false hope while he pocketed their hard-earned coins.

"You can barely keep your eyes open. Your lungs are damaged.

You're obviously in pain. Go get some rest."

"I'll sleep in the wagon while we travel. Alone." I drag in a breath and make sure my voice trembles as I say, "I need you and Heidi to be awake so you can make sure Ian doesn't . . . hurt me."

Having the two trackers for an audience will make my plan to kill Ian harder to pull off. Still, if Samuel feels protective of me instead of allied with Ian, it will be worth the extra risk.

Samuel doesn't reply. The incessant chirrup of crickets joins the soft, mournful hooting of an owl and surrounds us with the quiet nighttime noises of the Wasteland. The loneliness in my chest spreads through my veins until I want to shove the emotion into the bleak silence that still lurks in the dark corners within me. The last time I traveled the Wasteland with a virtual stranger, my best friend, Sylph, had just married the boy she loved, Logan was depending on me to rescue him from the Commander's dungeon, and the belief that my father was alive and could make everything right again was a brilliant flame of hope within me.

Now my father is gone. Sylph is dead. And if Ian is to be believed, Logan can't track me down until he finds a way around the Commander and his borrowed army.

I don't realize I'm crying until hot tears spill down my cheeks. Wrapping my arms around myself, I hunch over my knees and struggle to stop. To breathe. To believe that I can see this through, even if I have to see it through alone.

"Twenty-three years," Samuel says quietly.

I sniff and wipe my palms across my cheeks, trying hard not to look humiliated. It's one thing to act like a damsel in distress.

It's another thing to *feel* like one.

"What?" My voice sounds thick and unsteady. I clear my throat.

"I've been a tracker for twenty-three years. Joined the military for my mandatory three years of service straight out of school and was recruited for the tracker squad from there."

"Oh." I sit up, pulling my wounded arm close. My fingers press lightly against the burned flesh, even though I no longer need the pain as distraction. "So you're old enough to know Ian's father."

Samuel's jaw clenches, and he turns to examine the trees. I scramble to fill the silence with something that will grab his attention again.

"I thought you might be as old as my father. Maybe you knew him too? He visited Rowansmark at least twice a year as Baalboden's courier—"

"Jared Adams, the man who abused his diplomatic privileges and stole proprietary tech from Rowansmark."

"He didn't steal it. It was *given* to him."

"Through an illegal transaction that Jared, with his years of experience, would've immediately recognized as something that ought to be reported under the Diplomatic Trade Agreement. But he didn't report it. He kept it. So yes, I know who Jared Adams is. Every tracker knows who he is." Samuel's voice is flat.

"Was."

He turns toward me. "Was?"

"He's dead." The words are too easy to say. They roll off my tongue as if they don't carry the weight of all I've lost wrapped inside their syllables.

"How? A tracker?"

"Dad was too good to be caught by a tracker." I lift my chin and glare at him before I remember that I'm supposed to be gaining his sympathy. Dropping my eyes, I say, "He was trying to hide the device—the controller that Marcus had given him. The Cursed One attacked my dad and two Tree People who were helping him. He led the beast away from them and died saving their lives."

The silence between us stretches out, long and fraught with tension. Finally, Samuel says, "I'm sorry for your loss."

"You aren't sorry he's dead." The words are out before I can think better of them, but I don't want to take them back. I can accept sympathy from Logan. From Quinn. Maybe even from Willow. But I can't sit here next to a man who would've killed my father the moment he laid eyes on him and pretend his condolences mean anything.

"He committed treason against Rowansmark."

"It only counts as treason if he was actually a citizen," I snap, and then close my lips before I can say anything else. If I'm not careful, I'm going to alienate the only person who might be useful to me. "But yes, he ended up with stolen tech. However, he didn't know what Marcus had given him until we were already a day's journey away from Rowansmark."

"We?" Samuel's voice is sharp.

"I was with him."

"He was training you to be his apprentice?"

I choose my words carefully. "I'm a girl. From Baalboden. We weren't allowed to learn how to read or how to handle a weapon. We weren't even allowed to walk our city streets without a male

Protector in case we got the crazy idea that we could somehow be independent. So no, I wasn't his apprentice. I was simply his daughter."

My words are both true and utterly false. A Baalboden girl wasn't allowed to read, use a sword, or leave her house unattended, but my father never thought education was something to be feared. The fact that I've been trained to fight isn't something Samuel needs to know, though. The more he thinks I'm a typical Baalboden girl, the faster he'll drop his guard.

Unless Ian has already convinced him that I'm dangerous—a scenario that makes sense. Which means it's even more important for me to play up my injuries, my weakness, and be alert for Quinn's arrival.

"Dad got packages to deliver to the Commander all the time, but something about this one made him uneasy. Usually, he received his deliveries from James Rowan or from the state department. But that time, we were stopped in an alley just before we left the city, and a man gave him the package. So once we made camp for the night and Dad thought I was sleeping, he opened it."

When I don't continue, Samuel looks at me, his dark eyes glittering. "Did he know what it was?"

I shrug. "I don't think he knew for sure. Instead of delivering it to the Commander, we took a detour the next day so he could hide it near one of his safe houses in the Wasteland."

"Why not return it to Rowansmark?"

"And be late for his expected return to Baalboden?" I shake my head. "Have you met the Commander? He'd have been instantly suspicious, and in his eyes, suspicion is proof of guilt."

"But later? On his next trip to Rowansmark?"

Something moves in one of the maple trees to my left. A bough shakes gently and the leaves shimmer in the starlight. I look to the right in case Samuel is watching me and hope the movement I just saw was Quinn.

"The Commander never sent him back to Rowansmark. He got suspicious—I don't know how. Maybe he sent someone else to check in with Marcus and realized the tech had been given to my dad already."

My next words are rushed as I try to distract Samuel, who is staring intently into the thick copse of maples.

"Anyway, Dad was supposed to go to Carrington, but he never returned. I went to find him—"

"You?" Samuel's voice is sharp.

I curse myself for forgetting that I'm trying to seem harmless and inexperienced.

"Not by myself. The Commander sent me out with another Baalboden tracker because I knew where my dad's safe houses were on the journey to Rowansmark." I swallow against the sudden dryness in my mouth at the memory of Melkin's dark eyes burning into mine while he demanded that I give him the package or he would take it from me by force. "And because I told the Commander that I'd seen someone give Dad a package on his last trip to your city, and that Dad hid it instead of bringing it back."

"You said this even though you knew it would compromise your father in the Commander's eyes?"

His words arrow through me, but what hurts worse is the approval in his voice. He thinks I'm like him. Like Ian. That I would sell out my loved ones for the sake of civic duty.

He's wrong.

I told the Commander because if I hadn't, he'd have killed me before I had a chance to escape the city and look for my father.

The soft *thump-thump* of flapping wings echoes from the tree where I saw movement. Seconds later, a small animal shrieks—a piercing cry of pain that's cut off in seconds. I swallow my disappointment that the only creature inhabiting the trees near us is an owl. Quinn isn't here. Yet.

Turning to Samuel, I say, "My dad didn't steal from Rowansmark. He was used by the Commander and by Marcus McEntire. He died before he could make it right. How is it fair that I'm being punished for that?"

"You won't be punished unless James Rowan decides your actions make you guilty."

My laugh sounds wild and desperate. "Ian will punish me every chance he gets."

"You will arrive safely in Rowansmark." Samuel's voice is stiff.

"Will Ian be held accountable for destroying my city? For murdering my best friend along with many of the other Baalboden survivors?"

"Ian will be held accountable for completing his mission."

"For returning the controller." I wrap my arms around my chest as a gust of cold, damp air shivers through the trees. "No matter how many lives he took to get it back. No matter that he's using me as bait to destroy his brother, even though Logan hasn't done anything wrong. Where is the justice in that?"

Samuel looks at me, his expression carved in stone. "Justice requires sacrifice."

"But you can't possibly agree that killing innocent people—"

The tracker's voice is unforgiving. "Innocence is a relative term, Ms. Adams. Did you have the opportunity to return the controller to Ian before people died?"

"No." I lift my chin and glare at Samuel, all thoughts of pretending to be afraid vanishing beneath the tide of white-hot anger that surges through me. "He sent the Cursed One into our city while our gate was locked and killed thousands of people without ever once identifying himself or asking for the tech to be returned. And then he pretended to be one of the survivors and murdered our people—poisoning newlyweds and slitting the throats of *children*—across the Wasteland. All while leaving cryptic messages that made little sense. He never said who he was. He never demanded the tech. He played games with people's lives because he is sick, crazy—"

"You knew the tech was from Rowansmark when you found it in the Wasteland, did you not?"

"Yes, but—"

"You understood, based on your father's actions, that the tech didn't belong to the Commander. You knew about the bounty James Rowan placed on your father's head. You knew your father was wanted for treason against Rowansmark. You had all the information you needed. And yet you and Logan McEntire didn't return the controller to Rowansmark. You took what wasn't yours and because of that, Marcus McEntire's treason was discovered, and he died. Horribly."

For the first time since I met him, Samuel's voice trembles.

"I didn't know—"

"You knew enough." Samuel stands abruptly. "You can blame Ian all you want, but I know that boy. I've known him for his entire life. He's brilliant and driven and, up until a few months ago, wanted nothing more than to follow in his father's footsteps and make everyone proud of him. What he had to do to expunge the stain on his family's honor broke him. Do you understand me? It *broke* him. And he would never have broken if you and Logan McEntire had returned the controller."

Without another word, he turns on his heel and stalks off to do a perimeter sweep.

CHAPTER EIGHT

RACHEL

Heidi took over the watch at least two hours ago. I spent the first thirty minutes sitting near her, trying to start a conversation so I could build a possible alliance, but I might as well have been talking to the log I leaned against for all the response I got. Finally, I gave up and wandered over to lie by the ashes of our campfire, close enough to Samuel to feel marginally safe getting some rest but far enough removed that I feel cocooned in my own little corner of darkness.

I'm under no illusions. Heidi never looks my way, but she's aware of me just as I'm aware of her. Besides, an hour after Heidi took up the watch, Ian joined her. He never looked my way either, but Ian knows me. He'll be ready for anything I try.

So I lie on my back and watch the stars slowly drift by while Samuel curls up inside his bedroll and snores. Heidi and Ian stand beside the log Samuel used as a post for his watch, their heads close together. It looks like they're arguing about something, but only the occasional echo of their words reaches me.

Either they're being quiet to preserve their ability to be alert to dangers approaching the camp, or they don't want me to hear what they're saying. Or both.

I've tried to sleep, knowing I'll need to be ready for anything once we start traveling in the morning, but I can't seem to manage it for more than a few minutes at a time. My chest feels hollowed out, and everything in me longs to crawl away from this camp, disappear into the Wasteland, and make my way back to Logan. Missing him feels like something I was born to do. I breathe. I blink. I miss Logan. I couldn't stop it if I tried.

I don't try. I want the hurt. The ache that threads through my body until I can't separate the pain in my arm from the pain in my heart. Ian was right about one thing—pain reminds me that I'm still alive. Still here. Still moving forward even when it would be so much easier to stop.

I'm exhausted and on edge. Sleep feels impossible. I can't stop circling around the thought that, once upon a time, Ian was a boy with dreams not so very different from mine.

He deserves to die for destroying Baalboden. For murdering innocent people. Nothing will change that. But the boy with dreams also deserved to have his family remain whole. To follow in his father's footsteps instead of being the one responsible for ending his father's life.

I know all about the cruel ways life poisons the dreams we have and plunges us into darkness instead. I understand losing sight of the right choices because the wrong ones feel like the only salvation from pain that is too terrible to bear.

Something hot and wet slips down my face and drips onto my neck. I raise my good arm and wipe my cheeks. I'm crying.

Again. This is all Quinn's fault. Ever since he pushed me to crack the wall of silence inside and start feeling bits and pieces of the grief and guilt that belong to me, tears just . . . happen. It's like my body knows I need to grieve and refuses to wait for me to give in to it.

I sit up and blink away the tears, even as more form in their wake. This is ridiculous. I can't even think about Ian—the boy I want to *kill*—without feeling emotional and weepy. I scrub my face dry and glance at Samuel.

Still asleep. At least I don't have an audience for this. Even if it would reinforce my image as the girl who must be protected, I can't stand the thought of feeling raw and vulnerable in front of him again. Especially when I now know he blames me for Ian's brokenness.

Before more unwanted empathy for Ian can swamp me, I begin to count all the ways in which he and I are different. True, we both lost our fathers because of the treachery set in motion years ago by the Commander, but my father died a hero. Ian killed his father because his leader told him to. Before I can feel vindicated that I would never have obeyed orders like that, I remember watching Oliver die in front of me because I was too scared of the Commander to fight back.

A sob tears through me, and I shove my cloak against my mouth to muffle the sound.

Comparing my situation with Ian's is getting me nowhere. I need to take action and fix this before the entire tide of pent-up loss inside of me breaks loose. I glance toward Heidi and Ian. They've moved away from the log and are standing just inside the eastern edge of the Wasteland, facing away from the campsite.

Whispered snatches of their conversation float past me.

"*. . . other technicians . . .*"

"*. . . don't need it . . .*"

"*. . . Logan . . .*"

That does it. I need to know what they're saying. I lean toward them and hold my breath, straining to hear more.

As if Ian can feel the weight of my gaze, he turns his head in my direction. Quickly, I lie back down and hold perfectly still. My pulse thrums against my ears. My hands itch to grab the knife in my boot. My tears, thankfully, have dried. Nothing like a little spike of adrenaline to shove a girl into a warrior's mind-set again.

I count to one hundred, my back pressed against the rough dirt of our campsite, and then count to one hundred again for good measure. A breeze tangles with the oak leaves that surround us, and something skitters across a branch to the left of me. Samuel snores softly to the right.

When I finish counting, I slowly turn my head and look. Heidi and Ian are gone, though faint snatches of conversation still ghost through the night. They must've moved farther into the Wasteland. Apparently, they're willing to compromise their ability to guard me in order to keep me from overhearing them.

Now I really want to hear what they're saying.

I could take this opportunity to disappear in the opposite direction. Quinn should catch up soon. I wouldn't be alone for long. And then we could get Logan, Willow, Frankie, Adam, and anyone else who wants to join us in hunting down Ian and stopping Rowansmark from destroying anyone else.

I roll into a crouch and freeze, watching Samuel intently

for any sign that he heard me. Once I'm satisfied that he's still asleep, I stand carefully, wincing as my right arm brushes against my side and working hard not to let my smoke-scarred lungs breathe too harshly. Trying to escape three Rowansmark trackers in this condition would be difficult. I can't run. I can't climb a tree and leap. I'm not even sure I can stay on my feet for more than an hour.

Not that I'm averse to taking on nearly impossible tasks. Especially since I know that even if they caught me, the trackers would be committed to keeping me alive until Logan arrives in Rowansmark with the device. What's the worst they would do to me?

I think of Ian, of the terrible desperation in his eyes, and shiver.

Taking a second to let the searing pain in my arm abate, I look around to get my bearings. The log is about twenty yards east of me. Heidi and Ian are somewhere beyond that. I could go north and put a decent amount of distance between myself and the camp before daylight and then cut east toward Lankenshire. I could pray that Quinn finds me. I could bank on the fact that the trackers want to keep me alive and won't punish me too severely if they reach me first.

Or I could keep the promise I made to myself as Ian carried me away from the clearing where Quinn supposedly lay dying. I could be the warrior my dad raised me to be and head east to eavesdrop on the two trackers who seem awfully committed to making sure no one listens to their conversation.

In my head, I hear Logan's voice telling me I can't jump head-first into things without an exit strategy. If he were here, he'd have already considered every possible combination of things that could go wrong and come up with a way to handle it. I don't have the time or the clarity of thought to do that. Not when my head swims with exhaustion and pain crashes through me. If I get caught, I'll do what I do best—improvise.

Besides, it's not like they're going to kill me.

Moving as soundlessly as possible, I skirt the campsite and edge into the trees that line the northern side of the road. Moonlight pierces the canopy of branches above me in scattered pieces. I put my left arm out, my palm in front of me to keep from walking face-first into a tree, and then slowly start moving east, sliding my boots forward with care as I search for an unobstructed path.

I haven't gone far when my toe catches the edge of a rock, and I pitch forward. My left palm smacks into a tree trunk, and I dig my hand into the rough bark for balance. Motionless, I wait for a sign that Heidi and Ian heard me. When all stays quiet, I take a deep breath. The air is rich with the pungent smell of dogwood trees in bloom and the loamy scent of the forest floor. Releasing the tree trunk, I take a few more steps forward, and hear a whisper of sound ahead. Crouching, I slowly move another five yards through skinny tree trunks and rock-strewn dirt until the words Heidi is saying become clear.

". . . too risky, Ian."

"What's the risk?" Ian sounds furious. "She deserves it. You know that."

"Keep your voice down," Heidi whispers. "I'm not saying you don't have a point. But our orders are clear—"

"Our orders were to recover the device and punish the ones who stole it."

"Which we haven't done yet." Heidi sounds edgy. Like she's already explained this to Ian and isn't happy about repeating herself.

"It's as good as done. There's no way Logan will fail to bring it to us. He'd never leave Rachel behind. We don't have to worry—"

"I'm not worried. I'm just saying that I'm not walking into Rowansmark with nothing to show for our trip but your assurances that your brother will show up."

"We don't need Rachel anymore. He'll show up no matter what, don't you see that?" Ian's voice is impatient. "We can punish her now, and—"

"What does it matter if you punish her now or punish her later? The girl is dead either way."

"Because I can't stand to look at her! Every time I see her, I'm reminded that if she'd returned the controller to Rowansmark instead of taking it to Logan, my dad would be alive." Ian's voice shakes. "I want her *dead*. Not tomorrow. Not whenever Logan brings the controller to Rowansmark. I want her dead *now*."

A chill slides across my skin at the hatred in his voice. I understand that hatred. It boils and churns deep within me, waiting to lash out at the man whose actions ruined my life. Waiting for a chance to kill the Commander. That kind of bone-deep hatred is ravenous. The more you feed it, the hungrier it gets.

It can't be stopped. And it certainly can't be satisfied with slim assurances that the object of its bloodlust will pay her debt sometime in the future.

Ian is going to try to kill me the very second he thinks Samuel isn't watching. And with my useless arm and my crippled lungs, I'm going to need a miracle to fight him off.

It was one thing to threaten to kill Ian despite my injuries when I thought I had both Samuel and Heidi firmly on the side of keeping me alive. It's another to realize that Samuel blames me for Ian's craziness, and that Heidi can discuss disposing of me like it matters less to her than what she might choose to eat for breakfast in the morning.

A week ago, I would've welcomed the fight with Ian, despite the overwhelming odds against me. Maybe *because* of the overwhelming odds against me. A week ago—before the fire, before Eloise had Melkin's baby girl, before I cried over Sylph and started to feel real again inside—I didn't care if I lived or died.

I care now.

I'm not going to deliver myself to Ian on a silver platter. I'm going to do what Willow and Logan kept urging me to do as we traveled through the Wasteland—I'm going to be smart about this. I'm going to have a plan and an exit strategy. And I'm going to have to come up with it fast, because it won't be long before the trackers notice I'm no longer lying by the campfire's ashes.

Should I head east toward Lankenshire and hope to stumble into Quinn? Go north and then cut east after a few hours? Find a river or a creek to wade in so that I don't leave a trail? If I can just find Quinn, we can join up with Logan again. We can face all of this—Ian, Rowansmark, and the Commander—together. Logan will have a plan with five hundred backup scenarios just in case. We'll have tech and weapons. And I won't be going up against a madman with nothing but my left hand and a knife.

I'm pretty sure Logan would approve of this exit strategy.

I ease back, but freeze when Heidi says, "Maybe James Rowan

would be satisfied knowing that Logan will return the device. And that he can expect the Commander and Carrington's forces to follow the device straight to Rowansmark. We can give him that information, and it might be enough. But we can't predict if Logan will come alone, or if he'll bring troops. James Rowan is going to want Rachel as a bargaining chip in case Logan has an army of his own."

Ian's laugh is ugly. "It doesn't matter how many troops show up. Weren't you listening? The tech was finished just before we left Rowansmark. By now, it will be installed around the city's perimeter. Let Logan bring an army. The Commander, too. In fact, let every single city-state show up at our wall. We'll destroy them in the time it takes to push a single button."

My throat goes dry, and my hands tremble as I press my fingers into the dirt to keep my balance.

"If the tech works, yes, but—"

"It works. My father and I designed it." Ian's voice is proud. "One button, Heidi. That's all James Rowan has to push, and he can call an entire army of *tanniyn* to surface just outside our wall. Those who dare to march against us will be annihilated before they've had time to realize their mistake."

My heart knocks against my chest in quick, hard thumps as the escape plan I hatched sinks beneath a bloody vision of Logan, Baalboden survivors, and Lankenshire troops all decimated in seconds by an entire army of Cursed Ones. Until we arrived in Lankenshire, I didn't realize there was more than one beast still alive, much less enough to surround the city of Rowansmark, but I don't doubt the absolute confidence in Ian's voice.

The tech exists. The *tanniyn* exist. And Logan has no idea

that the trap he's walking into is far more dangerous than a single modified piece of Rowansmark tech can handle. Even if I escaped to warn him, what could we do? The only way to give us a fighting chance to break Rowansmark's tyranny is to get inside the city.

Forget escaping. Forget being afraid to die at Ian's hands. I'm going into Rowansmark, and I'm going to find that tech and destroy it before it takes the last of my family from me.

Ian can try to kill me, but he's going to fail.

Pushing my hands against the dirt, I start crawling backward, intent on returning to the campsite and pretending to be asleep before anyone realizes I'm gone. I've moved a little over fifteen yards when someone grabs the back of my cloak and hauls me roughly to my feet.

"Got you," Ian says.

I open my mouth to answer, but his fist slams into my face. Tiny lights explode across my vision, and then everything goes black.

CHAPTER NINE

LOGAN

Another Brute Squad guard, a blond man with freckled skin and eyebrows so pale they look nearly transparent in the torchlight, waits outside the dungeon's doorway as Willow and I walk out. A boy who looks to be about Rachel's age stands apart from the guard, his eyes wide as he stares at Willow's blood-stained tunic and the chains that bind my wrists. Something about the boy's dark eyes and hair, about the line of his jaw and the set of his shoulders, reminds me of Clarissa. A glance at the gold emblem that pins back his green travel cloak confirms that the boy is an emissary of Lankenshire. Probably the one who approached the Commander to lay out the terms of my "escape."

The Commander strides past me and stops in front of the boy. "Get us out of here."

The boy nods quickly. "The tunnel entrance is relatively close. I can return you to your army in about an hour."

The Commander grabs the boy's shoulder before he can turn

to lead us down the hall. "We aren't going back to the army. We're going to retrieve something from the Wasteland." He gestures roughly toward Willow. "The girl will tell you which direction to lead us."

"I have a name," Willow says, her eyes challenging as she meets the Commander's gaze. "And it isn't 'the girl.'"

The Commander steps closer to her and says with quiet menace, "You are nothing more than a tool I'm using to get what I want. I don't care about your name, your city of birth, your reasons for getting mixed up with Logan, or anything else you feel like sharing. Tell the boy where to take us."

Willow lifts her chin, her long hair floating behind her as she moves to stand toe to toe with the Commander. "My name is Willow Runningbrook, and you don't scare me."

The Commander's face twitches as if she'd slapped him, and I step forward, my chain links clinking softly. "We're wasting time. We need to *move*."

"I concur," the boy says. "The longer we debate amongst ourselves, the greater the chance of discovery by our mutual enemy Rowansmark."

His voice is both lyrical and precise, like a mathematician reciting poetry. I've never heard someone close to my age speak so formally, but now isn't the time to try to figure him out.

I nod toward Willow, and she says, "We need to exit northeast of the city."

The Commander turns to the blond guard who'd waited outside the dungeon. "Once we get into the tunnels, return to camp. Take Alford, Vale, and Roland along with extra horses and supplies. Meet us at the northeast tunnel exit."

The guard frowns. "I don't know where the northeast tunnel exit is."

"Do you know where northeast is?" the Commander asks, his tone biting.

"Of course."

The Commander chops his words up, each piece covered in scorn. "Then simply walk around Lankenshire's wall until you reach the northeast side and wait until you see us."

The Lankenshire boy leads us through the corridor until we come to a short, curved hallway that ends in a windowless brick wall. Without hesitating, the boy hurries down it and stops just near the end. Beneath his feet is a square of tile with a small iron ring set into its center. He crouches beside it and lifts it free. It opens on silent hinges, revealing a thick iron ladder that leads to the tunnels below.

"You first, Orion." The Commander gestures toward a short guard with a thick beard that completely covers the lower half of his face. "If either Logan or the girl tries to escape, hurt them."

Orion's dark eyes flick over me and settle on Willow. The speculative way he runs his gaze over her body makes me want to punch him.

"Show some respect," I snap.

Orion laughs. "Says the outcast to the Brute Squad guard."

"Or you could continue to disrespect her, and I'll show you how fast an outcast can beat you senseless." I step forward, and heft my chains. He takes a small step back. Maybe he's heard about the way I used the chains in the Commander's dungeon to attack his guards. Or maybe he's just a bully who doesn't know what to do when someone isn't afraid of him. Either way, he won't treat Willow the way guards in Baalboden were allowed to treat women. Not while I'm still alive.

"Stop talking to my guard as if he's your equal," the Commander says. He pauses as if waiting for a response from me, but I just glare at him. It isn't very satisfying, but I'm in chains, surrounded by guards, and I need the Commander's cooperation if I'm going to keep my promise to destroy Rowansmark's tech. Seeing that I don't plan to respond, the Commander turns away and says, "Orion, get down that ladder."

As Orion hurries to obey, Willow moves to my side and says quietly, "I can defend myself. I know how to take care of men like him."

My chest burns as I imagine the kind of things Willow endured at the hands of her father. She won't talk about her past beyond explaining the significance of the feather she wears on her ear cuff, but I see the weight of it when she doesn't think I'm looking.

"I know you can," I say as we move closer to the tunnel's entrance. "I'm not defending you because I doubt your skills, Willow."

"Then why?"

"Because we're family now. And because he shouldn't treat women like objects put here for him to use however he wants. I can't be the person I want to be if I let that pass."

The Commander grabs my shoulder and shoves me forward. "A useless sentiment clung to by those too weak to take what they want. Get into the tunnel."

My chains clang sharply against the ladder as I make my way

down each rung. The second my boots touch the tunnel floor, Orion grabs my cloak and shoves me face-first against the stone wall.

"Still think it's a good idea to tell me what to do?" he asks, his breath hot against the side of my face.

I tense and roll to the balls of my feet, but remain silent. Above us, the blond guard begins carefully descending the ladder, his torch held aloft.

"I'm talking to you." Orion shoves me harder.

I lift my hands to my chest as if trying to protect myself from the wall, but refuse to answer. He curses, and digs his fingers into my cloak.

"I asked you a question," he snaps.

When I still don't answer, he jerks me around. I plant my right foot and raise my fists as I spin toward him. The length of chain that dangles from my wrists whips out and lashes him across the face. His head snaps back. I raise my hands and pound the bulk of the iron shackles against his skull like I'm hammering a nail.

He stumbles back, but I don't follow him. The blond guard is nearly at the base of the ladder, the glow from his torch illuminating the craggy white-gray stone of the tunnel. Willow is climbing down above him. I don't need either of them trying to intervene. Besides, Orion has learned what I needed to teach him: I'm not a helpless outcast cowering in the shadow of the almighty Baalboden guards anymore, and anyone who wants to disrespect those I care about will have to go through me to do it.

"What happened to your face?" the blond guard asks as the

torchlight shows a trail of blood leaking from Orion's cheek and a bruise swelling around his left eye.

"Nothing. Mind your own business, Peter." Orion wipes the blood away and glares at me. I guess he doesn't feel like admitting that he took on the shackled prisoner and lost.

Willow steps off the ladder and looks at Orion. "Looks like your face ran into a wall. Don't worry, it's an improvement."

He gives her a look of pure hatred, and she laughs as she brushes past him to stand next to me. Moments later, the Commander, the Lankenshire boy, and the last guard, a rail-thin man with sharp cheekbones and a torch of his own, join us in the tunnel. The thin guard, a man called Gregory, lights a spare torch and hands it to the Lankenshire boy. The Commander sends Peter, the blond guard, back to the waiting army of Carrington soldiers and Baalboden guards, and then we begin moving toward the northeast exit.

The Lankenshire boy leads, followed closely by Willow and me. The Commander walks behind us, and Orion and Gregory bring up the rear. Walking with my back to the Commander makes me feel exposed, but I don't have much choice in the matter. Not if I want this uneasy alliance to hold.

The tunnel is just wide enough to allow Willow and me to walk side by side without touching. The air is dry and warm enough that my cloak is beginning to be uncomfortable. Here and there, the stone ceiling becomes a square of wood with another ladder leading up into Lankenshire, but the tunnel we're in twists and turns so much, I've lost track of what part of the city we're currently under.

"I'm curious as to our planned route once we exit the tunnel."

The boy breaks the silence as he leads us around a sharp right corner, his torch illuminating yet another long length of craggy gray-white stone.

"You're returning to your city once we exit the tunnel," the Commander says.

"Actually, I'm escorting you to Hodenswald as Lankenshire's official emissary." The boy's voice is calm, though his words tumble out too fast. I don't blame him. Correcting the Commander is a good way to get killed.

"I never agreed to that."

The boy gives a small, one-shouldered shrug as if to apologize. "The triumvirate intended for my presence to assist you in gaining support at Hodenswald. Our alliance with them is strong."

The Commander grunts and falls back a few steps, his only concession that the boy can continue on with us.

The boy waits until the Commander is closer to his guards than he is to us, and then says, "The triumvirate is under the belief that you're capable of dispatching our difficulty with Rowansmark."

"You talk like a character in an old book," Willow says.

The boy rubs the nape of his neck and casts a sideways glance at her. "Perhaps because I prefer spending most of my time with old books."

"Why?" Willow asks.

"Books are nicer than most people. I suppose that makes me appear weak to someone who can fight off a Rowansmark tracker." He squares his shoulders as if waiting for her judgment.

"My brother loves books, too—poetry mostly—and he's the best warrior I know," Willow says. "And this one"—she points to me—"thinks mathematical equations are better than kissing, and he's anything but weak. Worrying about what others think of you is a waste of time."

The boy flashes a smile. "I'm Connor. You've already met my mother, Clarissa the Great. And my sister, Cassidy the Soon-to-Be-Great."

Willow laughs. "Does that make you Connor the Also-Great?"

"Not exactly."

"I'm Logan, and this is Willow. And for the record, I don't think mathematical equations are better than kissing," I say as we turn yet another corner. The air is cooler in this portion of the tunnel. I wonder if that means we're closing in on an exit.

Connor grins. "I'd imagine it would depend on whom you were kissing."

I return his smile, but my heart isn't in it. My heart is somewhere in the Wasteland with Rachel. The last time we were separated, I was worried that Melkin would try to kill her on the Commander's orders. I was scared that she'd be forced to kill him instead. And I was kicking myself for not realizing earlier that Rachel—fierce, loyal, reckless, intelligent, beautiful Rachel—was the one person I couldn't bear to live without.

This time, I know what loving Rachel and being loved in return feels like. But instead of holding on to that like a lifeline, I'm shackled to the thought that Rachel's father knew who I was. That Oliver did too. That no one trusted me enough to tell me the truth, and all the respect I thought I'd earned, all the love I thought they'd had for me, was a lie. I sift through my memories of Oliver and Jared, and nothing *feels* like a lie, but feelings aren't the same as facts.

The fact is that I was the Commander's investment, stolen from Rowansmark with the intention to coerce my father into giving tech capable of weaponizing the *tanniyn* to the Commander.

The fact is that my Baalboden mother wasn't my real mother.

The fact is that Oliver took care of me, but so did the woman who pretended to be my mother. If she did so on the Commander's orders, maybe Oliver did too.

The fact is that Jared brought reports of my well-being to my father every six months. Every time Jared treated me like a son—every bit of training, every shared dinner, every moment I spent with him—was simply so that he would have something truthful to report.

And the fact is that Rachel, the girl who wears her every emotion for the world to see, is incapable of the kind of long-term dishonesty that keeping my secrets would take. Which means I can still trust her. I can still look at my memories of her without the taint of suspicion poisoning everything we had. The foundation I built my life upon might be crumbling, but Rachel is still my constant, and I'm not going to lose her.

I tracked her down once. I can do it again.

Best Case Scenario: The risky plan I've put in motion works.

Worst Case Scenario: The Commander tries to kill me before I'm ready for him, the northern city-states won't commit troops against Rowansmark, or I fail to find Ian and Rachel.

None of those are options I can accept. If I have to grovel before the Commander, if I have to wear chains, if I have to pretend to be nothing but the investment he wants me to be, I'll do it. Nothing is going to stop me from keeping my promises.

CHAPTER TEN

RACHEL

I wake to the jostling of the moving wagon. My mouth is dry, and my cheekbone aches where Ian punched me. I'm lying on my back in the wagon bed. Every bump of the wheels sends my head careening into something hard. In the few seconds it takes for my brain to convince my body that it's time to wake up and get moving, my face smacks against it three more times.

"Ouch." I force my eyes open and immediately wish I hadn't.

Ian sits near me, his hands clasped in his lap while he stares at me in the weak light of early morning. How long have I been unconscious? A few hours? A day? Are we still heading west? The wagon shudders again as the wheels roll across the crumbling road beneath us, and my head slams into a crate of supplies that rests under the bench to my left.

I dig my elbows into my bedroll and try to sit up, but I can't pull my legs into position. Something is wrapped around my ankles.

"I tied you to one of the posts on the back of the wagon." A ghost of his charming smile flits across Ian's face, though his eyes are hard.

"Good for you."

"You should see your face." He reaches out as if to touch my cheek, and I bare my teeth. He laughs, but there's no amusement in it. "I told Heidi and Samuel I want you tied up in the wagon because you'll try to escape, but they don't know you like I do." He leans closer. "You aren't the type who runs away, even when you should. I think you were eavesdropping instead. Learn anything interesting?"

The conversation between Ian and Heidi flashes through my mind in rapid snatches. Ian's desire to kill me as soon as possible. Heidi's careless attitude toward what she believes is my certain death.

And the tech that waits for Logan at Rowansmark. Tech that can summon an entire army of *tanniyn* to annihilate Rowansmark's enemies in moments. Tech that will set a trap even Logan can't plan his way out of.

Which is why, even though I want to pull the knife out of my boot, sever the rope that binds me, and escape at my first opportunity, I'm not going to do it. I'm going inside Rowansmark, because that's my best chance at disabling the tech before Logan arrives.

"Samuel and Heidi were right," I say as I rub my fingers against the dull ache that throbs along my bruised cheekbone. "I was trying to escape."

Ian's jaw muscles bunch. "You never try to escape. You run headlong toward whatever is most dangerous. Courageous stupidity. That's you."

I ignore him and scoot closer to the wagon's entrance so that I can sit with my knees pressed against my chest. A length of rope wraps three times around my ankles in a figure eight and then disappears out of the canvas flap that covers the entrance. I shuffle my boots against my bedroll as if I'm trying to get comfortable, and feel a surge of satisfaction when my knife moves slightly against my left ankle.

Ian must have searched me for weapons when he knocked me unconscious and took me from Lankenshire, and he's confident he doesn't need to search me again. It's the only explanation for why he hasn't discovered the stolen blade I carry. It doesn't explain why he let me keep the lightweight armored vest I wear under my tunic, but maybe he figured as long as he knows about it, my advantage is lost.

"It doesn't matter," he says.

I look at him, at his sharp profile, his close-cut hair, his eyes burning with miserable hate when he watches me. "What doesn't matter?"

"Whatever you overheard. Whatever you think you know. You can't escape your fate, Rachel." Ian leans forward and tugs on the rope that binds my ankles. It barely moves.

"Watch me."

He shakes his head. "Look at you. You can't use your right arm. Your lungs whistle when you breathe. You just slept through me hauling you into the wagon and tying you up because your body doesn't have what it takes to keep going. The only reason you're still making threats is because you don't know how to give up when you're beaten."

I want to argue with him. Tell him he doesn't have what it

takes to beat me, not on his best day, but the truth is he's right. I'm in no shape to fight him physically, and I can't risk inciting the rage that fuels him. I have to make it to Rowansmark alive.

"I guess you have me all figured out," I say, my voice quiet.

The skin between his brows puckers as he studies me. I look away. Let him think I'm cowering. I don't care. I'll do whatever it takes to stay alive long enough to get into Rowansmark. After that . . . well, after that I don't know. I'll have to figure out how to escape. And how to hide from every tracker inside the city's wall. And how to find and disable tech even though I understand tech about as well as I understand how to properly host a fancy dinner party.

Ian's right about me. I don't run away, even when I probably should. I rush headlong into danger if I think by doing so I can protect those I love. I operate on instinct—courageous stupidity, Ian called it—but instinct and courage might not be enough this time. Especially when I'm in no shape to win a fight. Or to run away if I start to lose. Since fighting and running are the two mainstays of any plan I've ever made, I'm going to have to think like someone else. Someone who can still see scenarios when none exist and who can grab small opportunities and leverage them into huge wins.

I'm going to have to think like Logan.

"You look awful, by the way." Ian's voice is casual. "You're dirty, your hair is an absolute mess, and I'm pretty sure if you don't get some medicine for that nasty wound on your arm, it's going to get infected. We wouldn't want that." The sly malevolence in his gaze sets my teeth on edge.

"Going to be hard to convince Logan to give you what you

want if I die before we reach Rowansmark," I say, as if I don't already know that Ian has no intention of letting me make it that far. Not if he gets a chance to come after me when Samuel is distracted elsewhere.

"Why do you even want to live?" he asks. There's a desperate curiosity in his voice. "Your family is dead. Your city is gone. Most of your friends are gone too. And you're to blame. You, Logan, and the Commander. Don't you want to just close your eyes and never wake up?"

I wrap my arms around my stomach as if the broken pieces inside of me might pierce my skin and fly away, but I know Ian isn't really asking why I want to live. He's looking for a reason of his own to keep going.

I don't want to give him one.

But Logan would. Logan would see this as an opportunity to soften his opponent. To gain a foothold. I'm not sure there's a foothold left to be found in Ian's madness, but Samuel's words still echo in my head, and I can't look at Ian the monster without also seeing Ian the boy with broken dreams.

"I have to believe that there are people still worth living for. That *I'm* worth living for," I say, remembering Oliver's words to me as we traveled to the Commander's compound for the reading of Dad's will. "Hope is precious, and it's worth clinging to."

"Even when it looks like there's nothing left to hope for?" His eyes are full of misery.

"There's always something left. There are second, third, and fourth chances. There are new friends." I think of Quinn, stoically dedicated to helping me heal, even when it meant stripping his own secrets bare. Willow, unafraid to tell me the truth no one else wanted to say. Frankie admitting he was wrong about Tree People. Thom taking Logan's place on the bridge. And then I think of Logan. Of the way he used to look at me when he thought Dad wasn't watching us. Of the way he looks at me now. "And there are old friends we've underestimated. There's a legacy of love in our lives that gives us value, even after we've made mistakes."

He stares at me for a long moment, his face pale and tense. "I don't think hope keeps you alive at all. I think you're still here because you're too stubborn to die." His long, pale fingers grip the rope and pull on it again. "I actually like that about you."

"I don't care what you like about me."

"You never care what anyone thinks of you. You never care what others think you should do." His fingers clench the rope with sudden force. "Even when it costs you. Even when it costs *them*."

The memory of Melkin's dark eyes pleading with me while his blood spilled over my hands cuts into me, and it's difficult to breathe.

"What did I cost you, Ian?" I ask, Samuel's words burning against the back of my mind. I don't want to think about Ian, broken and lost, trying to find a way to still see some of his dreams come true even if it takes more than his spirit can bear to pay. "What did I do to you that is worth going through so much trouble to hurt me?"

"You didn't keep your promise." He sounds hurt. As if he has a *right* to be hurt when he'd already murdered eight children and destroyed our entire city-state before I ever said I'd get the device from Logan and give it to Ian to use against the Commander.

I stare at the pain in his eyes and realize he truly believes he's the one who's been wronged. And maybe in the beginning that was true, but Ian's done too much between then and now to pretend his hands are clean. Maybe he isn't pretending. Maybe he believes what he needs to believe in order to keep what little sanity he has left.

"Think about what you're saying." I make an effort to keep my voice calm, but I can't quite keep the anger out of it. This is the boy who killed Sylph. Having a civil conversation with him feels like a betrayal of her. "You asked me to get the device while we were running for our lives from the Carrington army, and I was trying to get to my best friend, who was dying because of *you*."

"No, she was dying because Logan didn't—"

"She died because of you and your stupid pain atonement vendetta! Because you assumed Logan was loyal to the Commander. Because you *assumed* he knew about his background." My voice rises, and I clench my fists as grief and anger churn inside of me. My wounded arm aches, but I ignore it. "And because you couldn't be bothered to confront Logan at the start and clear the air, my city burned and thousands died. *Sylph* died."

"I was following orders! Whipping my father to death wasn't enough to reclaim our family's honor." His voice shakes. "To pay for his crime. Not with the tech in enemy hands. I had to reclaim the tech and punish those who took it. I had to make it clear that no one should mess with Rowansmark again. Sylph wouldn't have had to die if—"

"If you hadn't killed her to make a point!" I pull my arms tighter across my body to keep myself from lunging toward him. To keep him from defending himself and killing me before I get a chance to go after Rowansmark's tech. "Do you understand what you've done? You took mothers from their children. Sons from their fathers. You ripped families and friends apart and for *what*, Ian? So that Logan would feel pain? Is that really worth ruining so many lives?"

"Logan ruined *my* life!" The pain in his eyes disappears in a blink, replaced by the hard, vicious brilliance of undiluted rage. "Because of him, I've had to become the kind of person who could *do* those things. And then I saw a way out. You would give me the controller. I would take it back to Rowansmark, restore my family's honor, and I would be *done*. I could stop killing and walk away. But you didn't keep your word. And I couldn't stop. I couldn't stop!" His breath hitches, and two bright spots of color burn against the paleness of his cheeks.

I recognize his fury, the well of impossible darkness that stretches beneath his words, consuming logic and spewing lies in its place. A small voice in my head whispers that Ian is my future if I let the hatred I feel for the Commander and the deep need I feel for revenge become everything that I live for. If I run on desperation and vengeance, forgetting to count the cost to others and to myself, I'll dishonor the forgiveness Eloise gave to me for the death of her husband, the sacrifices Quinn made for me, and the steady belief Logan has in me even when it seems I'm proving him wrong.

Once upon a time, I would've ignored that voice. Shoved it into the silence inside of me and refused to consider it because it would only slow me down. I was so sure vengeance was the answer. So sure my pain would mean something if I could deliver the same.

I meet Ian's eyes and speak slowly as I fumble my way through something that feels like a truth I should've realized a long time ago. "Logan didn't ruin your life, Ian. When something is ruined it can never be rebuilt. It can't recover. The things others do to us can break us, but we can heal. But when we twist the pain and use it as justification for the choices we make, we lose ourselves. We hurt ourselves by shoving the pain away like if we just don't look at it, it won't exist. By using it as the fuel that gets us through every day."

"What a bunch of . . . I didn't hurt myself. Logan did." Ian sounds furious, but the pain is back in his eyes. "My mother was so busy grieving for her lost child that she never saw me. Barely spoke to me. I tried to reach her. I tried, but one day she just decided life without Logan was too much to bear. It didn't matter that she had me or that I loved her. She was gone."

His voice shakes, and a vein bulges in his neck. "And my father was so busy trying to get Logan back that he didn't care that his actions could leave us permanently disgraced. And what did Logan do after all of that? After my parents gave their lives for him? He took the controller back to the man who started all of this misery in the first place."

"Logan didn't know any of that. You've lost yourself, Ian." I let my arms fall to my sides, and though I still see the boy who killed Sylph, I also see the boy who only wanted his mother to love him and his father to think of him. "You took that misery, you multiplied it a hundred times over, and you spread it over people who never hurt you. Never wronged you. The Commander's actions cost you two people you loved. Three, if you count Logan."

"I don't love Logan."

"You would have if he'd been allowed to grow up in Rowansmark as part of your family."

He stares at me in silence.

"Ian, you lost two people. And you used the pain of that loss to justify killing thousands."

"You and I are the same." His chest heaves as if he's been running, and he shoves his words at me like he wants to hurt me. "We're the same, Rachel. You said as long as it didn't cost you the few people you loved, you'd do anything to destroy the Commander. You understood that justice requires sacrifice. Don't pretend to be better than me."

A chill spreads across my skin as I think of the narrow line between justice and revenge at any cost, and of how close I came to crossing it. How I didn't care that the line existed.

How having Logan, Quinn, Willow, and Sylph in my life saved me from making the kind of choices that would leave me just as broken and desperate as Ian. Ian needed someone to keep him from crossing that line, too, but all he had were fanatics who told him a pain atonement bloodbath during his quest to retrieve the missing tech would restore the only thing he still had left—his family's honor.

"You're right. I did say I'd do anything to destroy the Commander." I wrap my hands around my ankles and feel the comforting weight of the knife pressed against my left one. "But I was wrong. Justice and revenge aren't the same thing."

His laugh is cruel. "It's a little hard to take you seriously when just yesterday you promised to keep coming after me until you kill me to make me pay for what I've done."

I meet his eyes and raise my chin. "I meant every word I said. The difference between us, Ian, is that I'm not willing to kill anyone but those who absolutely deserve it."

"You're tied to a wagon, surrounded by trackers, and too injured and weak to even defend yourself. You're stupid if you think you can get the best of me." He gets to his feet, his legs braced against the constant motion of the wheels. "And I don't care what you say about hope. About second chances. You've used up your chances, Rachel. You and Logan both."

His voice drops until his words are nothing but a breath whispered across the space between us. "You and I are the same. You know it. I know it. Justice requires sacrifice. The moment Samuel turns his back on you, I'm going to deliver the justice you so desperately deserve."

Without another word, he leaps from the wagon, and I'm alone.

CHAPTER ELEVEN

LOGAN

Lankenshire is a distant gleam of white-gray stone on a hill behind us, only intermittently visible through the thick clusters of tall maples, hickories, and oaks.

It took us nearly three hours to work our way out of the tunnels. Once we reached the northeast exit and met up with the handful of soldiers and horses the Commander had requested from the vast army camped across the fields surrounding Lankenshire, Willow announced that the device was actually four hundred yards north*west* of the city. When the Commander cursed her for costing us extra time, Willow coolly asked him if he'd rather have had the location announced in the hearing of the few trackers who'd survived the dungeon assault. Covering the ground between our exit point and the device was slow going in the dark, even with the horses, because we didn't want to leave a trail beside the tunnel's entrance advertising our new direction.

I wish I had Jeremiah's map with me so I could figure out where we are in relation to Hodenswald, the next closest city-state, but the map, along with my bag of spare tech supplies, my extra clothes, and my weapons, is in my room at the hospital in Lankenshire.

The Commander will know how to get to Hodenswald from here. I just have to hope that once we recover the device, he still agrees that I'm necessary to his efforts to take down Rowansmark.

Actually, hope has nothing to do with it.

My horse's hoof slides through a damp patch of dirt, and I take a second to lean down and brush the print away with the leafy bough I'm carrying as I ride at the back of our small group. My left hand aches in dull throbs, and I handle the branch carefully to avoid bumping it against the stump of my missing finger. It isn't easy to carry the bough and keep my seat on my borrowed horse while my hands are wrapped in chains, but I'm not about to complain. I might need these chains for a weapon.

I fully expect the Commander to try to kill me as soon as we recover the device. Part of me wants to let him try. Let him take up his sword against me and learn a permanent lesson about what happens when a leader abuses his power and pushes his people to the breaking point. If I couldn't defend myself against him with my chains like I did inside his dungeon, Willow could simply shoot him with an arrow.

A shrill whistle interrupts my thoughts, and I look up to see Willow swing out of her saddle and leap into the cradle of a huge oak. Knots in the wood have created holes the size of my fist across the trunk. She looks from me to the hole closest to her and then back again.

We've found it.

The Commander and his men ease to a stop and dismount. "Where is it? In that tree?" he asks. "Bring it down."

Willow pauses, looking to me for direction. I understand her hesitation. Once we give him the device, our bargaining chip is gone. We'll have to hope he understands that he needs me if he wants to disarm the tech in the northern city-states and strengthen this device enough to have a prayer against Rowansmark's armies.

"If you're considering breaking the terms of our deal, think again." The Commander's voice cuts through the morning air. "I saw what you did with the arrows in the dungeon, girl, and I came prepared."

A knot forms in my stomach as two of the new guards whip arrows into their bows and aim them at Willow. She's stuck, her feet on a branch, her body wrapped around the trunk while she reaches for the hole that hides the device.

She'll never get out of the way in time.

The cold rasp of a sword leaving its scabbard stings the air and the Commander grabs my cloak, pulls me from my horse, and shoves me against the nearest tree, his blade already at my neck. I don't raise my hands to block him. I can't. If I make a single wrong move, both Willow and I are dead. The Commander already knows where the device is. Our leverage is gone. All I have left is the faint hope that his need to destroy James Rowan outweighs his need to destroy me.

"Perhaps we could discuss this matter with civility, rather than with weapons," Connor says as he spurs his horse forward so that he can grab the reins of the riderless mounts who stand quietly like the battle-trained horses that they are.

"Perhaps you should hold your tongue before I cut it out of your head," the Commander snaps.

"I told you it was a mistake to bring the old man out here," Willow says, her eyes on the two arrows aimed at her body. "I told you he'd stick a knife in our backs because he's too stupid to see the value of keeping alive the people who can actually stop this piece of tech from malfunctioning and who can disarm the tech in the other city-states."

"Better shut that little girl up, or I'll let my men teach her the same lesson I'm about to teach you." The edge of his sword catches against the skin on my neck.

"They'd better kill me on their first try," Willow says, her voice low and furious. "Because if they don't, I'll rip them apart limb from limb."

The Commander's smile is vicious, though he doesn't break eye contact with me. "Oh, they won't miss. The consequences for failing me are too painful for them to consider." His sword presses closer, and I struggle to hold still as blood seeps down my neck and into my tunic. His dark eyes bore into mine. "I don't allow those who disobey me to live. Your mother learned that the hard way. Now, so will you."

"She wasn't my mother." The words are poison running through every warm childhood memory I have. The scaly oak trunk behind me digs into my back as I do my best to shrink away from the Commander's sword.

The Commander's scar twitches. "I see you've learned a thing or two since we last spoke."

I swallow, wincing as my throat scrapes his blade. Choosing my words with care, I say, "I know I'm your investment.

Your insurance against James Rowan's plan to subjugate all of the city-states. I know my father finished the invention, but that it isn't the only one. It isn't even the strongest one. My brother had a controller with more power the day we called the Cursed One outside of Baalboden."

"You mean the day you tried to kill me."

"The day we tried to kill each other." I keep my voice calm even though I want to drive my fist into his face. Beat him until he falls to the ground and bleeds the way my Baalboden mother bled. Watch him tremble in fear the way Rachel trembled after she saw him murder Oliver in front of her. "My brother was tracking the package that was given to Jared. He followed us to Baalboden, and he sent the beast into your city. He destroyed everything you'd built. And while he was doing that, other Rowansmark trackers were approaching the rest of the city-states, offering them a deal."

"I know about the deal." His voice is angry, but he eases up a fraction on the sword.

"According to Clarissa Vaughn, all of the city-states took the deal. They paid the protection fee and allowed Rowansmark to install beacons throughout their towns."

"Not my allies." He sounds proud.

"Yes, your allies. Thorenburg and Schoensville committed troops to Rowansmark. Their armies are waiting for us there. And the city of Carrington is gone. Destroyed when they remained loyal to you." I meet his gaze while he glares at me, looking for a lie that isn't there. "We learned it hours ago from Clarissa Vaughn, leader of Lankenshire's triumvirate."

"He's right," Connor says. His eyes dart between me, trapped by the Commander's blade, and Willow, surrounded by guards ready to fill her full of arrows. "We received the news just before I brought the terms of Logan's deal to you."

The Commander's eyes flicker toward Connor, and I quietly wrap my hands around the length of chain that dangles below my wrists, tensing my legs in case I need to fight my way out of this.

Not that I *can* fight my way out of this. Not with a sword already slicing into my throat.

"If you kill us, how will you make sure this device doesn't malfunction when you arrive at Rowansmark?" I ask, keeping my voice as neutral as possible. If he thinks I'm challenging him, he'll drive his blade into my neck. "How will you convince the northern city-states to violate their protection agreements unless you can disable the beacons and promise them safety from the *tanniyn*?"

His lips curve into a sneer. "And I suppose you just want to help me out of the goodness of your heart. There isn't a single part of you that hopes to catch me off guard, steal the tech for yourself, and leave my body in the Wasteland."

"Not while the Rowansmark threat remains." I meet his gaze. "My brother destroyed my city and then murdered my friends as we traveled to Lankenshire. Now he's taken Rachel hostage, and he won't release her unless I show up at Rowansmark with the device."

"That girl isn't worth half the trouble she's caused."

My pulse pounds against my ears. "She hasn't caused trouble. Rowansmark has. The tech, the murders, the destruction . . . it all goes back to them. You knew this would happen when you heard rumors of my father's invention nineteen years ago. You know James Rowan can't be trusted with this much power." Neither can the Commander, but he won't live long enough to try it. Not if Rachel and I have anything to say about it.

His angry expression turns thoughtful, though his sword remains steady. "You really do want to take down James Rowan." He says the words like he's trying them on for size.

"I do."

"With me."

"Yes. There are three armies waiting for us. At least one controller that is stronger than ours. And we'd be fighting on the terrain Rowansmark uses as a training ground. We need your credibility with the northern city-states to convince them to give us troops. We need your military expertise to win the war. And we need my ability to disarm the beacons, strengthen our device, and if I have time, replicate it."

He leans closer, the blade sliding painfully against the scarred brand he gave me the first time I was his prisoner. "How do I know you won't betray me the second I take off your chains and treat you like an ally?"

"Because I would do anything to save Rachel." The words are heavy with conviction. With the one truth I have left. With Rachel.

His smile makes me feel sick inside. "Women have always been your weakness. First your mother, now Jared's daughter. You even defend the Tree Girl." He eases back a fraction, and I take a careful breath, trying hard not to let more skin catch against his blade. "A word of advice: Showing your weaknesses makes you easy prey. We do this my way, on my terms." He spits the words in my face. "I'm in charge. The very second you do something I don't like, I will torture the Tree Girl. You know I have ways of breaking a woman and making her beg."

"How about if you beg first?" Smithson's voice fills the air a millisecond before he bursts from the trees and slams into the Commander.

CHAPTER TWELVE

LOGAN

The Commander's sword nicks my throat as he stumbles to the ground beneath Smithson's weight. I raise my hands and press them against the wound. The rest of my closest friends rush out of the trees. Blood flows over my fingers as Jodi runs toward Smithson while Frankie, Drake, Adam, and Nola charge the guards who surround Willow, their swords raised.

One of the guards with a bow spins and lets an arrow loose. His arrow flies past Nola and buries itself in Drake's leg. He falls to the ground.

"No!" I yell.

The other guard shoots his arrow at Willow, but he's too late. She's already skimming the branches, nothing but a blur in the trees as she moves. Frankie and Adam collide with soldiers. I bend down, yank Smithson and Jodi off the Commander, and yell, "Help me before anyone dies!"

Smithson glares at me while the Commander snarls and struggles to his feet.

"Logan—" Smithson says.

"They aren't our enemies right now, Smithson. I just made a deal with the Commander."

Smithson stares at me as if nothing I'm saying is making sense. The clang of swords meeting fills the air behind us while I pull on his arm. "No one needs to die. *Help* me."

My words finally seem to reach him, and he lunges toward the melee where Nola, her back to a tree, is dueling with a guard whose movements are slower than hers, but whose brute strength is starting to wear her down, and where Adam and Frankie are fighting for their lives while four guards circle them. A fifth guard is still wasting his time trying to shoot Willow, though she never stays on one branch long enough for his aim to be worth anything.

"Subdue, but don't kill," I say as Smithson and I race into the fray, leaving Jodi to catch up to us. He raises the hilt of his sword and slams it into the head of the closest guard, and then kicks the guard's sword clear as the man falls to the ground in a daze.

I brace my legs as I swing the chain into the nearest guard. He jerks away from the metal lash, but doesn't fall. Panic is clawing at me. I have to get closer. Hit harder. Stop him. Stop all of them before anyone else gets seriously hurt.

"Stop!" I'm yelling, but no one is listening.

Lowering my shoulder, I duck beneath the guard's sword arm and crash into him, my shackled fists in front of me like a club. He coughs, gags, and slowly slides to the ground, the life leaving his eyes as he falls. I stare at him in shock. I didn't hit him hard enough to kill him. I was just trying to get everyone to stop long enough to realize that we're on the same side.

Long enough to go help Nola before it's too late.

The guard lands on his stomach, and I see Willow's arrow protruding from his back. Another arrow streaks through the forest and buries its tip in the back of the guard who shot Drake, and then a third arrow takes out the guard Smithson fought on his way to Nola.

Frankie and Adam are trading blows with two of the remaining guards, their swords moving with the deft grace earned from hours of practice as we traveled across the Wasteland, while Smithson is doing his best to subdue Peter, the blond guard busy fighting Nola.

Blood runs down Smithson's face, and I stumble over the fallen guard in front of me as Orion and Frankie crash into me.

"Stop!" I yell, shoving Orion away from Frankie. Orion turns on me, and it's all I can do to dodge his weapon. The chain dangling from my wrists isn't any help when I can't move my hands along the length of it to gain any leverage. He raises his sword, and Adam lunges for him.

They go down hard in a tangle of limbs and metal. I kick Orion's weapon away, but Gregory, the thin guard who walked the tunnels with the Commander, leaps for Adam while he's down. I lower my shoulder and drive it into him, knocking him off course before he can impale Adam on his sword.

"Don't kill them!" I say, but still no one listens to me. Adam is parrying Gregory's sword, blow for blow; Frankie is shoving Orion against the nearest tree, his sword to the guard's throat; Nola and Smithson have their hands full fighting Peter; and Willow is somewhere up in the trees, waiting for her chance to drop the next guard who steps away from us. "We're on the same side."

The Commander's voice punctures the air. "Stop fighting or she dies!"

The guards stop fighting, but keep their weapons up. My people and I spin around to see the Commander standing near the tree where just moments ago he'd come to a grudging agreement to work with me to bring down James Rowan. In one hand he holds Jodi, anchoring her by his side with a fist in her hair. In the other, he holds his sword to her heart. Blood gleams against his silver blade, and I quickly examine Jodi for injuries, but she isn't bleeding. Instead, I see Connor leaning against the tree behind the Commander, his hand pressed to a wound in his shoulder.

"Connor?" I take a step forward, and Jodi whimpers as the Commander presses the point of his sword against her chest.

"It's merely a flesh wound," Connor says, his voice tight with pain.

I glare at the Commander. "You *stabbed* the Lankenshire ambassador assigned to vouch for us at Hodenswald?"

The Commander's mouth twists with derision. "Foolish boy tried to rescue the girl who attacked me." He gives Jodi a rough shake. "I don't care where he's from. If you think you're man enough to draw your sword against me, then you're man enough to take what's coming to you."

I tear my gaze away from the blood dripping down Connor's arm, and look into Jodi's wide, terrified eyes. "Jodi, it's going to be okay. Don't move. Everything will be okay."

"You're a liar," the Commander says, malice dripping from every word. "A liar and a thief. These are my people. Look at their cloaks. Their boots. Baalboden made. They're *my* people, and you had them attack me."

"We aren't your people anymore," Frankie says.

I reach over and squeeze his shoulder, both in appreciation of his loyalty and in warning that now isn't the time to antagonize the Commander further. Jodi squeaks as the Commander yanks her hair back and raises his sword.

We can't stop him. He holds Jodi in front of him, an effective shield against Willow's arrows. The three guards surrounding us still have their weapons up. If we move, they'll attack. We'd never get to the Commander in time to save Jodi.

I scramble madly for a plan, but only one scenario presents itself. Slowly, I let go of Frankie's shoulder and raise my wrists.

"I'm not attacking you," I say as I take a small step forward. "I wasn't attacking your guards, either. I was trying to stop everyone. I was trying to tell them that we are all on the same side."

"We are *not* on the same side," Adam snarls from my left. "He had his sword to your throat."

"Logan's right," Connor says. "He was negotiating an alliance with the Commander to work together to assure Rowansmark's destruction."

Adam's shoulders drop, and he looks at Jodi with desperation on his face. I know the feeling. "You didn't know," I say quietly. "You were protecting me. All of you. It's not your fault."

"No, this is *your* fault," the Commander says. "Did you really think you could distract me with talk about Rowansmark and then have these traitors attack me so you could steal the device for yourself?"

I take another step toward him.

"I didn't know they were coming. I've been inside the Lankenshire dungeon since right after you arrived at the gate. None of them were allowed to visit me—"

"You expect me to believe this wasn't planned?" He bites his words off.

"Logan didn't tell us where to find him. Willow did," Adam says. "She sat beside me during Logan's trial, and she told me they were going to escape the dungeon and meet at the tree where she'd hidden the device."

The Commander's laugh is a harsh bark of disbelief. "And you just happened to know which tree she meant?"

"I've been here before. With Willow." Adam's voice shakes with anger. "I knew how to use the tunnels beneath Lankenshire and where to bring the people who wanted to help Logan fight this war."

I take a few more steps forward until I'm alone in the stretch of ground between the Commander and the group behind me. "It was a misunderstanding, and it won't happen again."

"This girl attacked me. I didn't misunderstand that. You know what I do to women who defy me." He pulls Jodi close, his sword pressed against her throat. His dark eyes are coldly furious as he looks at me.

I push away the memory of my mother's last moments and say, "Jodi thought you were trying to kill me—"

"You deserve it," he snarls.

"Maybe I do." I meet his gaze. "But James Rowan deserves it more. And so does my brother, Ian. We have to be able to work together if we want to bring Rowansmark to its knees. Trackers will be after us by now. We need to bury the dead and—"

"We?" He glares at me. "*You* follow orders, or you die."

I force myself to ignore my anger and my pride. They won't help me now. I have to give him what he wants—the belief that his power is above question—or he'll kill us all and try to take on Rowansmark himself.

Raising my hands in surrender, I force myself to say, "We aren't your enemies. James Rowan is. Together we can bring him down. You and I. Please. Let her go."

He stares at me for a moment, and then shoves Jodi away from him. She stumbles over to Connor and fusses over his wound, her fingers shaking. He awkwardly pats her shoulder, leaving bloody fingerprints on her tunic.

The Commander leans toward me. "A real man doesn't raise his hands in surrender. A real man doesn't beg for the lives of those who aren't his equals. You are a worthless example of a man, and we are not a team. I don't need a *team*."

"You did once."

He jerks as if I've cut him with my sword.

"When the Cursed—when the *tanniyn* first surfaced, you led a team down to the beast's lair to destroy it. You were the kind of man others could respect and trust. Your team followed you because they believed in you, not because they feared you."

"You know nothing about that."

"I know that leading people is difficult. That sometimes the choices you have to make are almost too hard to live with."

A shadow crosses his face, and he lifts the sword as if he might aim it at me.

"Listen to me," I say quietly, so that only the two of us can hear. "I know what it's like to hold the weight of lives in your hands and to know that your decisions will determine their fates. I know how it feels to have to quell dissension because you know unity is the only thing that will keep everyone alive."

He looks at me, his dark eyes glittering, his fingers white around the hilt of his sword.

"And I know the terrible shame that fills you when you fail—"

"I never failed."

"When you *fail* to save the ones depending on you."

His glare pierces me. "A world in shambles. That's what we came back to, my team and I. Cities, infrastructure, *entire governments* wiped off the planet like they were never there. We rounded up the survivors. We found the resources. We kept them safe. We did *not* fail."

"If you'd killed the *tanniyn* like you were supposed to, the world wouldn't have needed you to save it."

His face drains of color, and he presses his lips together.

"I'm saying I understand how it feels to try so hard to do the right thing only to have everything blow up in your face. You didn't kill the beast—"

"Because they couldn't be killed!" His whole body vibrates as if I've struck him. "Don't you think we tried? I lost half of my team in the bowels of the earth. Good people! All for a suicide mission, because there wasn't just one creature. There were scores of them. *Scores.*"

I stare at him while my stomach plummets. Ian was telling the truth about there being multiple *tanniyn*. The device I have calls and controls one. What if Rowansmark has tech that calls and controls a host of the creatures? Swallowing hard, I say, "Why did you let us believe there was only one beast left?"

"People must be dependent on their leader for him to maintain order and control. A manageable threat creates dependence. Anything more breeds terror, and terror gives way to anarchy. You know nothing of that. You understand *nothing*." Pain settles onto his face in furrows and creases.

"I understand that shame can either poison us slowly, turning us into angry, bitter men, or it can sharpen us into better leaders. You chose anger and because of that, you've ruled through brutality and fear. I'm asking you to make a different choice now. Please." The word cuts me as it leaves my lips.

"I killed your mother," he says softly. "And you cost me everything I'd been working for."

"Yes. But this is bigger than our personal vendettas. This is about the survivors of Baalboden. And your allies in the east. And every other city-state in Rowansmark's crosshairs. If we stand together, we can beat James Rowan. And when we beat him, you'll finally have what you've worked for all these years— absolute control."

At least until I take it from you.

His gaze locks on to mine. Gone is the harsh, predatory gleam in his eye. He looks withered, beaten, *old* for the first time since I've known him. Slowly, he straightens his shoulders.

"You can alter the beacons installed in each city-state and strengthen the device?"

"I can."

He looks as if he's just chewed a piece of rancid meat. "You speak to me of leadership, choices, and shame as if we're equals, but we aren't." The pain in his eyes sinks slowly beneath a wall of cold disdain. "You aren't good enough to lead anyone. You never were. You're the outcast whose family's dishonor brought death and destruction right to Baalboden's door. One day soon, those who follow you will realize the truth, and they'll turn on you like South Edge dogs."

A sharp whistle echoes from the trees twenty yards east of us. The Commander jerks his head up, but I'm already moving.

"That's a warning from Willow," I say. "Get to the horses. Now!"

I race toward Drake, who is sitting on the ground, his hands pressed against the wound in his leg. Nola and Smithson get there first. Smithson wraps an arm around the older man and lifts him to his feet while Nola rapidly uncoils the chains from my hands. Frankie and Adam disappear into the trees and return seconds later with travel packs, including mine, and a piece of tech I didn't expect to see again—Melkin's staff.

I frown at the staff, and Frankie says in a voice only I can hear, "Willow told me this walking stick can call the Cursed One. Figured we might need it."

"We've got a crowd of trackers approaching," Willow calls as she grabs the device from its hiding place in the oak and then leaps from a branch to land lightly beside Adam.

"Give me the tech." The Commander holds out his hand. Willow glances at me, and when I nod, she carefully places the cloth-wrapped device on the Commander's palm.

"If you're done worrying about things that don't matter, maybe we could focus on the trackers who are coming for us,"

Willow snaps. "Get on a horse or die."

No one argues. In less than a minute, we sling our packs and ourselves onto the nearest horses and spur our mounts deep into the northern Wasteland.

CHAPTER THIRTEEN

RACHEL

The wagon lurches to a stop, and footsteps crunch across the remains of the road. I barely have time to sit up before Heidi opens the canvas flap and pokes her head inside.

"Time to get out," she says.

The sky framing her head is already dusky with the purple-gray of twilight. Our fourth day of travel is over, and we're still heading west. I don't know how they expect to get to Rowansmark without going south, but I don't care. The longer we spend in the Wasteland, the better chance I have of Quinn, Willow, and Logan catching up to me.

Heidi bends down to untie the rope that secures me to the wagon post, and I take a second to be sure that my bootlaces are loose enough to allow access to the knife. Usually Samuel is the one who fetches me from the wagon each day. I don't trust Samuel much, but I trust Heidi even less. If Ian decided to attack me, I doubt Heidi would lift a hand in my defense.

When she looks up, the rope now held in her hands, I'm

sitting with my back to the bench, my laces loose enough to let me grip the knife hilt in seconds if I feel threatened.

Not that I can do much with it when my right hand is useless, but it's better than nothing.

"Let's go." She removes the rope around my ankles and then pulls me out of the wagon.

The evening air clings to my skin as I climb down the wagon steps, careful to keep my right arm tucked close to my body. The skin around my burn is yellow and puffy. My fingers keep swelling up when I sleep. I'm sure the wound needs to be thoroughly cleaned, medicated, and rebandaged, but I don't have the supplies for that, and if the trackers have a first aid box in the crates of supplies at the head of the wagon, they aren't saying.

I take a deep breath, grateful to smell something other than the hot, dusty air inside the wagon, and taste something bitter and dank on the back of my tongue. The air is more than humid. It's damp and carries with it the unmistakable tang of algae mixed with wet wood. We must be near a river or a lake.

"Hurry up." Heidi's voice is curt as she grabs my left elbow and propels me past a bank of cypress trees. The trunks are narrow at the top, grow thicker through the middle, and then expand at the bottom to stab the ground like a skirt of splayed silver-gray fingers.

"What's the rush?" I ask.

Heidi walks faster, and I stumble over a half-buried rock as I try to keep up. Her grip tightens painfully on my elbow. "I said hurry up. You need to eat fast. We don't have much time."

"Why not?" I ask, but she ignores me.

The wagon rests on the side of the crumbling road. We

haven't stopped in a clearing like we usually do. Instead of a fire for the night's meal, Samuel is ripping strips of jerky off a chunk of meat he carries in his pack while Ian sits on a tree stump, scraping the blade of his sword against a rock to sharpen it. Both of them frequently stop to study the surrounding forest.

"What's the rush?" I ask again, and Ian jerks his gaze to mine.

"We're waiting on the boat to arrive," Samuel says.

A boat. That explains the dankness in the air. It also explains why we've been heading west. Rowansmark is built along a river. A journey by boat will cut our travel time down from weeks to a few days.

"The boat should've been here already." Heidi shoves a strip of jerky into her mouth and talks around it. "I don't like waiting for it when we know we're being followed."

Quinn.

My heart beats so fast, I'm convinced Samuel can hear it. If I'm right, the trackers are about to be in a world of trouble.

"Could be Logan, if he used the tunnels beneath Lankenshire to leave the city without the Carrington army seeing him," Ian says. "Or Willow. Though if she was tracking us, she'd have found her brother's body, and we'd all have arrows sticking out of our necks by now."

The thought of Quinn, still alive despite Ian's best efforts, sends a blaze of triumph through me.

"Could be highwaymen. A Tree Village. A courier from another city-state who isn't happy with his leader's new protection agreement with Rowansmark." Heidi's voice is clipped. "Doesn't matter who's out there. What matters is getting the girl somewhere safe before we're forced into a confrontation that could jeopardize the mission."

"We can't wait here much longer," Samuel says. "If the boat doesn't show, we need to cut south and find a place suitable for setting a trap."

They aren't going to set a trap for Quinn while I still have breath in my body.

Heidi shoves jerky into my hands. "Get the girl into the wagon and tie her up. Ian and I will decide whether to wait for the boat or to start moving south with the wagon."

Samuel takes hold of my arm, and I slowly turn toward the wagon.

The road we're on climbs a gentle slope leading west. I can't see anything beyond the rise, but if we're stuck between Quinn and a river with no boat in sight, I'm about to be rescued, and Ian is about to wish he'd never been born.

Except I can't be rescued. Not when Rowansmark has the ability to call an army of *tanniyn* to destroy Logan and my friends.

In the distance, a low bellow fills the air and then rises rapidly in pitch. It doesn't sound like an animal. Or like the Cursed One. It sounds smooth and mechanical and like nothing I've ever heard.

"The boat! Get her in the wagon, and let's go." Heidi brushes past Samuel and heads for the rise just as something long and pale streaks out of the forest to our left and buries itself in her thigh. She swears and stares down at the shaft of a roughly hewn spear protruding from her leg.

Even though I know I need to remain a prisoner if I want to save Logan, I smile fiercely. Quinn is here. Anyone else would've aimed for the heart.

"Run!" Samuel yells.

He scoops me up and races for the wagon while Heidi struggles to pull the spear from her leg. Ian drops low and runs up the slope, moving from left to right and back again in an attempt to make aiming a spear at him much more difficult.

It works. Another spear streaks through the air, missing Ian's back by a fraction. Seconds later, Ian vaults over the top of the rise and disappears.

Samuel reaches the wagon, and I expect him to dump me inside and then move toward the driver's bench. I'm sure Quinn expects it, too. The only reason Samuel doesn't have a crippled leg right now is because he's holding me, and Quinn won't risk injuring me with his spear.

Instead of putting me into the back of the wagon, though, Samuel races for the driver's bench. He pushes me onto the seat and leaps in behind me. Shoving me to the floor, he throws his body on top of mine. By making it impossible to hit him without also hitting me, he's just saved his own life.

Of course, Quinn wouldn't actually try to kill him. Still, being left behind in the Wasteland with a crippling leg injury is nearly a death sentence in and of itself. Heidi will be lucky to last the night. Wild animals will smell the blood that soaks her clothing and come to finish her off.

I pull my legs toward my chest, and struggle to raise my head above the driver's bench so I can see what's going on.

"Be still!" Samuel barks at me. He slaps the reins against the donkeys, and the wagon lurches into motion. I wait to feel the wheels strain to carry their load uphill, but instead, they curve to the right.

"What are you doing?" I ask. Not that I *want* him to hurry toward the boat and cut me off from Quinn permanently, but Samuel just wants to do his job and live to see another day. Getting me onto the water and avoiding the painful consequences for failing his leader should be his top priority.

"I don't leave people behind," he says, gritting his teeth with exertion while he hauls on the reins and keeps his head below the wagon bench.

I don't either. The thought that maybe Samuel and I have more in common than I gave him credit for makes me uncomfortable.

"Heidi!" Samuel twists himself off my upper body and leans toward the ground, his arm outstretched.

Digging my left elbow into the wagon floor, I lift myself up and strain to see the southern tree line. I start to shake as I pull against Samuel's weight on my legs. Quinn is out there, somewhere. Close enough to throw a spear and hit his mark.

There's a blur of movement in the cypress trees. A flash of brown leather pants. A flutter of dark hair. I smile even as tears gather in my eyes, turning the landscape into a puddle of silver and green.

Quinn came for me. I'm not alone. For this one moment, I'm not alone. It will have to be enough, because I can't turn back now. I'm getting on that boat. I'm going into Rowansmark. And I'm going to bring them all down, because I promised myself that I wouldn't lose anyone else.

"Scoot down," Samuel says to me seconds before he heaves Heidi onto the floor beside us. Samuel lifts his weight off my legs briefly, and I tuck them toward my chest, wedging myself tightly between the bench and the front of the wagon.

My eyes are still on the southern tree line. Still watching Quinn move amid the bright-green leaves and the scarves of white moss draping the tree limbs. I've made my decision to not try to escape the wagon, but I still want to see his face, to feel connected to someone who cares about me before I go into Rowansmark alone.

A thread of defiance blazes through me, at once familiar and strange. I've spent so many weeks lost in a fog of depression and inner silence that I hardly know what to do with the bold spark of rebellion that I used to take for granted.

I'm not the same girl I was when I stood at Baalboden's gate beside Oliver, hoping my father would come home in time. I've seen things that will haunt me forever. I've done things I can't undo. And the lessons I've learned are carved deep into my soul.

I'm not going into Rowansmark as a mindless, rage-fueled weapon. I'm choosing to infiltrate the enemy's city and right a wrong because I'm a warrior, and that's what warriors do.

The wagon shudders as it goes uphill, and the wheels slow as the donkeys labor to pull the weight. I lift my eyes to the tree line again and catch a tiny flash of movement in a huge cypress only fifteen yards from the road. The lacy strips of moss sway gently, and a shadow slips along a thick, twisted branch, barely rustling the leaves as it passes.

"Tallyho!" someone shouts to the west of us.

"The boat's docked," Samuel says. "Keep pressure on that leg,

Heidi. We're almost there."

He slaps the reins against the donkeys' backs, but they don't move any faster as we crest the top of the rise. I push my left hand against the wagon floor and raise my head to see what lies in front of us.

The road coasts downhill for thirty yards, flattens out for another five, and then ends abruptly at the edge of a long wooden dock a few yards wider than the road. The dock is made of thick planks and rests on pillars as wide as the cypress trunks that hug the edge of the river. At the end of the dock, a huge white boat is tied to a pillar, ramp lowered for us to enter. There are two decks that wrap all the way around the ship. The lower deck has doors every five yards that lead into the ship's interior. The upper deck is lined with trackers, each carrying a crossbow aimed straight at me.

No, not at me. At the trees beside me.

They've seen Quinn moving through the cypresses, just like I have, and they're going to kill him the second he gives them a clear shot.

I press my arms against the wagon floor and pull myself to the side of the wagon until I'm free of Samuel's weight. Scanning the trees to my left, I look for the shadow that moves water-quick through the twisted branches. For the boy who time and time again has saved my life even when he didn't owe me a thing.

"Get down," Samuel barks.

A whisper of sound—the barest brush of a boot sliding against a branch—floats from the tree closest to us. Samuel jerks his head up at the same moment that the mossy fringe along a branch trembles.

He shouts, "Target, my ten o'clock, seventeen yards. Destroy!"

"Quinn!" I scream. "Down!"

A slew of arrows fly from the trackers on the boat, arc swiftly, and slice into the trees.

CHAPTER FOURTEEN

RACHEL

"Shoot again!" Samuel shouts. His hand digs painfully into my shoulder as he orders Quinn's death. I turn on my heels, leaning into the arm that holds on to me, and punch him in the face.

He won't let go of the reins, because getting the wagon onto the boat is his first priority, but he should let go of me to protect his cheekbone—it's instinctive self-defense. He doesn't. Instead, he absorbs the blow and then gives me a look that makes something deep inside of me shiver.

Any hope that I might one day count Samuel as a reluctant ally shrivels beneath the scathing contempt on his face.

Behind me, more arrows slam into the cypress tree. I twist my head around, frantically scanning the ground for Quinn's body. He isn't there. I look at the tree, at the arrows buried in its branches, terrified that I'll find him impaled by one of the weapons.

He isn't there, either. Or if he is, he's still hidden behind drooping moss and bright-green leaves. I scan the pale trunk and the dark forest floor for patches of blood, but I can't see any.

A hand wraps around my hair and jerks me to the wagon floor. I land heavily on my injured arm, and swallow against the bile that rises to the back of my throat as pain screams through me. Sweat beads along my upper lip, and my breath comes in short, harsh bursts as Samuel leans over me, his dark eyes pitiless.

"Whoever is in those trees speared Heidi. I don't allow those who attack my people without provocation to escape alive."

The wagon picks up speed as the donkeys hurry downhill. The momentum drags me forward, crushing me against the front of the wagon. I meet Samuel's gaze.

"He *did* have provocation." My tone is as pitiless as his. "You kidnapped me. Ian, whom you're so loyal to, killed innocent people—including *children*—instead of confronting the person he felt had wronged him. Any violence at this point can be traced straight back to Rowansmark."

"No." He slaps the reins, and the wagon barrels down the slope. "The violence can be traced back to your leader, Commander Chase."

"He isn't my leader." I twist my hips and try to pull my knees toward my chest, but Samuel's grip is relentless. "He's cruel, and he's a coward, and he deserves to die. I hope I'm the one who gets to kill him. But the Commander isn't in those trees. You're trying to kill a boy who only wants to save my life."

My words are falling on deaf ears. Samuel glances at Heidi, who lies in stoic silence at the end of the wagon bench, her eyes closed and her hands pressed hard against the bloody wound in her thigh, and then scans the forest again. Beneath us, the wheels bite into the wooden planks of the dock, and the dirty-fish smell of the river swamps me.

The wagon rocks gently to the left, as if all of the crates within its bed suddenly shifted to one side.

Or as if someone just leaped onto the left edge of the wagon's back step.

Quinn is on the wagon.

My heart pounds wildly as I see the realization dawn on Samuel's face as well. The anger in his eyes blinks out, replaced instantly by detached ruthlessness.

I twist my neck, trying to see the back of the wagon, but all I see is the side of the bench.

I haven't watched Samuel fight, but he's a tracker. He's going to have the same efficient, powerful technique that Rowansmark trackers are known for.

Quinn is efficient and powerful, too. Maybe they're evenly matched in strength and prowess. Maybe not. But Quinn won't take another's life. He'll fight to incapacitate or disarm.

Samuel will be fighting to kill.

And the dozen trackers standing guard atop the boat's upper deck will be ready to assist him.

Samuel lets go of my shoulder, grabs my hands, and loops the reins around my wrists so tightly, I can barely feel my fingers. The agony spiking up my right arm is nearly unbearable. I jerk against the strips of leather, trying to loosen them enough to get free, but he's left me no leverage.

"Get us onto the boat," he says.

I clamp my jaw against another wave of pain, and tug harder at the reins. I have to free my hands while there's still time to help Quinn. The donkeys squeal in protest, and the wagon wheels slow.

Samuel pulls a dagger from his boot. "Go ahead and stop the wagon, Rachel. You'll simply make it easier for my men to aim their arrows."

Without another word, he grabs the bench, vaults over it, and heads toward the back of the wagon.

Toward Quinn.

Bending my face toward my hands, I yank at the reins with my teeth. The leather tastes like salt and dirt. My teeth ache as I arch my back and pull as hard as I can.

The reins won't budge.

The wagon shudders, and something big slams into its bed.

Quinn? Samuel? Both? I have no idea. I'm useless sitting here trussed up like a boar about to be cooked over a spit, and the wagon keeps moving closer and closer to the boat. I have to cut the reins before it's too late.

My fingers, numb and swollen from lack of blood, fumble as I reach for my knife. The wagon shakes again, and someone grunts. My fingertips brush the knife hilt, but I can't grasp it. Gritting my teeth, I find the hilt again and shove my hands farther into my boot.

This time, I wrap the fingers of my left hand around the hilt and pull. The weapon slides free. I push the hilt firmly between my feet, grip it as tightly as I can with my boots, and start sawing the reins against the blade.

Something crashes behind me. Seconds later, the wagon's canvas covering rips—a rough tearing sound that turns my blood to ice.

Nothing cuts canvas that swiftly except a sword. The only person in the wagon bed who has a sword is Samuel, which means Quinn hasn't been able to disarm him, and now Quinn is fighting an opponent of equal skill in a small, contained area with nothing between him and a sword but his wits and his speed.

I saw the reins against the knife as fast as I can. The leather snags the blade and then slips, and I wince as the steel slices into my skin instead. Blood wells, slicking the leather, and I look toward the sky before the sight can remind me of pressing my hands to Oliver's neck. Of trying to seal the wound I made in Melkin's chest.

I don't have time to be distracted by ghosts. I have a friend to save.

The knife wobbles, and I push my feet together to hold it steady. Someone shouts from the boat, and I hear the steady slap of boots on the dock coming closer and closer to the wagon.

The trackers aboard the boat have sent help for Samuel. If I let another tracker join the fight in the wagon bed, Quinn won't make it out alive.

My breath heaves in and out as I desperately yank the reins against the blade.

"Break, you stupid piece of leather. Break!" I haul back, and the leather snags again. This time, the knife bites deep. A small tear slowly widens as I pull with all my might. With a snap, one of the reins splits completely. Quickly, I shake my hands, and the rest of the leather loosens around my wrists.

Another crash shakes the wagon as I grab the reins with my good hand and pull myself onto the wagon bench. Ian is rushing down the dock toward us, his face set in grim lines. His sword is already out.

Desperation churns through me. The second he sees Quinn, he'll know what Samuel has surely already figured out: that the only way Quinn could have survived the fight with Ian four days ago is if he's wearing armor, and that stabbing him in the chest is useless.

They'll be trying to cut off his head.

My muscles tighten, and my vision narrows. Ian isn't going to take anyone else from me. I may be too weak to join the fight, but that doesn't mean I can't change the odds. All I have to do is give Samuel and Ian something more important to think about than killing Quinn.

Something like trying to keep me in custody.

Something like trying to save their own lives.

Starting with Ian.

"Run!" I lunge to my feet and slap the reins against the donkeys repeatedly. They squeal and jerk their ears flat against their heads, but another few smacks gets them moving. Fast. The wagon careens down the dock as the donkeys race to get away from the lashes.

Bracing myself against the lip of the wagon, I lock eyes with Ian, drag the reins to the left, and aim the wagon straight for him.

Seconds before the donkeys crash into Ian, sending him

beneath their hooves and the steel-rimmed wheels of the wagon, the animals swerve sharply, throwing me against the bench as I struggle to keep my balance.

Apparently, donkeys prefer not to trample humans. Lucky for Ian. Not so lucky for me.

I clutch the reins in my hands, but I'm no longer in control of the wagon. No one is. The tiny sliver of dock between Ian and the river isn't big enough to give the donkeys anywhere to go. I have a split second to drag in a breath, and then we plunge over the side of the dock and into the river.

With a tremendous splash, the water swallows us and flings us downstream. I let go of the reins, blink my eyes until I can see in the hazy, dirt-filled water, and push off from the wagon with my feet. Beside me, Heidi lets go of her leg and struggles feebly against the river's current. She'll be okay. Ian is about to dive into the water, and I bet most of the other trackers will follow suit. They'll be looking for me, but if Samuel's loyalty is any indication, they won't leave Heidi behind to drown.

I hope they rescue the donkeys, too.

The current pulls at me, but I kick against it and grab the side of the wagon as it sinks slowly toward the riverbed. I wish I'd thought to reach for my knife as we went over the side of the dock, but I didn't, and the water has surely stolen it by now.

Working my way along the side of the wagon, using my left hand and my feet, I pray Quinn is still alive. Maybe going into the river gave Quinn an opportunity to disarm Samuel in the confusion.

Or maybe it gave Samuel the opportunity to kill Quinn, instead.

My pulse slams against my eardrums, and my lungs feel strained. I can't hold my breath much longer. Grabbing the jagged tear in the canvas, I pull it open and look inside.

It's empty.

Someone grabs my waist from behind and pulls me away from the wagon. I whip my head around, and something hard dissolves inside my chest when I find myself face-to-face with Quinn. His shoulder-length dark hair swirls around his golden face, and his eyes burn into mine. Relief gushes through me, loosening the knot of fear in my chest, and I latch on to him like I never plan to let go.

He nods once as if to tell me he's found me, and that I'll be okay, then jerks his head toward the dock, where a small gap of air hovers between the top of the river and the bottom of the wooden planks. My lungs are throbbing now, begging for me to take a breath. I kick my legs, struggling to move forward, but my right arm makes it difficult to swim against the current.

Quinn wraps his fingers around my left wrist and moves through the water with the same effortless grace he uses on land. I kick my feet to help propel us along, but he's doing most of the work. My lungs ache with the need for air. Just when I'm sure I'm going to have to let the gritty water gush down my throat, we surface beneath the dock.

I gasp for air, and when that doesn't satisfy my aching lungs, I gasp again. Quinn's chest is heaving as well. He keeps his fingers around my wrist as boots race down the dock and men jump into the water. Judging from the length of time they swim away from the dock before plunging below the surface, the current has dragged the wagon a good forty-five yards from where we first went in.

Close to the shoreline, the donkeys' heads bob as they swim for dry land. Someone must have cut them loose. I hope that someone also pulled Heidi to the surface.

"We can't stay here," Quinn says quietly, scanning our surroundings. "They're still searching for you by the wagon. We can use the confusion to swim beneath the dock until we reach shore and then run into the forest."

Above us, more boots tromp down the dock, but these men don't jump into the water. I meet Quinn's eyes and slowly shake my head.

We can't get away. If we try to escape into the forest at the edge of the dock, the men above will see us, and I'm in no shape to run away. Worse, they'll see that Quinn survived the fall into the river, and they'll hunt him down as well. I can tell by his labored breathing that he still hasn't recovered from the smoke inhalation he suffered in the fires Ian set. He won't be able to outrun healthy trackers either.

Our only option is to swim to the opposite shore, something that would be difficult to accomplish even if we weren't also trying to hide from any trackers who remain stationed on the boat's upper deck. I can barely swim on my own. The weight of the armor and my useless right arm make it impossible to fight the current for more than a few seconds. Quinn would have to pull me, and it's clear that pulling me once has already taken a huge toll.

We can't get away. But Quinn can. He can make it to shore

undetected. Especially if I provide the distraction. If they think he's dead, they'll stop hunting him.

Besides, I have to go to Rowansmark. Quinn will understand. He'll have to. I can't turn back now.

"Rachel." Quinn's voice is hushed. "We can't stay here."

I meet his eyes. "No, you can't."

Something like fear flashes across his normally stoic expression, and the grip on my hand becomes almost painfully tight. "I said *we*. We can't stay here."

Splashes and shouting echo across the river. I guess they've realized I'm not near the sunken wagon.

"I can't swim to safety," I say, and he's already shaking his head.

"I'll pull you."

"You can barely pull yourself."

"I can do what needs to be done. Trust me. Please." His voice is still hushed, still barely a whisper above the slap of the river against the pillars that hold the dock in place, but there's an intensity to it that pulls at me.

I understand that intensity. That need to fix something because if you don't, it's one more failure to shackle you to the darkness you're trying to outrun. I raise my injured arm and press my hand to his cheek.

"You don't have to save me, Quinn."

His eyes are desperate. "Yes, I do."

I shake my head. "I don't need to be saved. I'm choosing to stay here. To get on the boat. I'm choosing this, Quinn. I want you to leave me behind."

"Why?" The harsh emotion in his voice, so rare for him, makes me ache.

"Because James Rowan has the ability to summon an entire army of the beasts. An *army.* You can go back to Lankenshire and warn Logan, but I still have to go inside, find the stash of weaponized tech, and destroy it, because, otherwise, we're never going to be out of danger."

A donkey brays from the shoreline, and I glance over my shoulder to see trackers swimming toward the animals. More trackers are heading back toward the dock. We have less than a minute before they'll be close enough to see that Quinn is still alive.

I turn back to Quinn. "Go. I'm not going to lose another person I care about. You've saved me several times already. It's my turn to repay the favor."

His jaw flexes. "You don't need to save me."

"Oh, so now you're the only one with the right to make sacrifices for your friends? Don't be insulting."

"Don't be stubborn."

"I don't think I know how to be anything *but* stubborn."

He looks at the approaching trackers, and sinks a little closer to the surface of the water. "I can't just leave you."

"You have to. You once told me there was a difference between being a weapon and being a warrior. And you showed me that sometimes doing the right thing costs us almost everything." My hand lingers on his cheek for another second, and then I drop it and step back, my feet sinking in the rough silt beneath me. "I'm choosing to be a warrior, Quinn. I'm choosing to do the right thing. You of all people know better than to say I shouldn't do what needs to be done."

Grief shadows his eyes, but he gives me a tiny smile. "Using my own words against me is low."

"You know I'm right."

"I know you're convinced you're right." He glances again at the men who swim toward us with sure, steady strokes. "And I know that it's your choice."

Turning back to me, he meets my gaze. "And this is *my* choice. I'm going with you. I'm going to get on the boat while you distract them. You're right—it isn't enough to warn Logan. The tech still has to be destroyed, and we're going to do it. You can be a warrior, Rachel, but you don't have to do it alone."

His fingers squeeze my wrist once more, and then he sinks below the surface of the river and lets me go. Instantly, I splash my way toward one of the pillars, plaster myself against it like I'm terrified that if I let go I'll drown, and start yelling for help.

Boots crash against the planks above. The trackers already swimming toward the dock aim for me. Seconds later, hands grasp my arms and pull me onto the dock. I lie there, shivering and coughing as if I've swallowed too much water. Two of the men who are still dry kneel down, flip me to my side, and pound my back. The trackers who were in the water heave themselves onto the dock, panting.

I don't look for Quinn as the trackers who were pounding on my back hoist me onto their shoulders and carry me up the ramp. I don't look for him as the rest of the trackers make their way onto the dock, leading the donkeys, carrying salvaged supplies, and pulling Heidi on a narrow wheeled bed that belongs to the boat's medical bay.

But after we've set sail—after the steam whistles shriek and the giant paddle wheel at the back of the boat begins churning the water—as the last faint drops of sunlight gleam fiery orange against the Wasteland, I lean against the railing on the lower deck and take comfort in the fact that even though I'm at the mercy of my enemies, I'm not truly alone.

CHAPTER FIFTEEN

LOGAN

"What's taking her so long?" Adam asks as he spreads pine needles to cushion the ground beneath his bedroll. "The light is almost gone. If she doesn't hurry, she could get lost. Or hurt. Or both."

We've stopped for the day on a flat circle of land sheltered on one side by the sagging, moss-covered remains of a farmhouse and ringed by tall pines and clusters of flowering bushes. The Commander, along with Peter and Gregory, are staking out the perimeter, choosing the best sites to set up the evening's watch. Orion, the third guard, is busy setting up the Commander's small tent in the center of the camp. My people are scattered around, setting up their bedrolls, foraging for food, or, in Willow's case, backtracking through the treetops, searching for signs that the trackers who've been following us on foot are close enough to be dangerous tonight.

The horses are tethered on a small patch of grass to the west of the farmhouse, their saddles lying ready a short distance away in case we need to flee. Not that most of us can saddle a horse quickly, but we're faster at it now than we were four days ago when we began the northwest trek toward Hodenswald.

Adam lays his bedroll on the pine needles and then stands beside me, his fingers tapping a jerky rhythm against his leg. His nervous energy is spilling over onto me, and I carefully examine the trees around us, though I know there's no point. Willow will return when she returns.

"It takes time to search for signs left by trackers," I say quietly while I spread my own bedroll out and then grimace as Connor flaps his bedding, catches it on a shrub, and yanks it free, snapping off a small piece of the bush.

"Four days of travel and Mr. Big Words still doesn't know how to lay a blanket on the ground without announcing our presence to the trackers behind us. Thanks for that." Orion, the short, burly guard whose face still bears a bruise from our encounter in the Lankenshire tunnels, shoves Connor as he walks past us, sending the boy crashing into the bush.

"Idiot," Adam snaps at Orion. "Now you've broken half of the branches. The little piece might have been overlooked, but this? This is a red flag."

Orion turns toward Adam, a scowl on his face, and I thrust myself between the two before another fistfight—their third in the past four days of travel—can break out between them.

"That's enough." I keep my voice calm and measured. Adam takes a step back, but Orion sneers.

"Look at these people taking orders from you like a pack of trained sheep. What else do you have them do for you, Logan?" His eyes wander past us to land on Nola, who is gently cleaning her father's wound while Drake leans his head against a tree, his eyes screwed shut against the pain. Nola was able to find plants to disinfect the arrow wound in his leg, and another plant to help promote healing, but we don't have anything that can dull the pain. Nola used the plants on my stub of a finger, too, but there was nothing left to clean. The cauterized flesh is a lumpy, blackened scar that aches so often, I've willed myself to ignore it because it's a problem I can't solve.

Drake suffers the pain of his own wound without complaining, though his face is pale and sweaty every time he has to climb up and down from the horse he shares with Nola, and he can't put weight on his leg without the help of the crutch Frankie fashioned from a thick oak branch.

I'd offer him the use of Melkin's walking staff, but if he were to drive the tip too deeply into the ground, it would set off an infrasonic signal to call the *tanniyn*. Not only am I anxious to avoid the fire-breathing beasts, the staff is the one piece of tech I have that the Commander doesn't know about. Melkin told Rachel the staff was a gift, and there's no way the Commander would possess tech with the power to call the *tanniyn* and then give that tech to someone else. Melkin was tasked with a trip to Rowansmark after Jared's disappearance. It's possible that my father, desperate to rescue me once he realized his original device never made it back to the Commander, gave Baalboden's new courier the staff instead.

However Melkin came to own it, I'm grateful that Connor agreed to pretend the staff was his in order to keep the Commander from questioning its existence. Now he wears it strapped to his back when he rides, and keeps it beside his bedroll while he sleeps, and I ignore it in favor of working on a way to replicate the original controller with the scant tech supplies I have left.

I snap back to reality as Orion looks away from Nola and leers at Jodi instead. "I bet you got your eye on that little piece of pretty, don't you? She ain't too busy with her father, and she ain't climbing trees and pretending to track things at all hours of the day."

Jodi, finished with laying her bedroll beside Nola's, bends at the waist to dig some nuts and herbs out of her pack. My pulse hammers as Orion says, "Yeah, you got her trained, don't you? You got her visiting you in the middle of the night—"

My fist connects with his jaw, and he stumbles back even as I lunge forward. I snatch the front of Orion's tunic and shake him. His eyes blaze, and he spits in my face. Adam slams into Orion from the side, ripping him out of my grasp, and they both hit the ground hard.

Before I can react, Connor draws his sword, places his boot on Orion's wrist, grinding it into the ground to stop him from taking another swing at Adam, and says, "You would do well to mind your tongue around the ladies in our camp."

"Or what? You'll flap your bedroll at me?" Orion asks as he shoves Adam off him. Adam gives me a look asking for permission to punch Orion once more, but I shake my head. The Commander and his other two guards, while content to ignore yet another fistfight between Adam and Orion, began moving toward us the second Connor pulled his sword.

Connor's voice is cold. "Leave the ladies alone or else I will be forced to call you out on your dishonor and duel with you accordingly."

"I don't know what you just said, but I do know that drawing your sword against a member of the Brute Squad is asking for pain." Orion glares at us, using his free arm to push at Connor's boot.

"He said if you disrespect the women in our camp, he'll run you through with his sword," Adam says helpfully.

"Let him up." The Commander's voice is sharp as he stalks toward us. "And give me one reason why I shouldn't sever your tendons and leave you for the carrion birds to feast on."

Connor slowly removes his boot, and Orion scrambles to his feet, his face flushed red, his fists clenched.

I open my mouth to intervene on Connor's behalf—to say *something* that will stop whatever violence I'm sure the Commander has planned—but Connor beats me to it.

"As an official emissary of Lankenshire, I represent the triumvirate while on this journey. These people"—he gestures toward everyone but the Commander and his three guards—"are now Lankenshire citizens, and as such are under the protection of our leaders and our laws."

The Commander's eyes narrow, and his scar twitches.

"However, I recognize that this man is under your jurisdiction, not mine, and therefore I humbly beg your pardon for not bringing my complaint about his behavior to you, instead of acting in the heat of the moment." Connor manages to sound both contrite and unyielding, a skill I'm certain he learned from his mother.

"Are we talking about complaints now?" Orion's voice is surly. "Because I have a list of my own. Starting with the fact that you don't know the first thing about traveling without leaving a trail and ending with the fact that drawing your weapon because I looked at a girl—"

"You looked at her with dishonorable intent." Connor raises his chin, and suddenly seems every inch a leader. "Miss Jodi, Miss Nola, and Miss Willow are under the protection of Lankenshire."

"Appreciate it, but I can protect myself," Willow says as she drops out of a tree to the right of us and lands softly beside Adam. "And apparently, so can you. Nice work pinning his wrist with your boot." She smiles at Connor and then looks at Orion. "What have you done now?"

His eyes narrow as Adam's arm wraps around Willow's waist. "Just suggesting Logan share some of what he's getting with the rest of us, but I see he already has. Always did wonder what Tree Girl tasted like."

Adam lets go of Willow and jumps for Orion, but Frankie gets there first. Shoving himself between Orion and the rest of us, he looms over the guard and snarls, "I remember when you were nothing but a snot-nosed little brat always whining to your mama whenever someone didn't let you have your way. You're still whining, only this time, your mama isn't here to stop me from delivering the beating you deserve."

"You think you can beat me?" Orion sounds incredulous, which, given the size of Frankie's arms and the fury on his face, doesn't speak highly of Orion's common sense.

I glance at the Commander, expecting him to intervene on Orion's behalf, but he's staring at his guard with a cold expression on his face.

"This isn't Baalboden," Frankie says. "You can't drag me off to the dungeon if I look at you wrong. This is the Wasteland. If you push me, you'll learn that I'm not the same man you used to know. I have a new leader. New friends. And nothing to keep me from ruining you if you bother Willow, Nola, or Jodi again."

Willow stares at Frankie the way she often looked at Quinn—like she'd fight off an army for him because he's family now.

Gregory and Peter step closer to Orion, their hands on their sword hilts, and I lay a hand on Frankie's shoulder. His muscles bunch beneath my touch, but he slowly moves away from Orion without breaking eye contact with the guard.

I look past Orion to find the Commander watching me closely, his eyes narrowed as Smithson and Adam also obey my signal to disengage from the fight. Orion starts to say something, but the Commander cuts him off.

"This is finished." His voice is hard. "Everyone back to your jobs." He looks at Willow. "Any sign of the trackers?"

I'm not sure when the Commander decided Willow's skills made her worth treating with a bare modicum of respect, but his ability to put his team's survival ahead of his own prejudices when it matters is going to work to our advantage when we have to convince the other city-states to give us troops.

"Not anywhere close." Her eyes are locked on Orion. "The horses are giving us the advantage in speed, but they're also making it impossible to not leave a trail. If the trackers decide to push themselves to travel by night as well as by day, we're in trouble."

The Commander sweeps the group with his gaze. "Double the guard shifts. Use two-hour increments. We leave before dawn."

We begin to disperse, and the Commander snatches Orion's

cloak and spins the guard around to face him. Leaning close, he says, "If I ever see a man of mine taken down by an untrained boy again, I will drive my sword through his useless chest and invite the beasts of the woods to rip him apart limb from limb."

"But I—"

"Cooking duty, three days. Trail sweeping, four days. And if that doesn't motivate you to be better at what I've trained you to do, then I will kill you where you stand."

Orion's mouth snaps shut, and he looks at the ground. The Commander shoves the guard away from him, turns on his heel, and stalks toward Peter to join him in guarding the southern perimeter.

I take my ration of nuts, dandelion, and rabbit jerky and move to sit near the horses for the first shift of guard duty. Smithson sits nearby, though he doesn't really speak to anyone. Maybe he's been like this since we left Lankenshire. Maybe he's been like this since Sylph died, and I was too busy trying to keep everyone alive to notice.

Either way, tonight isn't the night to pry into his thoughts. I imagine they're filled with missing Sylph. With the ways he wishes his life was different. And since I'm part of the reason she's gone, I must be the last person he'd like to share his memories with.

Besides, I have memories of my own to consider as the first stars pierce the sky, and the horses whicker softly to one another.

Like the fact that the last time I saw Rachel, she was weak from her injuries and struggling to handle the sheer weight of the grief and horror of the last few months. I should be with her. I should be holding her when she wakes from her nightmares.

She's facing Ian alone, and she shouldn't have to. He's my brother. This mess started nineteen years ago with my father. Rachel shouldn't have to bear the brunt of that, but I can't save her from it. Not yet.

I know she can take care of herself. I *know* it. But that doesn't make it easier to imagine her alone in Rowansmark, surrounded by a bunch of fanatics who all believe in pain atonement.

And it doesn't make it easier to face each day without her by my side.

I *miss* Rachel. In my darkest moments, a voice in my head whispers that she might be gone forever. That no matter what I do, no matter how fast I travel, I won't catch up to her in time. That she'll die at the hands of my brother the madman, and I'll be left with the terrible emptiness that threatens to consume me whenever I consider a future without her.

Nothing can fix that. It's the one scenario for which I have no backup plan.

I have a lot of promises to keep—promises to deliver justice to Ian, to stop James Rowan, to take down the Commander—but the one promise that means more to me than all the rest is my promise to always find Rachel.

There is no best or worst case scenario for Rachel. There is only finding her before it's too late.

CHAPTER SIXTEEN

LOGAN

Hodenswald comes into view in the late afternoon of our fifth day of travel. Compact buildings in sturdy brown brick hug the ground behind a thick wall studded with stocky turrets that blend into the hills behind the city. The gate is plain, the field surrounding the city has been ruthlessly trimmed, and the sun gleams off a row of long metallic weapons fixed in regular increments along the wall. Hodenswald looks like a well-muscled warrior who has no intention of hiding his nature behind the pretense of decorative landscaping and fancy stonework.

"There it is," I say, because silence has stretched between the Commander and his Brute Squad and the rest of us for the better part of the afternoon, and it's time someone broke it. Even to say something painfully obvious.

"It's rather ugly, isn't it?" Connor asks with forced cheerfulness in his voice. "It reminds me of a freakishly large dog guarding a bone."

"It's serviceable. Not every city feels the need to sparkle." The

Commander brushes past us and moves his horse into the lead.

Orion laughs and bumps Connor hard as he passes by. "Get it? He said that because the stone in Lankenshire sparkles."

"Does it really? Allow me a moment to gasp in surprise. You'd think after living there for eighteen years I'd have noticed." Sarcasm barbs Connor's words, but Orion doesn't seem to hear it.

Gregory is another story. He urges his horse forward, ducks beneath a low-hanging oak branch, and reaches Connor's side. "Better watch yourself," he says quietly. "You're in over your head here, and Logan won't always be around to run to your rescue."

"Then I shall endeavor to rescue myself."

Gregory's laugh is ugly. "You? You're a puny excuse of a boy who has to use a big vocabulary because you don't know how to use a sword."

Connor abruptly reins in his horse and turns to face Gregory. His dark eyes are steady, but something burns within them. "Never mistake a man's intellect for weakness."

Gregory shakes his head, mutters, "Useless," and moves on.

"Maybe if you didn't sound like a walking library all the time, they wouldn't keep singling you out," Willow says as she spurs the horse she shares with Adam and moves abreast of Connor's mount.

Connor looks at her. "Would you alter your internal composition to avoid the occasional taunt from a small-minded adversary?"

"See?" Willow frowns. "I can't even figure out what you're saying."

"I'm asking if you'd change who you are in here"—he leans

forward and taps her above her heart—"just because some people are incapable of understanding you."

"He sounds like Quinn," I say to Willow.

Her jaw flexes as she meets Connor's gaze. "No, I wouldn't change. And I'd make sure I knew how to defend myself with more than just words. Better yet, I'd take the fight to *them*."

Connor's expression shutters. "There will always be someone who despises me for the books I enjoy, or the clothes I wear, or the way I express my thoughts. If I took the fight to them, I'd never stop swinging."

"Exactly." Willow grins as if Connor has discovered the secret to a life well lived, and then she and Adam move ahead of us as we crest the final hill before reaching Hodenswald. Drake and Nola are behind us, as are Smithson, Jodi, and Peter. Frankie moves his horse to Connor's side and looks at the boy.

"Don't you worry about them," Frankie says in a gruff voice. "There are two kinds of people in this world—those who are confident enough to treat others with respect and those who are miserable inside and spend their lives tearing others down because they think it will somehow make up for what they lack."

"I've spent my life learning how to avoid people like them." Connor nods toward Gregory and Orion. "It's just a bit difficult to do so when we're forced to endure one another's company."

"We're almost to Hodenswald," I say as my horse plods along beneath the graceful boughs of a pine tree. "You won't have to worry about the Commander's men much longer. Your part in the journey will be over." I glance at Melkin's staff, strapped to Connor's back, and wonder how I'm going to take custody of it again without the Commander becoming suspicious.

Connor follows my gaze and sits up a little straighter in his saddle.

"You can't carry the staff," Connor says quietly.

"I'll have to. If you give it to me as a parting gift—"

"Then the Commander will wait until you're away from Hodenswald before he takes it from you by force." Connor's dark eyes are steady as he looks at me. "He's bound to wonder why I would gift it to you, which means he'll take a closer look at it and realize it's made from the same metal as the Rowansmark device he carries."

"I'll carry it," Frankie says. "Let that brute try to take it from *me* by force. I dare him."

Connor smiles. "You have courage. Both of you. But I've observed the way the Commander and his men watch you when you aren't looking. They'll take the staff and the modified controller Logan is building. And then they'll take your lives."

"The Commander needs Logan to dismantle the beacons in the other northern city-states and work the tech once we reach Rowansmark," Frankie says.

I meet Connor's eyes and share a moment of perfect understanding. "The Commander will insist on observing how I shut down the beacons in Hodenswald, and he's arrogant enough to believe he can work the tech as well as I can. Connor's right."

He's right, and I don't know what to do about it. I need Melkin's staff. I can't hand over the modified Rowansmark controller to the Commander without also having a secret *tanniyn*-controlling weapon of my own. Not that the staff does more than call the beast, but still. If I can strengthen the signal, and if there are multiple beasts lurking beneath the Wasteland, I will have a weapon capable of getting my people out of a desperate place should the situation in Rowansmark turn against us. No one, not even the Commander, would be focused on killing us if the ground was getting ready to spew multiple *tanniyn*.

"I'll go with you," Connor says, snapping me out of my thoughts.

I stare at him, at his polished boots and the white shirt he meticulously whisks with a fabric brush each night before sleep, and say the first stupid thought to come into my head. "It's dangerous."

His mouth tightens. "I'm aware of the danger. As are you, but that isn't stopping you from committing yourself wholeheartedly to a task that might very well cost you your life, is it?"

"No one doubts your courage, boy." Frankie nudges his horse closer to Connor's and claps a huge hand on the boy's shoulder. "Logan just likes to make sure his people know the risks before they follow him."

"And also, I might be a little scared of your mother," I say. "But no, I don't doubt your courage. I just can't promise to protect you. I can promise to do my best, but if you were at my trial in Lankenshire, you know my best hasn't been terribly effective." I speak matter-of-factly, but it's hard to scrub the doubt and regret out of my voice. Every decision I make, every plan I formulate, every worst case scenario I consider carries behind it the weight of all the people I lost to Ian as I led our group across the Wasteland.

Frankie glares at me and opens his mouth as if to argue with my words, but Connor beats him to it.

"I'm of the opinion that any leader who cares about his

failings is a leader worth following. I'm going. I'll carry the staff and stand as Lankenshire's witness on your behalf. I wager killing you in an underhanded fashion will be more difficult for the Commander to accomplish with the specter of my mother looking over his shoulder. God knows my mother has that effect on me."

Connor nudges his horse forward, and I follow suit as I consider Connor's belief that the Commander is actively looking for ways to learn what I know so that he can get rid of me before the showdown in Rowansmark. I know Connor's right because I'd be doing the same thing, and the Commander is many things, but he's no fool.

He won't try to double-cross me yet, but the only thing keeping him from making good on his promise to reunite me with my mother is the fact that he doesn't know how to dismantle the Rowansmark beacons or how to replicate the tech that we'll need to protect our army from the threat of the *tanniyn*. The second he no longer needs me for either of those things, he'll do his best to kill me. Connor's presence will help, but the truth is the Commander's sword has been hovering over the back of my neck since the moment he walked into Lankenshire's dungeon.

Which is why I need to kill him first.

As the last of the thick oaks scattered across the meadow gives way to a stretch of grass dotted with hawthorn trees and clusters of wild blueberry bushes, I take a hard look at my options.

Best Case Scenario 1: Once the battle against Rowansmark has decidedly turned in our favor, and I no longer need the Commander to lead the troops, I bury my sword in his heart. This option depends on the Commander being focused on the battle, and on the Brute Squad paying more attention to the fighting than to protecting their leader. Which is unlikely to occur. It also depends on me being near him and not inside Rowansmark hunting for Rachel. Again, unlikely to occur.

Best Case Scenario 2: I challenge the Commander to a duel, thus forcing his soldiers to allow him to fight his own battle. He may be more experienced than I am, but he's also significantly older. I could take him, but could I trust the Brute Squad not to try to immediately avenge his death? I don't think so.

Best Case Scenario 3: I do what I told Rachel I would do—build tech that is specifically engineered to destroy the Commander. This option allows me the most distance from him, eliminating the need to take him by surprise or deal with his guards, but it's fraught with risk of its own. What if the tech malfunctions? What if the injury to him is minimal, and I'm left with no backup plan but my sword and the hope that I can kill him before his guards kill me?

Worst Case Scenario: Every plan I come up with fails, or the Commander manages to kill me first.

The thick stone gate guarding Hodenswald's entrance is barred shut. Two guards dressed in uniforms that match the brown stone of the wall stand on the parapet above, metal arrows loaded into crossbows and pointed straight at us as we approach. Long, spear-like weapons protruding from the two closest turrets are pointed at us too. A whirring sound—like a well-oiled chain running swiftly along its track—comes from behind us. I turn to find that four stone columns, all equipped with spring-loaded spears, have risen from hiding places beneath the meadow and are turned toward the gate. One wrong move and weapons will converge on us from multiple angles.

No one could escape from that.

I pause midstep and slowly scan my surroundings. Spears to the east, west, and south of us. Arrows to the north. A circle of destruction, impossible to overcome.

Impossible to survive.

My gaze rests on the Commander as he glares with an arrogance that dares the Hodenswald guards to speak to him.

A circle of destruction. Impossible to survive.

That's what I need. Not just my sword. Not just tech aimed at the transmitter in his wrist or at the necklace he wears to keep the *tanniyn* at bay. I need to surround him with weapons he can't outrun. Can't outfight.

Can't defeat.

"State your name and the reason for your visit," one of the guards, a woman with a square jaw and suntanned skin, calls down to us.

"Commander Jason Chase of Baalboden here for my yearly diplomatic visit with your leader, Lyle Hoden."

The same woman speaks again. "You aren't scheduled to visit for another two months."

The Commander's back stiffens, and his words are clipped. "I do not need to inform you when my schedule changes. Tell Lyle that I am here."

The guards exchange a quick glance, and then the woman's companion, a man with deep lines on his face and a few scraps of hair on his head, leaves. The woman watches us in silence, her crossbow held steady. The sun beats down on us without mercy while we wait.

When the male guard returns with orders to open the gate, the columns behind us sheathe their spears and slowly sink beneath the ground again as we walk into the city. I scan the compact brown buildings, see a scattering of Rowansmark beacons, and smile grimly as an idea hits me.

A circle of destruction. Impossible to survive. Aimed straight for Commander Jason Chase.

I know exactly how to build that.

CHAPTER SEVENTEEN

LOGAN
—

Lyle Hoden doesn't keep us waiting. A woman with long dark hair and a vibrant red dress that brushes against her ankles meets us just inside the gate. Her focus is on the Commander as she strides toward him with the kind of confident power that reminds me of Clarissa. One of the Hodenswald guards leads our horses away. I notice that Connor has removed his green Lankenshire cloak and emissary's pin—a smart move, making sure the trackers within the city are unaware of Lankenshire's affiliation with us in case something goes wrong.

I desperately hope nothing goes wrong.

"Commander, how nice to see you again. Welcome to Hodenswald. How many in your party?" She turns to scan the rest of us and falters briefly when she sees Connor. A tiny frown puckers the skin between her brows, and then she looks at the Commander again. "Will you require separate rooms for each of your people?"

He barely spares us a glance. "Do what you want with them. Where's Lyle?"

With another quick, sidelong glance at Connor, the woman turns on her heel. "He's waiting for you at his home. Please follow me."

The streets of Hodenswald are as straightforward and no-nonsense as the exterior. Dark stone paves roads that divide the city into neat sections. Tall lampposts made of iron hold oil lanterns on simple hooks and are spaced about twenty yards apart. We move quickly past buildings on either side, but everything is the same brown stone with little to no exterior adornment, and it's impossible to tell what each building is used for.

I move to walk beside Connor as the woman ahead of us makes a sharp left turn and approaches a compact building with three stories, a narrow front door, and black curtains blocking out the windows.

"She knows you," I say quietly as the woman marches up the low set of stairs leading to the building's front door.

"Yes."

"Who is she?"

The woman opens the door and steps aside to allow the Commander to enter. The Brute Squad follows closely on his heels.

"Her name is Amarynda Buehrlen. She's the sister of Clarissa Vaughn and the daughter of Lyle Hoden." Connor looks at me. "But I just call her Aunt Mandy."

Frankie and Willow disappear through the doorway with Adam close behind. I grab Connor's arm and slow his progress as we approach the steps.

"Are you telling me that the leader of Hodenswald is your grandfather?"

He grins. "Did you think Mom sent me on this mission because of my stunning expertise in navigating the Wasteland?"

"I didn't . . . no. No, I was wondering why Clarissa chose to send you, actually."

Something dark flashes in his eyes, and I hurry on before the hurt I just saw can take root and grow in him. "Not that I'm not happy to have you. You've already proven yourself to be both brave and smart."

"Not smart about the things the rest of you take for granted, but I have influence here. I won't be completely useless on this trip," he says quietly.

Jodi nods to the woman—Amarynda—and enters the building with Nola, Drake, and Smithson behind her.

I meet Connor's eyes, and we stop at the base of the steps. "You aren't useless. You came into this with a different skill set than the rest of us, but that doesn't mean you have nothing to offer. Besides, two months ago, nobody but Willow and I had experience traveling the Wasteland either. They learned, and so will you."

A corner of his mouth quirks up. "I can see why your people follow you."

My chest tightens, and I look away.

"Come on," I say, and take the steps quickly.

The interior is well lit and furnished with plain, utilitarian pieces. Amarynda leads us down another set of steps and through a pair of double doors at the end of a long hall. We find ourselves in a square, windowless room where oil lanterns glow against the white walls, straight-backed benches fill half the space, and a large table dominates the north end of the room. The benches are empty, but a man flanked by two Rowansmark trackers sits in a wheelchair at the table, watching us as we walk toward him.

"Jason! Excellent to see you as always." The man's voice booms out, shaky with age but still powerful. His broad shoulders and compact build remind me of the buildings in his city. He sweeps our group with a sharp gaze, and then turns his brown eyes on the Commander. "Right on time for our yearly trade negotiations. Punctual. I've always appreciated that about you." His glance darts toward the trackers who flank him and then returns to the Commander. "We must discuss how much you expect us to pay for corn this year, of course. The prices you wanted last year were highway robbery."

"Still getting right to the point, I see." The Commander gives no indication that he knows Lyle is lying for the sake of the trackers. "While we're laying our issues on the table, I'll tell you right now that the ale you sold to us last year was subpar for the price you charged. And I'll not be giving you a small fortune for oil, either."

Lyle laughs and reaches down to wheel his chair away from the table. "Subpar ale! You didn't think so when you were busy drinking my samples."

"And you didn't complain about the price of my corn."

Lyle rounds the edge of the table, and I see that the lower half of his body is shriveled and twisted. He catches me staring at his legs and smiles, though it doesn't reach his eyes. "Don't let the legs fool you, son. I can do more damage with my arms than most men could ever hope to do with their entire body."

I nod as if I agree with him. His eyes slide over Connor without pausing, and he rolls himself to the center of the room, right beside the Commander. I start to look toward them when I realize one of the trackers is watching me closely, a slight frown on his face.

"I trust you brought experts to test my samples this year?" Lyle asks the Commander.

The Commander glances at me and then says, "Of course."

"Well, then, what are we waiting for? Bring your experts, and let's go test my ale and your corn." He looks at Amarynda. "Have Jordan show the rest of Commander Chase's party to their lodgings."

"He'll be here shortly."

"Wait a minute." The tracker who keeps staring at me steps forward and addresses Lyle. "I'll come with you."

Lyle's face turns an alarming shade of red. "Think you can drink my ale for free, do you? I signed a protection agreement, not a standing invitation to raid my stores. If you want ale, you buy it at the going rate." His hands grip the wheels on his chair until his knuckles turn white. "I'm not running a charity here."

"I don't want to drink your ale, old man."

"Old man!" Lyle whips his chair around and speeds toward the tracker. "Pull your sword, fool. I'll show you what this old man can do."

"Father!" Amarynda rushes forward and jumps between the tracker and Lyle. "I'm sure Tracker Sharpe meant no disrespect."

"He meant every disrespect." Lyle's voice trembles with fury. "He called me old man. He wanted to drink my ale."

Amarynda looks over her shoulder at Sharpe. Her voice is

calm. "The ale is below us in the cellar. You've already searched that room. What is the harm in allowing him to conduct his trade negotiations as he always does?"

Sharpe's jaw tightens. "Fine. But we search the visitors before they go to the cellar."

I meet the Commander's eyes in a moment of shared panic. If they search him, they'll find the Rowansmark device he carries. If they search me, they'll find schematics for improving upon the device's design. And if they pay too much attention to Connor, I'll lose the staff.

The Commander's spine snaps into a rigid line, and he stares the tracker down while he spits his words at him. "I am Commander Jason Chase, leader of Baalboden. I am not in Rowansmark, nor is this city under Rowansmark's jurisdiction."

"Actually, we are the official protectors of Hodenswald—"

"In the event of a *tanniyn* attack. Yes, I'm familiar with your leader's protection agreement." The Commander steps forward. "I am not the *tanniyn*, but if you disrespect my authority, I will make you wish you were facing that creature instead of me."

Sharpe takes a step toward the Commander.

"Lay a hand on me, and you'll lose it." The Commander takes another step forward and stands toe to toe with Sharpe. "Furthermore, an act of aggression toward me during a diplomatic mission is equal to an act of aggression toward Baalboden and her allies. I'm sure I don't need to remind you of the Diplomatic Trade Agreement ratified twelve years ago by all nine leaders." His voice becomes dangerously soft. "You are in imminent danger of violating that agreement and thus giving me cause to start a war with James Rowan."

Silence falls, thick with tension, and then Sharpe lifts a hand as if he's going to pat down the Commander's chest, searching for . . . whatever it is they're searching for.

The Commander's sword slides free of its sheath with a metallic shriek. "Go ahead, boy. Give me a reason to start that war."

Amarynda steps to Sharpe's side, cold confidence pouring off her. "There will be no bloodshed on Hodenswald's soil. We are not in violation of our protection agreement, Tracker Sharpe, and these are our diplomatic guests. We will be responsible for their actions while they are inside our city."

A smug smile tugs at the scar on the Commander's face until Amarynda turns to him and says, "By the same token, Tracker Sharpe and his companion are simply doing their jobs. There is no need to antagonize them further."

Before either man can respond, she turns to her father. "Jordan is just outside the door. You take Commander Chase and his experts to the cellar, and once Jordan has the rest of the Commander's party well in hand, I'll be along to conclude the negotiations."

Lyle immediately starts rolling his chair toward a door in the far left corner of the room. The Commander glances over his shoulder at me and jerks his head toward Lyle as if to tell me I'm expected to follow. I grab Connor and Willow, and we head toward the door. Sharpe slaps a hand on my shoulder and pulls me to a halt as I brush past him.

"Have we met?" he asks.

I keep my expression neutral, though my pulse is pounding. In Lankenshire, the historian who was working with Jeremiah on the map recognized me as the lost McEntire boy from

Rowansmark seconds after meeting me because apparently I closely resemble my mother. Sharpe looks to be at least fifteen years older than me. Maybe he knew her before she died.

I glance at him like I'm not worried about being recognized and say, "I doubt it. This is my first trip to Hodenswald, and I've never been to Rowansmark."

He frowns as if trying to figure out how he knows me. I glance impatiently between him and the door, as if wondering what his problem is. Finally, he lets go of my shoulder and steps back. I follow the Commander, Willow, and Connor through the door. The trackers stay behind.

The door opens up to a gently sloping ramp that leads us down another well-lit corridor until we reach the cellar below. Lyle gestures for the Commander to open the cellar door, but he turns and stares at Willow as if he expects her to open it instead. Willow crosses her arms over her chest and stares back.

I swallow the pithy remark I want to make about his arrogant misogyny and open the door myself.

Lyle's cellar is stacked floor to ceiling with crates of ale along two walls. A third wall holds polished weaponry that I've only seen in the books Jared smuggled in from his trips outside Baalboden—rifles, pistols, bayonets. Relics from the past that were mostly destroyed in the fires that swept the major cities in the wake of the *tanniyn*'s arrival. A dusty table with a single oil lantern in the middle of it rests against the wall at the back of the rectangular room. Lyle wheels himself to the table, lights the lantern, and then barks, "Shut the door before those fools try to get my ale."

As soon as the door is shut, the Commander asks, "Since

when did you start letting Amarynda tell people what to do?"

"She's my heir. Who else is going to tell people what to do? Now, I'm pretty sure those trackers believed my offended old man routine, but we'd better make this quick. You arrived two months earlier than our scheduled meeting, and you have my grandson in tow." He nods toward Connor. "What's going on?"

The Commander stares from Lyle to Connor and back again with narrowed eyes. "*That's* your grandson?"

Lyle lifts his chin to meet the Commander's gaze. "Something wrong with that?"

"He can barely walk through the Wasteland without tripping over his own two feet."

Lyle's expression doesn't change, but a subtle tension enters the room. "He's smarter than the two of us put together, and you'd do well to remember it."

"I'm here as an official representative from Lankenshire." Connor steps past the Commander. "Like you, we've been under Rowansmark's control ever since we signed the protection agreement. But Logan"—he gestures toward me—"knows how to dismantle the beacons and replicate a device that controls the *tanniyn* like a puppet on a string. And the Commander has the combined might of Baalboden and Carrington at his disposal, plus the promise of one-fourth of Lankenshire's army as long as you also commit troops."

"One-fourth?" the Commander barks. "What's this one-fourth business? We need a full commitment of troops."

For once, I find myself in complete agreement with him. It's an unsettling feeling.

Connor is firm. "And if you fail, who will be left to protect my city? You get one-fourth if you gain troops from Hoden-swald—"

"If you're so worried about us failing, then give us more than one-fourth!" The Commander paces around the table like a predator stalking his prey. "All of my remaining guards are committed. Carrington's entire army is committed. For you to do less—"

"Forgive me, Commander, but neither your guards nor the army of Carrington have anywhere else to go. It's easy to commit when that's all you have left. We have a city to protect."

"Committed to do what?" Lyle interrupts Connor before the Commander can respond. "Why are the soldiers of Carrington, Baalboden, and possibly Lankenshire coming together?"

Connor turns toward him. "To wage war against Rowans-mark."

Lyle slaps the arm of his chair. "It's about time."

CHAPTER EIGHTEEN

RACHEL

I hate boats.

The deck refuses to stop swaying. The trees slide past on the shore too quickly for me to find my bearings. And the salty food the trackers keep offering me refuses to stay in my stomach.

I spent most of my first night aboard the boat with my head hanging over a bucket while I vomited until I had nothing left. When I tried to eat something for breakfast the next morning, I got to start the process all over again.

And now, at the end of our second day, I finally crawled out of the bathroom and took a few sips of water only to discover that my stomach still refuses to behave. I clutch the smooth railing along the lower deck and lean over the river as I gag and heave.

I *really* hate boats.

The only silver lining in the entire situation is that the trackers, convinced that I can't escape from the boat and that my bout of seasickness renders me harmless, are ignoring me. If I could just get my stomach to calm down, I could take advantage of that. I could look for Quinn. Make sure he has food and water. I could find a weapon to replace the knife I lost to the river.

I could be ready for Ian if he tries to kill me before we reach port.

I drop to the deck and lean my head against the railing while I slowly breathe in through my nose and out through my mouth. We're traveling quickly. At this pace, we should reach Rowansmark in another two days.

I need to feel better before then so I can figure out a plan for sabotaging Rowansmark that doesn't end with me receiving a pain atonement sentence at the hands of Ian or his leader. My hands shake as I press clammy palms against my aching head. My right arm feels swollen and itchy, but I've been too miserable to roll up my tunic sleeve and check my wound.

"Here. Chew on this." Samuel settles beside me and pushes a thick piece of peeled ginger root into my hand. "It'll help."

"I don't want to swallow anything." My voice sounds hoarse.

"Trust me. An empty stomach only makes it worse. Ginger will help."

I take the ginger and bite off a tiny piece. The peppery sweetness explodes across my tongue. Swallowing carefully, I wait for my stomach to rebel, but it doesn't. I take another bite and chew while I look at Samuel.

"Thank you."

"You could've killed all of us by driving the wagon off the dock like you did." His voice is calm and measured, but there's steel beneath it. I remember the way he looked at me when I punched him in the face to distract him from tracking Quinn's location. I'm long past pretending I'm helpless, but maybe I can still keep him guessing enough to convince him I'm not a threat while we're on the boat.

If I'm going to escape my captors once we're inside the city, I'm going to need to search this boat for a weapon. I can't do that if Samuel is watching me too closely.

"I didn't mean to drive it off the dock." I lift my chin and scratch at my right arm, where the burned skin feels tight and impossibly itchy. "I meant to run over Ian. Apparently, donkeys have issues with trampling people. They jerked to the side, and we went into the water."

He hands me another plug of ginger. "Yes, I heard that you tried to run Ian over. He'd have a thing or two to say about the matter if I wasn't keeping him busy elsewhere on the ship."

"Why bother? You don't care about me. Why don't you let him punish me one more time for how disappointed he is at the way his life turned out?" The bitterness of my words tastes like ashes in my mouth. I can see the boy with dreams who watched his entire world shatter. Who sees the blood of his father on his hands every time he looks at himself. But I can also see Thom's gentle smile and Donny's eager gaze following Willow's every move.

I can see Sylph.

Samuel's voice is cold. "No, I don't care about you. But I do care about *him*."

"Oh, right. Because he had a bright future, and losing those he loved broke him." I swallow the ginger, and scratch harder at my arm. It simultaneously burns like fire and provides some measure of relief. "You know what? I lost my dreams, too. I lost my family. But I didn't go out and purposefully kill innocents just so that someone could pay the price for my pain."

"He was charged with restoring honor to his family by returning the tech and by making an example out of those who took it. He had to punish the Commander, and Logan too if Logan was involved, in a way that would make it clear that the cost of challenging Rowansmark is too bloody to be worthwhile." Samuel leans toward me. "He was just a boy. It was too big a task—"

"Forget about the size of the task." I stop scratching my arm and sit up straighter. "Let's focus on the fact that it was *wrong*."

"I don't expect you to understand."

I laugh, but it sounds more like a sob. "Why, because I value the lives of those who died when Ian decided he couldn't be bothered to confront the Commander or Logan directly?"

"They were an unfortunate sacrifice in a larger—"

"They were my friends!" My words echo across the water and die inside the vast darkness that presses against both shores.

"And Ian is mine." Samuel's voice is rigid. "He's done too much already. I'm keeping him away from you because the opportunity to perform more sanctioned violence might cause him irreparable harm."

I stare at him while the paddle wheel purrs quietly and the boat's wake churns through the water behind us. I'm still staring as he hands me the rest of the ginger and tells me someone is watching to make sure I don't jump overboard.

He walks away while I sift through his words until I find the ones that send a chill across my skin and cause my heartbeat to thunder in my ears.

Sanctioned violence.

He's been saying it all along. Ian was commissioned by James Rowan to punish the Commander and Logan. To levy a sentence of pain atonement against the two by destroying everything and everyone they cared about so that no one would dare stand against Rowansmark again.

Ian might have destroyed our city and murdered our people, but he didn't do it alone. Someone had to be watching over him. Making sure he restored his family's honor while also making the innocents of Baalboden a bloody example of why Rowansmark's supremacy should be left unchallenged. Someone had to be keeping supplies, like the white phosphorous that burned me, in a wagon until Ian needed them.

A wagon like the one I sent to the bottom of the river.

Slowly I get to my feet as the truth ignites a gut-deep well of anger I no longer knew I possessed. Heidi, the tracker I'd hoped someone would save from drowning. Samuel, the man I've been trying to make my ally.

The two trackers who were waiting in the Wasteland outside of Lankenshire. With a wagon full of supplies.

Something drips from my right hand and splashes against the deck. I look down to see blood leaking from my wound, the flesh scratched open by my nails.

Raising my hand, I let the starlight glitter against the drops of blood on my fingertips and fight against the sudden panic that steals my breath.

This isn't a dream. The ghosts that haunt me aren't going to come for me while the sky turns to blood and ash and horror.

This is real. And so is the fact that Heidi, Samuel, and every other tracker on this boat who understands the true cost of James Rowan's pain atonement policy yet looks the other way have as much blood on their hands as Ian does.

It's time they understood that there's a price to pay for hurting innocent people.

And I'm just the girl to teach them.

CHAPTER NINETEEN

LOGAN

Darkness presses close as Willow, Adam, Jodi, and I ease out of the rooms we share on the top floor of Lyle Hoden's home in the center of the city. Frankie, Nola, and Smithson are staying behind to guard Connor, Drake, and the tech in case any trackers come snooping around. They're also prepared with an excuse for our absence—something about Willow teaching us how to track—in case the Commander visits our rooms.

The plan I laid out for Lyle and the Commander was for one of Lyle's soldiers to steal a beacon tonight so that tomorrow, under the guise of concluding our trade negotiations, I could show them how to disable it.

I have no intention of teaching the Commander how to do the one thing he believes he needs me for. I'm hoping he thinks I need someone to bring a beacon to me. I hope it never occurs to him that I'm willing to brave the rooftops in the middle of the night and find it myself.

"Ready?" I ask quietly.

"Let's break some tech," Willow says.

Silently, we move down the corridor to the stairwell at the far end. Unlike the lower level of Lyle's home where the Commander and his guards are housed, the oil lanterns here aren't lit. Faint starlight filters in through windows on either end of the hall, but for the most part, we're shrouded in darkness.

Lyle and Amarynda agreed that if I could render the beacons incapable of calling the *tanniyn*, they would commit troops to our cause against Rowansmark. Unfortunately, Lyle followed Clarissa's example and only promised one-fourth of his army. It's not enough, but the Commander couldn't bully him into promising us more. When I asked how we could possibly take soldiers out of Hodenswald under the very noses of the trackers, Lyle informed me that he was too smart to have only one way in or out of his city.

I'd stared hard at the Commander then, waiting for a flicker of realization on his face that if he'd had tunnels beneath his city or secret side-exits, many of his people would've survived the fires that destroyed Baalboden, but the cold stoicism of his expression never changed.

Adam reaches the stairwell first and holds the door open for the rest of us. The stairs are narrow and the wood is slippery with age. We walk slowly, muffling the sound of our footsteps as best as we can.

We step onto the flat roof above Lyle's home, and I pause for a moment to get my bearings. After spending the afternoon touring the city and paying close attention to the location of the Rowansmark tech, Connor drew a map of the city's roofs, marking each place where a beacon was attached to the eaves.

Willow and I committed it to memory so we wouldn't have to worry about reading it in the dark. Now I just need to make the map in my head match the layout of the city that surrounds me.

The city is laid out on a grid, the buildings evenly spaced boxes with flat rooftops. As long as we're careful to plan our jumps so that we don't have to move from a shorter building to a taller one, we'll be fine.

"Adam and I will take the east half. You and Jodi can do the west," Willow says.

"Do you remember how to disable the infrasonic frequency?" I ask, even though I drew her a diagram and made her repeat the process back to me until she finally snapped and told me she'd disable *me* if I doubted her one more time.

She rolls her eyes. "I yank out the wires on the left side of the transmitter and then rip out the silver mechanism. It's not hard, Logan."

"Actually, it's a very delicate process requiring precision and careful—"

"It requires me to know my right from my left and to pull out some wires." She pats my shoulder and moves toward Adam. "We're good. Meet you back here before dawn."

"Be careful," Jodi says. "You don't want to run into a tracker."

Willow flashes a dangerous smile. "No, the trackers don't want to run into *me*."

Seconds later, she and Adam leap, landing lightly on the neighboring roof. The fact that the buildings in Hodenswald are so close together is going to make this task much easier to accomplish.

"Ready?" I ask Jodi. She nods and moves to the western lip of the roof. I stand beside her and assess the jump. "Take a running start and aim for a spot at least two yards beyond the edge. You'll be fine."

"I know I will." Her voice shakes a little. I can't blame her. If she falls, if any of us fall, we won't be getting back up. She's the shortest in our group. I worry that her legs aren't long enough to give her the kind of distance she'll need, but she was adamant about coming, and if being around Rachel has taught me anything at all, it's that if a girl has made up her mind to do something, there's no point standing in her way unless you prefer to have your dignity, and possibly your nose, ruined.

"I'll go first so that I can catch you as you land."

"Okay." Her blue eyes are huge as she looks from her feet to the opposite roof.

"Just keep your eyes on me, and you'll be fine." I back up a few steps, run at the edge, and leap, my eyes fixed on a spot two yards past the lip of the opposite building. I don't hit my mark, but I do land safely past the gap that separates the two homes. Turning, I reach my arms out and say, "Run and jump. Don't look down; it will ruin your aim. Look only at me."

She takes a few steps back, raises her eyes to mine, and starts running. Seconds later, she lands lightly in front of me. I grab her arms to steady her, but she's already found her balance. She grins.

"That was fun."

"I'm glad you think so, because we're going to do that all night long."

It takes us seven leaps to get to the first building with a beacon attached to its eaves. I can't reach the tech by crouching down and leaning out, so Jodi lies on her stomach and eases over the edge of the roof while I hold on to her ankles. There's a sharp, metallic *pop*, and then she says, "Pull me up."

I help her wiggle her way back onto the roof, and she hands me the beacon. Quickly, I detach the back of the metal casing and use the soft glow of the moon to examine the transmitter inside. It's the same as the beacon I disabled in Lankenshire—ultrasonic frequency on the right, infrasonic on the left. I figured they'd be the same, but still . . . knowing that I gave Willow the correct instructions eases the knot in my stomach.

I carefully pull the wires on the left free from the transmitter and then snap the silver mechanisms that were set to the correct infrasonic frequency used to call the *tanniyn*. The beacon is now useful only to keep the monsters at bay.

My fingers slide gently over the powerful transmitter as I call up my memory of the map Amarynda drew for us. There are beacons approximately every seventy-five yards. A transmitter of this size is capable of sending out a signal for at least five hundred yards. Rowansmark must have put so many beacons in place to compensate for the possibility that a battery might die or a frequency might get corrupted. Or because they needed something strong enough to drown out the signal the leaders wear on a chain around their necks.

The bottom line is that Hodenswald doesn't need all of the transmitters they currently have in order to repel the *tanniyn*. My best estimate, calculating the size of the city and leaving room for some transmitters and batteries to fail, is that the city needs no more than twenty-eight beacons up and running on the western half. They currently have thirty-five. That leaves seven extra transmitters.

Seven might be just enough to help me build the circle of destruction I need to take down the Commander.

I slip the casing back into place and lower Jodi again until she can snap the beacon back onto its mooring. While she works, I run through the map of the city in my head, looking for places where I can remove a transmitter without creating a weakness in the blanket of anti-*tanniyn* ultrasonic frequency.

By the time Jodi's finished, I've picked the locations and am ready to move. We creep to the southern edge of the roof and assess the next jump, scanning the buildings laid out before us. Twelve jumps south, two jumps west, and another four jumps south will bring us to the next beacon. That's if the roofs remain equal in height. Those that are too high or too low will need to be circumvented, which will cost us valuable time. Already the moon is in the midpoint of its journey through the sky.

My legs tense, ready to leap forward, when Jodi snatches my arm and pulls me into a crouch.

"Look down," she breathes.

Carefully, I lean forward until I can see over the bricks and down to the street below. A dark shadow huddles on the street corner, just outside the glow of light from one of the hanging gas lanterns. I squint and try to figure out what I'm seeing. For a moment, I'm almost convinced that the shadow is nothing—a crate of trash, perhaps. A barrel of spare rainwater. But then the shadow shifts, and a sliver of moonlight illuminates a pale face before the shadow eases farther back against the wall behind it.

That brief glimpse is enough to make my breath come faster as I push back from the edge and look at Jodi. "It's Sharpe. The tracker who was with Lyle when he first received us."

"Maybe that's his regular post?"

I study the buildings, but they're so uniform, it's impossible to tell what they are. Maybe he's standing guard outside an important government building, but why would he? Unless he's worried we'll try to break in for some reason, but if that's the case, why wouldn't he just wait inside where it's comfortable? Maybe he's watching the streets to make sure the citizens of Hodenswald aren't trying to mess with the beacons.

But if that's true, then why didn't he say something when Jodi hung over the edge of the building and removed the tech?

"I don't think so. Something else is going on. Good catch."

She shrugs. "Rachel taught me to always treat my surroundings as if everything wants to kill me."

"Good advice," I say, and swallow the ache at the base of my throat. I hope Rachel is taking her own advice.

We watch Sharpe in silence for several moments. It's hard to keep my eyes on him because he sits so still, he's nothing more than an absence of starlight on a street that is already dark. When he shows no sign of leaving, I signal Jodi to move to the opposite side of the roof with me.

"We're going to have to go around him." I examine the rooftops around us. "It's going to add a few extra jumps, and we're already running short on time."

"We can hurry."

"We aren't going to hurry the jumps. I don't want us taking any chances there. We'll just have to disable the beacons faster." I take a moment to think through the map. "We're going to do three jumps north, cut to the east four jumps, and then head south to the next beacon. We'll have to cut back west at some point, but this way we can go around Sharpe."

"Let's go," she says.

I estimate it takes nearly twenty minutes to make our way to the next beacon. I lower Jodi, and she quickly grabs the tech. This time, I don't pull the wires free. Instead, I remove the entire transmitter and slide it into the inner pocket of my cloak. One transmitter stolen. Six to go.

When Jodi raises a brow at me, I say, "I've run the calculations. Hodenswald doesn't need all of these to be protected. And I have use for them."

She doesn't argue. Quickly, we replace the tech and head south again. It takes nearly two hours to alter twenty-nine more beacons and steal two more transmitters. We only have four more beacons to go. We've fallen into a rhythm. Run, jump, examine the streets for problems, assess the next jump, and then start all over again. At this rate, we'll easily finish and be back inside Lyle's home before dawn.

We hit the roof that holds the next beacon and head for the eaves. Jodi lies on her stomach. I grab her ankles and brace my boots against the lip of stone at the edge of the building. Then, she inches her way over the side and jackknifes at the waist in order to reach the tech. The beacon comes free of its moorings,

and then I hear something that freezes the breath in my lungs—
the soft thud of someone landing on the roof behind me.

I whip my head around and find Sharpe stalking toward
me, his expression a mask of cold, ruthless authority, his sword
already in his hand.

"Don't bother pulling her up," he says. "You'll be dead before
you can draw the breath to tell her she's next."

CHAPTER TWENTY

LOGAN

"Brace yourself!" I yell. Pushing my feet against the stone ledge, I haul Jodi up far enough that she can reach back and grab the top of the roof with her arm. Letting go of her ankles, I flip over into a crouch in time to see Sharpe skid to a stop in front of me, his sword already falling toward my neck.

Lunging forward, I slam into his knees, and send both of us flying onto the rough, gritty stone beneath us. He raises his sword arm and slams the hilt into my face. Pain explodes across my cheekbone, and I throw myself to the side to avoid the next hit.

Sharpe rolls with me, his sword flashing past my head in a swing so powerful, I can feel the breeze as the blade slices the air. For one second, the momentum of his missed strike keeps him off-balance. I ball up my fist and punch him in the jaw.

It's like punching the side of a wagon.

He shakes off the blow, and raises his sword arm again. I pull my knees up to my chest as his blade falls toward me, plant my boots on his stomach, and kick as hard as I can.

His sword nicks me as he skids backward. Fewer than five yards separate us. I lunge to my feet, and he does the same. Yanking my sword out of its sheath, I raise it and face him down even while I listen for evidence that other trackers might be closing in.

I don't hear anything, but that doesn't mean they aren't coming. Somehow, Sharpe followed us through the city. Somehow, he knew to come up to the roof. If he knows, others might know, too.

I need to end this soon, or we aren't getting off this rooftop alive.

"How did you find us?" I ask.

The cold ruthlessness of his expression has nothing on the viciousness in his voice. "When you expect people to behave like criminals, you take precautions in case you need to follow them later."

I remember the way he stared at me when we first met Lyle. The way his hand slapped my shoulder and held on tight while he asked me if we'd met. The way his fingers pressed too hard against the neckline of my cloak before he let me go.

"You put a tracking signal on me, didn't you?"

"You've led me on quite a chase tonight. Couldn't figure out why I was getting a ping off your signal but couldn't see you on the streets." He circles me, slowly edging closer. "Took me a while to figure out I needed to move to the rooftops."

His sword flashes, and I parry, spin, strike, and parry again before we break apart. The power of his blows reverberates up my arms. He's better than good. He's an efficient, well-trained machine with more experience and more strength than me.

"Why would you think to put a tracking signal on me in the first place?" I ask, mostly to buy myself a little breathing room. His swordsmanship is superior to mine. Maybe if I keep him talking, I can find a chink in his armor to use to my advantage.

He sneers as we dance around each other, looking for openings. "Liars always have the same tells. You and the Commander? You're both liars."

I sidestep a swing and slap the flat of my blade against his back as he passes. My face hurts like I ran cheek-first into a wall, and blood is steadily dripping off my jaw.

"I never lied to you." I slide to the right to mirror his movements. Out of the corner of my eye, I see Jodi move away from the edge of the building.

Sharpe jumps forward, his sword slicing toward my chest. I block the blow, but his leg lashes out and sweeps my feet out from underneath me.

I hit the ground and roll, but he's already on me. He lands with a knee in the middle of my back, grabs a fistful of my hair, and yanks, exposing my throat.

"You lied," he says while the moonlight gleams along the length of the blade he's raising toward my throat. "I recognize you. I can't place how I know you, but we've met. And you lied about it. You made sure you kept strong eye contact with me while you did it, too. You're smart enough to realize that liars usually glance away as they lie, but not smart enough to know that the really *good* liars try too hard to look you in the face."

"We've never met. If we had, you'd be able to place me. But I know why I look familiar to you," I say because his blade keeps coming closer. I can only hope that by telling him a piece of the truth, I'll intrigue him enough to give me an opportunity to kill him.

"Why is that?" His tone makes it clear he thinks I'm telling him another lie to buy myself more time.

He's almost right.

"Because I was born in Rowansmark to Marcus and Julia McEntire."

His sword freezes in midair, though the grip on my hair doesn't lessen. "You're the lost McEntire boy?"

"Yes. The Commander kidnapped me when I was a few days old. I was raised in Baalboden. I didn't know who I really was until recently."

He removes his knee from my back and twists me around to face him. Bringing the length of his sword beneath my chin, he studies me in what's left of the moonlight. Two yards behind him, Jodi crouches, her eyes locked on me, her expression a mix of calculation and defiance. She's going to intervene. Try to save me. And if she does, Sharpe will kill her.

Sharpe is going to kill her anyway if I can't find a way to defeat him.

Jodi presses her palms into the stone and looks from me to the edge of the roof on her other side and then back to me again. I blink, and she repeats herself. Me—the edge of the roof—me again.

"I can see it," Sharpe says, and I quickly meet his gaze before he realizes Jodi is a scant two yards behind him, clinging to the roof just inches before the building ends and the long drop to the ground begins. "You resemble your mother."

"You knew my parents?"

"Marcus was the one who recruited me into the tracking program. He was a good man." Sharpe's tone hardens. "Which doesn't explain why his son is on a roof stealing the tech Marcus worked so hard to build."

I can't tell him we're disabling the tech, and he'd never believe we were simply curious and decided to do a midnight rooftop dash through the city to pry open a few beacons and peek inside. Time to become what he's accused me of being all along: a liar.

I frown. "What are you talking about? This is Hodenswald tech."

He leans forward and says softly, "Every city-state has either signed the protection agreement with Rowansmark or has been destroyed. Your leader himself admitted he understood that our presence here is to protect against a *tanniyn* attack. You know what these beacons are for. Lie to me again, and I will kill you."

"You're going to kill me anyway."

His smile dries the spit in my mouth. "Lie to me again, and I will kill you *slowly*."

Jodi gestures behind Sharpe, and I let my eyes glance off her as I scan my surroundings. Two yards between Sharpe and Jodi. Inches between Jodi and a long, fatal fall.

I just have to tell the truth long enough to find an opportunity to take advantage of Jodi's position.

"Okay, fine. I know what they are. But you have plenty here. A transmitter that size? You've got this city covered and then some. I figured I could lift a few transmitters without anyone noticing."

His sword doesn't waver. "You thought wrong. What do

you need the transmitters for? Planning on using our own tech against us?"

It's hard to deliver a scornful laugh with a sword at my throat, but I try. "Why would I do that? I'm from Rowansmark, remember? If the Commander hadn't intervened, I'd be wearing a tracker's uniform right now."

The truth of that statement sits uneasily in my thoughts, and I push it away. "But he did intervene. He kidnapped me, stole the life I was supposed to have, and dumped me on the streets of Baalboden when I was six, after having my adoptive mother killed."

"A tragic story." Sharpe's voice is pitiless. "But still not an explanation for the theft."

"Don't you see? I hate him." My tone is as ruthless as his. "I *hate* him. I hate what he did to my family in Rowansmark. I hate what he did to the people I cared about in Baalboden. Everyone I've lost, everything that's gone wrong, can be traced back to him."

I drop my sword and raise my hands to show him that I'm not a threat, and then I slowly reach my left hand into my cloak pocket and pull out one of the stolen transmitters.

"The Commander, like all city-state leaders, wears a necklace to ward off the *tanniyn*. The transmitter inside that necklace is powerful enough to keep the beasts away from an entire city, which is why you needed so many beacons up, right? You needed enough transmitters to make sure you could override the leaders' signals if you needed to call the Cursed—the *tanniyn*."

He nods and watches me closely. I keep the transmitter in my hand, but raise my arms again in a posture of surrender.

"I know enough about tech to be able to amplify the signal in these transmitters. I only took a few. It shouldn't greatly affect your signal strength inside the city." Except for the fact that the only signal they'll be sending out is ultrasonic and therefore useless to Rowansmark's purposes. "I just needed enough to overpower the Commander's necklace."

"Why?" he asks, but he already knows. And he knows I'm telling the truth. I can see it in the way his shoulders relax. In the increased space between my neck and the edge of his blade.

"Because the next time we have an encounter with the *tanniyn*, I want the Commander to be utterly defenseless."

"If you want to kill him, why not just run him through with your sword?"

I meet his gaze. "Because some crimes deserve more than that."

I'm speaking the language of pain atonement, and it works. He steps back, though he doesn't completely lower his sword.

"You're telling me the truth," he says.

"Yes."

"That's a dilemma." He motions with his sword for me to stand.

I get to my feet and assess the distance between him and Jodi, still crouched near the edge of the building. "Where's the dilemma?"

"Pick up your sword."

"Why?"

"Pick up. Your. Sword."

Slowly, I lean down and pick up my weapon, though I don't raise it toward him. I want him off guard for as long as possible.

He opens his stance, but I remain still.

"The dilemma is this: You're telling the truth about who you are and about wanting the Commander dead. But you were caught stealing from Rowansmark. I can't let that go."

"That's unfortunate." I slowly shift my weight to my right leg.

"If you return the stolen property to me, I'll deliver your punishment, but I will spare the girl." He glances behind him at Jodi, who huddles on the ground as if too terrified to move.

I speak quickly to get his focus back on me. "You'll kill me over a few stolen transmitters?"

"Not kill." He looks at me. "Punish. You're tough. You'll survive it."

I swipe blood off my cheek. Jodi meets my eyes and then glances meaningfully at the back of Sharpe's legs. I nod as if I'm agreeing with Sharpe, and turn as if to reach into my cloak for the other transmitters.

"You can have them," I say.

His stance relaxes slightly, and his sword lowers a fraction.

Jodi lunges toward the back of Sharpe's knees, and I snap my leg up. My boot finds his chin just as Jodi slams into him. His knees crumple, and my kick sends him flying over Jodi's back. Sharpe hits the stone, skids backward for a few inches, and then goes sailing over the side of the building.

Jodi and I run to the edge of the roof in time to hear a thick, wet splat as Sharpe hits the bricks three stories below us. He lies sprawled in the moonlight, his legs at an unnatural angle, his eyes staring at nothing.

Seconds later, we hear the high-pitched whine of his internal trigger, and he explodes in a cloud of blood and bone.

"Disgusting," Jodi says as the bloody mist that used to be Sharpe floats through the air, darkening the pool of golden light beneath the closest gas lamp.

I whip my cloak off, find the tiny transmitter stuck on the neckline, and rip it free. Crushing it beneath my heel in case any other trackers in the city are also homing in on the signal, I follow Jodi onto the next rooftop and concentrate on getting the rest of the beacons disabled before dawn.

CHAPTER TWENTY-ONE

RACHEL

Darkness hides the shoreline as we sail down the river. The smells of damp bark and night-blooming jasmine drift through the air, and the occasional owl swoops across the starlit sky. Samuel has long since disappeared inside one of the doors on the lower deck. Occasionally, one of the trackers on the upper deck paces in his small compartment or leans out over the railing to look at me, but I haven't seen another person on the lower deck in hours.

I've sat against the side of the boat listening to the paddle wheel churn through the water and thinking about Quinn hiding somewhere on the boat, determined not to let me face Rowansmark alone. About Logan heading straight for Rowansmark to ransom me with the stolen tech with no idea that the trap he's facing—the tech that can call an entire army of the *tanniyn*—is worse than anything he'd even think to plan for.

And about how Samuel and Heidi were helping Ian all along. Carrying his supplies. Covering his tracks. Sanctioning his violence against the people I love.

I want to hurt them. To send the message that they can't treat innocent lives like collateral damage. I want to, but if I do anything to jeopardize my ability to get inside Rowansmark, Logan will die. I can't start trouble on this boat.

But if trouble finds me anyway, I can certainly be ready to finish it.

There are supplies on the boat. Food. Clean drinking water. Medicine. Weapons. Maybe Rowansmark tech. I might not intuitively understand tech like Logan does, but I bet if I press enough buttons, I can figure it out.

Quinn and I will find food and water after we escape the trackers. In the meantime, I need a weapon to replace the knife I lost in the river. Something big enough to do some damage, but small enough to conceal on my body. I need medicine, too. My arm, swollen and hot, still itches in a painful, throbbing way that makes it hard to think straight. I can't stand to scratch it. I can't stand not to. Blood runs down my hand in a slow, faltering stream. My throat is starting to ache fiercely like it did the time I got the flu so badly that Dad put off one of his trips to Schoensville because he didn't want to leave my side.

I swallow hard, grateful that the ginger Samuel gave me seems to have finally settled my stomach, and force myself to think about something other than my arm.

At this speed, we should reach Rowansmark sometime tomorrow. I have to be ready to escape my keepers and disappear into the city. To do that, I need to raid the boat for supplies, both for Quinn and for myself.

I listen for another moment, but only the creak of the boat's lower deck and the distant slap of the water against the shoreline meet my ears. Slowly, taking care not to bump my right arm against anything, I get to my feet. Then I move down the lower deck until I reach the first door.

This is the door Samuel used when he left me. I don't want to run into him, but I'm pretty sure this is the medical bay, and I need to bandage this arm. Some medicine for the pain would be helpful, too. The knob turns soundlessly, and I ease the door open.

The room is about the size of my old bedroom and contains two beds and an entire wall of labeled supplies stocked on metal shelves bolted to the wall. Heidi lies sleeping on one of the beds, her leg bandaged and propped up on a pillow. There's no one else in the room.

A lantern glows softly on a small table wedged between the two beds. A closer look reveals that the lantern is also bolted down. I step quietly past Heidi and examine the shelves.

Bandages. Burn cream. Pain medicine. Antiseptic paste. Herbs for curing stomach ailments and headaches. For curing blood clots. For flushing the body of poison.

I linger for a moment on the bottle of herbal blood clot medicine. Ian injected Sylph with ground castor seeds, causing the blood to clot inside her organs while thinning the blood at her extremities. There was no cure, no nice wall of neatly labeled shelves that I could turn to for help. Instead, I lay by her side and listened to her breath leave her body. She was my best friend, and there was nothing I could do.

My hands shake as I pick up the blood clot medicine. Something hot splashes onto my collarbone, and I realize I'm crying.

Tears of grief for the Sylph-shaped hole inside of me that nothing can ever fill. Tears of anger because she didn't have to die. If Heidi or Samuel had stopped Ian, if one of them had said *No, this is wrong*, she'd still be alive now.

The stopper is out of the bottle before I realize I'm going to remove it. I lift the dropper and stare at Heidi. At her bandaged leg, where a bloody wound would take this medicine straight into her veins.

It isn't poison. She wouldn't suffer the way Sylph did, but she'd die just the same. A blood clot can kill you when it reaches your heart. Or your lungs. Or your brain. Chloe Jarbonneau's father died of one. I remember how shocked we were because Chloe was only eight, and we had no idea our fathers could die when we were so young.

I stand over Heidi, my hands shaking. My tears falling. Blood on my hands smears across the jar's label, and I set the jar on the table before I drop it.

Can I do this? Can I poison a woman while she sleeps, even if she deserves it? Is it justified, or would it bring me one step closer to becoming the kind of monster I'm determined to stop?

I don't know. I wish Logan were here so I could ask him. So I could look in his eyes and see if he'd still love me once he knew what I'd done.

I reach for Heidi's leg and pull the top of her bandage aside. The edge of her wound glares at me, crimson and angry. The dropper in my hand, filled with clear liquid, quivers as I hold it above the injury.

She deserves this. She does. Melkin's dark eyes burn against the back of my mind, and I flinch. Maybe I'll see Heidi's face in my nightmares after this. But maybe it's worth it if I'm doing it for Sylph.

For Sylph, who loved everyone with equal measure but spared extra for me. Who took the pain of her family's death and turned it into care for others instead of letting it sour into bitterness.

Sylph, who wouldn't do this. Wouldn't stand over a defenseless person, even a guilty one, and poison her in her sleep.

My arm falls to my side, and a single drop of liquid leaves the dropper and splashes harmlessly onto the floor.

I can't kill Heidi in her sleep the way Ian killed Sylph, even though I believe she deserves to die for her crimes. There's something dishonorable about it, and the few pieces of myself that I've managed to salvage from my inner silence would be lost if I crossed this line.

The anger that burns within me beats against my thoughts with relentless fists. I raise my hands to cradle my head as if by pressing my palms against my scalp I can somehow find peace.

Heat radiates from my forehead. I slide my fingers over the rest of my face and find that even my cheeks feel crisp with fever.

My vision blurs for a moment as I tug on the blood-soaked sleeve of my tunic until I can see my entire forearm. The jagged seam of blackened skin is stretched tight over an angry red-and-yellow swelling that leaks blood and white fluid where I've scratched at it. My fingers are so swollen, I can barely move them, and red streaks run beneath my skin, heading from the wound toward my shoulder.

No wonder this itched so badly. No wonder I have a fever. It's infected. It must have happened when I went into the filthy water of the river. Turning back to the shelves of supplies, I search for something that will help me.

Moments later, I've smeared antiseptic and burn cream across the infection, wrapped a loose, sloppy bandage over it, and swallowed what I hope is enough painkiller to take the edge off.

My head now aches as badly as my throat, and I long to lie down, but I can't. Not yet. I have to find a weapon and some supplies.

Leaving the medical room behind, I creep along the deck until I come to the room where I tried unsuccessfully to swallow some breakfast. This room is much bigger than the medical bay. Eight round tables with four chairs each are sprinkled around a rug of brilliant red. Lanterns are bolted to each table, though only two of them are lit. Across the room, a door on the opposite wall leads out to the other side of the deck. The one side of the room closest to me is a simple kitchen with long counters, two stoves, and a metal shelving unit half-full of food supplies.

I head for the food. My eyes ache as I read the labels on jars, crates, and canvas bags. Flour. Rice. Honey. Dried tomatoes. Salted pork. A crate of sugared orange peels. Fruit, both fresh and canned. And several barrels of water.

Dumping a nearly empty canvas bag of flour into a half-used bag of rice, I fill the empty bag with pork, orange peels, apples, and two jars of cherry preserves. I also upend all of the jars of dried tomatoes into my bag and then fill the jars with drinking water. It's difficult to hold the jars steady with my swollen right hand while I replace the lids, but I manage. Then, holding my bag of food and my water, I creep out of the dining area, listening carefully for any activity on the lower deck. Everything is quiet, but still I move with care. If I'm caught now, they'll tie me to a bed for sure.

I need a place to hide this, but I've been too sick to really explore the boat. My only options are to start opening doors on the lower deck and hope I don't surprise a tracker, or to find a place for my supplies among the lifeboats tied to the back of the deck.

The lifeboats, a collection of wooden vessels the approximate size of a wagon that are stored upside down and tied to pillars at the back of the boat, are my best bet. I start toward them, but have to stop and lean against the wall when my vision tunnels toward black. The familiar noises—the slap of the water against the boat, the splash of the paddle wheel, and the hum of the insects in the Wasteland—suddenly seem unbearably loud. The starlight too sharp. I close my eyes and hug the wall while I suck in deep breaths of the dank river air.

I can't lose consciousness here. I can't succumb to the fever. Not until the bag of supplies is hidden beneath the lifeboats. And not until I've found a weapon.

I open my eyes, but the wooden planking beneath me swirls and the walls look like they're melting. Quickly, I close my eyes again and struggle to get my bearings.

Maybe this isn't because of my fever. Maybe I took too much pain medicine. Or maybe that wasn't pain medicine after all. I'm no longer sure of anything except the fact that I have to put one foot in front of the other until I reach the lifeboats.

Leaning heavily against the wall, I slide my boots forward, convinced that if I lift a foot off the floor, I'll fall. I slowly work my way past two doors, and my hand brushes against the outline of a third. Before I can move past it, the door opens, and I tumble forward into the open space.

Arms steady me, and then the door behind me closes. I open my eyes, but the darkness inside this room is so thick, I can't see who holds me. I can barely make out the fact that I'm standing at the top of a set of stairs that lead down to a room where stacks of supply crates and piles of rope are barely illuminated by faint moonlight filtering in past a single grimy window.

My vision blurs again, and my knees sag. The arms holding me tighten.

"I've got you," says a familiar voice.

"Quinn." I breathe his name, and have to swallow hard against the tears that thicken the back of my throat. "You keep making me cry."

He's silent for a moment, and then he says in a voice that sounds like he's suddenly realized he's standing on an explosive and any move could be his last, "I'm . . . sorry?"

"First you start making me face my grief, and then you tell me you killed your dad to save mine, and then you sacrifice yourself just to give me a knife—I lost the knife. I *lost* it." The tears are pouring down my face now, and I sob against his shoulder, while he pats my back in quick, awkward movements.

"We'll get you another one," he says.

"And now I can't stop crying over everything. Over Logan. And being alone. And even *Ian*." I push away from him and nearly fall before he grabs me again. "I cried because I felt sorry for Ian, and this is all your fault."

He gently pulls me down to sit on the top step, and then settles beside me. "Is crying a bad thing?"

Trust Quinn to sound calm and curious no matter what. I

shove the bag of food into his lap and wipe my face with my left hand.

"Yes, it's a bad thing. Maybe. I don't know. I'm not a crier. I've never been a crier until you made me start *feeling* things again, and now I can't stop."

"So . . . it's like when you cut off the circulation to your leg for a while and then it feels tingly and raw, every sensation overwhelming and unbearable for a while as it wakes up?" he asks.

"Exactly." The stairs feel like they're wobbling beneath me, and I clutch the edge of the step to keep my balance.

"Then I guess you either choose to keep waking up inside and trust that eventually the feelings won't be so overwhelming, or you cut the circulation again and choose to go back to the way things were."

"You make it sound so easy."

His voice is quiet. "Healing is the hardest thing you'll ever do."

My arm throbs in vicious spikes, and I scratch at it. "You used a weapon on that tracker when you were trying to rescue me."

"I did." He pauses as if thinking through his words, and then says, "I couldn't think of any other way to get to you. I wasn't trying to kill her, though."

"I'm sorry you had to break your principles for me."

"They're my principles to break." His voice sounds warm. "Besides, the point of not carrying a weapon is to remind myself to think through my actions and make careful choices instead of the choices I've been trained to make. I'm not going to sacrifice someone I care about simply to be able to say I never picked up another weapon."

He rummages in the bag of food, pulls something out, and takes a bite. The crisp, sweet scent of an apple floats across the space between us and makes me feel like puking.

"I don't think I'm doing okay," I say as sweat beads along my upper lip and my pulse roars in my ears.

"Of course you're not doing okay, Rachel. You've endured trauma after trauma with very little time to deal with any of it. You can't go back to the person you were before all of this started. Too many scars inside. But that doesn't mean you won't be okay. That doesn't mean you won't be happy."

I consider opening my mouth to tell him I wasn't talking about my emotions, but my teeth are chattering now, and it's all I can do to clamp my jaw shut tight and ride it out.

Apparently taking my silence as doubt, he bumps his knee against mine and says, "Take me, for example. When your dad gave his life for mine, I was devastated. He was a good man, who'd done good things, and he had a daughter depending on him. I was a trained killer who'd managed to get myself and my sister cast out of our village. I promised myself I'd do something to be worthy of that sacrifice. That I'd do what Jared couldn't do because of me. I promised I'd protect you. I'll be honest with you—it wasn't an enjoyable task at first."

He takes another bite, and I hunch my shoulders, curling in on myself as my body throbs and aches. He wraps a warm hand around my shoulder.

"No, don't take it like that. I just meant that at first it was a duty. You were Jared's daughter, therefore whatever happened, I would do my best to make sure you were safe. But somewhere along the way, I started wanting to keep you safe. Not because of

Jared, but because you're my friend. More than a friend, actually. It's like I gained another sister. And now I'm part of something much bigger than paying a debt to your dad. I'm part of something that matters. And that makes me happy, Rachel. For the first time in . . . well, in longer than I can remember, I'm happy."

He waves the apple under my nose and says, "Want some?"

I lean over and vomit onto the stairs.

He sits frozen for a second, his hand still wrapped around my shoulder, and then says, "I'll take that as a no."

"Told you I'm not okay," I mumble. My voice sounds far away, and I can't seem to get warm.

"Oh." Gently, he wraps his arms around me and lifts me up. "So here I am, talking about healing and happiness, and you just meant you thought you might puke."

My head falls against his shoulder, and he leans his cheek against my forehead and then swears. "You're burning up. You need help. Where's the medical bay?"

"Need a knife." My lips feel clumsy as I try to form the words.

His voice is urgent. "Rachel, where is the medical bay? I haven't been outside this room since I boarded the ship. I don't know my way around. You have to tell me."

"Got food. Water. Need knife." I try to make him understand that we have to be ready to escape once we make port, have to have our supplies in hand, but my thoughts feel like half-formed wisps floating in and out of my head like ribbons of fog.

"I'll get you a weapon. I'll take care of the food. But you have to tell me where to take you to get you the help you need."

"Left," I say. Or I think I say it. I'm not exactly sure if I opened my mouth or not.

He pushes open the door and eases out onto the deck. My skin feels stretched too thin, there's a furnace in my brain, and the ache in my arm refuses to relent. I consider sinking into the comfort of sleep as Quinn moves slowly toward the next doorway, but a thudding sound behind us jerks me into awareness again.

Trackers. On the stairs. They'll see us. They'll see *Quinn*.

"Put me down and go." My words run together, and for a moment, he keeps moving. "Put me *down*. They'll help me."

The boots are coming closer. Quinn has seconds to drop me and sprint back to the storage room. Bending swiftly, he lays me on the cold, hard deck and whispers, "If you need me, yell my name. I'll be there."

Then he's gone, and the boots are shaking the deck, and my head fills with tiny white sparks of pain.

"She's here!" a mustached man yells over his shoulder as he crouches beside me, a torch in his hand. More boots slap the deck, and then Ian and Samuel are crouched down beside me, too.

My vision blurs, and I have to blink several times to bring Ian into focus as he leans over me.

"The watchman went to check on you, and couldn't find you. Trying to sabotage the boat?" he asks.

My tongue feels too thick to allow me to swallow, much less talk. I cough and reach for my bandaged arm to scratch at the swollen, itchy skin.

"She's sick." Samuel places his hand on my forehead. I want to tell him to stop touching me. To leave me alone. But the fire eating away at my brain has taken my words as well. "She's burning up. Unwrap her arm. *Gently*, Ian."

Rough fingers tug at the bandage, and someone gasps.

"Well, that's ugly," Ian says.

"That's infected. If we don't treat that, she's going to lose the arm," the blond man says.

"So let her lose the arm. She likes the idea of sacrificing herself." Ian's voice is flat.

"Those streaks of infection are in her blood, and it's moving up her arm and toward her heart," Samuel says. "If we don't stop it, she won't just lose her arm. She'll die."

I want to tell them I'm not going to die. Not here. Not before Ian, James Rowan, and the Commander pay for their crimes. I open my mouth to say so, but my ears are buzzing, and a strange heaviness is pushing me down, pulling me under a blanket of darkness that promises me relief from the pain.

I meet Ian's cold gaze for one long moment, and then my eyes flutter shut.

CHAPTER TWENTY-TWO

LOGAN

"What do you mean, the beacons have already been disabled?" The Commander leans across Lyle Hoden's breakfast table, gripping his fork like he means to stab me with it. "We were going to do that this morning. We had an agreement."

I meet his gaze evenly while beside me, Frankie drops the sausage he'd been about to eat and grabs his butter knife instead.

"No, we had a *plan*," I say. "A plan whose success depended on no one outside of our inner circle finding out what we were doing. Considering the number of trackers currently roaming the halls of this mansion, I decided it was prudent to—"

"You decided! What gives you the right to decide anything?" Fury fills the Commander's face.

His guards glare at me. Lyle, seated at the head of the table, flanked by Connor and Amarynda, glares at me. Smithson, Adam, Nola, and Drake all set down their forks and pick up their knives. Willow pushes away from the table, her hand on the bow resting against her chair. The Commander looks like he wants to skewer me where I sit.

"The only people who knew about the plan are sitting at this table," Amarynda says, her voice cool. "If you're suggesting that one of us would leak news of your intentions to a tracker—"

"Sleeping in my house! Eating my food!" Lyle pounds a fist on the table. "And you dare imply that I'm not trustworthy?"

"Or maybe we aren't the ones you don't trust." Amarynda looks at the guards and then sweeps her eyes over the Commander. "Maybe you expected treachery from your own ranks."

The Commander looks at me. "I knew better than to trust you. I should've cut off your head when I had the chance." A vein in his neck bulges, and I scramble to think of something noninflammatory to say.

"It was my idea."

Everyone at the table turns to stare at Connor. He raises a brow and calmly spreads a healthy serving of blackberry jam over his piece of toast before offering the jam to Jodi.

"The trackers have infiltrated your city, Grandfather. It seemed reasonable to expect them to be watching us closely during the daylight. You needed to be above reproach or risk being found in violation of your protection agreement. I asked Logan to assist me, and we accomplished the task. Your beacons are disabled." He lays his knife against his plate and takes a large bite of his toast.

I'm impressed with his ability to lie with absolute conviction. I'm going to have to keep an eye on him. And keep him on my side.

"Where is the proof that the beacons are disabled?" the Commander asks.

"I did the task myself," Connor says.

Another lie delivered with flawless confidence.

Connor sets his toast down and smiles at Amarynda. "Delicious jam, Aunt Mandy. I wish Mother's cook had your recipe."

"I want proof." The Commander's dark eyes are locked on me. "I want to see the inside of a disabled beacon with my own eyes."

I bet he does. The sooner he learns his way around the Rowansmark tech, the faster he can betray me.

"Are you calling my grandson a liar?" Lyle's voice rises. "Because if you are, you can forget about using any of my troops—"

"Keep your voice down," the Commander snaps. "Do you want to be overheard?" He turns toward Connor. "Why wasn't I included in this?"

Connor frowns. "We had to jump from rooftop to rooftop in the dark. Forgive me, but I wasn't certain that would be a safe activity for a man of your age. Rest assured, the task is completed, and we can move on to another city-state. I assume Brooksworth is next on the agenda?"

The Commander slowly sits back in his chair, his expression cold and calculating. "I will say this once, and only once: I am the leader of the forces of Baalboden and Carrington. I don't care what city you represent, whose grandson you are, or"—he glares at me—"what motives you claim to have, if anyone goes behind my back again, it will be considered treason and therefore punishable by whatever means I see fit."

"And I will say this once and only once." Connor's voice is crisp. "I am an emissary from Lankenshire on official city-state business. I am subject to the laws ratified by all nine city-states, and to the laws of Lankenshire. I am not subject to you. Lankenshire has a stake in the outcome of this operation, therefore I am committed to seeing it through. I will take whatever actions serve our joint cause best. In this case, choosing the youngest team members, members whose loyalties are not tied to the same city-state but instead to the same cause, was the most expedient and safest course of action. If you disagree, feel free to bring it up to the triumvirate when we return to Lankenshire."

Once again, we all stare at Connor as he calmly takes another bite of his toast.

I suddenly understand very clearly why Clarissa sent Connor. He may not have the wilderness survival skills necessary to trek through the Wasteland alone, and he may not walk into a room and instantly command the kind of attention his mother and sister do, but he understands how to wield his influence at exactly the right times.

Lyle reaches over and pounds Connor's shoulder. "Well said! It isn't easy managing a room full of old men and their egos." He looks at the Commander, whose expression betrays none of his thoughts, and says, "Speaking of old men and their egos, you'd best let me approach Brooksworth. Hank isn't in his right mind. Hasn't been for years. Won't have much to do with any of us, but I have it on good authority he'd shoot *you* on sight. The older he gets, the more he blames you for Christina."

The Commander drops his fork to his plate with a clatter and shoves his chair away from the table. "Fine. You approach Hank. I'll head to Chelmingford. We leave in an hour." He stalks out of the room.

Connor looks from the Commander's retreating back to Lyle. "What was that all about? Who's Christina?"

Lyle picks up his mug of juice. "That's his story to tell, and if you're wise, you won't ask him for it. I think I'll go ahead and send a messenger ahead of you to Chelmingford, too. Tara Lanning, their leader, is on decent terms with Jason, but given his current frame of mind, it might be best to assure her that he does, indeed, have allies. Now go pack up your things so you can spend a little time with me before you leave."

An hour later, we stand at Hodenswald's gate, our travel packs freshly provisioned by Amarynda. A groom brings our horses out to us, and I pat my brown mare on the nose before strapping my travel pack and bag of tech supplies to the back of the saddle. Chelmingford is a five-day journey northeast if we push the horses. I'm anxious to get started. The faster we reach Chelmingford, the faster I can turn south and catch up with Rachel.

Amarynda pushes Lyle's chair to the gate so he can see us off. Connor rushes forward as they come to a stop, and Amarynda wraps her arms around him and whispers something in his ear. He clings to her for a moment and then gives his grandfather a hug as well.

When Lyle lets him go, I step forward and shake the leader's hand.

"Thank you for your help," I say. "You'll have no more trouble from the beacons."

"Nor from Sharpe, apparently." Lyle raises a brow at me. "He was reported missing this morning not ten minutes after someone else reported an unsightly mess of guts and bone all over the street in front of my favorite tailor's house."

I hold his gaze. "I wouldn't know anything about that."

"Of course not." His smile is sly.

The Commander looms beside me, his face set in a scowl. "We've done what we promised, Lyle. Time for you to hold up your end of our bargain."

Lyle's smile spreads. "One-quarter of my troops and a diplomatic emissary to Brooksworth to show Hank how to disable his beacons and to beg for armed forces in exchange. Plus, I'll send an emissary ahead of you to Chelmingford to hasten your discussions there. My courier can travel faster alone than you can with your group."

"How will your Brooksworth emissary know how to fix the beacons?" the Commander demands, cutting his eyes toward me.

"Connor explained the process to me," Amarynda says. "I'll go to Brooksworth myself. If I'm successful, Hank's troops will convene at Lankenshire in one week, along with ours. If he refuses me, then our commanding officer will let you know."

"Fine." The Commander and Lyle shake hands, and then the Commander mounts his horse and rides out of the city, the rest of us on his heels. Willow is already outside the gate waiting, having checked the surrounding Wasteland for signs that the trackers on our trail caught up while we were inside Hodenswald.

"We're clear," she says. The Commander rides past her without acknowledging her words.

Our horses leave hoofprints across the dew-soaked meadow as we head northeast to Chelmingford. The Commander and

Peter take the lead. Gregory and Orion guard our backs. My people are staggered in between. I wait until there's a sufficient distance between us and the guards and then say to Connor, "You surprised me at breakfast this morning."

Frankie grins. "For a moment, you reminded me of your mother. I don't mind saying that woman makes me sit up and pay attention."

"Yes, I'm well aware that my mother and my sister command everyone's attention and respect."

There's a shadow of bitterness in Connor's voice that has me looking closely at him as our horses climb over a half-rotten log with wildflowers peeking out of its cracks.

"Clarissa and Cassidy can be intimidating, but that isn't necessarily something to aspire to," I say.

"Depends upon whom you ask." Connor's dark eyes scan the ground, and he carefully maneuvers his horse around a cluster of moss-covered stones that would surely have captured a hoofprint. "I don't have the ability to make an entire roomful of people sit up and take notice when I enter the way Mom, Aunt Mandy, and Cassidy do, but sometimes the most valuable observations can be made when you're the kind of person everyone overlooks. Sometimes when you stay in the background, it lends impact to the moments when you choose to take center stage."

I smile. "Agreed. I spent years as an outcast in Baalboden. Most people wanted nothing to do with me. Sometimes being invisible gives you the space to sharpen your mind and *learn* while everyone else is busy running in circles trying to get noticed."

"And look at you now," Frankie says. I flinch at the pride in his voice—it's as if he's willfully forgotten how many of us died while I was in charge. "The leader of Baalboden's survivors and a boy who has the respect and trust of the heads of two other city-states." He leans across me and points a thick finger at Connor. "Just goes to show it doesn't matter who you are or what you come from. It only matters what choices you make now."

That's true for Connor, but who I am and what I come from matter immensely. If I hadn't been born to Marcus and Julia McEntire, the Commander would've taken no notice of me, I'd have grown up in Rowansmark, and my brother wouldn't have been driven to destroy thousands of lives in retaliation for the ruin of his own.

I can make all the right choices now. I can protect the other city-states from Rowansmark's beacons. I can make alliances and rally an army. I can see that justice finds the Commander and Ian for their crimes. But nothing I do will put Baalboden back together again. Nothing I do will wash away the blood shed by my brother. Maybe that's not my responsibility, but the survivors I promised to protect became my friends—my family—and they died under my watch. I can't let that go.

I don't realize I've been ignoring the conversation going on around me until Frankie's hand squeezes my shoulder.

"You all right?" he asks.

"Just tired." I make myself smile at him, and then nod toward Orion, who has spurred his horse forward as if hoping to eavesdrop on our conversation. "Mind crowding him until he gets back to his place?"

"With pleasure." Frankie moves his horse toward Orion, his face set like stone.

"You lied to him." Connor's voice is low, but still I glance around to make sure no one overheard.

"What are you talking about?" I ask quietly.

"I observe people. Study their interactions." He shrugs. "It doesn't make me a very scintillating conversationalist, and it certainly draws the scorn of those who appreciate a more . . . physical approach to life, but it does have its advantages."

"I'm sure it does."

Connor squints as sunlight pierces a gap between the leaves above us. "I know that Frankie volunteers to cook each night so that he won't have to sit quietly and think about whatever is inside his head. I know that Smithson seems like he's refusing to talk, but the truth is that he doesn't know what to say. I also know that the Commander is going to try to kill you sooner rather than later. Willow and Adam are in love, though neither of them is comfortable saying those words. Jodi is driven to prove that she's fearless, even when she's terrified—"

"I get it." I hold my hand up to stop the flow of words. "You study people the way I study technology."

"Oh, you study people, too. But you're less concerned with their inner emotional landscape than with their usefulness to your agenda and with any possibility that they might sabotage your plans."

I stare at him and nearly get smacked in the face by an errant branch for my trouble. "That's harsh."

He raises a brow. "It wasn't meant to be. Your ability to assess motives, strengths, and weaknesses makes you a good leader. The fact that you also have the integrity to not use that ability to harm those who trust you makes you great. And like all great leaders, you know when to keep your secrets, but Frankie seems to be a close friend of yours. Which is why I'm trying to figure out why you lied to him."

"You may not have your mother's skill at making people uncomfortable when you walk into a room, but you get there eventually."

"Indeed. So now I'm curious—why hide your true feelings from a close friend?"

"It doesn't matter. You're observant. I get it. And I'm glad, because we're going to need . . ." I can't finish the sentence, even though I've just proven him right. I *do* assess people's strengths, looking for how they can be useful to my plans.

"You're going to need my observations when you deal with Chelmingford, yes. It's not a crime to use your people's strengths, especially when they're freely offered." He looks at Frankie as we crest the hill we've been climbing and see the vast darkness of the northern Wasteland, ribboned with glittering bodies of water, spread out before us. "But you talk plans and strategy. Contingencies and fallbacks. You don't talk about why you never sleep well, or why Willow bullies you into eating enough, or why when you're lost in thought, you look like you're on the brink of losing everything that matters."

"Connor—"

He holds up a hand. "I'm not asking you to tell me the truth. I'm simply saying that a truth that eats away at you shouldn't be shouldered alone. Frankie cares enough to ask. Why not let him in?"

I take a deep breath of the spicy, pine-scented air and find that I have nothing to say. I don't know how to let people in. I never learned. Besides Oliver, Jared, and Rachel, every encounter I had with the people in Baalboden was guarded. Adversarial. I knew better than to show weakness, fear, or doubt.

I guess some habits are hard to break.

I turn away from Connor and urge my horse to move a little faster while I sort through my heavy thoughts. How to approach Chelmingford. How to transform the stolen transmitters hidden within my pocket into a weapon the Commander will never see coming. How to defeat the three armies waiting for us at Rowansmark when they have the advantage of knowing the terrain and when they must have a supply of tech that my handful of transmitters can't equal.

But mostly, I think of Rachel. Of missing her. Of how I can't keep secrets from her, but I don't know how to stop keeping them from everybody else.

I have no idea how to change that, and so I focus on the problems I can control and tell myself that the secret doubts I'm holding on to are better left unsaid.

CHAPTER TWENTY-THREE

RACHEL

Someone is screaming—raw, anguished sounds that flay the air and hurt my eardrums. I try to swim up through the layers of hazy darkness that keep dragging me into unconsciousness, but I can't get my bearings. I'm drifting. Spinning. Weightless and heavy at the same time.

Pain slices into my right arm, sharp and bright, jerking me through the layers of darkness and thrusting me into the harsh reality of consciousness.

The person screaming is me.

"She's waking up. Hold her down." Samuel's voice is calm.

"Might be easier to just knock her out again," Ian says.

"With what?" Samuel asks as more pain blazes up my arm and seizes my chest. "Get her legs before she kicks out my teeth!"

Something heavy lands on my legs, and I pry my gritty eyelids open to see Ian sitting on me while another man holds my right arm steady enough for Samuel to dig into my wound with a thin silver blade.

Blood and pus gush out of the wound and drip down my fingers. My throat feels thick and raw. I'm lying on the second bed in the medical bay. I can't see if Heidi still occupies the bed closest to the door, and I have better things to worry about than who shares the room with me.

Samuel lowers his blade, and brilliant agony sears me. I scream, arching my back off the mattress and doing my best to send Ian onto the floor. I claw at Samuel with my left hand, trying desperately to reach him. He evades my grasp, and seconds later Ian snatches my arm and anchors it to the mattress with his own. Samuel raises his knife again, and I crack.

"Stop. Please. Stop," I say. I hate to beg Samuel for anything, but I can't bear more of that pain.

"It's infected, Rachel," he says. "I've done my best to remove the bad tissue and squeeze the infected fluid out, but I have to get it all, or you aren't going to survive this."

"Give her some pain medicine," says the man holding my arm in place. I stare at him with his pale eyes and ridiculously large blond mustache and decide of everyone in this room, he's my favorite.

"No." Ian's voice is cold. "She swore she could handle any pain I could give her. Let her prove it."

"And what good will that do?" Samuel asks quietly.

"I'll feel better about the way she broke her promise. The way she chose to take what wasn't hers in the first place, just like her father."

"If a young girl's screams make you feel better, then you need help," Samuel says.

Ian swears. "I don't need *help*, Samuel. Not now. And certainly not from you."

Samuel sets the blade on the table and dabs his hands with a white towel. I look away from the blood that dots its surface and try not to think about Oliver's blood staining my white tunic while I sat in the back of the wagon trying to understand that he was dead.

"Give her some medicine," Samuel says to the blond man. "Once it kicks in, I'll finish."

Ian laughs, a mocking, bitter sound that seems to bow the set of Samuel's shoulders. "I see. Take care of the little Baalboden girl whose father helped destroy mine."

"Her father didn't intend the harm that was done."

I blink at Samuel in surprise. I never thought I'd hear him defend my father, especially when it meant going against his own leader.

The blond man offers me a pinch of gray-white powder, and I obediently open my mouth. I don't know what he's giving me, and at this point, I don't care. My arm hurts more than I ever thought was possible. I'll do anything to make it stop. The powder coats my tongue with a fine grit that tastes sour and is hard to swallow without water. As if he understands my thoughts, the man brings a cup of lukewarm water to my lips and tips a little of the liquid into my mouth.

"Did *you* intend the harm that was done?" Ian asks Samuel, a challenge in his voice.

Samuel looks at the blond man. "Thank you. Can you give us a moment, please?"

The man leaves without a sound, and Samuel grabs another clean towel and begins mopping up my arm, careful to avoid touching the open seam of flesh. I wish he wouldn't be so gentle with me. I can't reconcile this treatment with the man who would let Ian poison innocent people and trap an entire group in a ring of dangerous white phosphorous fire.

Finished with my arm for the moment, Samuel sets the bloodstained towel on the floor and presses a cool palm against my forehead. Until that moment, I didn't realize that the fever that turned my thoughts sluggish and my body weak is nearly gone. He must have given me something for that when I lost consciousness. I wonder how long I've been lying here, and if Quinn was able to return to the supply room without being seen.

"How long have I been out?" My voice is nothing but a hoarse croak.

"We found you on the deck just before midnight last night. It's now midmorning," Samuel says. "You were feverish. Delirious—"

"Kept calling for someone named Oliver. Does Logan know?" Ian smirks at me, his blue eyes hard.

I don't have enough spit in my mouth for the tirade of abuse I'd like to aim at him. I settle for looking away like nothing he has to say matters to me in the least.

It's not very satisfying.

"You'd tried to treat your wound yourself. Do you remember?" Samuel asks as he holds a cup of water to my lips.

"This is stupid." Ian jumps off the bed and grabs my face, knocking aside the cup. "You don't deserve water. You don't deserve medicine."

"Ian." Samuel's voice is still calm, but there's pain inside it.

Ian digs his fingers into my cheeks. "You deserve to be staked to the deck and left to burn in the sun until your skin peels away from your bones and you beg for relief that isn't coming."

"Ian!" Samuel wraps his hand around Ian's wrist, and Ian jerks away from both of us, his eyes wild. "She isn't to blame for everything that upsets you."

This from the man who told me if I had only returned the device to Rowansmark in the first place, Ian wouldn't have been broken.

Of course, he also told me that he's afraid of what more sanctioned violence would do to Ian's spirit. I look into Ian's eyes, at the light of furious need that burns inside him, and shiver. Samuel's right. Ian is broken, and every time he lashes out, hoping the pain he causes others will somehow soak up his own, he loses himself a little more.

I'm relieved that I chose not to put the blood clot medicine in Heidi's wound while she slept. I don't want to end up like Ian, spilling my hurt over others like a poison that has no cure.

"Then who is to blame? Who?" Ian yells and smashes his fist into a jar of something green and goopy. Viscous liquid slowly drips off the shelf, and blood wells from a web of cuts across Ian's knuckles.

"Me," Samuel says. His voice is quiet and full of the kind of guilt that once drove me into my inner silence. "I'm to blame, Ian. Me, and your dad, and James Rowan. We failed you, and

I'm sorry." His voice breaks. "I'm sorry."

Ian vibrates like a plucked wire. "You're sorry. What good does that do me now? He was your friend, and you didn't help him. You didn't warn him. You just let them come for him and sentence him to death."

"I know." Samuel looks at the floor. "And then I made it worse by allowing you to be the one to carry out the sentence. I should've protested. I should've volunteered. Found a way to convince James that I was the better person for the job."

"I did my job." Ian's jaw clenches. "I'm a good tracker. I'm a loyal citizen. I did my job. I didn't need you to do it for me."

"Yes, you did. And I failed you."

Ian whirls away and starts pacing the tight quarters while a warm fuzziness slowly encroaches on my thoughts. Whatever the blond man gave me is taking effect.

"And then I thought that if I helped you clear your family's honor, if I did what I could to make it easier for you to carry out the pain atonement against those who took the controller, it would make up for my failure. It would heal you—"

"I don't need to be healed. I just need to finish this."

"And then what? What will you have left after you're done? A string of murders to your name, starting with your father's—"

"I did not murder my father!" Ian leaps across the room, crashes into Samuel, and wraps his hands around the older man's neck. They slam into the wall beside me, knocking the table awry and sending the thin silver blade tumbling to the floor.

Samuel does nothing to defend himself. He just leans against the wall with Ian's fingers digging into his neck, and closes his eyes as if he's willing to die.

For a moment, the only sound in the room is the harsh rasp of Ian's breath, and then he curses and drops his hands. His voice shakes as he says, "Marcus McEntire broke the law and did not survive his pain atonement. His death was just."

"Ian—"

"It was just. It restored his honor. And everything I've done since then has been just. I only have to finish it. Just finish it." He sounds impossibly tired.

"Let me finish it for you." Samuel straightens slowly, but Ian is already backing toward the door.

The fuzziness presses down on me, and my eyelids flutter as Ian says, "I don't need your help anymore, Samuel. You were my dad's friend. You aren't mine."

The door shuts behind him as my lids close and the darkness takes me once again.

CHAPTER TWENTY-FOUR

RACHEL

When I open my eyes, I'm alone in the medical bay with Heidi, who lies propped up on the other bed, slowly lacing a boot on her injured leg. She glances at me as I lift my right arm and examine the crisp white bandage that covers my wound. A yellowish-brown stain lines the bandage on my inner forearm, but it isn't discharge from my wound. It smells sharp and bitter.

"It's goldenseal," Heidi says when I sniff the bandage. "Disinfects the wound and kills off bacteria that cause infections. You won't be smelling pretty for a while."

I cut my eyes toward her leg. "Your leg wound doesn't smell so great either, you know. He must've used the same stuff on you."

"I reckon." She bends toward her boot and winces as she brushes against her leg. "We're coming into port. Be off the boat in thirty minutes, more or less." She glances at my hair. "Might want to clean yourself up a bit before you meet James Rowan."

I have no intention of meeting James Rowan, cleaned up or

otherwise, but I'd be a fool to pass up the opportunity to bathe. I have no idea when I'll get another chance at clean water and some soap.

I push myself into a sitting position. My fever is gone, but my throat still aches, though this time, I'm pretty sure it's raw from screaming. My thoughts still feel a little bit fuzzy from whatever pain medicine the blond man gave me, but the room doesn't spin as I stand up. The evidence of Ian's attack on Samuel has been cleaned up, but I can still hear the terrible pain in Samuel's voice, the rage in Ian's.

"Bathroom's on the other side of the deck. Use the middle hallway to cut across. Masterson has been assigned to watch you," Heidi says.

"Fine." I wiggle the fingers on my right hand. They're still swollen, but at least I can bend them somewhat now.

"You're supposed to swallow that before you do anything." Heidi gestures toward the table between our beds.

I turn and find a small cup half-full of a pale-yellow liquid. It smells atrocious.

"What is it?"

"More medicine to fight the infection." Heidi straightens her injured leg slowly.

Another thing I can't afford to refuse. I hold my breath, toss the nasty medicine down the back of my throat, and head for the door.

"Don't go far. Just to the bathroom and back." Her voice is thick with warning.

"Where am I going to go? Overboard?" I yank open the door and step outside.

I've slept nearly the entire day away. Dusk hangs in the air, a mantle of purple slowly smothering the western sky.

I glance around the deck, hoping to catch sight of Quinn even though I know he'd be a fool to be out of hiding while there's still daylight left. I don't see him, but the knowledge that he's on the boat warms me.

The air carries the soft, musty scent of wet bark mixed with the sharp tang of the bright-green algae that blooms in the water. Ahead of us, the river spills into a huge lake. At the far end of the lake is the dam with its system of locks that keeps the enormous amount of water in the river from flooding the city-state of Rowansmark.

Heidi was right. If we're already nearing the first gate, it won't be long before we make port. I need to hurry.

Voices murmur above me, and a tracker with thick arms and unsympathetic eyes stands near the hall that bisects the lower deck. He looks at me, gestures toward the hall, and then watches carefully while I obey his silent instructions. I'm guessing this is Masterson.

I hurry past Masterson and find the bathroom. It's a small, windowless box of a room. Closing and locking the door behind me, I stare at myself in the mirror bolted to the wall above a small, pump-operated sink. I barely recognize the wild-haired, hollow-faced girl looking back at me.

Gone is the pride, the complete confidence that I could take on the entire world with nothing but determination and the things I learned from my father. In its place are shadows of grief and guilt and a weary understanding that there are few easy answers, and even fewer easy roads to walk. The confidence

I have now has little to do with my ability to win a fight, and everything to do with the knowledge that my choices have consequences, and that if I'm not prepared to face the consequence, then I have to make a different choice.

I pump some water into the sink and grimace at the floating bits of silt and algae that flood out of the pipe. This water must be pumped straight from the river. Pressing my lips closed to avoid getting any in my mouth, I grab the bar of soap sitting on the side of the sink and use my left hand to scrub clean as much of my skin as I can reach without stripping out of my clothes.

Then I finger-comb my hair and tame it into a long braid like the one Willow wears. I don't have anything to tie off the end, so I rip off a bit of the bandage on my right arm and use that.

The girl staring back at me looks more presentable now, though the hollows in her cheeks can't be fixed so easily. Nor can the hollowness in her eyes. I decide I don't want it fixed. I don't want to go back to the girl who glibly thought she could make life bend to her will if only she pushed hard enough. I don't want to pretend that everything is black and white, that people are either all good or all bad, and that I'm the one best qualified to tell the difference.

I want to remember the things I've learned. Remember that killing Melkin taught me that life is precious, and that the taking of a life is an almost unspeakable burden, even when the person seems to deserve it. Remember that Sylph showed me that prowess in battle takes skill, but choosing to love others in the midst of your own pain takes true strength. Remember the sight of Thom, quietly becoming a hero—not because he wanted to, but because the right thing was in front of him, and he chose to do it.

I need to hold on to Quinn's advice to face the things that hurt me so that I can keep chipping away at the silence within until it finally disappears. I refuse to lose myself again. I'm not going to dishonor those who love me by running away from the things that haunt me. I'm not going to dishonor *myself*.

The lessons I've learned have left permanent scars on my spirit, but the scars are proof that I'm not broken. I'm healing. And I'm not done with the hard things. Ian has to be stopped. Rowansmark's tech has to be destroyed. The Commander must die.

I'll do my part. When the right thing is in front of me, I'll choose to do it. And I won't lose myself, because I finally understand the difference between seeking revenge and seeking justice.

I push away from the mirror just as someone raps a fist against the door.

"Rachel?" Ian asks. "You aren't hatching any little plots in there, are you?"

"Plots like maybe slitting the throats of some children and poisoning a bunch of innocent people, then having the gall to call it just?"

His fist slams against the door, shaking it against its frame. "Masterson is a friend of mine. And Samuel is on the upper deck, supervising the ship's passage through the gates." His voice is low. "He won't be able to rush to your rescue before I do some damage."

"Haven't you done enough?" I ask.

"Not even close." He sounds cold. Empty. Like the emotion that propelled him to attack Samuel has been snuffed out.

He sounds like I did after I allowed the silence to fill me, completely cutting me off from my feelings. From myself. I thought I needed that protection to survive what was breaking me.

Maybe he does, too. But if he can't feel hesitation or guilt about hurting me, then I'm in trouble. I can't soften him and turn his fury aside if I can't reach the part of him that makes him human.

I'm surprised to realize that I want to find that part of him again. I saw it on our journey to Lankenshire when he stood up for Logan. When he flirted with the girls in camp. When he desperately wanted the device so that he could be finished with his task. Maybe if I'd found a way to give it to him in the first place, he would've stopped killing people.

Or maybe I'm trying to find excuses for someone who chose to become a monster.

Either way, if Samuel isn't around to intervene, Ian is going to keep his promise to kill me for the way he thinks I've betrayed him.

I have promises of my own to keep, as well.

My heart kicks against my chest as I quickly scan the room, looking for a weapon. Ian is coming through that door. There has to be *something* in this tiny space that I can use to defend myself.

The mirror is bolted down. So is the water pump, the little sink, and the chamber pot. That leaves the pile of clean cloths and a covered basket for used rags. Nothing useful. Nothing that can save my life.

The door shakes again as Ian pounds on it. My hands tremble as I roll into a defensive crouch. No weapon means fighting hand to hand. Which means I'll be using my one good arm.

Which means I'm going to lose.

I can barely hear Ian's fists against the door over the sound of my heartbeat thundering in my ears. I'm not ready to die. I'm not *going* to die. Not in a bathroom on some godforsaken Rowansmark boat miles from anyone I love.

There's a weapon in here. There has to be. I just have to find it. I look wildly around the room once more as Ian stops beating at the wood with his fist. The silence that follows raises the hair on the back of my neck. I don't know where he went, but I know he wouldn't give up that easily. Not with Samuel out of earshot.

I need a weapon. *Now.*

Mirror. Water pump. Chamber pot. Rags. There has to be *something* I can use. Mirror. Water pump. Chamber pot. Rags.

Mirror. Rags.

I snatch a clean rag, wrap it around my hand, and smash my fist into the mirror just as Ian's boot slams into the door and splinters it right down the center. Glass falls out of the mirror's frame in chunks and slivers. I crouch, wrap a piece the size of my palm in the rag I'm holding, and stuff it into my pants pocket. Even muffled by the soft cloth, the sharp edges of the piece bite into my leg.

Ian kicks the door again, and the wood shrieks in protest. I grab another rag, a piece of glass that looks like a crooked knife blade, and wedge myself into the small corner between the door frame and the wall.

Kick.

Widen my stance and crouch.

Kick.

Raise the glass and pray my left hand has enough strength to do the job.

Kick.

Breathe in through my nose and focus.

Kick.

The door explodes inward, sending shards of wood flying. Ian lunges through the doorway, and I attack. Slamming the heel of my boot against the side of his knee, I let the momentum of my strike carry me forward and slash at his back with the glass. His tunic rips and blood flows, but I haven't cut deep enough to do any real harm.

He pivots toward me, his fists flying toward my face. I drop to the floor and try to sweep his legs out from under him, but the room is small, and I can't get the leverage I need.

He leaps on top of me, pinning my legs beneath his weight. I try to scissor-kick my way to freedom, but he blocks me. I buck beneath him, and punch his ear with my right hand. He grabs my wound and wrestles my arm to the floor. When I gasp in pain, he swiftly pushes his forearm under my chin and leans on it. I yank at my trapped right arm, twist my head from side to side, and desperately try to get some air as he crushes my windpipe.

"You forget, I let you train me," he says in that cold, empty voice. "I know your moves. You've got no surprises left."

We'll see about that.

I flail with my right arm again, and he digs his fingers into my bandage.

Good. Let him be so preoccupied with the arm I've chosen to fight with that he forgets about my left. Let him see my lips turn white as the buzzing in my head screams for me to take a breath. Let him focus on beating me until the very last second.

Sparks flicker at the edge of my vision as Ian smiles, a desperate, horrible smile, and says, "You should've kept your promise."

I gather the last bit of oxygen in my lungs, tighten my abdomen, and whip my left arm up with as much power as I can.

The glass shard slams into the side of his face. He screams and rolls off me as blood pours from a deep gash running from his temple to his jaw.

I take a breath of air, meet his eyes as he presses his hands to his face, and say, "Oh, I'm keeping my promise, Ian. You can bet your life on it."

He lunges toward me, but someone grabs me from behind, knocks the glass out of my hand, and hauls me out of the bathroom before Ian can reach me.

"She has to be alive when we get there, Ian," a man says. I crane my neck to see dark skin and piercing green eyes. One of the trackers from the upper deck. This one has enough muscles that I'm confident he could rip me apart without even breaking a sweat.

"Get her out of my sight." Ian's voice is cold again, but his hands shake as he grabs clean rags and tries to stop his bleeding. "I don't want to see her until I get to deliver her pain atonement sentence."

Without another word, the man drags me down the hall and up the stairs. From the upper deck, I can see that we're in the first gate. The stone tunnel on either side of us is just wide enough to accommodate the boat. The water in the tunnel is slowly lowering, moving the boat level with the next gate. Ahead of us lie four more gates and then the warm red-brown brick of Rowansmark's wall. My stomach clenches. Being trapped on the upper deck, surrounded by trackers, while we enter Rowansmark's port isn't part of my escape plan.

In fact, it lights a blazing fire beneath my escape plan and turns it to ash. I'd hoped to play the sick, weakened Baalboden girl, to obediently walk off the boat without giving anyone any cause to tie me up or aim a sword at me, and then I'd planned to pick the right moment to make a break for it and disappear into the crowds that flock to the docks. Instead, I've got the attention of every tracker on the ship, and I've just proven that even with my injury, I can fight off one of their best.

Samuel is standing with his back to the deck, watching the transfer from the first gate into the second. He turns when the tracker holding on to me says, "Caught the prisoner attacking Ian."

"He attacked *me*." I glare at the tracker and try to jerk my arm free, but he simply squeezes his fingers until pain shoots down my arm.

"Then why is he the one with the bloody gash in his face?"

"Because he kicked in the bathroom door and attacked me." I enunciate my words carefully, as if trying to get a difficult concept across, and the tracker's expression turns mean.

"How did you cut Ian's face?" Samuel asks.

"With broken glass."

Samuel raises a brow. "There just happened to be broken glass in the bathroom?"

I jerk against the tracker's hold, but can't get free. "Look, this is stupid. Ian kicked in the bathroom door. He said you were busy up here and wouldn't be able to come to my rescue. He was going to *kill* me. I broke the mirror and defended myself."

It's the wrong thing to say. I know it the moment the words leave my mouth, and Samuel's expression goes from curious to cold and calculating in a heartbeat.

"You defended yourself against a Rowansmark tracker," he says, stepping closer to me and examining me as if searching for wounds of my own. "And came out without a scratch."

"Not exactly." I try to make my voice tremble, but it's clear the damage has been done. "He choked me and hurt the burn on my arm. He was on top of me. I just grabbed some glass—"

"From the mirror you had the presence of mind to shatter in a moment of panic right before Ian finished breaking down the door?" Samuel grabs my hands and turns them palm up. "No cuts from the glass you grabbed."

"She had it wrapped in a rag," the tracker holding on to me says.

"That kind of presence of mind in the middle of an attack shows training." Samuel looks at me, and we share a moment of silence. I don't even bother trying to look like a damsel in distress. It won't get me anywhere. Instead, I lift my chin and meet his gaze like the equals we are. His nostrils flare. "It appears I've badly underestimated you. Search her for weapons."

The tracker lets go of my arm and pats me down briskly. It doesn't take him long to find the palm-sized shard of mirror hidden in my pocket.

"Do you have an explanation for this?" Samuel asks.

"Other than the fact that I've been kidnapped by people who want to kill me? No."

Samuel holds himself very still. "You don't want me as an enemy, Rachel."

I look at him and see Baalboden burning. Donny's throat slashed ear to ear. Sylph bleeding out in the back of a wagon. Holding Samuel's gaze with mine, I say, "We were enemies from the moment you turned your back on innocent lives and let Ian murder whomever he pleased."

The tracker who searched me grabs my neck and shoves me to my knees. "Carson, bring me a rope," he calls.

In the time it takes the boat to transition from the second gate to the third, the two trackers secure my hands behind my back and then hobble my ankles while Samuel watches without expression.

When they've finished tying me up, Samuel turns away as if I'm of no more consequence than a crate of supplies. "Assign two more trackers to her. I want her surrounded at all times. We'll deliver her to James Rowan within the hour."

My half-formed plan to meekly follow my captors into Rowansmark, giving them no reason to tie me up or get suspicious until I saw an opportunity to break away and run into the city, is in shambles. I have no exit strategy, no weapon, and no ally.

I do, however, have my instincts, my training, and an advantage Rowansmark will never see coming: I have Quinn.

CHAPTER TWENTY-FIVE

LOGAN

We push the horses hard and make excellent progress on our first day's journey toward Chelmingford. The trail winds along banks of buckeye trees, climbs steep hills where maples cling to outcroppings that look like huge slabs of stone stacked haphazardly on top of one another, and plunges into valleys full of silent reminders of the civilization that walked this land before us—tall metal posts draped in ivy, brick buildings with flowering trees growing up through the floorboards, and broken chunks of smooth whitish stone that look like they were once a bridge that spanned the roads and buildings beneath them.

When the Commander calls a halt in a clearing beside a shallow stream, we quickly unsaddle the horses, tethering them close enough to the water to drink when they want to, and set up camp. We've fallen into a rhythm, uneasy though it may be. The Commander and his men establish the perimeter and choose the guard positions. Frankie, Nola, and Connor forage for food to supplement our dwindling supplies of jerky. Willow, Adam, and

Jodi tree-leap a thousand yards southwest, looking for signs that we've been followed. Drake and Smithson lay out the bedrolls, and I use my remaining daylight to work on tech. If anyone asks, I'm building something to amplify the device's signal—just like I said I would—but really, I'm wiring the stolen transmitters together so that I can create a weapon capable of protecting my people and destroying the Commander.

When Drake and Smithson finish with the bedrolls, they sit beside me. Drake breathes heavily and massages his leg, though he's quick to smile when I catch his eye. Smithson, on the other hand, sits locked in the same brooding silence that has followed him since Lankenshire. Connor thinks Smithson's silence means he doesn't know what to say. Maybe he doesn't. Or maybe he's silent because grieving for Sylph has become an all-consuming task. I saw what happened to Rachel when she locked herself inside her head with the ghosts of those she'd lost. I can't stand to see the same thing happen to Smithson. Pressure builds at the back of my throat as I try to figure out how to reach him.

"Smithson, I can tell that things are hard for you," I say, and then curse myself for stating something so obvious and stupid. "I mean . . . you're so . . . it's just that . . ." I drag in a deep breath and make myself meet his eyes. "I'm sorry. About Sylph. About not catching Ian in time. I wish—"

"I wish, too, but it doesn't do me any good." Smithson's voice is rough, and he looks at the ground.

"I'm sorry." My words are helpless to convey the depth of regret and guilt that churns through me.

"I know." He gets up and stalks toward the stream, where he leans against his horse. Nola approaches him, wraps a hand around his arm, and stands quietly beside him.

"She has a way with people," Drake says. "If anyone can help him, my Nola can."

I nod, but I don't know what to say. I've never known what to say. Words are so much harder to navigate than the clear-cut scientific principles I'm so at home with. Technology doesn't care if you say one thing even though you meant another. It doesn't search for hidden meanings, or dissect your body language looking for clues. It just obeys the rules that govern it. Simple. Uncomplicated. Easy.

I pull out one of the stolen transmitters and fiddle with the wires, grateful to have something I can actually fix. The last of the daylight is waning quickly. If I want to make any progress on the weapon I'm creating to kill the Commander, I have to work fast.

Frankie sits down across from me, unceremoniously dumping an armful of blackberries and clumps of edible roots on Drake's lap before picking up one of the transmitters and turning it over in his hands to examine the wires that dangle uselessly from its sides.

"You all right?" he asks me.

It's on the tip of my tongue to lie and say yes, to brush him off and keep my doubts and fears secret, but Connor was right. The things that keep me up at night are too heavy to carry by myself. It's time to learn how to let others in.

"No, I'm not." I scrub my hand over my face and try to find the right words. "I get sick every time I think about Rachel, alone with Ian, taking the brunt of his vengeance while I'm going in the opposite direction, hoping I can somehow scrounge up enough troops to give us a fighting chance to beat Rowans-mark. I'm afraid to sleep at night because the second I drop my guard, the Commander could betray us. I'm worried the tech I'm building isn't going to be strong enough to do the job." I look away from him. "And every time I close my eyes, I see the faces of those who chose me as their leader and then died because my brother wanted to hurt me."

"Logan—" Drake pushes the food onto his bedroll and claps a hand on my shoulder the way Jared used to when he could see I needed encouragement.

"I keep trying. Thinking. Planning." I make myself meet his gaze, and then turn to Frankie as well. "I want to believe that if I just try harder, think smarter, and plan better, I can fix all of this, but I can't. Even if we succeed in bringing Rowansmark down and in making Ian pay for his crimes, nothing will wash those crimes away. I don't know how to live with the fact that I didn't catch him in time. That I didn't save my people."

Drake's grip tightens. "You aren't responsible for Ian—"

"No, but I *am* responsible for the safety of our people." I glare at him, though he isn't the cause of my anger. "I took that responsibility when I agreed to lead us across the Wasteland, and I failed. More than that, I brought danger right to our door."

"The point is that you tried to protect us." Drake's voice is firm.

My fingers clench around the tech I hold until the blood drains from my knuckles. "Is knowing that I tried enough for Smithson?" I look at Frankie. "For you?"

"There it is," Frankie says. "I was wondering when we were going to get around to this."

Drake removes his hand from my shoulder and leans toward me.

"I got this one." Frankie carefully sets the transmitter down, raises his fist, and pokes his finger into my chest. Hard.

"Now, you listen here. That'll be about enough foolishness out of you."

I blink and sit up straighter, but he isn't finished.

"You don't fool me one bit. Sitting here thinking that all of our misery is yours alone to carry and that you've got to come up with all the answers. Thinking that we regret choosing you as our leader, and that if we'd known you were Logan McEntire from Rowansmark with a lunatic for a brother we'd have made a different choice."

His words strike deep, bruising an already painful wound. I open my mouth to answer, but he isn't finished.

Quietly he says, "Who you're related to and where you were born have nothing to do with this. We followed you because you took action against a tyrant when none of us found the courage to do it ourselves. Because you kept your head in a crisis and rescued us. Because you had a plan. You always have a plan. And because you're the kind of leader who feels responsible when someone on your watch dies, even though you weren't the cause."

His finger digs into me. "You *weren't* the cause. You hear me? We make our own choices. We're responsible for those choices and nothing more. And speaking of choices, you aren't the only one in this fight. You don't have to figure out how to watch the Commander, take down Rowansmark, and rescue Rachel by yourself. Why on earth do you think the six of us joined you and Willow in the Wasteland? You think we just wanted a tour of the northern city-states? We're here because we're in this together."

He drops his hand, and waits. When I don't respond, he says, "Are you just going to sit there looking like you got all the sense knocked out of you, or are you going to say something?"

I swallow and pick up the transmitter he dropped. "I don't know what to say."

"Sure you do. You just overthink everything all the time." There's a smile in Drake's voice.

Frankie smacks his hand against my knee. "It's actually pretty simple. The Commander and James Rowan got into a pissing match, Ian lost his mind, and the rest of us got caught in the middle. And now we're going to fix it or die trying."

Warmth fills me, loosening the ever-present knot of tension at the base of my neck. I might have a series of nearly impossible tasks in front of me, and I might have ruins lying behind me, but I'm not alone. "What would I do without the two of you?"

Frankie snorts. "Flounder around with nothing but half-baked nonsense in your head." He smacks my shoulder affectionately, and I shake my head even as I smile.

"Frankie and I can help you keep an eye on the Commander. We'll split up our guard shift so that one of us is always awake," Drake says. "As for your fears about Rachel . . . I can't tell you not to worry. If it was Nola, I'd be sick over it." His voice is quiet.

"That's hardly a pep talk." Frankie glares at him.

"It's reality." Drake's voice is calm and measured. "Rachel's in tremendous danger, but then again, so is Ian. Rachel knows how to fight, and she's got plenty of reasons to want Ian dead. We have to believe that Ian really does need her alive to compel you to bring the device to Rowansmark, and failing that, we have to bet on our girl to know how to defend herself and take him down."

"She's strong, even though she's badly injured," Frankie says.

"Now who's screwing up the pep talk?" Drake smacks Frankie's back.

"It's okay." It isn't, but I don't want to talk about Rachel. I don't want to imagine all the ways Ian could be torturing her. I don't want to think of her facing him down alone.

Drake gives me a gentle smile. "We'll do everything we can to get to Rowansmark in time to rescue her."

"And then what?" I ask.

"Then we show Ian what happens when you mess with the people of Baalboden." Frankie's voice is grim.

I nod like I agree with him, but that wasn't what I meant. What happens when this is over? When we defeat Rowansmark, destroy the tech, and punish Ian and the Commander for their crimes?

When all is quiet, and there are no enemies left to face, when it's just Rachel and me, will we be able to pick up the pieces of our lives and make them fit together?

I'm still wrestling with that question as the rest of our group returns, eats dinner, and settles in for the night. Still wrestling as Drake leaves his bedroll to join Gregory for a shift guarding the horses, while Nola, Willow, and Jodi take advantage of the darkness to bathe in the stream without worrying about one of the Commander's men leering at them.

Still wrestling when the first scream pierces the air.

CHAPTER TWENTY-SIX

LOGAN

I'm out of my bedroll, my sword in my hand, and running toward the stream before the echo of the scream dies. Behind me, Frankie, Smithson, and Adam stumble to their feet, cursing and grabbing for their weapons. Connor isn't far behind. I race past the Commander's tent as he lunges out of the flap.

"The stream!" I call as I race forward. Another scream splits the air, followed by a litany of vitriolic cursing that can only be one person.

"Willow!" I skid down the slippery bank and launch myself into the water. The horses tethered beside the stream throw their heads into the air and stomp their feet as I scan its dark, glittering surface.

I can't find Nola, Willow, or Jodi.

Fear pours through me. Where are they? I splash farther into the stream, and hoofbeats thunder behind me.

"Logan, down!" the Commander yells behind me.

I throw myself to the side as a horse gallops through the

water, narrowly missing my body. A glimpse of the rider makes my pulse pound. Bearded face, clothing patched together, and a belt full of weapons.

Highwaymen.

I twist away from the horse as its rider doubles back, aiming for me again. Onshore, I hear the clash of steel against steel and more hoofbeats as highwaymen pour out of the trees and charge toward us. Highwaymen on horseback streak through camp, chasing down those of us who were standing guard around the horses, while other highwaymen slash through the tethers and steal our mounts.

"Protect the horses!" The Commander's voice cuts through the melee, but I turn away. Let them fight for the horses. I'm going to find the girls.

After I take care of the highwayman currently yanking his horse around to face me again.

He spurs the animal forward, and I dodge to the left. Planting a boot in my chest, he sends me sprawling into the water. My sword spins out of my grasp, and I don't have time to find it. The horse is lunging for me again while its rider raises his voice in a sharp, high-pitched war cry.

A chill goes down my spine as the cry is answered all along the banks of the stream—from both sides—as well as from inside the Wasteland. This isn't the small, half-competent band of thugs we encountered on our way to Lankenshire. This is a huge, well-organized group of fighters. They've cut us off from one another, and if we don't figure out a strategy fast, they're going to kill us one by one.

The highwayman attacking me spurs his horse forward again.

I dig my boots into the slippery soil beneath me, pivot into the side of the horse, and grab the man's weapon belt.

He twists in the saddle, attempting to pry my fingers off the belt before I can drag him off the horse, but I'm not letting go. I need both the weapons and the horse.

I need to stay alive long enough to rescue my people.

He grabs a dagger and slashes toward my hands. I let the leather belt slide through my fingers and snatch his leg instead. He leans away from me, instinctively anticipating an attempt to pull him off the horse. I knock the stirrup away from his boot, hook my hands beneath his foot, and heave with all my might.

He goes over the other side, but doesn't let go of the reins. The horse crashes down on top of him. I snatch the horse's bridle, pull it to its feet, and scramble into the saddle. The man lies unmoving beneath the water.

Quickly, I take stock of the situation. The Commander, Frankie, Orion, and Smithson are fighting back-to-back against a pair of mounted attackers. Adam and Connor are at the edge of the stream, their swords drawn while more horsemen circle them. I can't see Drake, Gregory, Peter, or the girls.

I need weapons. I slide off the horse, reach beneath the water, and tug the belt of weaponry off the dead highwayman. Something bumps my foot, hard. I fumble for it in the dark and finally wrap my hands around the object. Pulling it free, I hold it up and time seems to slow down as I stare at Willow's bow.

A tremor runs through me. Willow wouldn't give up her weapon unless . . .

I refuse to finish the thought. She's alive and fighting

somewhere. The bow was probably on the bank of the stream while she bathed, and it got kicked into the water by a horse. That's a logical explanation. That's the *only* explanation.

It has to be.

Hauling myself up into the saddle, I sling the bow over my back and grab a machete with a wicked-looking blade from the dead highwayman's belt. Then I yell a war cry of my own as I spur my horse toward the shore.

The horsemen circling Connor and Adam wheel to face me. Adam lunges forward and drives his sword into the leg of the closest rider while I gallop straight for the other three.

Another cry echoes across the water, but this one is a high-pitched whistle like a farmer might use to call his dog. Instantly, the riders wheel about and spur their mounts northeast. All of our horses are gone. We're left with the horse I stole from my attacker and the horse beneath the highwayman Adam stabbed. The man jerks his reins, but Adam slaps the flat of his blade against the rider's hands. Connor jumps forward, his weapon slicing into the rider, and then I reach them.

I grab the man's heavy leather coat and throw him toward Adam. The Commander grabs the riderless horse's reins and glares down at the man lying on the ground. "Kill him."

"No!" I leap from my horse and shove the reins into Connor's hands. "We need answers first. They have our horses. The girls are missing. And who knows what else they took from camp?" I meet the Commander's gaze and see the moment he realizes that his tent was left unguarded while he dealt with the attack. The device could be gone. Anger floods me at the thought that everything I've worked for, everything I've sacrificed to find a way to rescue Rachel and take down Rowansmark, could be ruined by a band of thugs.

The man coughs out a pained laugh and says in a rough voice, "Why would I tell you anything? You're going to kill me either way."

The Commander crouches, grabs the man's face, and then says, "All he needs to be able to give us answers are his tongue, his lungs, his heart, and his brain." He looks up at Adam. "Carve the rest of it out of him, one piece at a time. Start with the eyes."

The man blinks, his gaze darting wildly between the Commander and Adam. I lean down, and the man's gaze lands on me.

"Do you know who this is?" I nod toward the Commander.

The man tries to shake his head, but he can't get free of the Commander's grip. "Just a small group of travelers with a few items of value."

"Where are the girls?" Adam asks, his voice shaking with rage. The point of his sword hovers inches above the man's left eye.

When the man doesn't reply, I say, "How much do you know about the city-states?"

"I don't—wait. Wait!" The man digs his heels into the ground and tries to push himself away as Adam's sword drops lower. "I know a little about the city-states. Some of them."

"What do you know of Baalboden?" I ask.

The man swallows. "It's . . . we don't go there."

"And why not?" the Commander asks, his voice a lethal slice of fury.

The man's eyes dart toward the Commander and then focus again on Adam's sword. "Because the leader won't give you a trial or time in the dungeon like some of the other leaders. He'll . . ." The man stares as the moonlight glides over the Commander's face, lingering on his scar. "You're Commander Chase."

"I am. And I'm very interested to hear what you think I do to those who anger me."

The man's voice is faint. "You make an example out of them. Carve them up and burn the pieces."

"And that's how I treat those who haven't wronged me personally," the Commander says. "Imagine what I do to those who kill my men and steal from me. Adam, the left eye. And then an ear, I think. After that, I'll ask my first question."

"No, wait! I'll talk. Please." The man's voice shakes. "Please, I'll tell you what you want to know. The girls—"

"I don't care about the girls. I want—"

"Yes, we do." I glare at the Commander. "We care about the girls. And the horses. And anything else your friends stole from us."

The man's words rush from him as if he hopes by talking fast enough, he can avoid the inevitable. "We took them to our camp. The girls, the horses . . ."

"Orion, check my tent. See if my belongings are there," the Commander snaps.

See if the device is still there, he means. If it isn't, he'll lead the charge to track down the highwaymen, and we'll have to pray the thieves don't decide to experiment with the tech. If they realize what they've got, there's no way we'll ever get close enough to their camp to rescue the girls.

No way we'll be able to ransom Rachel from Rowansmark either.

"It's gone!" Orion calls. No one needs to ask him what he means.

My heart sinks. Frantically, I start running scenarios.

"How far away is this camp?" the Commander snarls at the highwayman.

"A day's journey by horseback. Northeast. At the old city just south of the big mountain. You can't miss it. Please, let me go. I won't tell them you're coming. I won't even go in that direction. They'll never know—"

"No, they won't." The Commander stands, wraps his hands around Adam's, and drives the sword through the man's eye and into the ground beneath his head.

The second he stops twitching, I grab the sword from Adam, yank it free, and wipe it clean on the bank. "Adam, my sword fell to the bottom of the stream near the body of a highwayman I killed. The current isn't strong enough to have taken it. I need to use your weapon and ask you to retrieve mine at first light." Shoving the sword into my sheath, I meet his gaze.

"I'm going with you," he says.

"There are only two horses left. We can't all go. I need you to help Frankie. . . ." I look around, realizing I haven't heard anything from Frankie since the start of the fight.

"Frankie? Frankie!" I stalk toward the camp, my hands cold and shaking, as I see him hunched over a prone figure. It takes three steps for my brain to acknowledge that the person he's crouched beside is crumpled in an awkward angle no living person could achieve. Another five steps before I'm ready to acknowledge that the person I'm looking at is Drake.

Drake, who gathered a group of revolutionaries long before I even dreamed of standing up to the Commander. Who sent his daughter to save my life while I was locked in Baalboden's dungeon. Who stood by me and offered me quiet, consistent support and loyalty no matter what was going on around us.

Drake, who was my friend.

"Oh no." I sink to my knees beside Drake's trampled body. My throat closes and my eyes sting as I reach my hands out toward him as if I can somehow fix this.

Beside me, Frankie sobs once, and then curls over his knees and pounds the dirt with his fist.

"Who is it?" Adam calls from beside the horses, his voice shaky.

"Drake." I have to force his name past my lips. I feel like I've been punched in the stomach, my lungs refusing air even while I struggle to find words that won't be enough. That are never enough. An hour ago, Drake was sitting next to me, encouraging me, treating me almost like a son. Laughing with his longtime friend, Frankie.

Now he's one more in a list of people who've been ripped from us too soon.

"I'm sorry," I say, and swallow hard against the lump in my throat. "We'll have to bury him when I get back—"

"Go get Nola." Frankie raises his eyes to mine. "Get Nola and Willow and Jodi."

"Peter and Gregory are dead too," Orion says as he walks the perimeter of our camp. The Commander swears viciously.

"Here," Frankie whispers. He shoves something at me, and I wrap my hand around the slim outline of the Rowansmark device. "The highwaymen didn't get into the tent. I did. Figured it would be easier to keep the Commander in line if we had all the cards on our side. Now I want you to use it. You hear me? You do whatever you have to do to rescue the girls."

The device seems to weigh a hundred pounds as I move toward my bedroll, snatch my cloak, and shove the tech into an inner pocket. *You do whatever you have to do.*

He means that I should use the *tanniyn.*

I think of Jodi, tiny and trying so hard to be fearless. Of Willow, unflinchingly doing the right thing despite how she was raised. And Nola, gently reaching past Smithson's angry silence when no one else could. And I think of the stories about what highwaymen do to the girls they capture.

For the first time since Baalboden burned, I find I have no qualms about using the *tanniyn* as a weapon. I grab two of my transmitters and shove those into my pocket as well. And then, I return to the Commander and mount the horse waiting for me.

"Logan, it's Willow. I can't just stay behind. I have to do something." Adam stands beside my horse, his body vibrating with the need to act.

"Then help Frankie bury Drake and the others and then get the rest of the group to Chelmingford. If you stay on this trail and push yourselves, you should arrive in six or seven days. Don't sleep unless you have to. The trackers could be right behind us, and you no longer have the advantage of horses to increase your speed."

"That's not what I meant when I said I wanted to do something!"

I lean down. "I understand perfectly. Do you think I want to be traveling to the northern city-states looking for troops while

Rachel is in Rowansmark with Ian and a bunch of trackers? Sometimes we have to make hard choices, Adam. This is yours." I clasp his shoulder the way Drake clasped mine. "Willow's a survivor. The second they give her an inch, she'll make them wish they'd never been born."

He meets my eyes. "Bring her back."

"I will. I'll bring all of them back. And I won't leave a single highwayman alive to hunt us down again."

CHAPTER TWENTY-SEVEN

RACHEL

A crew of dockworkers greet us as the boat noses its way into a berth beside a long wooden ramp with thin handrails. The moment the paddle wheel stops churning, Samuel orders the hatch to be lowered onto the dock and gestures for the trackers assigned to me to escort me onto the ramp. They cut the rope that hobbles my ankles, but leave my hands bound. It feels strange to walk on solid ground again. I keep bracing my feet as if the walkway beneath me might sway like the deck of the boat.

"Do we have a carriage?" Samuel asks a dockworker whose ruddy skin is a sharp contrast to her steel-gray hair.

"Just up the top of the ramp and to the left, sir," the woman says as she grips a rope as thick as my arm and wraps it around a post, doing her part to secure the boat.

Samuel turns on his heel and marches up the ramp. The four trackers assigned to me shepherd me along in Samuel's wake. Behind us, boots tromp along the walkway. I glance back and see Ian, his face bandaged, stalking up the ramp. He meets my eyes, and the desperate hatred in his gaze makes me wish I still had a weapon. Behind him, I see a flash of dark hair and quick, graceful movements as Quinn quietly lowers himself off the deck and into the water.

My escape plan might be in shambles, but I still have Quinn. It might take him a while to catch up to me if we're using a carriage. He'll have to move carefully through the streets and ask questions to figure out where I am, but he's here, and no one else knows it. My knees feel shaky with the relief of knowing I don't have to face all of Rowansmark on my own.

Several docks line the river, all with long ramps attached. A scattering of oil lamps hang from poles, but most of the area is wreathed in shadows. The sluggish breeze that kicked up as the sun went down carries the scents of algae, rust, and damp wood on the air. The carriage looks like a shorter, fancier version of a wagon—all polished paint, big wheels, and plush seats. A golden fist wrapped around a dragon's tail—the official emblem of James Rowan—is painted onto the door. We squeeze in, three to a seat, and Ian hops up beside the driver. I'm wedged between two trackers. Samuel sits directly across from me, but he hasn't looked at me once.

"Where are we going?" I ask, just to force Samuel to deal with the girl he helped kidnap.

"Prison," he says shortly, his eyes scanning the landscape outside the carriage's windows. More oil lanterns spill light onto the sidewalk as we pass.

"I thought you didn't have a prison."

"You thought wrong."

Samuel turns away to examine the scenery again. I follow

his gaze and watch the streets of Rowansmark move past the window.

The neighborhoods near the docks are full of industrial buildings made of soot-stained brick or sheets of metal with patches of rust spreading from every nail. The carriage bounces over the dark-gray stones that pave the streets, and I brace my feet against the floor to keep from pitching headfirst into Samuel's lap. My hands, bound behind my back, are useless. The rope cuts into my wrists, and my fingertips are cold.

The industrial section gives way to a neighborhood that reminds me of South Edge—peeling paint, sagging gates, and the beaten-down air of people who've known nothing but poverty. The buildings are filthy and often crumbling. They look like structures left over from the previous civilization. People cluster on front steps or lean against lampposts, their eyes cast down as we travel past them, though I can feel their gazes on the back of the carriage once they're no longer in danger of making eye contact with a tracker.

The people in South Edge were the same. Afraid to look at those who were supposed to protect them. Tired of scrabbling for food and shelter and weary from the certainty that nothing they did would bring them a better life.

If I can escape from prison, this is the neighborhood I need to find. I can disappear here among people who don't feel an inborn loyalty to the leader who has consistently ignored their plight.

Of course, it's just as likely that someone might be willing to sell me out to a tracker for a meal, but if I change locations often, I'll be okay. Especially if Quinn is with me. I don't know how he'll find me when I'm being taken through Rowansmark in a carriage, but I don't doubt that he will.

I just have to stay focused, learn everything I can from my enemies, and watch for my first opportunity to escape and begin hunting for the tech that James Rowan will use to destroy Logan.

The crumbling buildings slowly give way to smaller structures, neat squares of grass, and clean streets. Oil lamps give way to iron braziers with cheerful little fires lit. The streets glow in the golden light. We turn a few corners, and enter the heart of Rowansmark—the place Dad and I stayed whenever we'd visit. A sudden spike of pain hits as I remember the last time we walked these streets, arm in arm, unaware that our lives were about to be ripped apart by Marcus McEntire's fierce need to rescue his missing son.

Blinking the sting of tears out of my eyes, I watch the familiar streets. If the slums resemble a beaten, mangy dog too tired to clean itself up anymore, the heart of Rowansmark is a regal woman wrapped in moss and draped with necklaces of ivy. The brick-and-mortar buildings have elegant lines, fancy scrolled-iron balconies, and pillars on either side of their doors.

Another left turn, and we drive through the marketplace. It smells of fresh-cut flowers, bitter coffee beans, and fried bread dusted with sugar.

Dad once took me to the marketplace while we were in Rowansmark on my birthday. He found a vendor who sold thick, honey-soaked cakes and frothy lemon drinks. We sat at an iron table in the shade of a pecan tree and watched the Rowansmark women, in their colorful silk scarves, bargain fiercely for bags of walnuts, sugar, strawberries, and more. At the time, with my father next to me and sweet treats to eat, it was easy to forget that three blocks over, near the grand mansion that houses James Rowan, a bloodstained stage was used to carry out pain atonement sentences on the same citizens who indulged themselves in silks and sugar and a life spent ignoring the ugliness that hovered just beneath Rowansmark's surface.

Maybe we were no better in Baalboden. We walked the streets with our Protectors. We wore our dresses. We gave up our education because that was the price of safety. That was the bargain we'd made with the devil we knew to escape the devil we didn't.

Until Dad decided that I should know how to protect myself. That dresses would hamper me in a fight, so I should have pants as well. That I needed to know how to read, how to write, and how to think for myself.

Maybe all the people of Rowansmark need is for someone to encourage them to think for themselves. To point out that the price they pay for safety is covered in their own blood.

Maybe, but I don't know how to send that message. And I don't have time to figure it out. I have to stage an escape from prison, find and destroy some tech, and reunite with Logan so that we can finish what we started.

The carriage rolls to a stop in front of a pair of huge scrolled-iron gates. Beyond the gates sits the sprawling brick mansion of James Rowan. Either I'm meeting with James Rowan before being locked in the prison, or the prison is somewhere on this property. A woman in the brown-and-red uniform of a city guard opens the gate and waves us through.

Magnolia trees with waxy flowers and pecan trees with branches coated in feathery patches of moss are strewn across the green grass. Huge, glass-enclosed oil lanterns are spaced evenly along the brick road that circles around to stop in front of the stately white columns that line the spacious porch of the mansion.

Ian hops down from the driver's bench and yanks open the door. His jaw is clenched, and he merely glances at me before saying, "Get out." Turning away, he begins pacing the driveway in short, tense circuits while the six of us inside the carriage make our way into the open. Samuel motions for the four men who accompanied us to remain with the vehicle, and then he and Ian flank me and we all move toward the house.

The front door opens soundlessly the moment we set foot on the porch. A man in a crisp white shirt and black pants bows slightly, his graying blond hair flopping forward over his eyes as he says, "Tracker Donnelson. Tracker McEntire. Our leader will see you in his receiving room now."

"No mention of seeing me. Guess that means I'll have to wait out here," I say.

Ian grabs my arm and jerks me forward so that I'm forced to match his pace as we move down a wide hall with gleaming wood floors and framed portraits of James Rowan in various semiheroic poses lining the walls.

"That's an awful lot of pictures of himself to keep around, don't you think?" I ask, and curse my voice for trembling as we near a set of elaborately carved wooden doors. I don't know what James Rowan will do to me, but I imagine any man who put in place the pain atonement policy and who rewards his trackers for brutality is going to have several creative ideas for how to punish a girl who helped steal his precious technology.

"You understand nothing about him." Ian's voice sounds just as shaky as mine. I wonder if it shakes from fear or from anticipation. "He's a great man. His people want to remember him when he's gone."

"Then maybe he should give these portraits to his people instead of keeping them in his own house."

The man who let us in frowns at me as if I've trespassed over sacred ground, and then stops before the double doors and says, "He will see Tracker McEntire first."

Once Ian enters the room and shuts the doors behind him, and the blond man disappears back to his post, Samuel meets my eye. "Rachel, there is no love lost between us. We're on opposite sides of an argument neither of us can afford to lose." He leans toward me and lowers his voice. "But for your own sake, I'm telling you now that you will not be allowed to show disrespect to our leader and get away with it. Swallow every rude, challenging thought that comes into your head and speak with deference if you want this to go well."

I straighten my spine. "I'll show respect when I see something worth respecting."

Samuel's expression becomes cool and detached again, and he waits in silence until Ian opens the door and motions us in. I can't tell from Ian's face if his interview went well, but I'm absolutely certain all of the blame for the fact that Ian still doesn't have either the device or his brother has now been firmly placed at my feet.

Turning away from Ian, I look around the room. Shelves filled with books line three walls while gold drapes bracket a bank of windows on the fourth. Light from multiple oil lamps floods the room with warmth and illuminates the face of the man standing near a side table that holds a pitcher of tea and some cookies on a platter. The room smells faintly of lilac and old books.

James Rowan is short, thin, and dressed in a plain blue tunic and pants. His dark eyes and olive skin remind me of Adam, and his age-spotted hands shake as he raises his arm in a snappy salute. Samuel returns the salute, his chest puffed out, his shoulders back. Samuel holds his pose until his leader lowers his arm.

"Be seated. Please." Rowan's voice is soft around the edges, like he enjoys lingering over his words. "Who would care for something to drink? It's been a long journey. I always appreciate a bit of cold tea after I've been traveling. Ian, cut those ropes off her. She can't hold a glass all trussed up like that."

Ian frees me from the ropes around my wrists, and then he and Samuel crowd me toward a cluster of simple chairs with straight backs that surround a short oval table, while James Rowan, leader of Rowansmark and instigator of the pain atonement laws, pours tea and sugar over cubes of ice. I feel off-kilter and uneasy as I slowly sink into a chair and accept a glass of amber liquid with tiny grains of sugar floating lazily toward the bottom.

The Commander would never serve his own guests. He would never allow the extravagance of ice for a guest he knew he'd likely throw into his dungeon. In fact, he wouldn't bother being polite at all.

I'm not sure what to do with a man who forces a boy to whip his father to death and then graciously serves that same boy a glass of tea. Ian and Samuel each sip their tea and thank their leader for it, but I lean forward and set my glass on the table in front of me. I'm not interested in gracious hospitality. It won't change why I'm here. It won't change what James Rowan has done. What Ian has done.

What I still have to do.

Rowan settles himself across from me, sets his tea down next to mine, and looks at me. I stare into his eyes. For a moment, his gaze is nothing but benign graciousness, but I narrow my eyes and lean closer, a clear challenge. He blinks twice, the creases around his mouth pinching close, and then I see it—powerful confidence edged with sharp intolerance for anyone who would dare stand in his way. Beneath the calm reception, behind the tea, the sugar, and the pretense, lurks the man who knows how to bend the will of others into a shape of his own choosing.

He's going to find my will impossible to bend.

He gives me a small smile, but I refuse to return it. Folding his hands in his lap, he studies me in silence, and then says, "You've caused us quite a few problems. Refusing to return our property, threatening my trackers when they're simply doing their job . . . I must say I'm disappointed in you."

I hold his gaze and slowly lift my chin. Swallowing hard, I will my voice not to shake and say, "I could say the same about you."

CHAPTER TWENTY-EIGHT

RACHEL

James Rowan's eyes narrow slightly—the only indication that my words have upset him. His smile remains friendly and paternal as he brushes an imaginary speck of dust from his tunic. The silence between us stretches so long, I begin to wish for a swallow of my tea just to keep my mouth from going dry. Dad used to use this technique on me when he was certain I'd done something I needed to confess. I always broke in less than two minutes, but I'm not going to break now.

Ian adjusts himself on the chair beside me, and his leg brushes against mine. I jerk away from him, and a tiny frown digs into Rowan's forehead, as if the tension he sees between Ian and me causes him concern.

"Ian was good enough to fill me in on the details of these past two months," Rowan says, his voice kind but firm.

I snort. "Was he good enough to tell you that he burned my city down, causing thousands of people to die, and then systematically murdered innocent people as we traveled to Lankenshire?"

Ian shifts in his seat and leans forward, but Rowan gives him a tiny warning glance, and he goes still.

"I see you have your pet dog on a tight leash," I say, and though I can't see his face, I can practically feel Samuel's disapproval radiating from his body.

Rowan presses his fingers into a steeple, and says, "I enjoyed a good relationship with your father. I'm sorry for his passing. My condolences."

"I'd love to explain to you in great detail where you can put your *condolences*."

Samuel's hand latches on to my shoulder and squeezes. Hard. "You will be respectful."

"Or what? You'll throw me in the dungeon? You'll kill me? I already know you're going to do both, so what have I got to lose?" My body vibrates with fury. How dare the man who created the kind of environment that kept Marcus from being able to go to him for help in rescuing Logan, the man who sent Ian after us knowing he would kill innocent people, sit there and pretend to mourn my father?

"I told you she was nothing like her father," Ian says, his tone smug.

I round on him and hurl my words at his face. "You know nothing about my father. He never blindly followed anyone's orders. He thought for himself. He stood for what was right, even when it cost him everything." I seal my lips before I can tell him that I may not be a hero like Dad, but nothing, not Ian, not James Rowan, not the stupid fire-breathing Cursed One, is going to stop me from doing the right thing.

Even if it costs me everything.

I turn back to face Rowan, who is watching me with speculation buried beneath his bland mask of concern, and say, "My father didn't steal anything from you. Once he realized the package he'd been given by Marcus McEntire was something the Commander shouldn't have, he hid it rather than bring it back to Baalboden. And you declared him a traitor. Then you sent Ian to kill *everyone*. . . ." My voice breaks as I remember Sylph's lifeless face. "Even though the people who died weren't responsible for any of this. So you don't get to sit there and tell me how sorry you are that my father is dead. Or how sorry you are that anyone from Baalboden is dead. Your condolences are useless to me."

"I imagine they are." His voice is still gentle, and it rubs against my anger like sandpaper. "But to be clear, I offered condolences for your father. I judged him based on the information I had once the tech went missing, and I was wrong. He was a good man. I did not, however, offer condolences for anyone else who died. Nor will I. Their deaths are just."

I open my mouth, but I can't seem to find the air to speak. My heart pounds against my skin, a hammer that wants to crush me from the inside out. I see Sylph's face. Donny's neck. I see the streets of Baalboden wreathed with flames while her people screamed for help that wasn't coming.

Rowan leans forward. "You see, your father made the right decision. But you didn't, did you?" He sounds like he expects me to confess my wrongdoing and ask for mercy. "And neither did your leader, Commander Chase."

"He isn't my leader." I grip the sides of the chair so hard my hands ache.

"Do you know why Baalboden had to burn? Why your friends had to die?"

"Because Ian is sick. Because *you're* sick—"

"Because justice requires sacrifice."

I lunge to my feet, knocking my tea over and sending the liquid splashing across the table. "You sacrificed innocent people!"

He stands, and suddenly he doesn't look so short anymore. "I sacrificed what mattered to Commander Chase. He thought he could steal from me. Subvert my technology for his own uses. Turn my citizens against me. A theft like that requires a strong response. He wanted to become the most powerful man in the world. I broke the seat of his power." His eyes bore into mine. "It was just."

"Nothing about you is just." I ball my hands into fists. "You destroy lives because your pride is wounded. That makes you a poor leader and an even poorer man. You don't care if you hurt those who are loyal to you or those who are loyal to someone else, as long as you get to say that you made your point."

"Loyalty is something a leader earns." His voice is still soft, but there's a thread of steel in it now. "My people are loyal to me for a reason."

"Yes, because if they aren't, you have them whip their family members to death."

"Shut your mouth!" Ian grabs my injured arm and spins me toward my chair. I plant my back foot and plow my left arm into his face as I turn. My momentum carries me into him, and we topple over backward, sending his chair skidding across the floor.

Ian scissor-kicks, wraps his arms around my head, and flips me onto my back. I punch as hard as I can with my left hand, aiming for his internal organs and his windpipe, but I'm not doing very much damage. Ian, however, is pounding his fists against my body like he thinks if he hits me hard enough, everything that haunts him will just disappear.

Someone is yelling for Ian to stop, but he doesn't listen. He drives his fist into my stomach, and I choke. I can't draw in another breath. I go limp as if I've been knocked out, and absorb another two punches before Samuel wraps his arms around Ian's chest and begins hauling him off me.

I wait until Ian is halfway between kneeling and standing and then draw my knee to my chest and slam my boot into his crotch. He shrieks in agony and falls to his knees when Samuel finishes pulling him away from me.

Coughing and gasping, I roll to my side and struggle to take a full breath. A shadow falls over my face, and then James Rowan crouches beside me. He reaches a hand out as if to touch me, and I wheeze, "Don't you dare."

His smile is a grim tightening of his lips. "I dare a great many things. Some of which you don't approve of."

"You mean like having Ian kill his father in the name of justice and then sending him on a mission to kill hundreds of others as well? You're right. I don't approve. Do you have any idea what you've done to him?"

He cocks his head and studies me. "Interesting. I detect a note of sympathy for the boy you seem to want to punish."

"Not sympathy. Understanding." Behind me I can hear Ian struggling to breathe past the pain I dealt him. I should feel satisfaction at giving him an ounce of the agony he gave to me, but I don't.

"Understanding." That awful sad little smile is back.

"Yes. I understand how living under your rules could twist a person into the kind of sick monster Ian has become."

"Come with me. I want to show you something." He extends his hand as if to help me up.

"Do I have a choice?"

"There's always a choice. Haven't you learned that yet? You can choose to defy me and take the consequences. Or you can choose to be civil and get up to look at my garden with me."

How about if I choose to pretend to admire your garden while I plot the best way to defy you? I think as I ignore his hand and climb to my feet on my own. He leads me to the bank of windows and gestures toward the garden beyond. The blooming bushes, trees, and flower beds are bathed in golden light from the oil lamps that surround the garden and cut through it along a narrow cobblestone path.

"What do you see?" he asks.

I roll my eyes. "Is that a trick question?"

"Humor me."

"Sure. Humor the man who destroyed my life. Sounds fun."

He sighs as if my insolence is another disappointment, and then points past a row of rosebushes. "Do you see that tree?"

I shake my head. "There isn't one."

He nods as if I've passed a test. "No, there isn't. Not anymore. Do you know why?"

"How in the world could I possibly know why there isn't a tree in your garden?" I snap.

"You're a smart girl, Rachel. Why wouldn't there be a tree?"

I cross my arms over my chest and glare out the window.

"Because there was never one in the first place."

"Wrong."

"What a shame. Are we done playing this game?"

"There was a tree. A beautiful old pecan tree. It was my favorite in the entire garden."

"Is this the part of the conversation where I parrot back your condolences?"

"Show some respect, Rachel," Samuel says from behind us.

Rowan waves his hand as if to tell Samuel not to worry. "Why wouldn't that tree—my favorite tree—be there any longer?"

"Because it blew down in a storm. Because you got cold one winter and chopped it up for kindling. Because you sent Ian after it before you sent him to Baalboden. Am I getting close yet?"

"Because it became diseased." His voice sounds just as regretful as it did when he told me he was disappointed in me. "I'd pruned that tree every fall. Cared for it every winter. Enjoyed its shade and its pecans every spring and summer. It was special to me, but then it began to rot from the inside out. By the time I discovered the rot, it was too late. The disease had spread from the branches down into the heart of the tree. If I didn't cut it down, it would continue to die until, one day, it might fall and hurt someone."

He waits as if I'm going to comment on the grand lesson I just learned, but I stay silent.

"People are like trees. I prune them. Care for them. Guide them. And enjoy them the way a father enjoys a son when he becomes what he's meant to be. But when I discover rot, I have to see how deep it goes. It isn't enough to just cut off the obvious branch. I have to test the core of the tree to see if it's still solid."

"And that's why you had Ian kill his father? To see if Ian was still loyal to you?"

"Exactly." His smile is full of regret. "Sometimes a father must hurt his sons if he loves them."

"And sometimes a son must hurt his father if he loves you." I turn to face him, this small man with the gentle smile and the incurable belief that people are pawns in a game that belongs only to him. "Why are you telling me this?"

His smile dies. "Because I respected your father, and he is no longer alive to see the rot that has spread inside his daughter. But I can see it. The disrespect. The inability to comprehend that your actions led to the very things you blame Ian for. Blame *me* for. I can see the rot, Rachel."

"So you're going to cut me down like your favorite tree?"

He meets my eyes for a long moment. "Yes."

CHAPTER TWENTY-NINE

LOGAN

The Commander and I reach the edge of the old city midafternoon the day after the attack. Our horses are worn out, their sides heaving, and their heads hanging low. We pushed them hard. I hope they can recover, but more than that, I hope the girls haven't been harmed. We weren't far behind the gang of highwaymen who attacked us. Now and then we caught glimpses of them, all riding horses—theirs and ours—as they traveled ahead of us. They couldn't have been back at their camp for more than an hour.

Hopefully, they used that time to stable the horses and settle in from their trip instead of using it to hurt the girls. If not . . . I try to run the scenarios, but I can't force myself to think of all the grim possibilities. Instead, I follow the Commander into a copse of birch trees on a rise just outside the city, tether my horse, and then move to the edge of the trees so I can study what used to be a huge city before the *tanniyn* surfaced.

The Commander joins me, and we stare at the sprawling

grid of collapsed buildings, twisted metal spires, and piles of crumbled stone held in place by the hardy tufts of wild grass growing from their depths. A few blocks west of the city's heart, the buildings are more intact, the streets cleaner. We can't see clearly past the debris and ruined structures, but it seems likely that the highwaymen are using that area as their base.

"They'll have lookouts," the Commander says.

"Yes."

"We could enter from the east once night falls. Move through the city until we reach them. Then take them out one at a time."

"Or we could walk right in and pretend to be interested in trading for some of their wares," I say because the girls have been in the highwaymen's custody for over twenty hours now, and I am not going to take all night to reach them. If the Commander disagrees, I'll enter the city alone, the Rowansmark device waiting in my pocket.

"Trading." The Commander snorts. "They'll take one look at us and realize we've got nothing to trade. Especially nothing worth three girls, seven horses, and a piece of tech."

"I have a plan."

He takes his time measuring me with his stare. "I'm listening, and I'd better like what I hear."

I hold my ground, though it takes everything I've got not to reach for my sword. "You're going to hate this plan until you hear how it benefits you," I say. "I just ask you to listen to me until I get to that part."

He lifts his chin in my direction, an indication to keep talking.

"We're going to trade ourselves. Or, more specifically, you."

His scar twitches as he curls his lip. "You're a fool if you think I'm agreeing to that."

"You haven't heard how it will work yet." I hurry on. "Rowansmark put a price on Jared Adams's head, remember? A huge price. We'll say that's you."

"You want me to pretend to be Jared Adams." His stare burns into me.

"Yes. I'll pretend to turn you over to them so that they can collect the bounty from Rowansmark. As a bonus, I'll tell them I've recovered the thing you stole from James Rowan."

"You don't offer something on the trading table that you can't produce," he says scornfully. "I don't expect you to understand how these kinds of things work, so let me set you straight. If you tell a pack of highwaymen that you have something, and then you fail to show them the item, they'll kill you. And then kill me because I was stupid enough to walk in there with you."

"I have the item."

His body goes still. "What?"

"I have it. The device. Frankie recovered it from your tent before the highwaymen could pillage it. He recognized how important it was to keep it from falling into the wrong hands. He gave it to me."

His hand grips the hilt of his sword. "And you said nothing about this? You dragged me an entire day's journey through the Wasteland because I thought we needed to recover the tech—"

"Exactly. You wouldn't have come, otherwise, and you wouldn't have allowed me to leave. Not without a fight."

He pulls his sword free, and I take a step back. "You'd better get to the part where this benefits me, because I'm about to see the benefit of cutting you down where you stand."

I meet his eyes and make my voice steady even as I offer up the last piece of leverage I have against him. "You want to know how to work the tech. I'm going to show you. Consider the high-waymen's camp to be a training ground for what you want to accomplish in Rowansmark."

And once he knows how to use the device, he'll feel free to dispose of me as soon as we secure troops from Chelmingford. There won't be any need for my technical expertise. He'll betray me. I'll just have to be ready.

He smiles, and I shiver.

"You're a fool," he says quietly. "I told you before that women are your weakness, and you've just proved me right. You're giving up the one reason you still exist for the slim chance that we can rescue those girls and get them out alive. Your life for theirs. Be sure you think that's a fair deal, because once we start this, there's no going back."

"Are you saying you're going to break your word and try to kill me before we take down James Rowan?" I raise a brow at him, though inside I'm shaking. He'll kill me, wipe off his sword, and walk away without thinking twice if I let him. "What will you do if our one piece of tech can't match what they have waiting for us there? What if we have to improvise or improve on it? How will you do that?"

He watches me for a long moment, and then slowly sheathes his sword. "We have a mission. Our task is to engage and sub-due the armies waiting for us and to remove James Rowan from power. Anything or anyone else is a distant second on our list of priorities. If you allow women you care about on your team, you'll worry over them. You'll make decisions based on fear instead of on strategy." There's a tremor in his voice, a first for him. "And then those decisions will cost you your mission and the lives of others who depend on you to make judgment calls without emotion."

I frown as the shadows lengthen around us. "Are we talking about me? Or are we talking about Christina?"

His mouth snaps shut, and he glares at me. "Who told you about Christina?"

"Lyle Hoden mentioned her at breakfast. Is that what this is about? You cared about a girl and made a decision you regret?"

"Let me tell you how leadership works." His words are curt. "You can't care about the individuals. You can only care about the group. The second you start caring about an individual more than the group, your ability to make decisions is compromised. You put one person above the whole, and it costs you the mission. It costs you the group."

"Caring about Christina cost you the group?" I stare at him. "Was she on your team?"

I don't expect him to answer me, but he does. His voice is weary. "She had talent as a soldier, but she hadn't seen combat before the beasts surfaced. We were sent down that shaft to destroy the nest and seal up the hole. We thought we were facing one monster. Maybe two . . ."

He stares at the ruined city where the late afternoon light lingers in pockets of golden, shimmering air. Finally, he says, "There were scores of them. Fat lizard things so big they could crush huge boulders beneath them. They were breathing fire and spewing smoke. We still might have been able to seal up the hole and get out, but Christina got trapped by some of the rocks the beasts were smashing with their tails."

"And you couldn't detonate the bomb to seal the hole because she would've been killed."

"Instead of detonating the bomb, I tried to help her. I tried to reach her. . . ." He touches the scar on his face as if remembering how he got it.

"She died anyway, didn't she?" I ask softly, feeling an uneasy sort of pity for him even while he visibly shakes off the effects of our conversation and squares his shoulders.

"She died. Half the team died. All because I put her ahead of the mission. I never made that mistake again, and neither will you, because if I think your ability to make decisions has been compromised, I'll finish you. I'm not interested in dying because you feel a misguided sense of responsibility for the few instead of for the many."

"You loved her, didn't you?" I know I sound too curious, too surprised, but I can't help it. The thought that the Commander was once capable of love is too foreign to wrap my mind around.

His eyes flash. "Let's get this done." He turns on his heel and stalks toward the city. I have to hurry to catch up.

CHAPTER THIRTY

LOGAN

We enter the city at midafternoon the day after the attack. I march the Commander in front of me, my sword out. I'm glad I don't have to see his face while I do it. His necklace, the one that marks him as the leader of a city-state and is capable of keeping the *tanniyn* at bay, has been left behind. Buried beneath a tree close to where we tethered our horses. I carry the Rowansmark tech in my pocket, wired to the two additional transmitters I brought.

The thought of demonstrating how to use it and then handing it back to the Commander makes my heart pound in quick, jerky thumps, but the thought of leaving Willow, Jodi, and Nola to the highwaymen is worse.

The city seems to tower over us as we enter. Everything is tall—the buildings, the faded metal signs now covered in moss and ivy, the broken pieces of road that inexplicably cross other roads like bridges over water. I stare at the underside of a road-bridge as we walk beneath it and wonder at a civilization that had so many wagons, they needed roads in the sky.

My pulse is pounding loudly in my ears as we walk. Every-thing inside of me is wound tight, a coil of anxiety that I have to willfully ignore. The girls will be okay. They have to be.

We haven't moved more than a few blocks through the ruins before three men materialize from behind a rusted hunk of metal that looks like an enormous once-yellow wagon with rub-ber wheels and glass windows all around the sides.

"State your business," one calls to us. The other two heft crossbows and aim them at our hearts.

"I'm here to make a trade." My voice seems to bounce off the half-crumbled brick storefronts that line this section of the city.

"What's with the weapon and the old man?" the speaker asks.

"He's my collateral."

One of the men snorts and shakes his head, as if marveling at my foolishness, but the third jerks his crossbow to the left and says, "Come with me. We have sentries posted throughout the city. Try anything funny, and we'll kill you."

Not before I kill you. My hand rests on the outline of the device sheltered in my pocket as grim resolution fills me.

It takes nearly an hour to wind our way through the wreckage of the city, dodging the craters left by the *tanniyn* and ducking around burned-out husks of buildings. When we finally reach the cleaned-up streets of the western side of town, another pair of sentries steps out to meet us.

"Whatcha got?" a thin, red-eyed man asks.

"The boy here says he wants to make a trade. Apparently, he thinks Rufus will be interested in the old man."

The red-eyed man spits on the cracked gray road beneath his

feet. "Seems unlikely, but let's ask him."

Leaving our original guide behind, we follow the red-eyed man into the highwaymen's base camp. Here, the debris has been cleared, and shaky structures are propped up with boards and branches. A few taller buildings gleam dully in the afternoon sun, their windows reflecting the clear blue sky beneath a layer of grime.

I search the windows of the buildings we pass, looking for Willow, Jodi, and Nola, but I don't see them. Here and there, a group of men in the ragged, patched-together clothing of highwaymen stare at us from inside a building as we pass, but for the most part, the street seems empty. When we turn left onto a wide street with cracked sidewalks, everything changes.

Horses mill about a large, flat square of the same kind of stone that makes up the old road beneath our feet. A fence encloses the square, and an awning covers the eastern side, sheltering piles of hay. A couple of men lounge in front of the makeshift stable, their eyes assessing us carefully as we pass. I remember the way the highwaymen attacked—the speed and precision with which they killed our guards, stole our horses, and left with the girls— and remind myself not to underestimate Rufus and his band of criminals.

Past the stable, the smell of roasted pig fills the air. One of the buildings has smoke curling up from a chimney, and as we get closer, the scent of baking bread and the yeasty aroma of a strong, dark ale mingles with the smell of the cooking meat and makes my stomach rumble.

I glance at the building where the food is being cooked, taking in the wide space where a window used to be, the cluster of round tables and chairs scattered across the floor inside, and the dozen or so men seated in those chairs who stop chewing to watch us as we walk by.

No girls.

"Here we are." The red-eyed man stops before a wide, low-slung brick building and raps sharply on a narrow blue door.

"Yeah?" a voice asks from inside.

"Traders here."

The door swings open, and an older man with greasy clumps of gray hair hanging from his head steps out.

"No weapons allowed inside," he says, seeing my sword still pointed at the Commander's back.

"If I don't keep a weapon on him, he's likely to bolt," I say.

The man comes closer to me, and I grimace. He smells like vinegar, sharp and sour. "If he tries to run past my boys, he'll be killed for his trouble. Weapon." He holds his hand out, and I reluctantly give up my sword.

"Inside." The man gestures toward the narrow doorway. When the Commander doesn't start walking fast enough, the man shoves him forward. Instantly, the Commander pivots, wedges his forearm beneath the man's throat, and crushes him against the wall.

"Touch me again and the next meal your boys eat will be you."

I hurry forward as the red-eyed man draws his sword and a pair of men from across the street start toward us.

"Let's go inside," I say roughly, though I don't touch the Commander. We may be temporarily on the same side, but I recognize the look on his face, and I don't want to be the one he kills.

The Commander steps back, straightens his tunic, and moves into the house as if he owns it.

"Told you I needed my sword," I say to the doorman as I push past him and follow the Commander.

The man slams the door and gestures toward a set of narrow stairs. His faded blue eyes regard the Commander with contempt.

"Go on up. And try to put your hands on Rufus, old man. He knows how to make you wish he'd kill you."

The Commander gives the man a withering stare.

"Let's go." I start up the stairs, my footsteps echoing hollowly on the warped wood.

When we reach the upper story, I notice three important things—Rufus looks like he could take Frankie in a fight, we're surrounded by men with machetes, crossbows, and knives, and Willow, Jodi, and Nola are tied to a hook in the far wall. I meet their eyes and work hard not to show the wild relief that rushes through me.

They look unharmed, which is more than I can say for the highwayman closest to Willow. His eye is swelling, and a cut splits the skin of his left cheek. He glares at Willow, and she smirks at him before looking back at me.

I don't give any sign that I recognize them. If Rufus discovers what they mean to me, their price will be more than I can afford. Looking away from them, I take my time sizing up Rufus as I wrap my hand around the Commander's upper arm and walk him to the middle of the room.

"I'm here to trade," I say.

"You got nothing I want." Rufus's voice is quiet for such a large man.

"I've got the thing every single person in the Wasteland wants."

Rufus raises a brow. "Is that so? And what would that be?"

"I'm sure you've heard the rumors out of Rowansmark." I push the Commander a little closer to Rufus. "The bounty they've placed on Jared Adams's head for stealing something very, very valuable."

"I've heard." Rufus leaves his chair and walks closer to us. "Are you trying to tell me this old man is Jared Adams, Baalboden's top courier? Because I ran into Jared once a long time ago, and I could swear he was my age. Red hair. No scar." He flicks a hand toward the Commander's face and begins circling us like a predator.

He gives me a look that dares me to lie to him. Dares me to make it easy for him to dismiss me, or worse, kill me. I scramble for a backup plan, and pray the Commander has the good sense to play along. If my next words don't convince Rufus, we're doomed. I can't call the *tanniyn* and rescue the girls while we're still inside this building. The entire thing would collapse the moment one of the beasts tunneled up through the floor.

"No, I'm not claiming this is Jared Adams. This is someone better. This is Commander Jason Chase."

Rufus stops circling us while beside me, the Commander clenches his fists and gives me a look of pure rage.

Rufus whistles. "I see. Is that true?" He looks at the Commander. "Are you Jason Chase, leader of Baalboden?"

The Commander draws himself up ramrod straight. "I am. And if you think I'm going to be traded off to you like some horse on an auction block, you can think again."

"I can see how that would be upsetting to you," Rufus says, and the light in his eyes tells me the negotiation has begun. "So tell me, what's it worth to you for me to kill the boy and set you free instead?"

Panic races through me, and I rush to speak before the Commander can decide that letting Rufus kill me would solve all of his problems. "He can't offer you anything."

Rufus grins. "He's the leader of Baalboden, mate. He can offer me the world."

"Baalboden is gone," I say. "Destroyed by the *tanniyn*."

The Commander divides his time between glaring at me and looking at Rufus as if he'd like to disembowel him. Slowly.

"So then what do I need with an old man who has no power, no money, and no one who would pay to take him off my hands?"

"Rowansmark will pay. The bounty that was on Jared's head is because the Commander had him take a piece of tech from Rowansmark. They want it back, and they want the Commander with it. James Rowan will pay you twenty times what you've earned in your entire life."

Rufus considers me in silence for a moment. "So why don't you just take him to Rowansmark yourself?"

I clear my throat and make a show of looking uncomfortable. "I'm not exactly welcome there."

Rufus scratches his chin, looks at a few of the men gathered inside the room, and says, "I'll give you a horse, your choice of five weapons from my cache, and the use of one of these fine ladies for the night." He jerks his head toward the girls, and I have to swallow against the tide of fury that wants to explode out of me.

"I'll take three horses, three weapons, and all three girls."

Rufus laughs. "You think you can handle all three of these ladies for the night?" He points toward Willow. "That one alone is more than you can take on by yourself."

I hold his gaze. "Not for the night. For good. I want to walk out of this camp with all three of the girls, along with a horse and a weapon for each of them."

Rufus's laughter dies. "One old man and the hope that I'll get paid handsomely at the end of a very long journey isn't nearly enough for that kind of trade."

"That's why I also brought the tech that was stolen from Rowansmark."

His smile is predatory. "Well, now we're getting somewhere. Let's see it."

I pull the device from my cloak pocket, careful not to loosen the wires attaching it to the transmitters.

"What is it?" Rufus asks.

"A weapon. If you have a practice range around here, I can give you a demonstration."

Rufus smiles slowly. "Or, my men kill you and we take both the tech and the old man." He steps closer. "I confiscated your weapons. Surrounded you with my crew. I hold all the advantages, my friend. You're holding nothing but an old man and a weird-looking flute. Why should I bother trading?"

"Because you're smart enough to want me as a repeat customer." I hope. "Why don't we step outside? Bring the girls and have one of your men go pick me out three horses. And while they're doing that, I'll give you a demonstration of the tech so you can assess its value. If you don't think it's worth my terms, I'll walk away."

"Counteroffer. You give me a demonstration. If it's worth your terms, you walk away with the girls, the weapons, and the horses. If you've wasted my time, I keep the old man, and you get nothing."

"Deal." I reach out and shake his hand while one of his men cuts through the rope that binds the girls to the wall. I notice the man is careful to avoid coming too close to Willow.

"Weapons," I say, and jerk my chin toward my sword and a stack of crossbows, daggers, and spears that line one wall in the room beside the front door.

"Three, like you said. Try to use them against us or run off with them before you've demonstrated how to use that tech, and my men will drop you where you stand." Rufus nods to the man who smells like vinegar, and he quickly moves toward the daggers.

"My choice." I speak firmly, thankful that my voice doesn't shake as the realization of what I'm about to do crashes into me. "Return my sword to me, and get me two daggers and"—I glance at Willow—"a crossbow."

The man looks at Rufus, receives a nod of permission, and hastens to grab what I've asked for. As we follow Rufus's men down the narrow stairs and out onto the street, I consider my options. I don't trust the Commander to watch out for the girls while I'm trying to control the *tanniyn*. Plus, I promised he could stick close to me and learn how to use the device. I need the girls to be free of the city before I call the beasts, but Rufus isn't going to release them until I give him a demonstration.

I'll have to simply call the *tanniyn* and use the distraction of its impending arrival to my advantage.

Sliding my sword into its sheath, I gesture for the girls to precede me out the door and to the middle of the street and then hand them their weapons. Willow's hand instantly tightens on the bow, and I breathe, "Not yet."

Her grip doesn't lessen, but she doesn't whip the bow up and start shooting either.

Rufus laughs, though he doesn't sound amused. "If I were you, mate, I wouldn't give that girl anything she can use to hurt you. Not until you break her spirit a bit."

I hold Rufus's gaze for a long moment, my jaw clenched against my anger, while his crew brings three horses to stand nearby, waiting to see if I can deliver on the terms of our deal.

"Well then, get on with it." Rufus gestures toward a line of targets bolted to a building fifty yards away. "Show me what this tech can do."

I meet Willow's eyes and mouth, "Run," and slam my finger down on the button that will call the *tanniyn*.

CHAPTER THIRTY-ONE

LOGAN

Before I have time to wonder if the additional transmitters will make a difference, the ground beneath my feet trembles. Rufus backs away from the Commander and me, his hands out in front of him as if to ward off whatever the device has just done, while the girls race for the horses. One of the highwaymen holding their bridles pulls a sword as if to stop the girls from taking their mounts. Willow sends an arrow into his chest, yanks the reins from his hands, and vaults into the saddle. Nola and Jodi scramble onto their horses seconds after her.

"What did you do? What is that?" Rufus asks as dust begins sifting from the rooftops around us and the few panes of glass that remain rattle in their berths.

The Commander turns a vicious smile toward Rufus. "That is the sound of unlimited power."

The ground heaves, and jagged cracks begin forming a web around our feet. Highwaymen scramble for the relative security of the buildings, but I know they won't find safety there. The only way to avoid what's coming is to be in control of the beasts or to be out of range.

"Logan?" Jodi calls to me as her horse dances nervously.

"Go!" I shout as I run toward the side of the street while behind me chunks of the road crumble and slide into the ever-widening maw that is opening in the ground.

"Not without you," Willow snaps, urging her horse toward me.

"Yes, without me. It's going to take all of my concentration to work the device. I can't worry about whether I might accidentally kill you." I look in her eyes and understand her struggle. Willow is a fighter, not a runner. "Get Nola and Jodi to safety." I lower my voice as the Commander strides toward us, his eyes on the tech. "If he's the only one who comes out alive, shoot him."

Willow leans down and grabs my shoulders in a rough half embrace. "Come out alive, Logan." Then she wheels her horse around and takes off at a gallop, Nola and Jodi on her heels, while behind me the ground erupts with a deafening roar.

It sounds like a wall collapsing. Like a thousand snarling cougars.

Like death.

Beside me, one of the tall metal poles that line the street snaps at its base and crashes down, pinning a man beneath it. He screams, but the sound is lost in the gut-churning thunder of the *tanniyn* that explode out of the ground in a mass of glistening black scales and puffs of smoky air.

Chunks of the road rain down on the surrounding buildings. Glass shatters. And the beasts pour out of the hole and into the street.

Everywhere I look there are huge, black, glistening creatures with milky eyes and spikes running down their backs. Streams of fire scorch the air as the creatures strafe the road. There are so *many*. A dozen. Maybe more. The ground trembles beneath them, and it's hard to keep my footing.

If this is what happens when I amplify the device's signal with two transmitters, I shudder to imagine what will happen when I attach the rest of the transmitters to Melkin's staff and use it against the Commander.

A circle of destruction. Impossible to survive.

I back away from the road and move my fingers over the buttons to send the beasts south. They surge forward, crushing metal poles, snapping trees, and barreling through brick walls and into buildings that immediately become blazing infernos as the creatures spew fire.

Men leap from second-story windows, landing hard in a tangle of limbs. Most are quickly crushed beneath the monstrous creatures. The *tanniyn* are nearly the size of a small house. Twice as big as the long, rusted yellow vehicle we saw when we entered the city. In moments, the entire south side of the street is burning.

"Turn them west," the Commander says, his eyes on the device.

"I plan to turn them in every direction," I say. "I promised not to leave a single highwayman alive to hunt us down."

My fingers are steady as I press the buttons to send the beasts east where warehouses and wagons line the street. The beasts roar, spitting fire at one another and anything else that moves as they twist and claw their way up the street away from us. Behind them, the buildings they plowed through sway uncertainly and then begin to crumble, raining ash and flaming debris.

"Get back!" The Commander's hand is rough as he shoves me aside seconds before another metal pole slams into the ground where I was just standing. My back hits the wall of Rufus's home, and the shock of the impact is nothing compared to the shock of being saved by the Commander twice in twenty-four hours.

I start moving toward the stables. In seconds, the *tanniyn* will have destroyed the eastern edge of the camp. I want to be near my escape plan before I have to turn them back toward us. Especially as it's clear that while the device might be powerful enough to call over a dozen *tanniyn*, and its signal might be enough to drive them in the direction of my choice, the effects are short-lived. Seconds after my fingers leave the device, the beasts turn in whichever direction they please. Another sonic signal from me jerks them to the east again, but not for long. Soon, four of them plunge north into the city streets. Another two return to the wreckage in the south.

Five more turn toward us.

I swallow hard against the smoky air and accept the facts. I can call them. I just can't truly control them.

This would've been good information to have before I decided to see if the transmitters would bring up more than one creature.

Before panic can strike, obliterating my ability to plan my way out of this, Rufus launches himself from the doorway of his house and slams into me, knocking us both to the ground.

"Stop!" he screams as he grabs my hands and tries to wrest the device away from me.

"Get off me." I elbow him. "They're coming, you idiot. Get

off me before they crush us both!"

Suddenly, Rufus grunts, his eyes glazing with pain. I stare past him at the Commander, who yanks his sword out of Rufus's back and shoves the man off me with the toe of his boot.

"Get up," he says, reaching down to help me to my feet.

I stare at him. "You saved my life. Again."

His scar twitches. "I saved the device and held to our mission. Now get those beasts away from us so we can leave."

I hit the buttons to send the beasts east again and freeze as the *tanniyn* who were crashing through the south side of the street whip their heads toward us. Their claws dig into the rubble as they shudder, jerking their heads east and spewing billows of smoke from their nostrils.

"They aren't moving," the Commander says.

"I know that."

"Send them east."

"I'm *trying*. It's like the longer they hear the signal, the better they can resist moving away from it."

The *tanniyn* shake their heads and roar, a deafening rumble that nearly sends me to my knees as the ground shivers beneath me. The Commander stumbles, and I catch him before he can fall.

The irony that two people who so desperately want to kill each other are busy saving each other instead isn't lost on me.

"Try harder!" he snaps as more *tanniyn* surge toward us. Their milky eyes and glistening scales reflect the flames as they crunch over the ruins of the road.

Beyond them, the city blocks that we can see are in flaming ruins. Black monstrous things heave themselves into the air and crash into buildings, leaving jagged holes or toppling structures that were already shaky. Metal rends apart with earsplitting shrieks, and one of the road-bridges topples beneath the weight of three *tanniyn*, who crush the rubble beneath them as they slither toward the next row of buildings.

We aren't going to get out of here alive if I don't *do* something. Abandoning my efforts to make them go east, I hit the button that will send them back to their nest instead. The Commander and I back slowly down the street, while the creatures roar and shudder and lash out with their tails, sending walls, trees, and sometimes one another flying.

I press relentlessly against the button that sends the infrasonic signal and pray that it works. The creatures closest to us finally dive back into the ground. I don't wait around to see if the rest follow. At this point, fire has spread from the eastern edge of the camp and is eating through the north side of the city. The Commander and I are the only people left on the street. Those hiding in the buildings are either going to burn to death or run from the city with only what they can carry.

With their leader dead and their supplies destroyed, I'm not worried about being followed. Quickly, the Commander and I hurry away from the camp and through the city. When we reach the outskirts, he turns to me.

"The device?" He holds out his hand. Reluctantly, I hand over the tech. He strokes it with loving fingers, and a vicious smile spreads across his face.

"It didn't control them very well when we used the transmitters," I say. "It works better when you're just trying to control one at a time."

"It will work well enough for our purposes." He looks back toward the city, and I follow his gaze.

Fire consumes entire city blocks. Buildings lean against one another or simply crash to the ground in a hail of metal and stone.

"No wonder the previous civilization didn't stand a chance," I say. "If this was what happened in every major city, and no one knew that the right infrasonic frequency would send them away, they'd be defenseless."

The Commander's voice is quiet. "It was like this all across the globe. Chaos. Panic. Someone in our air and space department figured out that the beasts could be repelled with the right sonic pulse. We could still communicate with other nations using satellite phones." He glances at me. "Phones were devices that allowed us to talk to others over great distances and—"

"I've read about phones." When his brow rises, I add, "Jared brought back books when he traveled."

He grunts. "We shared what we knew with the leaders of nations we could still reach by sat-phone and coordinated the effort to send teams down to destroy the nests of *tanniyn*. You know what happened after that."

"I know what happened here. What about the other teams? Were any successful?"

He shrugs. "No one ever answered their sat-phones again." His hands tighten over the device. I leave him there and start up the bluff, one ear tuned to the sound of his footsteps coming up behind me. There's nothing to keep him from driving a sword through my back now. He knows how to use the device. He's seen firsthand what it can do.

I'm expendable now.

I reach the top of the bluff while the Commander still stands at the base, staring at the city. Maybe he's lost in the memories of watching his home burn so many years ago. Maybe he's trying to decide if he should kill me now or when we reach Rowansmark.

Willow is standing on the bluff, the crossbow cradled in her arms, its arrow pointed at the Commander. Nola and Jodi flank her, their daggers in their hands. The horses are tethered with the two that the Commander and I rode.

"I'm here," I say. Nola runs to me and hugs me. I hold her tight and wish with everything in me that I didn't have to tell her about Drake. When Nola lets go, Jodi launches herself at me. I wrap my arms around her and meet Willow's gaze.

"Are you . . . did they . . . are you hurt?" I ask, my cheeks burning a little when she looks at me.

"I'm not hurt. Neither are Jodi or Nola." She shows no inclination to hug me, but her eyes glow with something that looks like relief.

"I found something of yours." I retrieve her bow from my bag. "I don't have any arrows, but—"

"That's okay. I can make some." She straps the crossbow to the back of her saddle and takes her bow, running her fingers across it like it's an old friend. She meets my eyes. "Thank you for the bow."

"You're welcome."

"And for coming back for us."

"We're family now, Willow. That's what family does." I brush a strand of hair out of her eyes and smile a little, though now that the girls are safe, the pain of losing Drake is settling into me.

She raises a brow at me. "You aren't going to hug me too, are you?"

I gently bump my fist against her shoulder. "No hugging."

"Good. You creep me out when you get all mushy."

I refrain from mentioning the fierce half hug she gave me when she wasn't sure I'd live and try to find the words to shatter Nola's world.

"He's coming," Nola says.

I turn to see the Commander climbing the bluff.

"Now that he knows how to use the device, he might use it against us," Nola says.

"We have his necklace to counteract the signal. It's buried there." I point.

"I can get it." Nola moves toward the tree, but I stop her with a hand on her arm.

"Let Jodi get it." I pull Nola to the side while Jodi digs up the necklace, and the Commander slowly climbs the bluff.

"What is it?" Nola asks, fear edging into her voice. "What's wrong?"

I look at her wide, dark eyes and wish I didn't have to be the one to do this. "During the attack, those who were guarding the camp were killed." She starts shaking her head. "I'm so sorry, Nola. Your father . . . Drake is gone."

She sways forward, and I catch her before she can crumple to the ground. Sobs tear through her, and I let her cry against me while Jodi runs to us and wraps her arms around her friend.

"He died a hero. I know that doesn't make it easier to bear, but it's the truth. He was a good man, and I'll miss him. I'm sorry," I say, though I know from experience how inadequate those words are. "I'm sorry" doesn't bring anyone back. It doesn't close the awful hole that opens up inside of you when someone you love dies. It doesn't really help, but it's all I have to offer.

Nola turns to Jodi as the Commander reaches the summit and starts toward us. When he spots Nola crying, he scowls. I head him off before he can demand that we leave for Chelmingford before Nola is ready to ride.

"Give her a few minutes," I say. "She just learned that her father is dead."

He turns away from me and looks out at what's left of the highwaymen's city. "She can have five minutes. Then we're leaving. If we ride hard, we can be at Chelmingford in two days."

His eyes follow me as I move to Nola's side again, and the expression in them makes the hair on the back of my neck rise. In his mind, I'm a dead man walking.

I smile grimly. If adding two transmitters to the device caused this much out-of-control destruction, imagine what will happen when I wire five of them to Melkin's staff and drive it into the ground beside the Commander. He'll rely on the device to control them. But the staff's signal will be too powerful. Too overwhelming.

There's no way the Commander will come out of that alive.

CHAPTER THIRTY-TWO

<u>RACHEL</u>

The sun is melting over the ramparts of Rowansmark's wall as Samuel and Ian lead me outside to the garden. I spent the last night sleeping on a cot in a room no bigger than my back porch while a pair of soldiers stood guard outside my door. I tried to escape through the room's one window, but it seemed to be welded shut. Night turned into morning, and I expected someone to come for me, but instead, I spent the day locked in the room until finally, just before sunset, Samuel and Ian came for me.

Now I walk through the garden, where roses in sunset hues of red, orange, and gold line a stone path that circles a fountain with a moss-covered statue of a woman whose plump arms are raised gracefully above her head, as if she was captured in stone mid-dance. Beyond the fountain, the path cuts through wispy purple rhododendron bushes and azaleas bursting with pink flowers and then leads to a square of dirt, where James Rowan waits beside a thick wooden post, a brown leather whip in his hand.

The air is clogged with moisture and heat, and my hair clings to the back of my neck as sweat beads along my skin. Ian's hand digs into my right forearm, sending shooting pains through my wound, but I hold my head high and refuse to flinch.

If these men think they're going to cut me down to size like James Rowan's precious pecan tree, they're wrong.

I've survived the Commander, the loss of almost everyone I love, physical injury, and kidnapping. I've walked through my own personal hell and come out the other side. I am my father's daughter, and I *will* survive this. For Logan. For my dad. But most of all, for myself. I came to Rowansmark with a mission, and I'm not finished yet.

"Tie her to the whipping post," Rowan says in that soft, regretful voice of his. Like he cares deeply about me, and hates to be the one to point out the error of my ways.

I glare at him and silently swear that I'm going to be his last mistake.

Ian shoves me against the wooden post, grabs the rope that is tethered to the post by a thick iron ring, and says, "Hold your hands up."

"Why should I make it easy for you to hurt me again?" I'm proud that my voice doesn't betray the way my knees shake or the way icy frissons of fear skate up my spine, threatening to make my teeth chatter.

How many lashes will Rowan give me? Or will he hand the whip to Ian and let the boy who killed his father do his best to kill me too?

I tell myself it doesn't matter as Ian yanks my arms over my head and pins my wrists together so that Samuel can wrap the rope around them like he's securing a boat to its dock. I can take whatever they give me. I can breathe through the pain—scream through it if I have to.

"How many lashes?" Ian asks in the same cold, empty voice he's been using since his confrontation with Samuel on the boat.

"Oh, I think fifteen should do it." Rowan steps around the post until he's standing eye to eye with me. I'd like to spit in his face, but my mouth is as dry as the wood I'm pressed against. "Ten to teach her not to take things that aren't hers and five extra to remind her that she should be respectful to those in charge."

Fifteen. Fifteen is enough to disfigure my back. Enough to cut my flesh from my bones and let infection set in if I'm not given first aid afterward. Fifteen is enough to incapacitate me, but not enough to kill me.

My armor would protect me from the worst of it, but no one gets whipped without baring her back. They're going to see that I have armor, and then they're going to take it from me and hurt me.

I set my jaw to keep my mouth from trembling, and meet Rowan's gaze with as much defiance as I can muster. He just smiles sadly and steps a little closer, the whip still coiled in his hands. The leather is cracked, and the tip is stained dark from the blood of all the people who've had the misfortune to be punished by him.

"Your father didn't bring the controller to his leader," he says. "You did. You knew about the bounty on your father's head. You understood that the tech hadn't been given to him through official channels and that we were searching for it. Your father didn't try to use what didn't belong to him. You did. You are as much at fault in this as Marcus McEntire and the Commander. Your father isn't here to correct your actions. That duty now falls to me as the person you've wronged. I'm sure your father would be disappointed to see the kind of person his daughter has become."

I'm stretched on my tiptoes, leaning hard against the post in an effort to keep the rope that binds my wrists above my head from cutting off all the circulation to my hands—not exactly the most defiant stance—but I lift my chin and speak in a loud, clear voice that would make Dad proud.

"I am exactly who my father raised me to be."

Rowan shakes his head and then looks past me. "Which of you wants the privilege of purging Rachel from the dishonor of her actions?"

Ian says, "I should be the one—"

"I'll do it." Samuel brushes past me and takes the whip. His expression is distant, his mouth set in a thin, firm line. But his eyes meet mine for a second, and I take scant comfort in the steady confidence he exudes. He's just doing his duty. Just trying to protect Ian from more sanctioned violence.

He won't be trying to kill me.

I hope.

My wrists hurt where the rope digs into my skin. My heart pounds, and the air feels too thick to breathe as Rowan says, "Bare her back."

Ian presses close to me and slides his dagger down the back of my tunic, rending the fabric until it hangs from each shoulder like a pair of tattered wings.

"She's wearing armor." Rowan sounds surprised.

"We took some from a band of highwaymen on our way to

Lankenshire," Ian says. The casual way he uses "we," like we're still on the same team, still allies, makes something inside of me ache.

We faced down the highwaymen just after the bruises from Ian's poison showed up on Sylph and the others who'd been injected. The night we defeated the highwaymen, we celebrated our tiny victory, only to quickly lose heart as those with purple bruises on their bodies started dying while we were helpless to stop it.

Gaining the armor was the beginning of losing my best friend, and I can't bear to hear Ian talk about it like it was nothing. Just one more event in a long line of things that somehow ended up with me tied to a whipping post in Rowansmark when I should be searching the city for the army headquarters, for the tech labs, for the weapons stash before Logan arrives, and it's too late.

"Get it off of her." Rowan nods to Ian.

"No," I say as Ian begins unknotting the rope around my wrists.

Rowan's expression is so full of condescending patience, I want to wipe it off his face with the bottom of my boot. "You cannot be cleansed by pain atonement unless we remove the armor."

Ian finishes untying me and pulls me away from the post. I grab the front of my tunic to keep it in place.

"You sentenced me to fifteen lashes. Not to be stripped by one of your trackers. Turn your backs. I'll remove it myself."

Rowan raises a brow and gives me a look that almost feels approving and says, "As you wish. If you try to escape or to hurt one of us while our backs are turned, Ian and Samuel have my permission to whip you until you are dead. Do you understand?"

"Perfectly."

I wait until they turn their backs and then let my ruined tunic fall to the ground while I wrestle with the armor. My fingers are still clumsy from lack of circulation. It's hard to grip the thin metal, but I force myself to grab hold of the bottom hem and then lift while I twist my body like a snake shedding its skin. The armor peels away from me, leaving only the silky undertunic that Logan found for me in the hospital at Lankenshire. The fabric whispers against my skin as I pull it over my head as well. I can't feel the satiny smoothness of the undertunic without remembering the way Logan's breath caught in his chest or the way my heart thundered in my ears as he stood so close behind me. I wonder if I'll still have the power to make Logan forget how to breathe once he sees the scars Samuel is about to give me.

I snatch my outer tunic even as I let the undertunic and the armor fall. The air that seconds ago felt too warm now sends chills over my exposed skin. I feel vulnerable—cracked wide open in front of my enemies—and I have to blink rapidly to stem the sudden tears that sting my eyes as I pull my tunic over my chest and face the post again.

"Secure her wrists," Rowan says, and Ian springs into action. In seconds, I'm once more trussed up, my cheek pressed against the scratchy wooden post while I stand on my tiptoes to ease the bite of the rope on my wrists. Once Ian steps back, Rowan says, "Rachel Adams, in accordance with the laws of Rowansmark, I declare you a thief and an insurgent who needs to learn how to respect authority. The penalty for your actions is fifteen lashes with the whip and a stay in my personal dungeon until Logan McEntire returns the controller and faces the consequences for his actions as well. Do you have anything to say for yourself?"

What could I possibly say that would convince him that none of this would've happened if Marcus McEntire hadn't been afraid to come to his leader for help when his newborn son was kidnapped by the Commander? That using Ian against his own father has poisoned him from the inside out? That no one man—not James Rowan, not the Commander—should have unlimited power over others, because too much power softens the goodness inside him until it turns to rot?

If I could go back to the moment when I first held the controller in my hands, I would change most of my choices. I would find a way to handle Melkin's desperation without killing him. I wouldn't insist that Logan and I try to use the device against the Commander, thereby giving Ian an opportunity to send the Cursed One into Baalboden. I would ask for advice. Listen carefully. And trust that I'm not the only one who knows what has to be done.

But I wouldn't bring the controller back to Rowansmark. I wouldn't give the man standing before me the exclusive use of tech that can turn the beasts into weapons. And I'm not going to lie and say that I would.

My voice is low and clear as I say, "I have nothing more to say to you."

He manages to appear both crestfallen and self-satisfied.

Looking beyond me, he says, "Begin her sentence."

I stare at the pecan trees that rim the garden, focusing on the way the dying sun paints their twisted branches with splashes of orange and gold. Drawing in a deep breath of humid air, I brace myself, but I can't control the terrible sound I make when the whip slashes across my back, trailing a stream of blistering pain in its wake.

One.

The whip cracks again, a sharp snap of sound that almost drowns out my scream.

Two.

I barely get another breath in before the leather tip eats into my skin again.

Three.

Pain spreads across my back in hot, wet spikes.

Four.

My face grinds against the wooden post as I writhe against the restraints that hold me there.

Five.

I scream, and my throat feels like it's bleeding. The pain is unrelenting. The whip falls, and another bright stream of agony sears me.

Six.

The whip leaves, and still the pain throbs, burrowing in, sinking toward my bones until I can't tell where my wounds end and the rest of me begins.

Seven.

I choke on my scream and it becomes a sob. I can't take this. I can't. I dig my toes into the dirt and strain against the ropes, but there's nowhere to go where the whip can't find me.

Eight.

My body shudders. My teeth chatter, and a low moaning cry keeps trying to strangle me as I struggle for air. I want to beg for mercy. But there's no mercy here. Not for me. Not for anyone.

Nine.

The pain shoots down my legs and my knees give out. I sag against the post, the rope cutting into my wrists, and stare at the pecan trees through a film of tears. Blood runs warm and wet down my back, over my legs, and drips onto the ground beneath me.

Ten.

I close my eyes and try desperately to ignore the way my back burns like it's on fire. I can do this. I *can*. A sob tears through me as I dig my fingernails into the post above me and slowly get back to my feet.

I'm not going to break. Not like this.

Eleven.

I suck in another breath and hold it, pressing my lungs against my chest in a futile effort to stop the bite of the whip from wrenching a scream from my lips. My legs give out again, and I lean against the post, using it for leverage as I slowly push myself upright once more.

Twelve.

This time, I can't push myself back up. I can't seem to make my legs obey me. My fingernails dig in, but it's no use. I dangle from the rope and lay my forehead against the post. Three more. That's all I have to endure. Three more, and this will be over.

Thirteen.

"Ask for mercy." Rowan squats in the dirt beside me and brushes my hair out of my eyes. "Show me you've learned your lesson, ask me for mercy, and it will be granted."

My breath sobs in and out of my lungs, and I can't seem to bring him into focus. I blink hard and try again. He kneels, his head outlined in a fiery nimbus from the setting sun, his dark eyes full of a concern that's almost fatherly.

I laugh, but it comes out a choked cough instead, and pain shivers down my body as if every inch of me has been flayed.

Who is this man to offer mercy to me when he wouldn't offer it to Marcus McEntire, who only wanted to rescue his son? When he wouldn't give it to Ian, the boy with dreams, and instead turned Ian into a cold, cruel shell of himself?

"Rachel, you've had enough. Ask for mercy," Rowan says.

I meet his eyes, lick my lips with a tongue as dry as sandpaper, and say, "You first."

Scorn mingles with the false disappointment on his face, and he stares into my eyes as he says, "Finish it."

Fourteen.

I bite back the scream and watch his face. Looking for weakness. For flaws. For the foothold I'll need to figure out how to destroy him. Just the way Dad taught me. And I promise myself that I'll survive this. I'll get out of James Rowan's dungeon, I'll turn his city upside down hunting for the tech that threatens Logan, and then I'll come back for the man who thought he could break others in his pursuit of power without any of them ever striking back.

Fifteen.

My body sags limply against the post, rope biting through

my skin, and I moan as tears pour down my face. Samuel cuts me loose and carefully lifts me over his shoulder, my bleeding back open to the air, and then he carries me toward the dungeon, leaving Ian and Rowan behind in the garden.

CHAPTER THIRTY-THREE

<u>RACHEL</u>

The dungeon is a long, narrow room on the bottom level of James Rowan's mansion. A single window is set in the far wall, allowing the muted shadows of dusk to seep into the room and color it gray. Wooden slats like the boards on sheep crates divide one side of the room into six cells. A thick length of iron chain coils around a hook beside each doorway, waiting to bolster the flimsy doors once someone is inside the cell. As far as dungeons go, it isn't very secure. A healthy person at full strength could probably kick her way through one of the walls in a matter of minutes.

But healthy people aren't imprisoned here. Why would they be? Rowansmark law states that anyone surviving a pain atonement sentence is then free to go with honor restored.

Anyone except the girl James Rowan still needs as a bargaining chip.

Samuel carries me past the first four cells and enters the fifth. The door to the sixth cell is closed, its chain looped through a hole above the doorknob and locked down tight.

I guess James Rowan needs someone else as a bargaining chip, too.

"Who's there?" I wave weakly at the room beside us and instantly regret it as pain flares along my shoulder blades and throbs viciously.

"I don't know," Samuel says as he gently sets me on a narrow bunk that is attached to the far wall. The mattress is thin but clean, and a thick blanket rests at the foot of the bed.

"James Rowan might whip his people half to death, but never let it be said that he makes his prisoners go cold." My voice cracks, and I hiss in a breath as I try to straighten my back. It's impossible to find a comfortable sitting position.

Samuel puts a hand on my arm to stop my movements. "Wait until I get your wounds cleaned up."

I stare at him. "You're going to clean the wounds *you* inflicted?"

"Would you rather it have been Ian?" He turns away without waiting for an answer and leaves my cell for a moment. I take the opportunity to look around me. The room is small, almost half the size of Oliver's tent in Lower Market, and mostly bare. Beside the bed I'm sitting on, there's a wooden bucket in the corner for me to relieve myself in and a pair of iron rings embedded into the wall behind the bed. Since the wall behind me is part of the original room and is therefore the only side of the cell not made from flimsy wooden slats, I'm guessing those rings are used to secure the chains of unruly prisoners.

I wouldn't be surprised to see Samuel return with a pair of chains for me, but instead he steps back into the cell with a piece of fabric and a small metal box in his hands.

"Can you lie on your stomach?" he asks.

I slowly lower myself to the bunk, pressing my lips together to keep from crying out as my every movement reopens the slashes across my back, sending burning pain cascading down my nerves until tears clog my throat. Samuel's hands are careful but firm as he cleans the wounds, covers them with a salve that instantly takes away half of the pain, and then puts bandages into place.

"You need to move every few hours, even though it hurts," he says. "Make yourself get up and walk. It will feel like the worst thing you've ever done to yourself, but it will help you heal much faster."

I scrub my palms over my face, erasing the last of my tears, and slowly sit up. The salve helps, but it still feels like my back is coated in fire whenever I move. Once I'm sitting, clutching my ruined tunic to me, I meet Samuel's eyes. His expression is calm and distant, as if he hadn't just whipped me and then gently tended my wounds.

"Why are you helping me?" This time, I'm not asking because I'm hoping he'll become my ally. I'm asking because I can't understand a man like Samuel obeying James Rowan without question.

Or maybe taking care of my wounds was Samuel's small way of rebelling against his leader. Of keeping his own humanity intact.

If so, I wish he'd found a way to rebel when it really counted—before Ian burned down my city and started killing off my friends.

Samuel sets the first aid box down and picks up the piece of fabric. He unfolds it, and I see that it's a tunic sewn from rough, unbleached cotton. He offers it to me, and turns his back in an unspoken acknowledgment that even though it will hurt to pull a new tunic over my head, I absolutely refuse to allow him to help me get dressed.

"I'm done," I say, and he turns back to face me, his expression as impassive as ever. "Are you going to tell me why you're helping me?"

"It's over now. You've faced your punishment. You survived. There's no need to prolong the pain." A muscle in his jaw flexes. "If you were my daughter, I'd want someone to take care of you." He crouches and picks up my ruined tunic and then meets my eyes. "It's *over*, Rachel. Wait it out. Move often enough to heal well. And once the controller is returned, you'll be free to leave."

"You really believe that." I don't know whether to laugh at his blind faith in his leader or cry for a man who has goodness in him but fails to stand up for others when it really matters.

The creases at the corners of his eyes tighten. "I believe it because it's true."

He moves as if to stand, and I lean forward, gasping when pain shoots across my back, and grab his hand. He stares at my hand, white and smudged with blood against his dark skin, and I say, "It's not true, Samuel. I'm dead, and you helped kill me. Just like you helped kill thousands of people in my city. Just like you helped poison my best friend and slit the throats of children and light white phosphorous fires that killed or disfigured inno-cent—"

"Stop." He pulls his hand away from mine and stands.

"On the first night of our trip from Lankenshire, I went to

sleep beside you at the campfire once Heidi took over the watch. How then did I end up in the wagon with a bruise on my face?" I ask.

"You decided to sleep in the wagon." He takes a step toward the door.

"And I just happened to punch myself in the face first?"

He stops.

"I got up and sneaked away from camp while you were sleeping—"

"Heidi had the watch. She'd never allow you to get more than five steps."

"Heidi and Ian were busy talking on our first night of camp. She left her post so that they could talk without being overheard. Since part of their conversation included how fast they could get away with killing me once your back was turned, I'm pretty sure the person they were trying to keep their conversation from was you."

He frowns. "And you just happened to overhear them?"

"Of course not. I told you, I sneaked away from camp. I had every intention of trying to escape through the Wasteland, but I figured anything Ian and Heidi didn't want you to overhear was important enough to risk getting close enough to listen. Ian caught me and punched me in the face, but not before I was able to eavesdrop for a few minutes."

"You could be lying." He watches me carefully.

"I could, but what would be the point?"

"Because you think you can somehow convince me to help you escape before James is ready to let you go."

I shake my head. "Don't you get it? *No one* is letting me go.

Ian was convinced that James had given him permission to kill me once I was no longer needed as bait. Heidi agreed with him. They also discussed the fact that Ian and his father had recently finished inventing tech that could wipe out Logan and anyone with him before Logan ever has a chance to set foot inside Rowansmark and return the controller."

Samuel's eyes narrow, but he says nothing.

I lean forward, ignoring the way the movement pulls at the scabs forming across my back. "You're an honorable man, Samuel. I don't know how you convinced yourself it was okay to stand by while Ian hurt so many people, but you did. It hurt you to see Ian break. It hurt you to see the cost of something that started nineteen years ago when James Rowan and the Commander got in a contest to see which of them could be the most powerful man in the land."

"You don't know anything about how I feel." He's working hard to wear his distant, cold expression again, but there are cracks of doubt at the edges now.

"I know you're more than a man who simply does his duty. You have a conscience. If you didn't, Ian and Heidi wouldn't have had to hide from you the fact that I was dead as soon as they captured me. You wouldn't have protected me to keep Ian from destroying more of himself. You wouldn't have taken the whip tonight to spare both Ian and me and then treated my wounds."

He doesn't say anything, but the doubts are growing in his eyes.

"You try hard to be a man of honor. Tell me, where is the honor in keeping me alive as bait and then killing me? In promising Logan that if he returns the controller, I'll be returned to him alive, only to already have a plan in place that will kill him before he can make right something he didn't start in the first place? Examine the facts, Samuel, and then look me in the eye and explain to me how any of that is honorable."

"Why keep you as bait if he already has tech that can destroy Logan?" Samuel asks, his tone impatient.

"You tell me. You know your leader. Is he the kind of man who likes to have contingency plans in case something goes wrong?"

His lips sink into a thin, hard line, and he turns on his heel and leaves the cell, closing the door and fastening the chain behind him. I listen to his footsteps stalk across the dungeon floor and then pound the stairs that lead back up to the main level of the mansion.

Maybe he'll think about what I said. Maybe he'll start asking the right questions. And maybe the next time it matters, he'll choose doing the right thing over doing his duty.

Or maybe he won't, and it's going to be just Quinn and me against the entire might of Rowansmark as we fight to disable the tech before Logan arrives.

Of course, for it to be Quinn and me against Rowansmark, I have to get out of this cell.

I sit on the edge of the bunk, my hands gripping my knees, while I concentrate on breathing past the pain in my back. Even with Samuel's first aid, the pain is a constant, vicious ache that spreads from the top of my scalp to the backs of my knees. I can't escape this dungeon if I can't even bear to draw a full breath. And staying locked up at the questionable mercy of

James Rowan isn't part of the plan.

I have to get up. I have to move. I have to be ready to fight when I get the chance.

The sound of Samuel's footsteps is long gone when I finally convince myself to get off the bunk. I whimper as I slowly clamber to my feet, bent at the waist because straightening my back feels impossible. Carefully, I take a step forward and suck in a breath as the flayed muscles along my spine send hot spikes of pain throughout my body. I set my jaw, take another step, and nearly stumble when my legs start shaking.

Nausea roils through me, and I gag, but that only makes the pain worse. I take another shuffling step and grasp blindly for the wall beside the bunk as my knees give out. My fingernails scrape along the flimsy, wooden-crate wall that separates me from the locked cell beside mine, but I can't keep myself on my feet. I scream as my knees hit the stone floor, sending another wave of agony through me, and then rest my forehead on the ground and try hard not to cry.

"I can do this," I whisper. I don't sound convincing, even to myself. Sobs gather at the back of my throat, but I swallow hard. "It's just pain. I can do this."

In the cell beside mine, a man's hoarse voice mumbles, "Absorption. Absorptivity. Which element? Neutral solution. Need a neutral solution. Neutral!"

Slowly, I stretch my body forward and start to crawl. The back-and-forth motion of my hips as I move my legs feels like someone is sawing away at my spine with a piece of metal, but I move nearly a yard before the pain forces me to stop.

Easing my face to the floor again, I let the stone cool my

flushed cheeks and tell the contents of my stomach to stay put.

"Not a neutral solution. Not that element. What is the heat capacity?" The man's mumbles become incoherent ramblings, and I suck in a breath of air, determined not to vomit from the pain.

"I can do this." I sound better this time. Like I believe it. "I'm Jared Adams's daughter, and pain isn't going to stop me. Nothing can stop me. I can do this."

The man's mumbling halts abruptly. Something scratches the wall beside me, and I turn my face toward it as the voice says, "Jared Adams's daughter is Rachel. Rachel. Rachel knows Logan . . . Logan . . . *Logan.*" The voice rises, trembling, as if latching on to Logan's name with all its strength, and suddenly a bright-blue eye blinks at me through a crack between one slat of wood and the next.

I jerk away from the wall and gasp as the quick movement sears my back.

"Don't go. *Don't.* Rachel Adams?"

I stare at the blue eye, and it blinks rapidly, and then the man shifts, giving me a quick glimpse of a scarred face, before he brings his other eye to the slat. This eye is covered in white film and the skin around it puckers and swells, part of a long scar that stretches beyond the piece of him that I can see.

"Doesn't work. Doesn't. Can't see you. Logan? Please, my son? *Please.*"

My breath comes in hard pants as ice slides through me, leaving a clammy chill on my skin as I slowly inch my way closer to the crack in the wall. Time feels sluggish, even though the thoughts in my head are spinning like a kaleidoscope of images that refuse to make sense.

The film-covered eye disappears, and the blue eye returns.

"My son? Rachel, Jared's daughter, my son?"

"Your son?" I whisper the words, and he jerks as if surprised to hear me speak to him.

"They took him. Jared promised he's good. He's fine. They took him away." His voice climbs again. "They took my sons. My *sons*. Please."

"Do you mean . . . Logan and Ian?" My tongue feels clumsy as I form the words. As I try to wrap my mind around what I'm seeing.

"Ian." His voice breaks, full of the kind of terrible grief that I once shoved into the silence within me because I was sure it would shatter me if I let myself feel it. "Gone. Everyone gone."

My skin feels cold and my fingers shake as I ask, "Are you Marcus McEntire?"

"Was. Now I'm . . ." The eye blinks once and looks away from me as if searching for the answer. For a way to sum up the person he's become since losing all of his loved ones. Since having his leader force his remaining son to whip him to the point of death. I know that feeling. That awful darkness that presses against your skin from the inside out and whispers that you have nothing left to live for and only yourself to blame.

"You're still Marcus," I say gently. "And you haven't lost everyone. They're alive. Your sons are alive."

Though one of them deserves to die.

He looks at me, his gaze feverish with desperate hope. "You know my sons? Know Ian? Know him?"

I swallow hard and keep my voice even. "I do."

He makes a choked sound, and then says, "Good boy. Good son. James will punish for what I did. *I* did. Ian? My son is good?"

I stare at him, and realize that all he knows of Ian is the boy with dreams. The boy who just wanted his mother to notice him and his father to be proud of him. He doesn't know that the moment Ian was forced to take a whip against his father, he started on a long, slippery slope that ended with murder and madness.

I can't tell him. I can't rip away the hope he's clinging to. I close my eyes and think of Logan. Of the way he takes the time to listen to others because what they have to say matters to him. The way he refuses to let anything but his own integrity define him. The way he fights for those who can't fight for themselves, even if they aren't ready to thank him for it.

Holding Logan in my mind, I open my eyes, look at Marcus, and say, "Yes, your son is okay. He's a good man. You can be proud of him."

He pulls back from the wall, and I see what looks like a smile on his ruined face before he disappears into the depths of his cell, humming a strange, broken melody and whispering Ian's name to himself.

Marcus McEntire is alive. One more thing James Rowan lied to Samuel about. Lied to Ian about. I wonder what either of them would do to their precious leader if I could figure out a way to show them the truth.

CHAPTER THIRTY-FOUR

LOGAN

Willow drops from the tree behind me on our second day of travel from the highwaymen's camp to Chelmingford and takes her lunch portion from Jodi's outstretched hands. "We're being followed."

I freeze in the act of taking another bite. "Highwaymen?"

"Trackers. Four of them. My guess is this is the group that followed us out of Lankenshire. We have maybe forty minutes before they arrive."

I force myself away from the fear that if the trackers are after us, they might have caught up to the rest of our group while we were at the highwaymen's camp.

"Maybe we can reach the ferry to take us out to Chelmingford before they catch up to us." I get to my feet and start packing up the tech I was working on. "Let's go."

The Commander shakes his head and reaches for the device. "We're too far away. I'll call the beasts and burn the trackers."

My chest tightens at the way he casually suggests using the

tanniyn as a weapon once again. More confirmation that neither the Commander nor James Rowan can be trusted with that sort of power. "You'd burn the rest of the Wasteland too while you're at it," I say.

"We'll set a trap." Willow is already scanning the small clearing we're in. It's maybe ten yards wide and surrounded on all sides by enormous oaks and pines. It's not big enough to stage a battle, and the trackers could approach us from any direction.

"A trap?" The Commander is scornful. "You don't trap Rowansmark trackers, girl."

"Maybe you don't. But *I* do." She cranes her neck to look at the branches that straddle the sky above us. "We've got everything we need. It'll be simple. I've done this so often, I could do it in my sleep. Now, who wants to be bait?"

Thirty minutes later, Nola, Jodi, and I are sitting against a large oak tree, facing west, when we hear the soft slide of a boot against the ground. We've collected berries and nuts in our laps as if we're doing nothing more than having lunch, but we haven't managed a bite in at least fifteen minutes. The tension of waiting for the trackers to arrive makes it impossible to eat. Willow is in a tree nearby, holding herself so motionless, I haven't heard a sound since she settled in. The Commander is hidden in a thicket several yards to the north of us, his sword out in case he needs to come to our assistance.

I think it's just as likely he'd leave us to the trackers. He has the device. He believes that Connor knows how to disengage the Rowansmark beacons at Chelmingford, a fact he's reminded me of twice in as many days. I think the only reason he hasn't tried to either kill me or leave me behind is that he doesn't know for sure if Connor and the rest of our group made it to Chelmingford. It would be shortsighted of him to betray me when he might still need me, and the Commander is nothing if not focused on doing whatever he must to achieve his own goals.

Another slight sound drifts toward us from the west. Beside me, Jodi stiffens and stares into the trees.

"Eat," I say softly, and put a berry into my mouth even though the fear racing through me leaves a stain of bitterness across my tongue that renders the sweet fruit tasteless.

Jodi blindly selects a nut and shoves it into her mouth, never taking her eyes from the western Wasteland.

"Do you want more berries?" Nola asks, tilting her head so that her curtain of curly dark hair masks her face as she does her part to make it look like this is a normal meal break. Her golden skin seems pale, and there are circles under her eyes, but she's holding herself together during the day. At night, I hear her crying, grieving the loss of her father. Jodi is always quick to go to her and offer comfort. Willow and I have left them to deal with that while we take turns standing guard. We don't talk about it, but neither one of us is willing to let the Commander out of our sight. Especially at night.

A whisper of sound seems to come from directly to our left. Jodi jerks her shoulders back and aims an expression of terrified defiance at the trees.

The cold prick of a knife blade bites into my neck and a voice behind me says, "Found you."

Nola jumps, spilling berries across the ground, while Jodi leaps to her feet and scurries away from me and toward the center of the clearing.

I slowly turn my head, careful not to scrape my skin against the knife, and come face-to-face with a Rowansmark tracker. Her brown hair is short, her eyes are keen, and her expression is ruthless as two more trackers step out of the trees on either side of her.

Three trackers surrounding me. That leaves a fourth in the wind.

"Did you really think you were going to get away from us?" the female tracker asks while the two who flank her draw their swords.

I swallow audibly, and tug on the neckline of my tunic as if I'm nervous.

Which I am.

Because if this plan doesn't work, I'm about to die.

"You've really screwed things up for yourself, you know that?" she asks, her knife held expertly in her left hand while she draws her sword with her right.

"How so?" I ask as Nola crawls away from me toward Jodi, who hovers in the middle of the clearing like a little bird too frightened to flee.

The female tracker shakes her head, her eyes never leaving mine. "You had one chance to give up the controller without losing the people you love. One chance, and you blew it."

"I can't help that the Commander broke me out of prison," I say. My voice sounds hoarse, and I clear my throat while to my left, a shadow moves in the trees. The other tracker? The Commander?

"I'm sure that would be true if it wasn't obvious that you aren't a prisoner now." The tracker levels her sword at me. Beside her, the other two do the same.

This time I swallow because my throat has gone completely dry.

"Besides, that's not what I meant. You care about that red-headed girl. That's why Ian took her. And you had one chance to ransom her life. But you didn't take it." She cocks her head as if studying me. "Guess you didn't care as much as Ian said you did."

I can't tell her how much I care about Rachel, so I settle for glaring at her instead.

She laughs. "I see I've struck a nerve. How strange that you care enough to be upset about the fact that she's dead by now, but you didn't care enough to go to Rowansmark when—"

"What do you mean she's dead now?" I scramble to my feet, ignoring the sword aimed at my chest.

"You went north. It was obvious you had no intention of going south, either because the Commander wouldn't let you, or because you chose not to make the trade." She shrugs, though her eyes are locked on mine with uncomfortable intensity. "Either way, we sent a messenger to James Rowan telling him you'd made the wrong choice. If he didn't get the message already, he will in a day or two, and then your girl will be of no more use to him."

Rachel.

The image of her bleeding to death at Ian's feet fills my head, and my knees won't hold me. I sink slowly to the earth, groping blindly for something to ground me to reality again, but the only reality left to me is that I didn't count on the surviving trackers in Lankenshire sending a message to James Rowan that I wasn't interested in trading the device for Rachel's life. I didn't count on her usefulness to him ending before I even had an army ready to march to her rescue.

I didn't count on failing.

There's a distant roaring in my ears, and a desperate need to do something to fix this, even though it's too late. I'm weeks away from Rowansmark, and it's *too late*.

Everything I've lost—Oliver, my mother, and now Rachel—wells up within me and hardens into a blaze of fury so absolute, I don't hesitate. Grabbing my sword, I charge the tracker.

"Logan!" Nola screams, but I'm not listening. I can't listen. All I can do is hack and slash and fight until somehow I vanquish the awful pit of loss that wants to ruin me.

The trackers converge, swords swinging, and then the soft *thwang* of an arrow disturbs the air, and the female tracker stiffens and falls.

"Get away from her!" Jodi yells as the anatomical trigger in the tracker's body starts beeping, but I don't care.

Ducking under the sword arm of the tracker on my right, I snatch his cloak and pivot to put him between me and the explosion. He attacks with cold efficiency, but I punch and pummel my way into him because he's part of what killed Rachel. He's part of it, and I have to destroy it. All of it. Before it destroys me.

The female tracker explodes, but I barely feel the bits of bone and blood that hit me. The third tracker grabs me from behind, locking his arm under my throat. I slam my head against his face, drive my heels into his shins, and raise my sword to pound the hilt against his head. The tracker in front of me lunges forward, sword raised, and another arrow buries itself in his chest.

I don't even bother trying to get out of the way of the explosion. Let it come. Let it cover me in the blood I should have shed weeks ago to find her. To save her.

"Let him go." Nola hurtles into the tracker holding me, and he grunts in pain. His grip slackens, and I twist away from him. I raise my sword to swing at him, but he's clutching the dagger Nola drove into his neck. I reach up and yank it out. Blood gushes, and I hand the dagger back to Nola and walk away.

One more tracker. I scan the clearing, and he steps out of the trees closest to where Jodi still stands, doing her part to be exactly where Willow asked her to be. He's a tall, lean man with squinty eyes that assess me without any discernible emotion. He has a wicked-looking machete in one hand and a curved knife in the other.

"Where is it?" he asks.

I let my eyes glance off Jodi and then back to the tracker as if I'm hoping he didn't notice the direction of my gaze. "We don't have it."

He pivots toward Jodi and raises his weapons. Jodi lunges to the right, takes two running steps, and grabs a low-hanging branch even as Willow springs from the tree behind the tracker and tackles him. He hits the ground and instantly grapples for a hold on her, but Willow isn't interested in fighting him. She digs her fingers into the pressure point behind his ear, and in seconds, he goes limp.

"Kill him," I snap as I stalk across the clearing. "Better yet, get out of the way and let me do it myself."

"No." Willow ignores me in favor of whipping the tracker's hands behind his back and trussing him up like a pig—hands and ankles both tied with the same rope.

"What do you mean, 'no'?" I crouch beside her, my sword still out. "You heard what they said. If you aren't going to kill him, I will."

"No, you won't." Willow gives me a sharp look. "Don't you want to see if what they told you is true? See just how much time we really have?"

"The female tracker said—"

"She could've lied." Willow tests the ropes and, satisfied that she's taken every inch of the tracker's mobility, shoves him onto his back and smacks his face. "Wake up!"

"What's to stop this tracker from lying too?" I ask, my voice hard because I can't allow the hope to seep into me. I can't let myself start to believe that I haven't lost Rachel only to realize all over again that she's gone.

"I'm very good at getting people to tell me the truth." Willow sounds haunted even as she calmly asks Nola for her dagger. I remember the way she looked when she said her first kill had been at age eight—her test to see if she was ready to take part in the family business—and the way her eyes went cold when she talked of her father, and I put my hand on her arm.

"Willow, you don't have to do this."

"You need the truth." She slaps the tracker again, and he stirs. Her voice is drained of all emotion.

"I don't want you to do this."

She turns on me. "Look at yourself. Covered in blood.

Destroying our plan because you couldn't see anything but the fact that a tracker told you Rachel is dead. You aren't thinking clearly, and you won't start to unless we know the truth. I can get the truth."

"So can I," the Commander says behind us. "And it won't take me half as long."

Willow moves aside without argument, her face as stoic as her brother's.

"Why would you care if a messenger told James Rowan I wasn't coming?" I ask as the tracker's eyes flutter open and awareness snaps back into his gaze.

"Because that messenger would also tell him about my army, and about my trip north, which could only mean that I'm trying to gather more troops. The more we know before we go into battle, the fewer risks we unknowingly take." He crouches beside the tracker, draws a knife, and says, "I think we'll start with the hands."

I reach for the stub of my little finger, for the pain that grows less each day, and wince as the Commander chops off two of the tracker's fingers in one blow. The man screams, and the Commander smiles grimly.

"You know who I am, don't you?" he asks.

The tracker pants heavily.

"Answer me, or lose the entire hand."

"Yes."

"Good." The Commander flays a piece of skin from the tracker's cheek. Blood puddles on the ground, and the man goes white, his lips drawn tight against the pain. "Every time I have to ask a question twice, you'll lose another piece of yourself. Understood?"

The tracker nods.

"Did a messenger leave from Lankenshire to tell James Rowan that Logan McEntire and I went to the northern city-states?"

The tracker glares, but quickly nods as the Commander's knife hovers above his neck.

"When do you expect that messenger to arrive at Rowansmark?"

"How should I know?" the tracker asks, his voice shaky.

The Commander slices through the tendon on the man's elbow. Nola gags and disappears into the trees. Jodi drops down from her perch and joins her as the man curses and moans.

"Once more: When do you expect the messenger to arrive?"

"I don't know." The man's eyes widen as the Commander reaches for his stomach. "Wait! Ian took the boat before our messenger arrived so he had to walk. He probably won't arrive for another week, though if he hurried, he could cut that down by a couple of days."

The vise wrapped around my chest eases, and I take a deep, steadying breath. I still have time. I'm weeks away by land, but if Ian took a boat to Rowansmark, I can too. Chelmingford is on an island. I can convince Tara Lanning, the leader of the city, to give us a boat. I can push my people to move faster. Sleep less.

I can still get to her. I can save her.

As the Commander drives his blade into the tracker to end the man's suffering, I grab some leaves, scrub the blood off me as best as I can, and mount my horse.

"We aren't stopping again until we're on a boat heading toward Rowansmark," I say.

No one argues with me as I spur my mount forward and set a course for Chelmingford as fast as my horse can travel.

CHAPTER THIRTY-FIVE

LOGAN

The rest of our group is waiting for us at the little wooden dock that usually houses the Chelmingford ferry. I'm relieved to see that Frankie, Connor, Smithson, and Adam made it safely. Less relieved to see that Orion made it as well, but he's the least of my concerns. The ferry isn't here, but a small boat with the name *Myra* painted in bold blue letters on the side is tied to the dock. The captain agrees to ferry us to the city once he realizes we're the group Lyle Hoden's emissary told Chelmingford to expect.

The *Myra*'s engine is powered by steam. On a normal day, I'd be fascinated by the way the engine propels the boat through the water like a knife slicing through butter.

Instead, I'm preoccupied with wondering what tech Rowansmark is using against Chelmingford, since the *tanniyn* won't surface underwater. Wondering what Tara Lanning is like and if she'll agree to help us.

Wondering how far away I am from Rachel now, and how

fast I can get to Rowansmark so I can keep my promise.

I lean against the bow with Connor on one side of me and Frankie on the other, my hands gripping the rough, splintery railing beneath me, and watch the blue-gray water lurch away from the boat's nose as I think of Rachel and how desperately grateful I am to know that I still have a chance to see her again. Of the way something burned in my stomach, like I swallowed a live coal, when I'd watch her spar. How I didn't know where to look when she'd catch me watching. Remembering the way her body flowed from one movement to the next makes me feel like the live coal in my stomach is slowly melting into my bloodstream.

I close my eyes and imagine that the railing beneath my hands is Rachel's hair instead. Hair that shimmers like a flame and suits the intensity with which she lives her life. The intensity in her eyes when she looks at me. The intensity in her kisses— like I'm a challenge she enjoys trying to conquer.

Thinking about kissing Rachel is doing nothing to stop the heat that is spreading through me. It pools in my stomach, spirals through my chest, and burns against my cheeks while I try not to remember the way her breath catches in between kisses. The way her fingers dig into my shoulders. The way she presses against me like she can't stand to have a single sliver of air between us.

Frankie slaps a hand on my shoulder, and my eyes fly open.

"Feeling okay?" he asks, his thick brows furrowed.

"I'm fine."

"If you're going to puke, aim it over the rail. I ain't cleaning that up."

"I said I'm fine."

"You sure?" He studies me. "You look flushed, and you're out of breath all of a sudden."

"I feel fine. Really. I was just thinking. About Rachel. I mean, not *just* about Rachel. About a lot of things. A lot of . . . things." I make myself stop talking before more inane nonsense can pour out of my mouth and ignore the knowing gleam in Frankie's eyes.

"About how kissing Rachel is eminently preferable to working through mathematical equations?" Connor asks, a sly smile on his face.

I'm silent a beat too long, and Frankie laughs, a great belly laugh that I haven't heard from him since the day Thom died. Connor joins him. It's nice to hear Frankie sound like he did before the people he cared about started dying, so I shrug off my embarrassment and smile for his sake.

"Chelmingford on the horizon!" the boat's captain calls out.

I turn back to the railing and see a silver mountain that seems to rise up out of the water ahead of us. As we get closer, the mountain becomes a collection of tall, narrow buildings in silvery stone with steeply slanted roofs resting on thick, algae-covered stilts. A collection of narrow bridges in the same stone connects one building to another.

"I thought Chelmingford was an island," Frankie says, the humor completely drained from his voice.

"It used to be." Connor shades his eyes with his hand. "But then a dam north of here from the previous civilization broke and the land Chelming built on was completely submerged." He gestures toward one of the thick stone stilts as we sail past it.

"Thankfully, he built his city on stilts because he figured the higher off the ground they were, the less chance they'd be visited by the *tanniyn*."

"The Commander said that the *tanniyn* don't surface underwater," I say as the boat slows.

"Well, I suppose Aaron didn't figure that out until later. At any rate, his city was on stilts, so when the dam broke, most of the buildings remained intact."

"Most of them?" I look around the city and find children sitting on the bridges, their legs dangling over the water while they stare at us.

"The dam broke to the north of them, and the power of the water swept away some of their northern buildings. That's how Aaron died and left his daughter in charge."

"This isn't natural." Frankie sounds shaken.

"Well, it's not unheard of for a child to succeed her father in the leading of a—"

"I don't care about who leads what. I'm talking about *those*." Frankie points to the bridges above us. "One misstep and we'll fall to our deaths."

I squeeze his shoulder as the image of Thom facing down the Carrington army on an old, rickety bridge seconds before he triggered the explosion that killed him fills my mind.

"You can stay here if you'd like," I say quietly while the boat approaches a wide ramp that disappears into the water. Thick metal rings are attached to the ramp every few yards. A woman stands on the ramp, her legs braced.

"I'm not staying anywhere unless it's by your side." Frankie jerks his head toward the Commander, who is stalking toward the bow, his eyes on the woman. "Not with that one still breathing."

"Toss me your rope," the woman calls out in a husky, smoky voice that makes the heat still lingering in the pit of my stomach burn a little warmer. Her dark hair is coiled around her head like a thick, braided crown, and her warm brown skin glows in the sunlight. Laugh lines bracket her eyes, and her full lips look like they're used to smiling. She catches the rope Frankie tosses to her with a lithe strength that suddenly makes her petite, curvy frame seem incredibly intriguing.

Connor makes a small noise at the back of his throat, and I punch him in the arm. "Stop staring," I say.

"You first."

I *am* staring. I blink and look at Frankie instead. He isn't nearly as interesting, but at least this way I don't feel like I'm being disloyal to Rachel for finding another woman beautiful.

Especially a woman old enough to be my mother.

Now *that* is an uncomfortable thought.

"Requesting permission to enter your city," the Commander says in a tone of voice that makes it clear he doesn't feel he should have to ask permission for anything.

"Of course, Jason," the woman says, and I catch a hint of power—not the turn-a-boy's-stomach-warm kind, but the I'm-in-charge-and-don't-you-forget-it kind—in her voice. Another woman joins her and lowers a ladder for us to use in climbing up to the ramp.

"We'll need a meeting," the Commander says, and then climbs the ladder first.

The woman watches him, her eyes narrow, and then slowly

examines the rest of us while the Commander steps past her and onto the ramp. When her brown eyes land on me, I have to work to maintain eye contact. Something about her makes me feel like she's just taken my measure and is deciding what to do with it.

She waits, her boots braced against the ramp, until we've all climbed the ladder. Then she gestures for us to precede her up the ramp and onto a wide walkway that seems to soar through the middle of the city. Every few yards, a narrow bridge stretches from the walkway into a line of buildings. Below us, the river swirls past the stilts that hold up the walkway. The land that anchors the stilts in place is too far below the surface to be seen.

Frankie looks like he's going to be sick. He clutches the ornately carved railing that brackets the walkway and refuses to look down. Connor and Orion have death grips on the railing as well. Willow, Adam, and Jodi move up the ramp as if it's a tree branch they're leaping, but Smithson moves carefully, one hand on the railing and the other wrapped around Nola to keep her from slipping. Even the Commander looks ill at ease, though he doesn't hold on to anything. I give two seconds of thought to taking a page out of the Commander's book and pretending that I'm not worried about falling into the river, and then wrap my hand around the railing too. Better to be honest about my fear than to see it come true.

"It's been a long time since your last visit, Jason," the woman says.

"As I said, we need a meeting with you. Quickly."

The woman nods, but then she notices the brooch on Connor's cloak. "You're the representative from Lankenshire?"

"Connor Vaughn, son of Clarissa Vaughn. I'm here represent-ing Lankenshire's interests." He reaches into his pocket for the letter bearing Lyle Hoden's seal. "I'm also the grandson of Lyle Hoden and am here in his stead as well."

"Indeed. Lyle's messenger arrived yesterday saying to expect you and that he supported you." She reaches for the letter and says, "Tara Lanning, daughter of Aaron Chelming and leader of Chelmingford. I'm pleased to meet you, Connor, and I admit I'm tremendously curious as to what business could bring Baal-boden, Lankenshire, and Hodenswald to my door at the same time."

"If we can meet somewhere private, we'll explain everything," I say. Tara assesses me, as if wondering what role I play in all of this that would give me the right to speak for everyone, but then she turns on her heel and leads us over the walkway and into the heart of the city.

We walk past shops with brightly colored banners hanging from their windows, narrow homes with boxes of pink, yellow, and purple flowers blooming in crates bolted to the walls, and even a playground that resembles a giant planter filled with dirt and grass, balanced securely on stilts. Children run and tumble over the playground, and Frankie makes a choking noise even though an iron fence wraps around the area, keeping anyone from falling into the swiftly moving river below.

"This way. We can talk at my house." Tara turns left onto a slender bridge that arcs from the walkway to a bright-blue door nestled in the front of yet another narrow house. We follow her, most of us clinging to the rail, and enter her home.

In moments, she has us settled around a long oval table with an arrangement of dried flowers resting in a vase at its center. The flowers are brown and crumbling, a stark contrast to the cool blues, whites, and yellows throughout the rest of the home. Tara swings in from the kitchen, a tray of dried fish in one hand and a pitcher of water in the other, and follows my gaze.

"My father's funeral bouquet," she says, and in that moment, I feel connected to her in ways that have nothing to do with her smoky voice and smiling eyes. She understands loss, and the lengths we'll go to keep the memories of our loved ones alive. She keeps her father's funeral bouquet. I kept my mother's necklace in my pocket for thirteen years until the day I realized that Rachel was my new family and gave the necklace to her instead.

The pain of missing Rachel twines around the hole that was carved in me when my mother died, and suddenly it's hard to breathe. It's painful to think about how much I loved my mother and to wonder if she felt the same. It's even harder to know how much I love Rachel and to wonder if I can get to her before James Rowan receives the message that I'm not coming.

Tara sets a plate of salted, dried fish in front of me and squeezes my shoulder briefly before moving on. I realize I'm still staring at the dried flowers, and I quickly look at my plate.

When everyone has been served, Tara sits at the head of the table and says, "I apologize for the lack of fresh food, but our mainland farms have recently been destroyed. We're busy rebuilding in another location, of course, but for now, we're relying on the last of our winter stores."

"Who destroyed the farms?" I ask, and Tara's gaze pierces mine.

"Interesting. You ask who, not what." Her voice is steady, but a spark of anger lies beneath it. "I have a question of my own. You sit here representing Baalboden, Lankenshire, and Hodenswald. Are you not allied with any other city-state as well?"

"Carrington," the Commander says. "But what you're really asking is if we are allies with the Rowansmark trackers who ruined your food supply."

Tara leans forward. "So you know about Rowansmark."

Quickly, the Commander fills her in on the fact that both Baalboden and Carrington have been destroyed, that Schoensville and Thorenburg have committed troops to Rowansmark in exchange for protection, and that Lankenshire and Hodenswald are infested with trackers, but that I've disabled the beacons that would call the *tanniyn* to attack them.

"I can fix any beacons in your city or your farmland as well," I say, even though the Commander seemed sure Chelmingford wouldn't need my services. "I can guarantee the safety of your city and your farms. And in return, we'd like to request that you join us in attacking Rowansmark and destroying the tech that gives them the ability to terrorize the rest of us."

Tara's smile is fierce. "There are no beacons in this city. There are no trackers either. I allow couriers and leaders from other city-states safe passage across the river, but a group of trackers can have no good purpose for coming to Chelmingford."

"You killed them?" the Commander asks.

The fierceness in Tara's smile reaches her eyes. "Indeed we did. They thought they could destroy our farms as a warning that they meant business. In return, my farmworkers allowed them the exclusive use of our ferry. I'm not sorry to report that the ferry never made it to Chelmingford."

"Where did it go?" Connor asks.

"To the bottom of the river." Tara presses her hands against the tabletop. "Anyone who believes that I haven't put contingencies in place for any possible threat to my city is making a grave mistake."

Even the Commander doesn't sneer at this. I shift in my chair as I realize we may have come all the way out to Chelmingford for nothing. Tara's city is safe. She has no incentive to help us now.

Her eyes meet mine, and I say, "I'm glad there aren't any beacons in your city or on your farmland."

I am. But I'm also scrambling to think of some way I could be of service to her in exchange for troops. We're facing three enormous armies on Rowansmark territory with only a partial commitment of soldiers from Lankenshire and Hodenswald. We need all the help we can get.

"And I'm sorry that Carrington and Baalboden were destroyed, and that Lankenshire and Hodenswald live in fear." She turns to the Commander. "What is your plan?"

"I know James Rowan and his military methods. He's too aggressive on the front end, leaving his reserve troops and supplies exposed. I'm going to take a combined army from four city-states, bait him into an aggressive frontal attack, let Logan use their own tech against them, and then flank the reserves with superior numbers to finish them off and leave the attacking unit surrounded." He sounds like his plan couldn't possibly fail, but I can see pitfalls at every turn. Not that I have a better plan, but still. So much could go wrong.

Apparently, Tara agrees with me. She picks up her cup and

swirls the water inside. "And what happens if the tech they have within their city is far superior to the tech you've stolen from them?"

"Logan can alter the tech. Boost it. Make it better. He's good at that." The Commander sounds irritated, and he glares at me as I stare at him in shock. I never thought I'd hear a compliment from his mouth.

"And if James decides to retreat to the river? If he has troops on the water? Supplies?"

The Commander opens his mouth. Shuts it. Looks at me like maybe I have a magic solution waiting in my pocket.

I don't. But Tara does. She rises from the table and invites us to follow her upstairs. We climb a steep set of steps, past the second floor, past the third floor, and into a small, round room completely surrounded by glass walls. Frankie stays rooted just inside the doorway, but the rest of us approach the eastern wall with Tara. My skin feels clammy, like it did when I had to climb to the top of the tall metal-and-glass building in the ruined city, and my chest hurts when I breathe, but I force myself to approach the wall and look where Tara is pointing.

Her home is near the eastern edge of the city. Beyond her windows is another row of houses. Beyond that is a huge walk-way that surrounds the city and separates it from the river. Small ramps branch out from that walkway every few yards and lead down to a collection of boats—no, not boats. *Ships.*

Silvery-gray ships as tall as a three-story house with graceful lines and tremendous sails line the water as far as I can see.

The Commander steps closer to the window-wall. "You have—"

"An armada. Yes."

"None of the other leaders know this." He makes it sound like an accusation.

"Of course not. The only way to see our ships is from the top floor of a house on the eastern edge of the city. I've always entertained other leaders in the bottom story of the town center in the west. One of the best ways to plan for any possible threat is to make sure those who might threaten you don't know your true strength."

We need her armada. If we could trap Rowansmark between an army on the river and an army at their wall, we'd have a much better chance of winning. The problem is, Tara doesn't need to help us. We have nothing to offer in exchange. Still, I have to try.

"I can invent things," I say. "I can build tech. Sonar. Tracking devices—"

"I don't need those."

"Well, maybe—"

"You can't bribe me to help you." Her voice is calm, but her eyes are fierce. "I'm helping you of my own accord. You owe me nothing for my trouble."

"You are? We don't?" I ask.

She meets my gaze and then looks at the Commander. "I hate bullies. I hate those who abuse their power and hurt the ones they should be protecting. And I believe that if I have the power to stop an injustice, and I choose to look away instead, I'm as guilty of that injustice as if I'd done the harm myself. So yes, I will help. It will take you two days to return to Lankenshire—"

"More like two weeks," Connor says.

She smiles. "Not if you take a boat. You can disembark a

mere day's walk from the city. Then if you head west for another four days, you'll reach the branch of the river that will take you straight to Rowansmark. I'll send half of my armada to pick you up." She looks at the ships. "It will be a tight fit, but we should be able to accommodate your soldiers."

"Only half?" the Commander asks.

"If the battle doesn't go our way, I'm going to need to be able to protect my people. Half for the battle, half for Chelmingford."

"I suppose that makes sense," the Commander says grudgingly.

"Of course it does." Tara claps her hands sharply and turns away from the window. "So, two days to Lankenshire. Four days to the Rowansmark branch of the river. And another three days to reach their port. We'll be at war in just over a week."

"We need to leave tonight," I say, because she's right. We have just over a week's worth of travel ahead of us, and a week might be too long. I need to get to Rowansmark before James Rowan decides no one cares enough to ransom Rachel.

Before he kills her.

I meet Tara's eyes. "We're on a tight schedule. A messenger has been dispatched from Lankenshire to warn James Rowan. We have to leave *now*. Every moment counts if we want to have a chance to save . . . to win this war."

She nods once, and within the hour, we're on a boat sailing south toward the drop-off point closest to Lankenshire, and I'm once again alone with thoughts of Rachel. Of loving her. Of kissing her.

Of being too late to save her.

CHAPTER THIRTY-SIX

RACHEL

I'm *hungry.*

I've been locked inside this cell for eight days now, and while I've been given water, I've received only two meals, both of which were half the size of what I'd normally eat.

I guess James Rowan doesn't need to keep up the pretense of wanting me alive to trade with Logan when there's no one but Marcus McEntire, with his incoherent ramblings and his strange humming, to see me slowly starve to death.

Twice a day, Rowan's butler comes downstairs, inspects my cell, gives me water, and empties the bucket I use to relieve myself. He has no weapons I can steal. He watches me closely while my cell door is open. And the lack of food combined with my injuries ensures that I don't have the strength to kick my way through one of the thin, crate-board walls while he's gone.

I'm trapped. Unable to escape. Unable to fight. Unable to do the one thing I swore I'd do when I reached Rowansmark: disable the tech in time to save Logan.

I've spent my days alternating between resting and following Samuel's advice. I've paced my cell. Stretched my arms above my head. Leaned down to touch my toes. I've cursed him, Ian, James Rowan, and the entire city of Rowansmark with every agony-laced breath I've taken, but I've done it. My scabs pull against my skin like too-small pieces of cloth stitched onto me with a needle and thread. I'm still unable to curl my right hand into a fist, thanks to Ian's stupid fires. And the lack of food makes my head spin. But Logan is coming, an ambush is waiting, and I can't let my body rest until I've done everything I can to save him.

As dawn sends weak shafts of sunlight into my cell, I flex my back, swallowing a whimper as my muscles burn. I haven't seen Rowan since the day he ordered me whipped. I haven't seen Samuel or Ian either, but considering the fact that Marcus McEntire—the man both Samuel and Ian believe to be dead— is locked in the cell next to me, mumbling nonsensical madness at all hours of the day, I wouldn't be surprised to learn that James has ordered both of them to stay away from me.

It wouldn't do to have two of his most faithful followers realize that he's a liar.

Pushing myself to my feet, I shuffle toward my cell door, where the light from the hall's window is the strongest. My head feels woozy, my thoughts sluggish. If I'm going to get out of here, I have to do it today. There's nothing helpful in my cell, unless I count the sewage bucket, but what could I do with that? Throw it at the butler and hope the two seconds it gives me are enough to let me outrun a healthy, well-fed man?

Reaching the cell's door, I push against it. The chain that

locks me in clinks softly. If I lean hard, I can give myself a small crack to look through. I scan what little I can see of the hall—past the empty cells beside me and to the foot of the dungeon's stairs—but I don't see anything that wasn't there the last time I checked. Gray stone floor, bleached white walls, the splintery slats of wood that divide half of the room into cells, a water pump similar to the one I used to pump by hand to fill our bathtub, and beside it a half door set into the wall beneath the stairs.

A large pipe is hidden behind the half door, ready to carry the contents of the sewage buckets into Rowansmark's main sewer line. In Baalboden, we'd haul the buckets to the far corner of our property and toss the contents into a deep hole. In Rowansmark, you can't dig a deep hole without hitting water, and no one wants to throw raw sewage into the same water that also supplies the city's wells. Instead, one of the city's engineers devised a system of pipes—one for each house—that lead to a large main pipe that carries the sewage hundreds of yards into the Wasteland.

The butler empties our buckets into the pipe and then uses the pump to rinse the sewage away. The pipe is just large enough that I think I could fit, but only if I want to be dumped into Rowansmark's main sewer pipe, where once a day a flood of water from the dam that holds the river at bay rushes through, sending anything inside of it gushing into the swampy mess that is the southern Wasteland.

As an escape plan, it's useless. I'd be outside Rowansmark, unable to help Logan. Unable to destroy the tech that can call an army of *tanniyn* in seconds.

My other option is to break down part of the walls that hold me in, something I've already tried to do and failed. My first night here, I kicked the wall between my cell and the empty one on my right until part of a board splintered, but by then my back was a mess of blood and pain and weakness, and I couldn't make enough headway to do any good. I've tried again and again, but the rough boards are stronger than they look, and every hour I go without food weakens my efforts further.

Besides, even if I could break out of my cell, where would I go? The pipe is out—I need to be inside Rowansmark disabling tech or, failing that, lighting all of the barracks, armories, and tech labs on fire. The stairs are out, too. I have no doubt that at least one guard is posted on the other side of the dungeon's door. I'm weaponless and weak. Fighting my way to freedom isn't an option.

That leaves the window beside Marcus's cell, but it's barred. I'm trapped, growing weaker by the day, and I'm no closer to saving Logan than I was when I first decided to remain Ian's prisoner instead of let Quinn take me into the Wasteland—a decision I'm trying hard not to regret.

The door at the top of the stairs creaks open, and footsteps stomp down the stairs. Quickly, I lean against the wall beside my door, where I have the best chance of seeing the window once the butler enters my room, and wait.

In seconds, the chain across my door rattles, and he comes in carrying a mug of water. Seeing that I'm beside the door frame, he grabs my left arm with his free hand and pulls me away from the door. Spinning me toward my bunk, he propels me forward and then shoves me forcibly onto the bed.

"Think you're going to just walk out of here, do you?" he asks, his tone brisk and impatient.

I close my eyes to stop the room from spinning and to keep him from seeing the tears that threaten to fall. "No," I say quietly. "I know I'm going to die here."

Something skitters along the wall between my cell and Marcus's, like fingernails dragging along the wood. The butler turns his head and snaps, "Stop that!"

Marcus hums loudly, a wild, discordant tune that sounds worse than his fingernails did.

The butler mutters something under his breath and then gives me the mug of water. "Here. Drink."

"Why bother?"

There is no way out. I'm going to die in here, and then Logan is going to be killed on a fool's errand to rescue me, and no one will be left to stand up for those who have no power to fight back.

"Giving up already?" the butler asks in a voice that says he really doesn't care. "Took that one five times as long to lose hope." He nods toward Marcus's cell, where he is muttering what sounds like a complicated math equation over and over again.

"Did it take him that long to lose his sanity, too? Or did he snap when his own son was forced to whip him almost to death?" My words are bitter, but it isn't just for Marcus's sake. Every loss, starting with my father and ending with Sylph, every sacrifice, and every promise I swore to keep was all for what? So that the men who started this nineteen years ago could survive to rule the world at the expense of everyone else?

The silence within me shivers, tempting me to seal up the cracks I made in it when I grieved for Sylph. When I held Melkin's baby girl. I could shove the desperation and the crushing sense of failure into that black hole inside of me and feel nothing at all as I slowly starve to death.

Or I could take a drink of water, move my back before my wounds stiffen up, and keep thinking of another way out of this.

Another way to make the losses and the sacrifices count for something.

The butler shrugs and starts to take the mug away, but at the last second I snatch it from him with shaky hands and drain it dry.

Maybe I am trapped. Maybe I'll die here. But it won't be because I gave up. Oliver once told me that hope is precious, and that it's worth hanging on to even when all seems lost. I'm going to take him at his word.

Quinn is inside Rowansmark looking for me. Logan is smart enough to realize there's an ambush here even though he has no idea how dangerous it really is. I'm a fighter, both by nature and by choice.

And I am getting out of this dungeon.

An idea hits me just as the butler is closing the door of my cell.

"Do you know Samuel?" I ask, keeping my voice breathy and faint. Not difficult, since the water sloshing around in my empty stomach makes me painfully aware that I need food badly.

"I know several Samuels." He shuts the door and begins lacing the chain through the lock.

"The Samuel who brought me here. Who whipped me. The one who arrived on the boat with Ian. He's a tracker, dark skin and gray hair. Do you know him?"

The chain links clank together as he finishes securing my

door. "I know him, girl, but that isn't going to help you any. You're a prisoner because you've wronged Rowansmark. No loyal citizen is going to want anything to do with you."

"I know. I . . . please, wait." My voice rises as he moves toward Marcus's cell. "I'm dying. We both know it. I can't go without food for much longer. Samuel is a good man. He respected my father. I want to tell him where my father is buried. That's all."

The man snorts. "And why would you do that?"

"Because I want to be buried beside him." My throat closes and my eyes sting as I remember that cold, ash-coated plot of dirt. The white cross Quinn carved. The way everything in me emptied out while I lay across Dad's grave and the way a shell of the girl I once was rose in my place.

I'm a liar. I don't want to be buried beside Dad. I don't want to be buried at all. Not yet. I want to get out of this cell. Stop the Commander, James Rowan, and Ian. Kiss Logan for a hundred years. And live out my days knowing that even though I was broken, I chose not to be lost.

"Will you ask him to come see me before I'm too far gone to remember what I want to say?" I ask in a quiet, pleading voice that does nothing to soften the butler's reply.

"We'll see."

It's better than a no. I wait until he finishes his tasks while in the cell beside me, Marcus hums his strange little melody and mutters to himself about wave function and thermodynamics. Once the door slams at the top of the stairs, leaving Marcus and me alone again, I lower myself to the stone floor and crawl slowly toward the crack in the wall between my cell and Marcus's. My head feels too heavy, and sparks dance at the edge of my vision as my stomach cramps in a miserable plea for food.

Laying my cheek against the floor beside the crack, I whisper, "Marcus, I'm going to die."

His muttering stops abruptly.

"Rachel? Jared Adams's Rachel?"

"Yes. I'm Jared Adams's Rachel." The words, following so closely on the heels of the memory of my father's grave, are bittersweet.

"Dying? No . . . no."

"Logan is in danger. I'm the only one left who can help him. I haven't had anything to eat in days. They're refusing to feed me. I can help Logan, but not if I starve to death first."

"Don't. Don't die. *Don't*. Logan? Ian? My sons?"

"Listen to me, Marcus. You and Ian invented tech that can call the Cursed . . . the *tanniyn*, remember?"

"Gave it to Jared. James knows. He *knows*." His voice cracks.

"It's okay. I don't mean the device you gave to Jared. I mean the tech you and Ian built that can call an entire army of the monsters. Do you know what I'm talking about?"

He's silent for a long moment, and I bite my lip as I pray that somewhere in the damaged morass of his mind, he can still grasp enough reality to help me. Then he says, "Summoners? Call them all. Summoners?"

A chill slides over me at the name. Summoners. "Yes. The summoners. James Rowan knows about Logan. He's going to kill Logan using the summoners unless I can stop it."

An eerie wail tears its way out of Marcus's throat and bounces off the walls of the cell. It's the sound of a wounded animal backed into a corner. If Logan dies, everything Marcus sacrificed, every loss he suffered, will be for nothing. I know the feeling.

"Wait! Marcus!" My voice snaps out with more strength than I realized I had left. "I can stop it. Do you hear me? I can save Logan. But I need your help. Okay? I just need your help, and we can save Logan."

The wail tapers off, and I hear the swish-slide of Marcus scrambling across the floor seconds before his bright-blue eye blinks at me through the crack in the wall.

"Ian too? Save him? Save both?"

I open my mouth, but nothing will come out. How can I promise to save Ian when I'm the one who wants him dead? But if I don't promise, will Marcus still help me? Maybe I can convince him that Logan is the only one who needs my help.

"Ian doesn't need to be saved. James Rowan is happy with him." All it took was the destruction of my city and the murder of my friends.

Marcus blinks rapidly. "My sons. Never safe with James. Not anymore. Save Ian, too? Promise?"

I clench my jaw tight. Save the boy who took almost everything from me? I'd rather swallow nails.

But Ian had dreams once. And none of them included ripping his father's life away from him or being forced to cover his hands in the blood of those who'd never wronged him. And if I don't promise to help Ian, I'll lose Logan, too.

The words taste like ashes in my mouth as I say, "Yes. I'll do my best to save Ian, too. I promise."

He pulls away from the crack, babbling softly to himself, and then he returns and shoves something through the sliver of space. I stare at it for a moment, and then reach out slowly to pick it up.

It's a pecan, broken in half so that it can fit through the crack between our cells. Another half follows and then four more. I grab all of them and shove them into my mouth. Their buttery flavor explodes across my tongue, and I nearly choke as I swallow too fast.

Marcus's blue eye returns to the crack as he shoves another few nuts through. "Don't die. Jared's Rachel. Don't die."

I scoop up the rest of the nuts. "I won't. And neither will your sons. Now, tell me how to find and disable the summoners, and then I'll tell you how you can help me get out of this dungeon."

CHAPTER THIRTY-SEVEN

LOGAN

We've been on the water for three days now. Four, if you count the day it took us to sail on a small boat from Chelmingford to the drop-off closest to Lankenshire, where we rejoined the Commander's troops, met the soldiers from Hodenswald and Lankenshire, and received the disheartening news that Brooksworth had refused to commit to our cause. The Commander wasted no time marching his army west to the river where the armada waited for us. I pushed hard for us to march faster, go farther, and the Commander didn't argue. He didn't want to lose the element of surprise.

I don't want to lose Rachel.

Our army is stuffed into fifteen silver-gray ships. The Commander and his ranking officers are aboard the armada's flagship vessel, along with my own people and the ranking officers from Chelmingford. I've done my best to avoid the Commander at any cost. Partially because I wanted to finish transforming Melkin's staff into a weapon that will make the device the Commander

351

holds look like a toy, and partially because my usefulness to the Commander is finished, and I don't have time to deal with a double cross. I have a promise to keep.

At the moment, the Commander is locked in the captain's quarters, going over strategy with his officers in preparation for docking tomorrow just above Rowansmark's dam. Nola is resting, trying to make up for the nights she spends grieving for Drake instead of sleeping, and Jodi decided to stay on the lower deck to watch over her. The rest of us headed up to get some fresh air and a brief respite from the Commander's constant scrutiny.

Willow, stripped to her undertunic, shinnies up the tallest mast, her hair whipping in the wind as the ship cuts through the murky green water of the river that leads to Rowansmark. Smithson wanders toward the prow of the boat, while Frankie, Adam, Connor, and I lean against the rail and watch Willow treat the upper rigging of the boat like it's a collection of tree branches.

"So we land tomorrow. I admit, I'll be grateful to partake in sustenance that isn't fish," Connor says. "I've never been overly fond of it."

"Sustenance." Frankie laughs and shakes his head. "Boy, you are a walking collection of words I never heard before."

"Sustenance. Noun. A means of sustaining life through . . . do you *see* that girl? Amazing." Connor's eyes light up as Willow races to the end of a long metal pole and leaps onto a rope ladder that will carry her to the very top.

Adam punches Connor's shoulder. "She's taken."

Connor rubs his shoulder. "I was only commenting on her athletic prowess."

Frankie laughs again. "Lots of boys notice Willow's . . . athletic prowess."

Connor's cheeks turn pink, and Adam scowls. Willow reaches the top and pulls herself up while sunlight glows against her dusky skin.

"Still admiring her prowess?" Adam asks. "Or have you moved on to other areas?"

"I wasn't—she's very—" Connor tears his gaze from Willow and looks at Adam. "Um . . . well equipped. Athletically speaking. Very fit. Very. Um . . . fit. I said that already. I'm done talking now."

"You'd better be," Adam says, though there's no real threat in his voice.

I roll my eyes at Adam. "Are you joining Willow, or will you be staying down here to torture Connor?"

Adam grins and begins climbing the mast like he was born to it.

"He's a bit territorial, isn't he?" Connor asks. "I was simply commenting on her—"

"Athletic prowess. Yeah, I heard that." I elbow him.

"Well, she's an admirable specimen of the female persuasion." Connor tugs at the collar of his shirt as if it's become a noose.

"I think you just called her cute." Frankie laughs while Connor's cheeks darken again. "I'd give a lot to see you say that to her face."

"And have Adam rearrange my internal organs? No, thank you."

I sling an arm over his shoulder and turn him away from the mast. "Once you fall in love with someone, you'll feel like that, too. But a word to the wise. Girls get pretty irritated if you act like you own them. I've made that mistake with Rachel plenty of times. I thought I was being protective. She thought I was being an idiot. If Willow had overheard that conversation, she'd have taken it out of Adam's skin."

Frankie nods wisely and nudges Connor in the ribs. "Girls like to feel special. Protected. But there's a fine line between feeling protected and feeling like a fence post being marked by a stray dog."

Connor ducks out from under my arm and shakes his head, though he's smiling. "On that memorable image, I think I'll take my leave and go see if Jodi wishes for some company."

"Is Jodi also a fine specimen of the female persuasion?" I ask. Connor walks away.

"Remember!" Frankie calls to his retreating back. "Don't piss on the fence post!"

I laugh, and it feels good even though I miss Drake and worry about Rachel. Connor shakes his head and moves toward the stairs that lead to the lower deck.

Frankie and I lean against the metal rail in companionable silence. The warmth of the early summer afternoon bakes my skin, and I lift my face to catch the breeze, which carries the scent of damp bark, wildflowers, and freshly caught fish.

"The Commander ain't taking us with him tomorrow," Frankie says. "Not that I want to go to war, mind, but if the Commander has decided we're useless, I figure he means to kill us."

I nod and squint against the bursts of sunlight that ricochet off the river. "I know. I've got a plan for that."

"Care to share it?" His tone is careful, and it hits me that he expects me to say no because I've said no so many times in the past. I shared my plans with Rachel, and then with Drake. But they aren't here, and I'd be hard-pressed to find a more faithful friend than Frankie.

"I've been talking with Corey Burkes, the captain of the armada. Tara Lanning gave him permission to engage in the conflict as he saw fit. The Commander is using the ships simply as transportation and a backup plan in case Rowansmark retreats to the river." I look at Frankie. "Rowansmark won't retreat up the river. They'd have to go through the locks, one ship at a time, before they could get to the top of the dam."

"So basically the armada is useless to us."

"Not exactly." I glance over my shoulder in case someone has joined us on the upper deck, but other than Smithson, who is now pacing along the railing toward the middle of the deck, we're alone. "The Commander wants to remove James Rowan from power and take over the city as his own, keeping the tech for himself."

Frankie snorts. "Sounds like exchanging one devil for another."

"Exactly. I want to remove James Rowan from power, keep the Commander from taking over, and destroy as many of the *tanniyn* as we possibly can. If the Commander doesn't call the beasts, I'm sure James Rowan will. The *tanniyn* don't surface underwater. Which means they can't breathe underwater."

"So you're aiming to flood Rowansmark?" Frankie's brows come together. "There are innocent people living there."

"Rowansmark regularly gets flooded, even with the dam.

The city has an evacuation plan put in place for this. Plus, all of their homes have three stories with balconies so that if necessary, people can get to their roofs. I won't willingly put the Rowansmark citizens in danger."

"And you've got Captain Burkes on board with this?"

"Yes. When the Commander makes his move, we'll be ready."

Frankie meets my eyes and grins like someone just bet on him in a fight. "I can't wait."

CHAPTER THIRTY-EIGHT

RACHEL

I finish the last mouthful of pecan halves that Marcus shoved through the crack in our cells and smile for him while he blinks anxiously, asking me over and over again not to die.

"More?" he asks. "Have oatmeal. Julia loves."

"Was Julia your wife?" I ask, though I already know the answer. He talks to her night and day, mumbling about Ian growing taller and having big feet, about not remembering to clean the stove between meals, and then reassures her that he still knows her song by heart.

"Julia. Song." He hums a few bars of his favorite discordant melody again. I'm guessing that's his version of Julia's song.

He disappears, scuttling toward his bunk, and then he's back, shoving two fingers coated in oatmeal through the crack. I reach out, scrape the oatmeal from his skin, and put it in my mouth. It's cold and gummy, but I swallow it gratefully.

"Music?" He hums for me and waits as if encouraging me to hum along. I try a few bars, copying his wandering notes as best as I can, and he rewards me with a flash of a smile.

"I'm sorry," I say softly. "I'm so sorry that Julia is gone. And that Ian . . ."

"Ian." He breathes the name like a prayer, and I shift uncomfortably, welcoming the stab of pain in my back to distract me from the anguished devotion in Marcus's voice.

"Mostly I'm sorry that Logan was taken from you, even though that means I wouldn't have known him." The thought sends a tendril of aching loneliness through me. What would it be like if I'd never known Logan? Never sparred with the boy who didn't mind the fact that I could beat him or argued with the boy who challenged me because he respected my intelligence?

Never kissed the boy who makes me feel like fire runs just beneath my skin?

"Know him? Know Logan?" Marcus watches me closely.

"I know him," I tell him again, just like I have every day since I've been in the dungeon. "I know Logan." Three little words that don't do anything justice. I know the look on his face when he's so busy thinking about an invention that he doesn't hear a word anyone is saying. I know the roughness of his calloused fingers. The way his skin smells like ink and paper. I know the lengths he'll go to keep his promises.

I know the smile he gives to others and the one he gives only to me.

I don't realize I'm smiling too—a drifting, dreamy sort of smile—until Marcus makes a soft hooting noise and asks, "Love him? Logan? Love?"

"I do," I say, and Marcus hums wildly. "And you love him, too. That's why you worked so hard to finish the invention that would ransom his life. I want him to meet you. I want him to have a family. But to do that, I have to know where the summoners are located and how to destroy them before Rowan can use them against Logan when he arrives to rescue me."

Marcus falls silent, his eye blinking rapidly as his gaze flits from my face to the floor and back again. "Know. Don't know." He shakes his head and speaks louder. "Know it. *Know.*"

I try to sound calm and soothing. "It's okay, Marcus. We'll take it slow. Please. You and I are the only ones left who can save your son."

He quiets, and then says in a low voice, "Sons. Save my sons. James? Punish them? You promised. *Sons.*"

I close my eyes and try not to think of the way Sylph's heart-beat slowed and then stopped as Ian's poison coursed through her veins. "Yes. Your sons. I promised. We'll do one question at a time, okay? First, do the summoners actually work?"

He mutters something that sounds like "inverse" followed by a string of unintelligible sounds that might be scientific equations or might be nothing at all.

"Did you say 'inverse'?" I ask, leaning my face against the wall so I can watch Marcus. His ruined face contorts, the scar tissue that covers what's left of his features pulling his mouth into grotesque angles while he mumbles and keens. He grabs his hair—still thick and dark blond like Logan's, but with gray at the temples—and yanks on it so hard, I expect to see his scalp start to bleed.

I'm running out of time. If Samuel takes the bait and visits me, I need to be ready. I bite back the surge of frustration, and try again.

"The summoners work by using inverse?" I ask. That doesn't sound like an actual thing, but he keeps repeating it, so it must be important.

Outside the dungeon's window, a drum begins pounding, and what sounds like hundreds of boots slap the pavement in time to the beat. I've heard the same sound every morning for the past four days. I assume it's Rowansmark's army running drills. Dad and I visited Rowansmark fairly often, and I don't remember seeing soldiers march in formation in front of James Rowan's mansion, but then again, I wasn't concerned with the military, the trackers, or anything else inside the city walls. I had Dad, so I was safe.

But I don't have Dad with me now, and I can't ignore the fact that even though James Rowan has tech at his disposal that can call and control an army of the *tanniyn*, he's still prepping his army for war.

Which means he feels the need to have a backup plan.

Which means the tech can be destroyed, if I can just get Marcus to tell me how.

"Listen to me," I say, cutting off another stream of mutterings that sound both mathematical and full of nonsense. "Where are the summoners?"

"Don't know. Don't. Do I?" He crawls to the wall and blinks at me, uncomfortably close. "Summoners?"

"Yes. Where are they?" My knees dig into the floor, and my back aches.

"Lab? No." He stares past me. "After? Ian." His eye finds me again. "After Ian."

I put the pieces of his thoughts together and come up with

the answer, my stomach sinking. "You don't know where the summoners are because they moved them from the lab after Ian . . . after you were hurt?"

"Below? Yes. Below."

"Below what?"

He huffs out a little breath. "Ground?" Patting his hand on the floor, he says, "Below?"

My chest hurts as the implication of his words hits me. "The summoners are buried somewhere? That's how they work?" I shake my head as he starts muttering "inverse wave function anomaly Julia" over and over again. "Of course that's how they work. Melkin's staff didn't call the Cursed One until it was driven into the ground. But if the summoners are buried, how will I find them? How will I destroy them?"

The rattle of a chain being pulled from its lock drifts down the dungeon stairs seconds before the door creaks open.

My voice is harsh as I whisper, "Marcus, someone's coming. Listen to me. How do I destroy the summoners?"

"Can't? Can't. Below. Inverse. Waves?"

Pressure builds in my head, an ache that begs to be released in tears as boots slap the stone steps. I can't get the answers I need from Marcus. I can't find the summoners because they're buried. And even if I could find them, how would I destroy them when all Marcus can say is *inverse*?

"Ian? Knows. Inverse. Summoners inverse."

My jaw clenches. "Ian knows how to destroy the summoners using the inverse of something?"

Marcus blinks rapidly while the chain on my door slides free. It's too early for the butler to be bringing us our second ration of water. Either Samuel took the bait, or Logan is on the horizon, and Rowan wants me visible so that I'll draw Logan close enough for the summoners to do their job.

Turning away from the wall, I watch my cell door open while Marcus hums and mutters to himself. Instead of Samuel, though, Ian enters the room, his eyes weary and his face as pale as if he's been the one locked up and starved for days instead of me. Instantly, I clamber to my feet, cursing the wounds on my back for making my movements slow and cumbersome. If Ian is here, it must mean that James no longer needs me alive and has given Ian permission to kill me.

Marcus continues to hum in loud, discordant bursts. I wonder how long it will take him to pay attention to the conversation in my cell. I wonder what he'll do when he recognizes Ian's voice.

More than that, I wonder what Ian will do once I tell him his father is alive.

If I'm lucky, it will reach the part of him that used to understand right from wrong and keep him from killing me. If I'm *really* lucky, it will distract him enough to give me a chance to escape.

"Quinn is still alive." His voice is cold. "But then I suppose you knew that. Considering the damage he's done over the past week, he must've arrived in the city the same day we did. Won't take us long to corner him, now that we know who we're looking for."

"What damage?"

"Someone burned down the armory last night. We lost hundreds of weapons." He speaks without much inflection, like the effort it takes to breathe life into his words is beyond him now.

"Before that, it was my father's lab. Before that, one of the army barracks. Yesterday, he got careless and was spotted just before a fire started in the trackers' main training center. Longish dark hair, leather pants, looks like he belongs in a tree. It's Quinn."

I blink. Burning down armories and barracks and labs doesn't sound like Quinn. Either he's using the blazes as a distraction while he hunts for me, or he's decided to start taking Rowansmark apart from the inside out without me. Or both.

"I bet you think he's helping your cause, don't you?" Ian asks, stepping closer to me. Marcus stops humming abruptly, and I hear the swish-scrape of his pants against the stone as he crawls toward the wall again. "I bet you think you're going to be rescued, and that you're going to turn the tables against a city-state—against an army of *three* city-states—and against the *tanniyn*, because if nothing else, you are recklessly confident in your own abilities."

"And I bet you think you're here to kill me, but you aren't." I speak softly, trying to keep Marcus from overhearing.

Ian laughs, but there's no humor in it. Instead, he sounds impossibly tired. "We heard from Lankenshire. Logan isn't coming. He went north instead, and now you're of no use to us. I have to finish this. I have to restore my family's honor. You can't talk me out of this, Rachel. Don't even try."

"Maybe I can't talk you out of taking another life, but I know someone who can."

Ian swallows hard, and something that looks like regret flashes briefly in his eyes before the light inside of them winks out, replaced by dull purpose. "Samuel already tried, but he isn't my leader. He isn't the one who can restore my father's name."

He draws his sword and steps closer. "I want you to know that even though I think you deserve this, it won't bring me any pleasure."

"James Rowan is a liar," I say, holding Ian's gaze while behind me, Marcus whispers Julia's name over and over again. "He's a liar who made you do his dirty work. Who convinced you that getting blood on your hands was somehow justice, when really it was a way to destroy the Commander's people so he could become the unrivaled leader of the city-states."

He shakes his head sharply, his eyes glowing pits of misery. "Justice requires—"

"Sacrifice. I know. But who was really sacrificed here? The only person who did anything wrong was the Commander, when he stole Logan and blackmailed your father. Every person after that has been an innocent caught up in circumstances beyond their control. Including you and me."

I move closer to him. He tightens his stance as if I'm going to attack him, but I keep my hands down at my sides and say quietly, "Tell me, Ian, would you have killed anyone if your father had survived his pain atonement?"

"Don't you dare speak of my father to me." His chest heaves as if he's been running, and bright spots of color darken his cheeks. "I did what was just." He raises his sword, his expression desperate. "I did what—"

"You did what James Rowan wanted you to do because he made you believe you'd lost everything. That you had nothing left except the faint hope that with enough Baalboden blood on your hands, your father's death wouldn't be in vain."

"Stop talking about my father!" He lunges toward me.

"Ian!" I scream his name, and Marcus falls silent for a second as Ian aims his blade at my heart.

"Ian? Son. My son? Mine? *Ian!*" Marcus's voice cuts through the space between Ian and me, a wavering knife of anguished hope.

Ian freezes, his sword hand shaking, and looks at the wall behind me. "Who is that? Who's in there?"

"James Rowan lied to you." I step to the side so that Ian can see his father's bright-blue eye blinking through the crack in the wall. "Your father is still alive."

CHAPTER THIRTY-NINE

RACHEL

Ian's sword hits the stone floor of my cell with a clatter. He stands frozen in place, his mouth open, though no sound comes out.

"Ian? Mine? Ian?" Marcus sounds like he's begging.

"That's not . . . it's not possible." Ian's voice shakes.

"Go to him," I say. Go to him and leave your sword behind and the cell door wide open. Please.

"It's not . . ." Ian lowers himself to the cell floor in unsteady increments. "It can't be. I saw him fall. He didn't get up. James pronounced him dead. I *saw*—"

"You saw what James Rowan wanted you to see so that you would be so ruined inside, you'd do anything he told you." I take a tiny step back from him, but he doesn't notice. He's staring at the strips of scar tissue covering what used to be Marcus's nose.

"Ian? Please? *Ian?*" Marcus presses his face against the wall, his gaze locked on his son.

Ian's fists clench, and he leans closer to the crack, his entire body trembling. "Dad?" His voice breaks, and he reaches one hand toward the wall.

"Ian. Ian? *Mine.*" Marcus sounds buoyant and upbeat for the first time since I've been listening to him speak. "Good. My son. Good boy. *Good.*"

Ian's chest heaves as he presses his palm to the crack in the wall. A long wail of pent-up anguish rips its way past his lips, and he sobs while Marcus croons over and over that Ian, his son, is good.

"No, Dad." Ian sounds desperate. "I'm not good. I've . . . done things. I *hurt* you. And then James sent me to Baalboden to deliver a message of pain atonement to the Commander and his people, and I *did* it. I . . ." He lays his head on the dungeon floor and cries.

I bend down and try to pick up Ian's sword. The weight of it sends stabs of white-hot pain through my back, and I drop the weapon. It hits the floor with a harsh clang, but Ian is too caught up to notice.

"Okay. Okay? Ian." Marcus tries to reach his hand through the crack, but there's only room for his fingers. "Okay, Ian."

"It's not okay!" Ian shouts. "It will never be okay. I've done terrible things in the name of justice, because you were dead, and it was all I had left, but it was a lie. Everything was a lie."

Ian has a dagger. I see the hilt peeking out of the boot closest to me. I may not be able to pick up his sword, but I can handle a dagger. I move swiftly, closing the short distance between us and ignoring the painful sting of scabs pulling against healthy skin as I crouch down and reach for the dagger.

"Forgive. Ian? Forgive you? All gone. All." Marcus's voice is gentle. "Forgive all, Ian."

A sudden flash of anger burns through me as I pull the dagger from its sheath and get to my feet. Why does Ian get the happy ending? Why is his father alive and ready to offer absolute forgiveness, while mine is dead, and I'm left alone to deal with the things I've done? I want to rail against the unfairness of it. I want to be the one lying on the floor, crying over my guilt and my grief, and hearing my father say that it's okay.

"I don't deserve forgiveness," Ian says, his face pressed to the floor like he can't bear to look into his father's eyes.

"No, you don't." My voice is brittle, and I hold the dagger steady in my left hand while I back away from Ian.

He lifts his face and looks at me. Where moments ago there had been nothing but dull purpose to fill the emptiness in his gaze, regret and anguish now war with hope in his eyes. I look away.

"Forgive? Forgive," Marcus says, as if forgiveness is that simple.

I look back at Ian, who stares at me in silence, his expression haunted. I'm struck by the fact that the guilt and horror I see on his face are similar to what lived inside my silence until Quinn helped me unlock it. Similar, but not the same. I made choices that hurt others, but I didn't knowingly hurt them. I didn't set out with the intention to take hundreds of lives.

My unshakable quest for vengeance never cost others what Ian's has cost me. Does that make me better than him?

"I thought he was dead," Ian whispers.

I take another step toward the open cell door. Outside, a trumpet blows, and the earthshaking sound of hundreds of soldiers marching in unison fills the air. I can't get out of the mansion unseen when three separate armies all seem to be running drills on the grounds at the same time. I don't even know if I can get out of the dungeon unseen. Who knows how many staff members and guards are lurking in the house?

"Your father is a good man. I've spent days listening to him ramble on about his family. That's all that matters to him. That's all that ever drove anything he did." I tuck the dagger behind me, but Ian doesn't seem to notice. "What drove you, Ian?"

"Rachel . . ." Ian looks lost as I back away.

"Ian. Mine? Forgive all. Ian?" Marcus pushes his fingers through the crack as far as they can go, and Ian slowly reaches out and lays his hand over his father's fingers.

"My dad is dead. For real." My voice shakes a little. "I know what that's like. It was bad, and I wasn't the one who killed him. But I found out about his death right after seeing the Commander murder Oliver, my grandfather, because the Commander was sure that if he broke me, I'd do what he wanted. So I know, Ian." I back up a little more and bump into the open cell door. "I know loss and anger and the desperate need to avenge yourself against those who wronged you because you think that will somehow make it easier to get through another day."

"I thought he was *dead*. I thought . . ."

"Okay, Ian. Rachel? Okay?" Marcus sounds worried.

I force myself to let the anger drain out of my voice. "We're okay, Marcus. We're just talking. Don't worry about it."

"Okay, Logan? Mine? Logan?"

I meet Ian's eyes and say, "Not yet. But he will be. Won't he, Ian?"

Ian stares at me and then at the crack in the wall where Marcus is babbling, "Inverse. Summoners? Below! Ian inverse? Transmitter wave? Below? Ian!"

"I don't understand. . . ." Ian looks from me to his father and back again. "I don't understand what he's saying."

I grip the dagger so hard, the handle bites into my palm. "You *have* to understand. You have to figure it out. Marcus said you knew how to destroy the summoners."

"He doesn't seem to be saying much of anything at all," Ian says quietly.

"He says enough." I step into the open doorway. "You just have to learn how to decode it."

"Decode?" Ian stares at his father as if trying to figure out where things have gone wrong inside Marcus's mind.

"That's all that's left of him now. James Rowan saw to that, and to a lesser extent, so did you, though Marcus doesn't blame you. You were just being a loyal citizen, after all. Isn't that the line Rowan fed you? Restoring honor by helping to destroy your father?"

Ian remains silent, but I find I still have plenty to say.

"Whatever his mind was before he was nearly whipped to death and tossed into the dungeon for months with nothing but the ghosts of his family to keep him company, it's gone. The scientific genius, the grand inventor, the man who could occupy one of the highest positions in Rowansmark's government, is gone. But you're lucky, Ian, because the best of your father remains. He has nothing left but love and devotion for his sons. If you listen carefully, you'll learn to figure out the things he can't quite say, but you don't have to listen carefully to hear that he loves you and forgives you. If you don't protect that, if you don't get him out of here and become worthy of the gift he's given you, then you are spitting his love back at his feet."

"How can he forgive me after all I've done?" Ian's voice is rough and pleading. Marcus's fingers tighten around his son's, and he croons softly through the wall.

"He doesn't know. And somehow I think even if he *did* know, he'd still choose to love you." I step into the hall and walk to Marcus's door, since Ian shows no signs of getting up off the cell floor. The chain running through Marcus's lock is heavier than it looks, and I suck in a pained breath as I carefully slide the dagger inside my boot and then struggle to remove the chain.

"Why didn't you tell him?" Ian says behind me.

I stop pulling on the chain and look at him. "Because he's been through enough. He loves you. He thinks the world of you. He doesn't deserve to have that ripped away from him."

"I don't know what to say." He sounds confused as he takes the chain from me and begins unwrapping it.

He's not the only one. I want to punch him in the face. I want to break down and cry because it isn't my dad behind this door. I want to stop feeling empathy for the boy who killed my best friend.

"I don't want to hear anything you have to say." I step back as the door swings open. "I just want you to help me save Logan."

"Jared Adams's Rachel? My sons? Save? Promised," Marcus says. "*Promised. Inverse.*"

"You promised him we'd save Logan?" Ian doesn't sound happy.

I turn toward him and snap, "No, I promised him I'd save you *both* from James."

"Why would you want to save me?"

"I don't. But it was the price of getting him to tell me about the summoners. Marcus says you know how to destroy them. We have to do that before Logan gets here."

"You forget that Logan went north. With the Commander, apparently. He isn't coming."

I meet his gaze. "He's coming. I promise you. If he went north first, he had a good reason, but he's coming to get me, and we are going to destroy the summoners before he gets here."

Ian steps into his father's cell, but keeps his eyes on me. "I don't know where they are or how to—"

"Inverse! Summoners below inverse transmitter music? Wave function! Ian? Ian!" Marcus shuffles toward us, his back permanently hunched, his gait unsteady. I'm guessing he didn't have medical care after his whipping.

"What is he saying?" Ian demands.

"He's saying you know how to destroy the summoners. Something about inverse." I move away from the cell, though I don't yet know how I'm getting out of here. "Just tell me, and I'll figure out where they are. I'll search the entire city if I have to. Just—"

"I don't know!" Ian shouts. "I don't know what he's saying or where the summoners are, and I don't know if I should help you even if I could."

"Ian!" Marcus's voice is wounded. "Help? Help Logan? *Help.*"

"Yes, Ian, help." My lips curl around the words, though for Marcus's sake, I try to keep my tone even. "Help your brother. You owe him that. You owe us both."

"Inverse! Transmitter? Ian?"

"I don't speak tech. What is he saying?" I ask as I glance at the dungeon's window. The bars gleam dully in the morning light, and I can just make out the lines of soldiers parading across the grounds. Soldiers in Rowansmark green and brown. But also soldiers in gray and blue. Soldiers in dark blue and white. A combined army that is so much bigger than anything Logan and Lankenshire can pull together.

Not that the army will matter if Rowan's summoners call a host of *tanniyn* instead.

"Summoners? Logan? Inverse? Wave!" Marcus stumbles, and Ian rushes to his side. The moment Ian touches his father, Marcus turns and wraps his arms around his son, holding him tight while he croons Julia's broken melody and smiles.

"Inverse . . . wave? Is that what you mean?" Ian looks at me. "It could work. Using a sonic wave that's the inverse of the frequency emitted by the summoners would, in theory, negate their signal."

"Would you need to know the exact location of the summoners to use an inverse sonic wave?"

"No, sound travels. The wave is amplified using transmitters, so theoretically, as long as you were in the vicinity and had a stronger sound wave, you could nullify the signal." He slowly leans his cheek against his father's shoulder, as if worried the resting place he seeks will disappear as soon as he gets there.

"So all we need to do is build a device that can send an inverse of the summoners' signal, right? You can do that, can't you, Ian?" My voice is a hard slap.

"I can't." His blue eyes challenge mine. "Remember how I said that Quinn burned down the lab? Years of research, equipment, supplies, and proprietary tech . . . gone."

Up until a few moments ago, I'd have been overjoyed to learn that the lab was destroyed. I'd planned to do it myself. Now, I'm terrified that the destruction of the lab means there's nothing I can do to save Logan.

"What can we do?" I ask. Fear trembles through my voice.

"Logan? Save? Promised. Mine. Logan?" Marcus pulls back to look at Ian.

Ian looks at the floor. "We don't know where the summoners are buried, and we don't have the supplies to build another controller. We can't stop this."

I stare at him, my chest burning, my eyes stinging, and feel something powerful surge through me. Maybe Ian can't stop it. Maybe he's willing to look at all the obstacles standing in our way and admit defeat. Or maybe he just has no intention of trying to save Logan after spending so many months hating him.

I don't care. I'm not giving up. If I can't save Logan from inside Rowansmark, then I'll just have to escape into the Wasteland and stop him from ever arriving at Rowansmark in the first place.

"I'm leaving," I say to Marcus. "I'm going to find Logan and help him. He's going to be okay."

"You can't get out of Rowansmark," Ian says. "There are soldiers on every corner. And the moment the guards find the dungeon empty, every single soldier will be on the lookout for you."

"Don't worry about me. I've got a plan. Besides, I can't stay here. You came down with orders to kill me. If you don't do it, Rowan will just send someone else. You get your father to safety." I meet Ian's eyes. "And if you happen to see Quinn in the city, don't kill him. Don't report him. In fact, do your best to help him. You owe him that. You owe all of us that."

"You're leaving him?"

"Oh, we'll be back for him." And when we find a way to return for Quinn, we'll finish wreaking the havoc he started. We'll break the city's power base and remove James Rowan from leadership. Permanently.

It makes me sick to think of leaving Quinn behind, but I don't know what else to do. I can't move freely throughout the city. I don't have time to look for him. Logan, and anyone else with him, will die if I don't meet them outside the city and tell them what they're facing. Quinn would understand. In fact, he'd tell me to go. I just hope if Willow is with Logan, she understands my decision before she decides to put an arrow in me for abandoning her brother.

Turning, I hurry down the hall until I get to the sewage closet. Opening the door, I gag at the sharp stench. I don't know when the dam floodgate attached to the main pipe is opened to allow a thorough rinsing of the system, but I need to be out of the pipe before the water hits.

"You'll need this." Ian walks toward me and holds out his cloak. I narrow my eyes, and he glares. "I owe you. Remember?"

I take the cloak and wrap it around myself. It smells of

smoke and fried cinnamon cakes.

"This too. Unless you want to accidentally stab yourself in the foot." He hands me the sheath to go with his dagger.

"Why are you doing this?" I ask. "And don't say you owe me, because up until a few minutes ago, the only thing you thought you owed me was death."

He clenches his jaw and glances back at Marcus, who leans heavily against the wall outside his cell. "I just want to be the son he thinks he has."

I don't have an answer to that, so I grab the edges of the pipe and try to lift my legs inside. My back spasms, and I gasp as pain sears me.

Ian wraps his hands around my waist, and I snap, "Don't touch me. Don't *ever* touch me."

He lets go, and I bare my teeth against the pain and work to get my legs into position.

"It lets out in the swamp just south of the city. The water runs through at sunset. If you aren't out of the pipe by then, you'll drown." Ian's voice sounds distant, though he's still right beside me. "There are alligators in the swamp, though they won't be close to the pipe, since they can't survive the toxic water there. The fastest way out of the swamp is to the east."

I can't make myself say thank you, so instead I look at Marcus and say, "I'll keep my promise."

"Logan? Love? Mine. Love?"

"Yes. I'll tell him you love him." I sit in the pipe and hold its sides tightly for one more second, and then I take a deep breath, release my grip, and slide feetfirst down the shaft.

CHAPTER FORTY

LOGAN

The morning we dock above the Rowansmark dam, I wake to find the Commander standing over me, his sword pointed at my chest, his dark eyes glaring. I jerk in surprise and swallow hard against the sudden fear that floods me.

"Get up."

I obey. Orion and two other soldiers are in the room standing over Frankie, Adam, Smithson, and Connor. I imagine the same scenario is being played out in the room shared by Willow, Jodi, and Nola. The Commander has decided our usefulness to him has come to an end. I just hope the plan I put in place with Captain Burkes is enough to save us.

"Move." The tip of his sword jerks toward the door.

I get up and put on my cloak, thankful that I hid the transmitters along with Melkin's staff in the boat's engine room two days ago.

The air is already warm—the damp, clinging warmth that Rowansmark is known for—as I step out of my room and find

Willow, Jodi, and Nola waiting on the deck. Nola's arms are crossed over her stomach, and she stares at the deck while Jodi wraps an arm around her shoulders, but Willow glares at everyone in the general vicinity. The Commander shoves me next to her, and she hisses, "They didn't even bother threatening me. Just threatened Nola. What was I supposed to do? They'd have killed her if I attacked them. Look what happens when you have friends."

I give her a tiny smile and nudge her boot with mine as Adam hurries to her side and gathers her close. "Yeah. Look what happens when you have friends."

"Be quiet." She rolls her eyes. "I've been taken captive at sword point *twice* in one trip. Quinn is never going to let me live that down."

"He never has to know." I scan the deck for Captain Burkes, and my stomach drops when I don't see him. If he doesn't show up now, we're in trouble.

"Where's the captain?" Frankie asks.

I shake my head and keep watching the lower deck as if I can will him to appear.

"Change of plan, then. What will it be?" Frankie asks softly from my other side as he shields Connor from the rough hands of the Commander's first lieutenant. "Charge the lot of them and fight to the death, or go over the rail and swim for shore?"

I look around us and realize the boat is anchored just off the shore above Rowansmark's dam. If we jumped, we might be able to swim against the river's current. We might be able to dodge the arrows the Commander will surely fire at us.

But I can't leave the staff behind. Not if I want to truly deliver justice and protect my people at the same time. I have one chance to put my plan into place. I have to take it and hope the captain comes through.

"Jump. Count of three." I take a step forward to put distance between myself and my people. If I distract the Commander, they'll have a better chance of escape.

"Wait a minute." Frankie's hand descends on my shoulder. "Either we all go or none of us go."

I turn to him as the Commander says, "On your knees."

"I need the staff." I mouth the words, and Frankie squares his shoulders.

"Then we fight," he says, even though none of us have our weapons.

"Halt!" The captain's voice slices through the morning air. Relief hits hard, and my hands shake as I raise my eyes to his.

"This is no concern of yours," the Commander says brusquely.

"My ship, my concern." The captain, a tall man with leathery skin and short red hair, stalks up to the Commander, radiating authority. "What is going on here?"

"Mutiny." The Commander turns back toward us.

"Are these people subject to your authority?" the captain asks.

"No, we are not." Connor's voice is clear and crisp. "We are citizens of Lankenshire, allied with the Commander in the effort to defeat Rowansmark. We are not subject to the Commander's authority outside of military operational matters."

The Commander snarls, "They're from Baalboden—"

"The seal on my cloak says otherwise." Connor steps forward, and I feel a rush of pride for him.

"There will be no bloodshed on my boat." The captain looks at the Commander. "You have bigger issues at hand than dealing with these eight people. I'll keep them behind while the army goes ashore. Once the battle is over, we can sort this out."

The Commander looks like he wants to argue, but short of challenging the captain's authority, a move that could cause the armada to turn around and head back to Chelmingford, soldiers still onboard, there's nothing he can do.

"Don't let them leave," he snaps at the captain. "Especially this one." He points at me. "Soon, I will be the new leader of Rowansmark. If I return and find them gone, the consequences will be severe."

The captain nods solemnly. "Of course." Then he claps his hands and yells, "Lower the boats!"

In moments all fifteen ships are lowering rowboats filled with soldiers and sending them to the shore. I stay at the rail to make sure the Commander and every last officer in his army is off the boat, and then I hurry to the engine room and retrieve the staff.

I return to the group in time to see Frankie and Connor finish packing up the travel bags. Captain Burkes waves me over to him.

"You know the plan?" I ask, to be sure, one last time, that I have every contingency in place.

He nods. "If I see a smoke signal from that direction"—he points to an area in the Wasteland just north of Rowansmark—"I open every floodgate on the dam and let the water into the city."

"That's right." I tie the staff to my travel pack and pull out the tracking device I built months ago to use in case I ever needed to find Rachel. It worked well for me once. I'm praying it will work again. She's somewhere inside Rowansmark if she's still alive—I refuse to accept the alternative—and I'm going to find her.

"You be absolutely sure before you send that smoke signal," the captain says. "I can't see the city from up here, so I won't know what's going on. I don't want to flood a city that hasn't been evacuated, you understand me?"

"I understand." I shake his hand, and then my people climb into a rowboat and head for shore. Jodi smiles at Connor as he discusses how much the forests of the southern Wasteland remind him of a poem he loves. Nola and Smithson both look worn and tired, but they put their heads together and talk quietly. Adam and Willow look at each other like they'd be kissing if they didn't have an audience.

"How are we getting into the city?" Frankie asks.

"I don't know." I look down at the tracking device, but it's dark. Rachel isn't near the river. "We can't walk in the front gate. We'll have to find another way in."

The army has disappeared into the Wasteland. I imagine the Commander will set up camp north of Rowansmark so he can survey the city and assess the military threat that waits for him. And stare at the device he so desperately longs to use again. He can't keep an army of that size secret for long. Rowansmark must be sending out trackers to check the city's perimeter. I estimate we have no more than two days before the Commander attacks.

I couldn't care less. I just want to find Rachel. I need to know that she's alive. Once I've found her, once I know that I'm not too late, I can focus on helping to bring down Rowansmark and then on annihilating the Commander once and for all.

The rowboat bumps gently against the shoreline, and Frankie hops out to haul the boat onto the sand and tie it to a tree. I follow him, and then reach my hand back to help the others get out of the boat. Willow rolls her eyes and leaps lightly onto the shore, as does Adam. Smithson takes my hand briefly, and then turns to help Nola himself.

That leaves Connor and Jodi and the job I've asked them to do. There's no way I'm bringing Connor on a surreptitious trip inside Rowansmark with the intent to stage a jailbreak and then kill the city's leader. Clarissa stuck her neck out for me enough by sending troops. She doesn't need me to risk her son's life. Plus, Connor has exactly the skill set I need in the person who will take the watch and send a smoke signal to Captain Burkes—he's calm under pressure and he thinks fast on his feet, just like Jodi.

I help him from the boat and then clap a hand on his shoulder. "I'm glad you came with us."

He smiles. "As am I." He reaches for Jodi, and she hops out.

"You know what to watch for?" I ask.

"When the clock tower in the center square burns, we send the signal," Connor says.

"We'll need to find a tree high enough to see over the wall." Jodi sounds cheered by the prospect. Connor goes pale, but smiles gamely.

"Sounds lovely."

Jodi laughs. "You don't mean that, but don't worry. I won't let you fall. We'll find a tree with a nice stable cradle big enough for the two of us, and then we'll just sit up there together until we see the signal."

"Sounds lovely." Connor's voice is full of enthusiasm this time, and Jodi smiles shyly.

I tell them to be safe, and then I join the others in a trek toward Rowansmark, the tracking device gripped tightly in my hand.

CHAPTER FORTY-ONE

RACHEL

The sewage pipe that runs beneath Rowansmark is wide enough for a wagon and twice as tall. By the time I climb out of it and into the swampland south of the city, the sun is well on its way toward the western horizon, my boots and the hem of Ian's cloak are covered in sewage, and the energy from the little bit of food Marcus gave me for breakfast has long since worn off. I ease out of the pipe and fall a few feet into the thick, murky swamp below. My feet instantly sink into the muddy ground, and I have to hoist the cloak and wade through water that reaches my thighs.

The entire place smells like raw sewage, moldering trees, and dank, stagnant water. Taking Ian's advice about moving east quickly so that I don't wander into any alligator-infested areas, I push through the molasses-thick swamp water until I reach a lip of dry land covered in fine, gritty dirt that is anchored by patches of wild grass.

I can't see the shadow of Rowansmark's wall to the north, but

I know it's there. And somewhere north of that, Logan is coming. I don't believe the report that Logan went north. I know him. He'd move heaven and earth to find me. I don't know how long it took him to get around the Commander's army. I don't know if he took a boat or had to travel by land, but he's coming for me.

I can't afford to assume that it will take him much longer to get here. Knowing his mind, and all of his interminable worst case scenarios, I have to assume that somehow Logan will find a way to arrive in Rowansmark before anyone expects him to.

Which means I have to *move*.

I don't waste time wiping the sludge off my clothing. My boots and cloak will be easier to clean once they're dry. My pants . . . I'll figure out how to clean those later.

I slip into the dense greenery of the Wasteland and move as quickly as my injured back will allow. My stomach rumbles in protest, but I don't stop to look for food. Not yet. I want to be north of Rowansmark by nightfall.

Lacy strips of Spanish moss drip from gnarled oak branches while clusters of fetterbush swipe at my cloak as I walk. Insects sing in the treetops, and the soft soil swallows the sound of my footsteps.

I am utterly alone for the first time since I tried to escape over Baalboden's Wall and got caught by the Commander. Unease skates down my spine in prickles of ice, and I slowly crouch, gritting my teeth against the pain that stabs through my back, and remove the dagger from its sheath.

Not that I'm in any shape to use it, but it's better than walking through the Wasteland completely defenseless. There are predators in this forest. Coyotes. Wildcats. Highwaymen. I have to be prepared.

The dagger doesn't help me feel any better. As I walk forward on legs shaky with hunger and pain, the sensation of being one tiny speck in a vast, unknowable land presses down on me with relentless force. The back of my neck itches as if trying to warn me that I'm being followed. I slip behind a thick tree trunk, close my eyes, and listen.

A flock of birds chirps incessantly to my right, and the leaves above me sift and sigh in the gentle late afternoon breeze. A branch creaks, reminding me of the old floorboards in Oliver's kitchen.

There's nothing to cause me alarm. Nothing to explain the unsettled feeling that coils through me until I want to curl up on the ground, wrap my arms across my chest, and hold myself silent and still until somehow I feel less alone.

Maybe that's what this is. Maybe I've spent so much time focused on what I have to say or do or be to those around me, that when I finally have a chance to be alone with myself, I don't know how to do it. With no immediate threats, no conversations, and no task other than to put one foot ahead of the other, I'm stripped of everything I've used to distract myself from the grief and longing that live inside of me.

I miss my dad. I miss Oliver, too.

An ache throbs at the back of my throat, and I swallow hard as I make myself keep walking. Keep moving, because even if there's nothing to keep the ghosts that haunt me at bay, I still have a job to finish. I have a boy to save.

Thinking about Logan eases the ache in my throat and

settles some of the unease that lurks within me. I think of his ink-stained fingers and how safe I feel when he wraps his hand around mine, pressing our palms together. I think of the way his eyes crinkle at the corners when he laughs. The way he watches others so carefully, as if he thinks that with enough data, he can predict who will hurt him and who will love him instead.

I wonder if he predicted the way my heart thuds against my chest when I think of his body leaning against mine, his breath tangled in my hair, his heat soaking into me like a blanket I wear beneath my skin. I wonder if all the years he spent observing me at Oliver's, and later at my own house, prepared him for the way he lives in a space inside of me that feels like it was always meant to be his.

I hope he knows that I would push myself to my limits to find him because he matters more to me than making Ian pay for his crimes, or taking James Rowan out of power, or even killing the Commander. The last time I spoke to Logan, we were rushing to get out of Lankenshire's hospital so we could find Ian. I didn't have a chance to tell him why I'd become so distant after Sylph's death, and that I was fighting to break through my silence and feel again. I couldn't show him that even though I'm far from better, I've found the courage to face what hurts me so that I can overcome it.

I duck beneath a curtain of rubbery kudzu vines, and catch a glimpse of Rowansmark, illuminated by the westward moving sun that spreads across the city's wall like golden syrup. Using the dagger, I slice off a long length of kudzu and wrap it around my waist several times. I don't have rope, so the thick kudzu will have to do.

My stomach growls, and I have to grab on to the trunk of an ancient walnut tree as my head spins. I need food, but I'm in no condition to hunt. The walnuts in the trees that are scattered around me won't ripen until September. The acorns on the oak trees would require blanching, and I don't dare try to light a fire. Clusters of mushrooms grow out of fallen tree trunks throughout the area, but I'm not sure if they're edible or not. Dad and I never traveled south of Rowansmark, and we usually steered clear of mushrooms anyway, because one wrong choice could mean a painful death.

Doing my best to ignore the ache in my stomach and the slight ringing in my ears, I push forward, holding on to tree trunks for balance as I wade through thick underbrush. The sun is just beginning to set when I finally find something I can eat.

A field of wild grass is choked with thistles. A stream runs through it, and the water looks clear and tastes clean. I strip off my clothes, rinse them, and then rinse myself as well. Laying out my clothes to dry as much as possible, I go after the thistles. It will take work to get to the edible part of the plant, but it's better than starving. I crouch beside a few plants and saw through the base of them with the dagger. Then I carefully use the dagger to strip away the outer skin and reveal the stalk inside each stem. The stalks are tough to chew, and the taste is bland, but they're filling. I eat my way through two small plants before stopping.

With my stomach satisfied, I pull on my damp tunic and pants and then turn my attention to finding a place to set up camp. I need to be able to see movement in the Wasteland north of Rowansmark. I don't know how else to track Logan. I don't have a tracking device for him. I don't know exactly which path he'll take through the Wasteland. All I can do is climb the highest tree around, pay attention, and hope.

I move west until stars are pricking the sky, and Rowansmark is a silent bulk of stone and lit torches less than two hundred yards behind me. I'm far enough into the Wasteland not to worry about being seen by guards patrolling the city's wall, but close enough to where the Wasteland meets the field of flat, damp ground that surrounds the city on three sides that if anyone approaches the city through the forest, I should hear them before they show themselves to the guards.

I find an oak tree that stretches so far toward the sky, I can't see the top of it from the ground. Putting my dagger back into the sheath inside my boot, I reach up toward the lowest branch and jump.

My hands wrap around the rough bark for a split second, and pain tears through my back and explodes throughout my body. I cry out and drop to the ground, cradling my right arm against me and breathing through my teeth as something warm and wet soaks through the back of my tunic. I've torn open some of my wounds, and the muscle in my right arm won't grip anything for very long. Tears gather in my eyes and spill down my face in salty trails as I slowly push myself to my feet and pull my bloody tunic away from my skin for a moment.

Logan is coming. I have to be able to warn him. I am going up this tree no matter what it costs me.

Careful not to tear through any more of the healing wounds on my back, I bend down and retrieve the dagger. If I can't jump up to the lowest branch and swing my body into the tree, I'm going to have to climb it the hard way. It will leave an obvious trail, but I don't have another choice.

Driving the dagger into the trunk of the tree at eye level, I wrap both of my hands around its hilt, letting my left hand take the brunt of my weight, and pull myself up. Hugging the trunk with my right arm and my legs, I pull the dagger free with my left hand, climb by digging the weapon into the bark for leverage, and then shinny my way up, inch by painful inch.

It seems to take forever to reach the first branch. My blood-soaked tunic is stuck to my back, and every move I make feels like someone is scraping sandpaper over my wounds. I crawl onto the limb, rest my face against the trunk, and clench my jaw to keep from crying.

"I can do this," I whisper into the gloomy twilight. "It's just pain."

Just pain. Just pain. I repeat the mantra to myself as I get to my feet, stab the dagger into the tree, and start climbing again. By the time I reach the highest cradle, the one that will let me see out over the Wasteland in every direction, I've given up trying to keep the tears at bay. I crawl into the small nesting spot supported by two branches at my back and another two on either side and struggle just to breathe without sobbing.

The stars are silver dust scattered across the sky, and the moon is a low-slung wedge that spills white light across the treetops like a path made of liquid diamonds. I position my back so that the bleeding wounds are between the two supporting branches, peel my tunic away from my skin as best I can, and tilt my head back to stare at the sky.

The last time I lay out beneath the sky near Rowansmark,

Dad was sitting near me, the package from Marcus in his hands. If I close my eyes, I imagine I can smell the remnants of our campfire and the gamey scent of the rabbit meat we'd wrapped in leaves and hidden in my pack to keep for morning. I can hear Dad humming quietly, the same lullaby he sang for me when I'd wake as a child from nightmares that now seem dull in comparison to the terrible things real life can bring. With my eyes closed, I can hang on, just for a second, to the absolute peace and security I always felt whenever he was near.

My eyes open, and I raise shaky fingers to wipe tears from my cheeks. I don't know if I'm crying because I hurt on the outside or because the ache of missing Dad feels more real in this moment than it has since the day I lay weeping on his grave.

"I miss you," I say softly, my voice breaking over the words because they are too small, too ordinary, to sum up everything he meant to me. "It was you and me and Oliver against the world for so long. And now it's just me. Me and Logan."

My words are quiet against the chorus of crickets and the quiet *shush-shush* of wings as an owl passes by overhead. I sit for a moment, staring at the stars, and then say, "I want you to know that I understand why you went back for the package. Why you didn't take it to Baalboden in the first place. And I'm proud of you for saving Quinn and Willow, even though it cost you . . . even though . . ."

My throat closes. I let the grief rush out of the silence, split it wide open, and consume me. I let it have me, and I *feel*. I feel the bright shard of pain in my chest when I accept that I will never pick up my Switch and spar with Dad again. That Oliver will never call me Rachel-girl, and I will never be forced to swallow

Dad's terrible cooking, and my little yellow house in Baalboden will never be filled with laughter and fairy tales and the good, cinnamony scent of Oliver's sticky buns.

I cry until I have no more tears, and then I raise my face to the heavens, to the place where I know Dad and Oliver are looking down on me with the same fierce love that I will always feel for them, and I say, "Thank you for raising me to think for myself. Thank you for telling me fairy tales but also for teaching me how to face the battles I'd need to win in real life."

I grab hold of a branch on my left and slowly reach my right hand toward the sky, imagining I can feel the whisper-soft touch of my family in return. "I love you both. I always will."

I swallow hard and let a painful kind of peace fill me as I say the last word I need Dad and Oliver to hear—the most compli-cated, powerful word I know.

"Good-bye."

Then, as my last word to my family floats across the endless expanse of trees in front of me, I use the kudzu vine to anchor myself to my perch, wrap my cloak around me to try to keep predators from catching the scent of the blood drying on the back of my tunic, and pray with everything in me that I will hear Logan before he gets caught in James Rowan's trap.

CHAPTER FORTY-TWO

LOGAN

"Keep moving," I say quietly as we carefully skirt a cluster of thick, flowering bushes growing in clumps in the shadow of giant hickory trees. "If we stay in one spot for too long, the sentries will find us."

We spent the night up in the trees, lashing ourselves to the branches with rope and keeping as silent as possible to avoid detection by the Rowansmark sentries who make regular rounds to check the city's perimeter. I kept the tracking device in my hand so I could check it every few minutes, even though logic would indicate that unless Rachel was moving toward us, the screen would remain blank.

We've spent most of the day slowly circling the Wasteland north of the city, noting the routine of the guards at the gates, avoiding sentries, and trying to find other ways into the city.

So far, I don't have any workable ideas. Rowansmark is clearly expecting an army from the north. The city's wall is bristling with soldiers and cannons. There's a triple guard at the entrance.

If we're going to get into the city, it won't be through the gate.

"We need to move east through the forest and then cut south. The city shouldn't be as heavily guarded there. We'll have a better chance of getting in." I hope. I have no idea if there are multiple entrances to Rowansmark, but I do know wandering around north of the wall is getting us nowhere. And every second we waste trying to find a way in from the north is another second that Rachel is in danger.

"Let's go," Willow says as she swings her body into the nearest hickory and starts moving. Adam follows her. Frankie walks beside me while Smithson and Nola bring up the rear.

I check the tracking device for what feels like the fiftieth time in the last hour, but it remains stubbornly dark. No sign of Rachel's wristmark signal. I tell myself it's because she's deep inside the city, too far for me to track.

I can't consider the other alternative. Not if I want to stay focused.

"Anything yet?" Frankie asks.

I shake my head, but don't bother coming up with excuses for why I still can't find a trace of her. Frankie's heard them already. Multiple times. Repeating myself in a desperate bid to keep my flagging hope alive is more than I can take.

Frankie repeats them for me. "Just means she's in the southern edge of the city or to the east somewhere. Maybe they're holding her deep underground where the signal can't reach."

I can't answer him. Not because I can't imagine Rachel in a deep, dark hole, but because I can. I can see her suffering under Rowansmark's pain atonement laws. I can see her turned over to Ian to do with as he pleases. I can see her dead.

Shoving that thought away, I pick up the pace and check the tracking device again out of habit.

It glows a faint blue.

My knees give out. I have to grab the nearest hickory trunk and hang on to keep my footing as relief, bright and giddy, rushes through me, chasing away the dark specters I couldn't bear to face.

"We're on the right track." My voice shakes, but I don't care because I've finally found her.

Frankie squeezes my shoulder and says softly, "Told you she'd be okay."

I meet his gaze for a second and then start half walking, half running east. The light on the tracking device flickers for the first few yards but then grows steadily stronger.

Willow drops out of a tree and lands in front of me, and I nearly plow into her.

"Slow down," she says sternly, grabbing fistfuls of my cloak when I try to move past her. "It could be a trap."

"I know."

"Then *slow down*. Sheesh. Being in love knocks the common sense right out of you, doesn't it?"

I glance up at Adam and grin. "I don't know, Willow. You tell me."

She rolls her eyes, but pink glows in her cheeks. "Use your head for a few more minutes. Once you find her, you can kiss her and tell her all the mushy things I know you two say to each other. Just do the rest of us a favor and make sure you're alone when you do so. I like to keep my dinner in my stomach."

Now I'm the one rolling my eyes even as I slow my pace and

walk past her. "So last night you weren't kissing Adam up in a tree? Because I could swear I heard—"

She smacks my back hard enough to make me stop talking. I raise my hands in mock surrender and keep moving east.

The sun is drifting to the west when the tracking device glows a deep, brilliant blue. We're at the northeastern edge of the Wasteland overlooking Rowansmark. If we climb a tree, we can still see the city, shining gold and brown in the late afternoon sun.

She's here. I scan the trees, the clumps of bushes, and the pads of moss lying underfoot, but I don't see anything out of place.

"Spread out," I say, and my people move through the trees, looking for signs.

Five minutes pass without a single trace of her other than the steadily glowing light of the tracking device, but then I hear a faint voice say, "Logan?"

It could be a trap. I know it could. But I can't stop myself from rushing forward to find her. I duck behind trees and look over my shoulder, searching for a threat, but I can't take my time. Everything inside of me yearns to see her. To touch her and assure myself that she's real.

"Found her!" Willow calls from my left.

I sprint, but when I get to Willow, I don't see Rachel. "Where is she?"

"Near the top of the tree." Willow points, and I follow a series of deep gouges in the trunk of a huge oak until I see a glimmer of red in the uppermost cradle.

"Rachel!" I press my palms against the tree trunk as if I can somehow reach through it and touch her instead.

"I'm up here." Her voice hitches as if she's crying.

I want to tear the tree down, branch by branch, to reach her, but I make myself take a deep breath and say calmly, "You can come down now. It's safe."

She's quiet for a moment, and the leaves near the top of the tree rustle, but then she cries out, a sharp sound of pain that hits me like a punch to the stomach.

"I'll go see what's wrong," Willow says.

"No, I'll go." I'm already wrapping my hands around the lowest branch.

"I'm faster—"

"I'm *going*." I swing my body onto the branch and start climbing as fast as I can.

It takes less than three minutes to get to Rachel. It feels like a lifetime. I see her hair first, glowing like fire in the afternoon sun, and it's like coming home for the first time in weeks. She's lashed herself to two branches in the uppermost cradle using kudzu. The cloak she's wearing isn't hers. Grabbing the branches she tied herself to, I haul myself into the cradle beside her and just stare into her beautiful face.

I want to find the words to tell her what it means to me to see her again—that a hollow space that opened up inside of me when she disappeared is whole again—but I'm suddenly out of words. There aren't any for what I feel. I lean forward and press my forehead to hers, close my eyes, and just take her in one breath at a time.

"*Rachel.*"

"You came," she whispers, and tears spill down her cheeks. "I knew you'd come, no matter what Ian said."

"Of course I came. I told you I'd always find you." I raise my hand and gently wipe the tears from her face. "I expected you to be inside Rowansmark. Why are you up in a tree in the middle of the forest?"

"I escaped because I had to find you. I had to warn you." Her eyes find mine. "You can't go near Rowansmark. Marcus—your dad—invented these things called summoners that can call an entire army of the *tanniyn* at once, and Rowan plans to unleash them on you or anyone else who threatens Rowansmark. I tried to figure out how to destroy them, but they're buried, and Ian didn't know how to break them, so Marcus said if we used an inverse signal—"

I pull back while a tight ball of heat presses against my chest from the inside out. "Wait a minute. I thought Marcus was dead. And what do you mean Ian didn't know how to break them? Why would you even ask him?"

Quickly, she tells me about being imprisoned in the make-shift dungeon below James Rowan's house, about my father with his broken mind but loving spirit locked for months in the cell beside hers, and about Ian breaking down when he realized everything he'd done to restore his family's honor had been based on a lie.

I'm not sure how to feel about the news that my father is still alive. Alive or dead, he's a stranger to me. Ian, however, is no stranger. The fact that he's suddenly realized he made the wrong choices doesn't take those choices away. This information doesn't change what we need to do—it just means we have to find a way around the summoners.

"Are you going to say anything?" she asks.

I shake my head. I could talk strategy or discuss the depths of crazy that inhabit my family tree, but after weeks of being apart, I'm finally with Rachel again. I'm not going to waste time talking scenarios when we could be kissing. "I'd rather kiss you."

Before she can say a word, I lean forward and kiss her the way I've dreamed of every night since we've been apart. When I pull back, we're both breathless. She looks me over as if trying to memorize me in case we're separated again, but then she frowns and grabs my left hand.

"What happened?" She nods toward the stub that used to be my little finger.

"A tracker cut it off." I try not to flinch at the memory of searing pain and the surreal sight of my finger separated from my hand.

"I hope you made him pay for that." Her voice is fierce.

"Willow slit his throat."

She pulls me to her and kisses me. Her kisses are just as fierce as her voice. When she pulls away, I grin.

"I'd love to keep kissing you, but maybe we'd be more comfortable on the ground?" I ask. "Besides, our friends want to see you."

She grins, but makes no move to leave the tree.

"Rachel, can we climb down now?"

She firms her lips and slowly reaches toward the branch closest to her, but before she can grasp it, her face pales, and she hisses in pain.

"Is it your arm?" I look at her burned forearm, but it's bandaged, so I can't see how bad the injury is.

"No, it's . . . there's one other thing I need to tell you about my stay in Rowansmark." She tries to adjust herself and winces. "James Rowan decided I was guilty of a rebellious attitude and of taking things that didn't belong to me, so he sentenced me to fifteen lashes."

"Fifteen . . . with a *whip*?" Anger is sharp and lethal inside of me as she leans forward, and I gently peel her tunic away from her back. The skin is a mass of partially healed strips. A few of the scabs have pulled away from the skin and are bleeding. "You're—that's—how did you climb this—I'm going to kill him, Rachel. I'm going to kill James Rowan for doing this to you."

"Actually, we're going to kill him because he does this to everybody, and because he thought he could just take over the world, and everyone would have to go along with his plan." She reaches for me, and I wrap my arms around her, careful to avoid pressing against her wounds.

She brushes a kiss along my jaw. "So . . . how am I going to get down?"

"I'll carry you."

"Down a tree?" She sounds alarmed.

"It can't be that hard."

"It sounds impossible."

"Nothing is impossible." I grin at her with as much confidence as I can muster, and then I wrap her arms around my neck, hoist her onto my back, and very carefully make my way down the tree. All the while my joy at finding Rachel wars with the fury I feel at the man who ordered her whipping, and I vow that summoners or no summoners, I'm going inside Rowansmark.

Best Case Scenario: I enter the city undetected, and James Rowan learns what I do to those who abuse the girl I love.

I don't even bother planning for a worst case scenario, because nothing is going to stop me from making James Rowan pay for hurting Rachel. Nothing.

CHAPTER FORTY-THREE

RACHEL

I hang on to Logan as tightly as I can without choking him while he slowly climbs down the tree. Being connected to him again is like finding the piece of me that was missing and putting it back into place. Willow meets us halfway and keeps a hand on me as we descend. I'm not sure she could catch me if I slipped, but I appreciate the sentiment. I just hope she continues to feel friendly toward me once I tell her about Quinn.

When we reach the ground, Frankie takes me off Logan's back so that Logan can drop down from the last branch. My cloak slips from my shoulders and falls to my feet. I lean against Frankie's big chest for a moment, then Nola steps forward and gently lifts the back of my bloodstained tunic, and Frankie swears viciously.

"Who did this? Ian? I'll tear him apart limb from limb."

"Not Ian." I cringe as Nola's fingers skim over my healing wounds. "James Rowan. This was my pain atonement for not taking the device back to them when I first found it. And I think he added extra lashes because I wasn't properly respectful to him and insisted on calling him a murderer."

"That's my girl," Logan murmurs, but there's a distance in his voice that wasn't there before he saw my back. A coldness that makes me shrivel a little bit inside. I knew my back would be horribly scarred, but I'd convinced myself Logan wouldn't care.

Now I'm not so sure. His eyes darken when he looks at me, and when I catch his gaze, he looks away.

"This needs cleaning. I'm going to look for plants to use," Nola says.

"I'll help." Smithson gives me a tiny smile and then follows Nola into the woods.

"Where's Quinn?" The words burst from Willow as if she'd been trying hard to hold them back for as long as possible. I realize that her restraint—her choice to help me down the tree and to hold her tongue until Nola had checked out my wounds—isn't like the Willow I first met.

"He's inside Rowansmark." I realize my mistake as Adam wraps a protective arm around Willow while her face blanches. "Not in the dungeon! He wasn't caught or whipped or anything. He's fine. In fact, he's become quite the revolutionary." Quickly, I tell them about how Quinn confronted Ian and pretended to die so that he could give me a knife, how he followed me onto the boat, and then how he's waged a campaign of fire against Rowansmark's important military buildings.

Willow's brows rise. "My brother is burning down buildings?"

"Apparently."

She blinks and then shakes her head. "Wonders never cease. Well, we have to go back into the city and get him. How did you escape?"

"I climbed out through the sewer system."

"Perfect. We'll go back through tomorrow." Willow nods as if it's settled, and I cut my eyes toward Logan, but he's staring toward Rowansmark.

Frankie looks between me and Logan, and then says, "Willow, you and Adam go find us something to eat. I'll set up camp somewhere down there." He gestures toward the south and starts walking.

Willow frowns at Logan, who is still staring at Rowansmark as if he's forgotten we're with him, and opens her mouth as if to say something, but Adam hooks his arm through hers and pulls her away before she can speak.

I wait for a moment, hoping Logan will look at me. Speak to me. But he stands motionless, shoulders stiff, watching the city.

"We might as well just say it so that it isn't awkward." My voice sounds calm, but hurt throbs beneath my breastbone as he slowly turns to look at me.

"I'm not sure I want to talk about it." His voice is quiet, and he won't hold my gaze.

A spark of anger flames to life inside of me, and I move toward him, wincing as my back protests. "Well, it isn't going to go away, so I don't see how ignoring it does any good."

A muscle in his jaw clenches, and he lifts his gaze to mine. Misery is etched in his eyes, and he looks away again. "I've been trying to figure out how to say this."

I cross my arms over my chest. It hurts, but I manage. "You could just come right out and say, 'Wow, Rachel, between your back and your arm, you're really scarred, and I don't find you pretty anymore.'"

His gaze whips up to mine and stays there. "Excuse me?"

I bite my lip to keep it from trembling. "I saw the difference in you. You were so happy to see me until you saw my scars, and then you got all distant, and I get it. It looks bad. But you know what? I earned those. Every one of them. I'm not the same girl you fell in love with back in Baalboden. I've got scars inside and out, and a lot of it isn't pretty. If you can't handle that without suddenly being unable to look me in the eye—"

He takes two strides forward, grips my upper arms, and pulls me against him. Hard. A dangerous light gleams in his eyes as he bends his neck and kisses me. Something in me relaxes.

When he pulls back, he says, "Do you really think your scars make you less beautiful to me?"

"Well . . . yes."

"When I see those scars, I see courage. The kind of courage most people only dream of having. I see proof that the girl I love is fierce and strong and unshakable when it really matters. Your scars are beautiful because they're part of you, Rachel."

Before he can kiss me again, I ask, "So then what happened?"

His expression becomes distant again, and I smack his shoulder lightly. "Stop doing that. Stop going inside your head and shutting me out. Just *tell* me."

He takes a deep breath and meets my eyes. "Ever since I learned who Ian was—who I was—I feel like who I am and where I come from contributed to the awful things that have happened." He lets go of me. "Like your scars. If Ian hadn't wanted to hurt me, you wouldn't have been burned or whipped. I'm not saying I'm responsible. I'm saying I know that who I am is wrapped up in everything you've lost. Your dad, Oliver, our city, Sylph . . . I don't know if you can look at me without being reminded of that. And if you can't, then—"

"What are you talking about?" I glare at him.

"Everyone who's ever said they loved me can't be trusted anymore. Except you."

"I don't understand."

"My mother—" His voice chokes off, and he clears his throat. "She wasn't my mother. She lied to me. All that time, all those reassurances that I was her whole world, and I was nothing more than someone else's child thrust into her care."

"Logan—"

"And Oliver." The words pour out as if he can't bear to hold them back any longer. "He said he loved me, too. But look at the facts. I was nothing more than the Commander's long-term investment. Do you really think the Commander would make me an outcast and not have an insurance policy in place to keep me alive until his investment paid off? No wonder Oliver was feeding me. Someone had to make sure I was still alive."

He looks at his feet. "And then there's Jared." His voice is so full of pain, it makes me ache too. "He carried regular reports of my well-being to my father. How could he not tell me who I was? I thought I'd earned his love and respect, but he was simply keeping an eye on me because that was part of his job."

He presses his fingers to his eyes. "I can't believe I'm telling you this. I don't want to tarnish the memory of the family you've lost. You'd been through so much. Most of it because of who I am. I'm so afraid that you won't be able to love me anymore, either."

His breath catches in his throat, and he falls silent. My heart thrums against my rib cage as slivers of the dreams I once had for us slide softly back into place. I understand being afraid that the wreckage in his life makes him unlovable now. And I can see the flaw in his reasoning. I step to his side.

"Logan?"

He nods, his fingers still pressed to his eyes, his shoulders bowed.

"For someone so smart, you sure are thickheaded about relationships."

He slowly raises his head. "Is that supposed to make me feel better?"

"It's the truth. And I'm learning that truth is the only thing that makes us better." I reach up, ignoring the twinge of pain in my back, and cup his face in my palms, holding him so he has to look me in the eye. "Some families are built through blood. Some are built through choice. It doesn't change what you mean to one another."

He doesn't reply, but he's listening.

"Your mother—"

He makes a strangled noise and lifts a hand as if to protest, and I glare at him.

"Your *mother* loved you. Does it matter where you came from? Or does it matter that once she had you, she did everything in her power to take care of you, even when it meant risking her life?" I lean closer. "People don't give their lives for others unless love is involved."

He opens his mouth to speak, and I shake my head. "I'm not done."

"I can see that."

"Oliver wasn't capable of deception, and you know it. When he said he loved you, he meant it. I don't know if he was being paid to watch out for you or if he chose to do that on his own, but how you two became connected doesn't matter nearly as much as the fact that he grew to see you as the son he never had. Can you honestly tell me you think Oliver would lie to you about that?"

"No, Oliver wasn't a liar." His voice is quiet.

"And as for Dad, well . . ." I pause to gather the right words, and Logan's jaw tenses beneath my hands. "I can't say he didn't keep secrets from you. He might have known all along what was going on. Or he might have simply delivered unopened messages and been none the wiser. But he loved and respected you, and I can prove it."

"*How?*"

I press close to him until I can feel the heat of his skin on mine. Until nothing stands between us but a few breaths of air. "Because when he knew he wasn't returning to Baalboden, he wrote a will. And in that will, he asked you to take care of one thing. Just one thing. What was it?"

"You," he breathes, and then his arms are around me, and my fingers are in his hair, and his mouth is on mine. His kiss is fierce, rough lips and desperate hands, and my skin hums as something bright and glorious rushes through my veins.

When he raises his head, there's a wild light in his eyes that I know burns for me alone. "I love you," he says.

I reach up and hold the necklace he gave me when he promised he would always find me, and I smile. "I love you, too. Always."

And then he kisses me like he's desperate for me, and I let go of his necklace and hold on to him instead.

CHAPTER FORTY-FOUR

LOGAN

As darkness falls, I lead Rachel away from where the others have made camp for the night. Nola smiles as we leave. Frankie wiggles his brows and laughs as I roll my eyes. And Willow tells us not to get so distracted that we forget to be on our guard.

I find a spot on the crest of a hill a short distance from the others. Close enough to hear them if they run into trouble, but far enough away that Rachel and I can talk without being overheard. I have so much to say, and suddenly I don't think I can find the words for any of it.

As I spread my bedroll out, trying to make it big enough for two since Rachel doesn't have one of her own, I examine my options. I want to tell her that I missed her, but that doesn't begin to describe the way I ached for her while we were apart. I could tell her that I thought of her often, but that's a lie. It would be better to say that I never stopped thinking of her. That every breath I took was filled with how much she means to me.

Behind us, the trees creak and rustle. Above us, the stars give off a cold, glittering light that bathes us in silver. And beside me, Rachel is slowly lowering herself to the bedroll, her movements stiff and unsteady. I wrap my hands around her upper arms and support her as she sinks to her knees. She hisses in a breath as she leans forward, stretching the wounds on her back while she crawls toward the top of the bedroll.

"Can I help? Let me help. I want to help," I say, though what I'm really saying is *I wish I could've protected you when you needed it.*

She laughs as she eases onto her stomach and then rolls to her side. "It's fine. It's good for me to move around. Helps it heal faster."

"I'm sorry. I should've been there. Or you *shouldn't* have been there. None of that should've happened. I promised I'd protect you, but I didn't, and—"

"Logan, it's fine."

I crawl onto the bedroll and stretch out beside her on my back, my face to the sky as anger boils through me. "It's not fine. There is *nothing* fine about a man abusing his power by whipping a girl. *He* should be whipped." I'm talking too loudly, but I can't seem to stop. "He should beg for mercy, just like my mother. . . ."

She reaches for me and lightly draws her fingers down my cheek as my words linger in the air between us.

"Are we talking about James Rowan? Or the Commander?" she asks, her thumb rubbing light circles across my cheek.

"Both, I guess." I sigh as her fingers find the tension in the side of my jaw and massage it away. "I can't keep failing those I love."

Her fingers still. Her voice is a snap of impatience. "That's ridiculous."

I open my mouth to reply, but she beats me to it.

"You didn't fail me. I chose to go into Rowansmark."

"You were kidnapped and badly injured."

"Please. You know me well enough by now to know that I wasn't cowering in a wagon waiting around for rescue. I spent my time assessing my opponents, gathering information, and looking for my opportunity to escape."

She shifts closer to me, cradling her head on her arm. A breeze sifts through her hair, lifting the strands to dance in the starlight. The warmth that gathers in my chest has nothing to do with the anger I feel toward those who've hurt her and everything to do with the way the silver light glows against her skin.

"And I had opportunities, Logan. Twice."

"And you didn't *take them*?" I stop admiring the curve of her cheekbones and glare at her. "You could've been killed. Ian is sick. You know that. He could've tortured you. He could've killed you. He—"

"He tried."

"Rachel." I reach for her, careful not to touch the wounds on her back, and pull her close until her head fits against my shoulder. Then I bury my hand in her hair to hide the way my fingers tremble.

"You're only upset with me because you were worried about me." She nuzzles closer to me, and I swear I can feel her heart beating strong and sure against my chest. "But I promise I was planning to escape. I was thinking about exit strategies. I just changed my strategy because I learned something important. You didn't fail me. I went to Rowansmark because I chose to, even though I knew the risks."

I hold her against me in silence for a moment while I struggle to find the balance between fear for her safety and pride that she is a fierce, smart, formidable girl who chooses courage every time. Finally, I say, "Okay, two things. One, I'm proud of you. You scare me because I know you'll choose to face danger instead of running away, but that doesn't mean I'm not proud of who you are.

"And two . . ." I gently tilt her chin up to face me. "Saying that I feel worry for you when you're in danger is like saying a starving man feels like having a snack. I don't worry, Rachel. I'm consumed. You're in every breath I take, and so I don't worry. I agonize. I plan. I reassure myself. And then I plan some more, because I'm not going to stand idly by while men who've been corrupted by their fear or their greed destroy the only family I have left."

She smiles, though it looks like there are tears in her eyes. "I love you, too."

I lean down and kiss her. A long, slow, sure kiss that leaves my pulse racing and my heart pounding. When I pull back, she says, "We need to talk about your family."

"I'm willfully ignoring the fact that Ian is related to me."

"I'm talking about your father."

I listen as she describes the man my father has become. As she tells me his only thought was for the safety of his sons.

For me.

By the time she starts explaining how Ian came to her cell to kill her only to break completely when he realized our father was still alive, my heart is pounding, a painful rhythm that sends jolts of energy through my veins, though I don't know what to do with it.

"Marcus isn't . . . stable. Mentally. But he's sweet, and he loves you, Logan. He really does. He loves Ian, too."

I move restlessly when she mentions Ian, and she tilts her head back to look in my eyes. "The things Ian did are monstrous. He deserves to be punished. But the boy Ian was before the Commander's actions caused your mom to commit suicide and your father to ignore everything but his frantic need to ransom you, the boy Ian wanted to be before James Rowan forced him to whip his father and feel responsible for his father's death—that boy isn't so different from us."

"He's *different*. Neither one of us murdered innocent people because we were angry or in pain."

"I did." Her voice is steady, but the hand pressing against my heart trembles.

I cover her hand with mine. "You were defending yourself. There was no time to ask questions, and we know Melkin was tasked with killing you and taking the device."

"He wouldn't have done it."

"Maybe. Maybe not. But there was no way for you to know that."

She smiles, a small, bittersweet lifting of her lips. "Logan, I'd just found out my father was dead. And I was still reeling from losing Oliver. I was running on nothing but rage and grief and the desperate belief that if I could just make the Commander pay, my pain would be worth something."

"And yet you were still defending yourself." I roll onto my side so I can face her. "Rachel, no matter how much pain you felt inside, you never deliberately took an innocent life. I can't imagine a situation in which you would make that choice. That's the difference between us and Ian." My voice hardens. "He's not my brother. He's a killer who hurt the people I was responsible for. The fact that he used to be something different, something better, doesn't change what he's done."

"I know." She brushes a kiss across my lips. "But you should've seen the awful expression on his face when he realized he'd done so much harm to make his father's death mean something, and it was all a lie. And then he helped me. He could've killed me, or turned me in, or just walked away. But he gave me his cloak and his dagger. He told me how to get safely out of the swamp. And he defied his leader so that he could rescue your father."

I absorb her words for a moment, but I can't find it in myself to soften toward Ian. "I'm glad he helped you, but he has a long way to go before he could ever make up for the things he's done. He deserves to be punished."

"Yes, he does. But your father forgave him, and made me promise I would save you both."

I stare at her. "You promised to save Ian? Why? From *what*?"

"From James Rowan. And I did it because I needed Marcus's help to learn about the summoners." Quickly, she explains that they're buried somewhere near Rowansmark—probably a safe distance outside the city's wall, if I had to guess—and that neither Marcus nor Ian knew how to find and destroy the tech.

"So you went into Rowansmark hoping to find the tech

before I walked into a trap our little stolen device couldn't possibly handle." I lean my forehead to hers and close my eyes as the gift of her love for me, a fierce, indestructible love that would drive her to sacrifice her life to save mine, pours across the broken foundations of my life and lends it strength. "Rachel . . ."

Her voice is a whisper of sound between us. "If you're about to tell me you feel bad because I put myself in danger for you when we both know you'd do the same for me—"

I press my lips to hers, swallowing the rest of her words as I fist my hand in her hair and draw her as close to me as she can go without sinking beneath my skin.

When I lift my head to draw a breath, she says in a breathless voice, "Are you just trying to shut me up, or—"

"I'm trying to thank you." I kiss her again, and it's like diving underwater. The cacophony of insect noises in the forest behind us becomes a muted hum. The brilliant starlight is a distant glow that can't touch us. Nothing can touch us. We're floating in a world that belongs only to us, and I don't ever want to surface.

Rachel breaks our kiss and says, "We could disappear, you know. We could walk into the Wasteland and never look back."

I lean my cheek to hers as I let myself imagine it. Rachel and me and peace. The seemingly endless expanse of the Wasteland ours to explore and conquer. No more fighting. No more fear. No more risking everything we have left to make sure those who deserve justice get their due.

But if we do that, who will stand for the innocents still in Rowansmark's path? Who will remove both James Rowan and the Commander from power? The weight of responsibility that lifted briefly at her words settles back on my shoulders, heavier than it was before.

"I want to," I say.

She smiles. "So do I, but we can't, can we? Not yet. We have to go back inside Rowansmark and find Quinn. We have to stop the summoners from destroying the troops you gathered. We have to get James Rowan out of power and get rid of the tech that uses the Cursed Ones as weapons. And we need to find your father, because he'd really love to meet you."

"And then, we finish what we started with the Commander," I say. "We finish it, and we do our best to live quiet, peaceful lives."

She laughs, and warmth coils through my body. "Do you really think you and I are capable of quiet, peaceful lives?"

"I'll settle for a life that doesn't involve bloodshed."

Her laughter dies, and I see the warrior she's become in the steady intensity of her gaze. "But first, we have more blood to shed."

"We do. But not tonight. Tonight, I have other things to worry about." I lean down and kiss her again, keeping my hands gentle as I hold her, though there's nothing gentle about the way she holds on to me. "Tonight, I have you."

"You said I don't worry you." She traces my jaw with her lips.

"You don't." I'm breathing too fast. Or too slow. I can't tell, but my chest is tight and my pulse is racing, and I'm underwater again. If this is how it feels to drown, I can't wait to suck the water into my lungs and let it take me.

"You said I consume you." Her lips find the pulse on my neck and press while my heart hammers inside my chest.

"You do." My voice is rough.

"Prove it."

I smile as I hear the challenge in her voice, and then, as the moon drifts across the sky above us, I dedicate myself to the task of kissing Rachel until she runs out of air, and we drown together.

CHAPTER FORTY-FIVE

We're up and moving south toward the swamp below the city before dawn. Logan has no idea how soon the Commander will attack Rowansmark, but it's too difficult to hide an army that size for long. Sooner or later, a tracker, a sentry, or a traveler through the Wasteland will see the forces gathered outside Rowansmark and report it to James. The Commander must know this, so he won't wait.

Which means we have to get back into the city today and stop the summoners.

Except that Logan doesn't seem to think we can.

"I told you," I say as I accept a handful of blackberries and some peeled thistle—our breakfast for the day—from Nola. "We can't find the summoners because they're buried somewhere, and we aren't going to have time to search every inch of dirt around the city's wall. There are three full armies running drills inside and out of that wall all day long. We'd be caught in a second. And if we can't find the summoners, we can't destroy them. According to Ian, our only option is to send an inverse signal to nullify the sound wave the summoners produce."

"We don't have anything capable of sending an inverse signal. That would require a device set exclusively to the opposite of the infrasonic wave, and all we've got is a staff set to infrasonic and enough transmitters to amplify it for hundreds of yards," he says as we follow Smithson and Nola through the woods. Frankie is at our backs, his hand on his sword, and Willow and Adam tree-leap far ahead of us, searching for danger.

None of them say it, but I can see their concern for me in the way they've surrounded me as we travel. The way they bring me food and watch for traps and basically treat me like my injuries mean I'm one slippery step away from being an invalid.

I'd argue that I had these same injuries when I escaped Rowansmark's dungeon, hiked through a sewer pipe and a swamp, and then traveled north of the city and climbed a tree, all while starving, but the reality is that it's nice to feel loved after weeks of being reviled and abused.

"The device could send an inverse signal," I say.

"The Commander has the device."

I blink at the bitter anger in his words, though I know it isn't directed at me. "Okay, then you can build something."

He gives me a tense, lopsided little smile. "While I love the faith you have in my abilities, the truth is that it would take days to put together a piece of tech capable of sending an inverse signal powerful enough to nullify what the summoners must be able to do. And that's *if* I had the right supplies, and *if* I wasn't also breaking into Rowansmark."

I frown as I skirt a thorny bush. The sun is a faint blush in the early morning sky, and the path through the Wasteland is cloaked in grays and purples. I reach out and run my fingers down the cold length of Melkin's staff, strapped securely to the back of Logan's travel pack. Near the top, a small section of the metal slides open—a battery compartment, I assume. The compartment is open by just a fraction, and a thin bundle of copper wires stretches from the opening and into Logan's pack.

It's the modification he spent the last few weeks working on so that he could do what he promised me—make a weapon capable of destroying the Commander.

So that I could finally close my eyes and dream of something other than blood.

"What about using Melkin's staff?" I ask as we pass the grove of ancient, twisted walnut trees I stopped at on my way north less than two days ago.

"The staff can only send an infrasonic signal."

"Which means what?"

"Which means it can only send the same type of signal that the summoners send. It would call the *tanniyn*, but instead of one sonic pulse, it uses the transmitters I stole from Hodenswald to emit a constant, unremitting infrasonic signal with an amplified strength capable of reaching a minimum five-hundred-yard radius." He wraps his hand around mine as we leave the walnut grove behind and approach the swamp. The sharp, fetid fumes lie heavy in the air and sting my eyes as we come closer. "I'm sorry, Rachel, but I don't know how to stop the summoners. We're going to have to stop James Rowan instead."

I think over his words as we reach the edge of the swamp and stare at the wide mouth of the pipe resting to the west of us.

"Fine. But we need a backup plan in case something goes wrong." I look at Logan. "You're usually the one with the multiple backup plans. What've you got?"

He slowly shakes his head. "If we can't stop James in time and he activates the summoners to call the *tanniyn* outside the city's wall, then we're out of options. The beasts will destroy the Commander's army."

"Unless we use the staff." I meet his eyes. "Maybe we can't nullify the summoners, but we can outdo them. If James triggers the tech before we can stop him, we can use the staff. A sustained, powerful infrasonic signal might draw all the *tanniyn* inside of Rowansmark instead of outside the wall. You said yourself that you'd put a plan in place with the armada's captain to evacuate the city and then flood it once you used the staff, right?"

"Only after the battle outside of the city was won. After the Commander came through the gate." He turns to me as the rest of our friends line up on either side of us and consider the distance between the sandy shore of the swamp and the mouth of the pipe.

"I built this weapon to take out the Commander."

"I know, but this is important, too."

His blue eyes bore into mine. "Rachel, this is a one-time-use weapon. We have to drive it into the ground and then run, because the *tanniyn*—every single one of them living anywhere near Rowansmark—will come bursting through the ground where the staff is located. If one of the monsters doesn't crush the staff, it will fall down into the depths of the earth. If we use this inside Rowansmark, there is nothing left to go after the Commander with except our swords, and he's surrounded by an army of soldiers ready to protect their leader. If we do this, you may be giving up your chance to get revenge."

I meet his gaze and swallow hard as the memory of the Commander's ruthless expression while he stabbed Oliver to death in front of me fills my mind. Reaching up, I run my fingers over the leather pouch I wear around my neck. The one with dirt from my father's grave and ashes from my childhood home. The one that commemorates everything I've lost because of the Commander.

Finally, I say, "Revenge won't help me. We'll find another way to bring him to justice. I want him dead, but I want to save the lives of the soldiers in his army more. Let's go."

Logan smiles, a breathtakingly beautiful smile that warms his eyes and sends a frisson of pleasure across my skin. He leans close. "I love you, you know."

I grin. "I know. Now, let's go wade through this mess and get inside the city before we're too late."

It doesn't take long to hike up our cloaks and wade through the swamp. Willow and Adam make snarky remarks about knowing all of Rowansmark's dirty little secrets. Nola and Smithson endure the stench quietly, as do Logan and I. But Frankie takes three steps into the thick, murky liquid and starts gagging like he's about to revisit every single thing he's eaten in the last decade.

"You okay, Frankie?" I ask.

He nods brusquely. "I'm"—*gag*—"fine." He bends at the waist and heaves, splattering the swamp with partially digested thistle stems swirling in a sea of purple blackberry juice.

"It gets better inside the pipe." I hope. The pipe was rinsed at sunset. How many people could've emptied their chamber pots already this morning?

Frankie curses and then vomits again.

"Need some help?" Logan asks.

"Worst thing"—*gag*—"I've ever"—*heave*—"smelled." He curses and gags and coughs until he's doubled over at the waist again.

"I wouldn't lean so close to the smell, if I were you," Willow calls from the mouth of the pipe, where she and Adam are already waiting. "Especially now that you get to smell both poop and puke."

Frankie promptly vomits again and then glares at Willow like it's her fault. She laughs, but it doesn't sound unkind.

"Come on, old man," she says. "Plug your nose and get over here before I have to go out and fetch you. You know I'd never let you live that down."

He obeys, hiking his cloak even higher, burying his nose in the heavy cloth, and then stumbling his way to the pipe just ahead of the rest of us. Willow helps him climb in, and then asks him if he wants some more blackberries.

He gags again, and glares at all of us. "Never speak of this to anyone. Do you hear me? Never."

Willow grins, but there's a tightness around her eyes, a stiffness in her shoulders, that says the fear of what we'll find when we get inside Rowansmark and look for Quinn is wearing on her.

"Let's go," I say, and we start the long, slippery trek through the bowels of the Wasteland and into the heart of the city.

This time, I'm not starving, and my back is a dull ache instead of sharp pains. I'm able to keep up with the group, though I suspect they're moving slower than they normally would simply to allow me the dignity of not having to ask them to wait for me.

I can tell when we reach the city limits because smaller pipes branch away from the main pipe, and the contents of chamber pots rest in sloppy, stinking piles beneath some of those openings.

Frankie curses again and wraps his cloak around most of his face.

"How far in do we need to go?" Willow asks, her voice a tangle of hope and fear.

"We need to get as close to James Rowan as possible," Logan says. "We should surface near the square, and then we can split up. Half of us can look for Quinn while the other half go after James."

It takes us another thirty minutes to reach what I estimate to be a building close to the square. Frankie lifts Willow into the smaller pipe above us. The rest of us follow her lead, and then Smithson reaches back to help Frankie crawl into the pipe as well. Bracing our arms and legs against the slick metal, we slowly work our way out of the pipe and into what looks to be the hall of an office building.

To the right is a corridor filled with doors. To the left, a window vibrates with the sound of a crowd chanting. Willow hurries toward the window and wrenches it open, letting in the fresh morning air and the deafening bellow of hundreds of Rowansmark citizens screaming in unison, *"Punish him! Punish him!"*

Willow makes a small, agonized sound and reaches for her bow. I rush to her side and look across the throng that fills the square to see James Rowan standing on the pain atonement stage, whip in hand, while beside him, stripped to the waist and chained to a post, is a boy with golden skin and dark hair.

Quinn.

CHAPTER FORTY-SIX

LOGAN

"Quinn!" Rachel calls, but he can't hear her.

The crowd chants, *"Punish him! Punish him!"* They sound excited. Hungry to see Quinn bleed. It makes me sick.

"I can't shoot the people holding him captive. It's too far." Willow looks at me, her eyes wild. "We have to rescue him."

"Find the door!" I yell, and we race through the building's basement.

The door is at the far end of the northern corridor. We sprint forward and burst onto the porch. People are pressed against the wrought-iron fence that encloses the building's tiny yard, staring at the stage where a short, older man with olive skin and a crisp military jacket is unfurling a whip to the wild delight of the crowd.

"Move. *Move!*" Willow shoves past people, spilling their drinks and causing panic as they take in our swampy clothes, our weapons, and the furious determination on our faces.

She reaches the edge of the yard, grabs the fence, and vaults over. The rest of us immediately follow suit. The crowds on the other side of the fence are worse. Densely packed. Cheering and screaming. Making it nearly impossible for us to move toward the stage.

The sharp crack of a whip fills the air. Willow starts shaking as she shoves another person aside only to find three more blocking the path. I crane my neck to look at the stage and see Quinn's back, still unmarked. The man with the whip cracks it again, close to Quinn without actually touching him, and the crowd screams, *"Punish him! Punish him!"*

"He's not hurt yet," I say because Willow looks like she's about to start shooting arrows at everyone between her and the stage. "We can still make it."

"But he will be," Rachel says. Her voice trembles with anger and fear. "The man with the whip is James Rowan."

My heart speeds up even as time seems to slow down. "That's the man who had you whipped?" Who ordered my father's pain atonement. Who sent Ian to destroy us.

"Yes. Come on. We'd better hurry." Rachel elbows her way to Willow's side, and together they push and shove through the crowd.

"Punish him!"

I try sliding around a large man with a fistful of fried bread, but he blocks me.

"Get out of my way," I snap.

The whip cracks.

The crowd closes in, a throng of frantic revelers smelling of sweat and sugar.

"Punish him!"

I lower my shoulder and ram the man out of my path. Pushing past him, I find that Willow and Rachel have only moved forward another few yards. The crowd is impossible. Behind me, Frankie, Smithson, Nola, and Adam have been swallowed up by the heaving, chanting sea of people.

Lunging forward, I grab Rachel and Willow. "Move to the side." I nod toward the very edge of the town square, the strip of sidewalk shaded by the buildings on that side of the street. The crowd is thinner there.

Together, we claw and shove our way toward the side while around us people scream in our ears, throw fried sugared bread in their mouths, and then scream some more.

Just as we reach the far sidewalk, the whip cracks again, followed by a sharp whistle. The crowd quiets almost immediately, and we hold ourselves motionless. To move toward the stage while everyone else is standing still would be to invite instant death from the solid wall of trackers who line the front of the square.

"People of Rowansmark!" James Rowan's voice echoes across the crowd. "Today is the day we display our true power. Our true honor. Today is the day we defeat our enemies once and for all! We have caught the criminal responsible for burning our government facilities." He points to Quinn.

"Punish him! Punish him!" The crowd screams for his blood.

"You aren't going to reach him in time." A familiar voice speaks quietly behind us.

I spin on my heel and come face-to-face with Ian. His eyes are shadowed, his expression grim.

"Punish him!"

I grab my sword hilt, and Rachel asks, "Where's Marcus?"

"Inside." Ian nods toward a rooftop just visible beyond the edge of the square.

"Punish him!"

"They won't let you up on the stage, Logan. They'll kill you—all of you—before you come within fifteen yards of Quinn. You can't get to him."

"I'm not wasting my time with this lunatic," Willow snaps. "You deal with him, Logan. I'm going after my brother." She takes a step toward the stage, and Rachel grabs her arm.

"He's right. Look at this crowd. Rowan won't even have to ask his trackers to lift a finger. We'll be crushed by a glut of people who came determined to see blood today, and it would give Rowan an excuse to kill Quinn."

"Punish him!"

James Rowan's voice fills the square. "We will punish the criminal as is just. But he is not the only enemy that must be dealt with. Today, Commander Chase's army marches against us, hoping to steal our technology and take over our city. Hoping to dishonor us."

The seething mass of people boo and jeer. I lock eyes with Ian and pull my sword from my sheath, the memory of all the people we lost across the Wasteland a lightning rod to the anger burning within me.

"It's like I was meant to find you today," Ian says quietly. The cocky confidence is gone from his voice. Weariness and resignation have taken its place.

Willow's voice is desperate. "If you think I'm just going to stand here and watch that man whip my brother—"

Ian turns on her. "You can't save him. You'll be instantly identified as an outsider come to rescue him, and you'll be killed. Only someone from Rowansmark could get close enough." He looks at Rachel. "Tell Marcus I became the son he thinks he has."

"What are you doing?" Rachel's voice is sharp.

"I was lied to, and I did things . . ." Ian looks at the stage and then back at me. "Take care of Dad. Promise me."

I don't even know how to answer him.

"Promise me!" His voice shakes.

"I promise," I say. My sword is heavy in my hand as I raise it. "But I also promised I would deliver justice for the people you killed."

"You won't have to." Ian squares his shoulders and pivots toward the stage. "I'll do that myself."

CHAPTER FORTY-SEVEN

LOGAN

As Ian stalks toward the stage, James Rowan says. "We will *not* be taken. We will *not* be dishonored. Our enemies have met their match." His voice rises. "We will teach them a lesson they will not soon forget. Starting with this criminal. Judge and be judged!"

"Judge and be judged!" The crowd takes up the chant, swelling in volume until I can feel their words in my bones. *"Judge and be judged!"*

The whip cracks, and the crowd screams in glee as a bloody welt rises on Quinn's back. Quinn's face is stoic, but his lips are pressed tight, his fists clenched against the pain.

"Logan! Let's go!" Willow grabs my arm, and together with Rachel, we edge our way closer to the stage, keeping to the fringes of the seething mass of people. Behind us, Frankie bellows at someone to remove themselves from his path or be ground to dust beneath his boots, and in seconds, the rest of our people have caught up to us.

We're still too far from the stage to get to Quinn, though. Pushing and ramming, we manage to move forward another ten yards before becoming stuck behind a wall of people who look like they've been drinking ale since sunrise.

Flashing the tracker insignia on the front of his cloak, Ian parts the crowd like water. The whip snaps again, and another bloody wound opens across Quinn's back as Ian vaults onto the stage.

James Rowan frowns. "What are you doing up here?"

"What I should've done the last time I was here. Stopping you."

Ian draws his sword. Instantly, the soldiers who surround the stage grab their weapons and surge toward him. He has seconds to either run, fight them off, or kill James Rowan.

I grip my own sword with bloodless fingers as Ian raises his weapon while the soldiers rush forward. His eyes meet mine for a moment, and then he turns and slices his weapon through the ropes that bind Quinn to the whipping post.

Quinn rolls away from the post and comes up in a crouch. The soldiers converge on Ian, their swords slashing. He doesn't try to defend himself. He simply drops his weapon and holds my gaze while they drive their blades into him. Pain flashes across his face, but in seconds it's replaced by peace. He opens his mouth to say something, but chokes instead, blood leaking from his lips while his knees give out and his body crumples to the stage.

My heart slams against my chest, and my throat tightens. Unexpected grief mixes with my anger until I can't tell the difference. I want to rush the stage and pull the soldiers away from

Ian. So I can scream the truth about the pain he caused. So I can hurt the man who turned my brother into a monster. So I can tell Ian I wish I could go back in time and save us both from all of this.

Tears sting my eyes, and I can't tell if I'm mourning the boy who would've been my brother if life had dealt us a different hand, or the boy who gave his life for us because he understood he'd made the wrong choices and that justice requires sacrifice.

When the soldiers step back, Ian lies bloody and unmoving, his eyes staring up at the sky. Seconds later, he explodes, and there's nothing left of him. I swallow hard and look away from the bloody mist that coats the stage.

The crowd panics, shoving one another to get away from the stage and the terrifying sight of a tracker standing up to their beloved leader. Quinn, free of his ropes, is caught between James Rowan's whip and the trackers who just killed Ian.

Using the panicked crowd to our advantage, we let Frankie bulldoze his way through to the stage. Willow leaps onto the platform and dashes toward Quinn. "Run!" she screams at him as the trackers turn toward them.

The rest of us vault onto the stage, draw our weapons, and scramble to get between Quinn and the trackers' weapons. On the city wall behind us, someone blows a long, low note from a horn, and soldiers begin running toward the gate or climbing ladders up to the cannons along the wall.

James Rowan locks eyes with me and smiles like he just found gold.

He whistles again while the trumpeter on the wall plays another long, low note. The crowd obediently falls into an uneasy quiet, and in the wake of their screaming panic, the unmistakable sound of hundreds of boots marching toward the city filters over the wall.

The Commander is here. Rowansmark is under attack.

"My people, the traitors sent against us are already in our midst. Evacuate now."

The people scatter, racing into buildings, climbing ladders, moving quickly but without the panic they displayed before. They've clearly been drilled on what to do in the event of an emergency. A bell begins tolling in the center of the city, warning residents who weren't at the stage.

Ignoring the movement around him, Rowan drops the whip, pulls a small black box with a raised button in the center from his pocket, and raises it high. His gaze finds mine, and his smile turns my stomach.

"Today, we call forth an army that cannot be defeated. Today, we sacrifice our enemies on the altar of justice. Today, we show the world what we are capable of!" he yells as he slams his finger down onto the button.

CHAPTER FORTY-EIGHT

RACHEL

A deep *boom* shakes the ground around the city's wall and rattles all of the buildings.

"He used the summoners," I say as the trackers onstage close ranks and lunge toward us. "The *tanniyn* are coming. He's going to destroy the army."

Seconds after the boom dissipates, the ground outside the wall sounds like it's shaking. The *tanniyn* are going to surface outside the wall and crush all of the innocent soldiers who got caught up in this war because they obeyed orders from their leaders. Leaders who simply want to stop James Rowan and destroy the tech that would enslave them all.

I look at Logan as Adam, Smithson, and Willow meet the first wave of trackers, swords clashing. "We have to use the staff."

Before he can answer me, a tracker slams into him. Logan barely keeps his footing and parries the blow in the nick of time. All around me, my friends are battling for their lives. The only reason I'm not yet fighting a tracker is because I'm in the center of the stage, and none of them can reach me yet.

Outside the wall, a rumble grows. We don't have much time left before the *tanniyn* destroy the army, and with it, our chance to break Rowansmark's seat of power.

Making my decision in a heartbeat, I lunge toward Logan, grab the staff, and wrestle it free of its ties while Logan fights.

"Rachel, I've got it," he says, but he doesn't have it. He's got his hands full defending himself against a tracker. So does everyone else. The only one who can call the *tanniyn* to surface inside the city is me.

Finally, the right thing to do is in front of me, and I don't have to think twice. Pivoting to put Frankie's bulk between me and the trackers, I race along the back of the stage and leap to the cobblestones below.

"Not so fast." James Rowan coils the whip that is once again in his hand and snaps it toward me.

I flinch, but suddenly Quinn is there, letting the leather tip hit him so that he can grab it, wrap it twice around his forearm, and yank the whip out of Rowan's grasp.

"Good to have you back," I say. "I was getting really tired of constantly saving myself."

Quinn laughs, but then he grasps the handle of the whip and gives Rowan a look that should fill the man with terror.

"Stay away from her. From all of us." Quinn's voice is coldly furious.

Rowan laughs. "Or what?"

"I'll stop you." The absolute certainty in Quinn's voice raises the hair on my neck as I hurry toward the edge of the square, where Rowan's gracious lawn meets the cobblestone pavement.

The ground quivers, and outside the wall, screams are rising as a few of the beasts surface.

I certainly hope there's more where those came from.

Across the square, Logan drives his sword into the tracker he's fighting, and turns to help Smithson and Nola. His eyes find mine, and for a second, there's only the two of us, but then I turn away, raise the staff, and drive it into the ground.

CHAPTER FORTY-NINE

RACHEL

This time, the boom doesn't stop. It's a rolling wave of deafening thunder that pulses from the staff every few seconds. The ground shudders and twists, throwing me to my knees as cracks split the grass and race through the cobblestones like snakes.

"No!" James Rowan screams and runs toward me. "What have you done?"

I push myself to my feet as Quinn leaps in front of Rowan to stop him from reaching me.

"What I had to do."

Rowan's voice shakes with rage. "You stupid girl. You've ruined us!"

The ground heaves, throwing all three of us onto our stomachs. I land on a crack that splits with a rending noise like the earth is tearing itself apart.

"Move!" Quinn shouts, dropping the whip so that he can crawl toward me. The dirt writhes, tossing him away from me and into Rowan.

The older man attacks, swinging his fists at Quinn's face. Quinn deflects the blows with cold precision, his entire focus on the crack that is widening beneath me in quick jerks.

"Hold on," he yells. As if I'd planned to let go.

I dig my hands into the ever-shifting ground and try to push myself away from the crack before it swallows me. Grabbing on to one side of the split, I hang on as it shudders and belches damp, loamy air tinged with the acrid stench of smoke.

I have to *move*. Roll to the side. Do something before the *tanniyn* surface and either slice me to shreds with their razor-sharp talons or burn me to a crisp.

Shoving my boots against the crumbling cobblestones behind me, I scramble frantically for leverage, but the ground crumbles beneath me. The cobblestones turn to dust. The grass buckles and shudders like a living thing.

Rowan is screaming, but I can't make out the words. I think Quinn is yelling at me too, but all I hear is the terrifying roar of the *tanniyn* barreling toward the surface directly below me.

CHAPTER FIFTY

LOGAN

Another tracker slams into me, and I struggle to keep my footing on the stage as his sword nicks my side. Ignoring the blood and the pain, I shout, "The *tanniyn* are surfacing inside the city. Stop fighting and get out!"

The tracker jerks his head toward the square and curses. I shove him out of my way, and then my blood seems to freeze as I take in the scene before me.

James Rowan crawling toward Quinn, the whip in his hands. Quinn stumbling toward Rachel and falling to his knees every few seconds as the ground gives way beneath him.

And Rachel fighting to pull back from the edge of a break that widens faster than she can move.

"Rachel!" I scream even though she can't hear me, and leap from the stage.

Adam and Willow streak past me, heading for the clock tower to give Captain Burkes the signal. I want to call them back. Tell them to wait. Tell them they can't flood the city while our people are on the ground, but I can't. We have to destroy Rowansmark's power and the *tanniyn* along with it.

I'll just have to reach Quinn and Rachel in time.

I race across the cracked cobblestones toward the wide expanse of green that leads up to the mansion and pass James Rowan first. He's got the whip and is on his feet, but I don't stop. Not when Rachel is holding on by her fingertips and Quinn is in danger of falling into one of the cracks every time he reaches for her.

"What have you done? What have you done?" Rowan screams at my back as the ground caves in around me.

The dirt beneath me disappears, and I slam my palms onto the edge of a crack in the cobblestones. Digging my fingers in, I fight for purchase while below me *tanniyn* bellow in fury.

From the corner of my eye, I see Rowan pull himself onto the grass above the cracks and hurry across solid ground toward Quinn and Rachel. Digging my elbows into the ground, I scramble onto the cobblestones. My boots slip as I try to push away from the crack.

"Got you." Smithson grabs a fistful of my cloak and hauls me to my feet while behind me, one of the beasts explodes out of the ground.

CHAPTER FIFTY-ONE

LOGAN

The *tanniyn* spew out of the ground like a nest of monstrous vipers. They writhe, digging clawed limbs into one another as they fight for purchase while more just keep coming. Everywhere I look I see sightless, milky-white eyes, puffs of gray smoke pouring from snouts, and sharp yellow talons crushing the cobblestones.

Smithson and I run toward the grass. Heat blazes along our backs as the beasts roar and strafe the square with fire. Flames rush across the stone, leaving scorch marks and smoke.

I've lost sight of Quinn and James Rowan. I've lost sight of Frankie and Nola.

I've lost sight of Rachel.

Desperation pounds through me, clouding my thoughts with panic, as the *tanniyn* whip their tails, smashing the cobblestones and flinging debris that slices into us as we race for safety. One beast slams into a gracious, two-story brick building, and the upper balcony rips free of its moorings and crashes to the ground.

Fire licks at the building's porch, and in seconds, the flames are racing inside to consume everything in their path.

At the far end of the square, the clock tower bursts into flame, and my heart feels like it's hammering against my throat. Adam and Willow have set the signal.

In moments, Captain Burkes will open all of the floodgates on the dam, drowning the *tanniyn* and anyone else on the ground.

A beast spews fire, sending a streak of flames shooting across our path. Throwing my arm up over my face, I drop to the ground to crawl beneath the heat. Smithson hits the cobblestones beside me, and I slap at his cloak to extinguish an errant flame.

"I'm going after Rachel and Quinn," I say as we drag ourselves onto the grass. "Find Nola and Frankie."

He nods, and I claw my way up the grass hillside until I'm free of the cracks and can see the square in its entirety. What I see dries the spit in my mouth.

The beasts have ripped a massive hole into the northern side of the square, starting from where Rachel drove the staff into the ground and spreading to encompass most of the ground beneath a brick building with yellow-and-white bunting fluttering from its balcony. The building tips precariously to the left, dangling over the hole as if a slight breeze would send it sliding down that dark shaft until it was swallowed up by the center of the earth.

Rachel, Quinn, and James Rowan are trapped on the building's porch, surrounded by a writhing, fire-spewing mass of *tanniyn*.

CHAPTER FIFTY-TWO

RACHEL

There's nowhere to hide. I heave quick pants of the smoky air and try to hold myself steady even though the terror blazing through me makes it impossible to stop shaking.

I'm trapped. Stuck with Quinn and Rowan on the porch of a building close to where I called the *tanniyn*. To the left, a huge hole threatens to swallow the house and us with it. Metal shrieks and wood snaps as the building slowly tips toward its side. To the right, a long crack is splitting the cobblestones, widening with every passing second. Below us, the porch shudders as if straining against the bonds that hold it to the house. We have to get away from here before the house comes apart at the seams, but we can't. The *tanniyn* are *everywhere*.

Wherever I look, I see huge black bodies, streams of fire, and white eyes daring me to make a sound so that they can find me. I press my back against the wall behind me and clench my jaw to keep my lips from trembling. I want to think about courage or sacrifice or justice, but my mind is stuck on a single, inescapable thought: *I don't want to die.*

Quinn stands next to me, blood flowing from the cuts on his back and on his face. Beside him, Rowan glares at us with hatred, his whip clutched in his hand. I ignore Rowan and reach for Quinn's hand. He closes his fingers around mine and squeezes. Tears gather in my eyes, and I lift my chin. I don't want to die. I don't want Quinn to die. There has to be a way out of this. I start looking for a miracle.

The staff has long since been swallowed up by one of the cracks in the ground, and we can no longer feel the thunderous pulse of its sonic frequency, but it doesn't seem to matter. The beasts are here, and they aren't going away until they destroy everything.

The creatures roar and lash their tails, sending other beasts crashing into the buildings around them. Iron balconies tear apart, brick crumbles, and decorative pillars tumble to the ground, where they explode into piles of white dust. The noise is unrelenting—a fierce, predatory snarl that shakes the air. But beyond that, another roar is building. A wet, wild rumble of noise that rushes closer with every second.

I grip Quinn's hand tighter.

"What is that? What else have you done?" Rowan yells.

The *tanniyn* closest to us whip their snouts toward Rowan, gray smoke pouring from their nostrils. Quinn pulls me against his side, and we cling to each other as the beasts slither toward us.

I drag in a shaky breath and force myself to *think*.

If the creatures strafe James Rowan with fire, we'll be hit too.

I don't want to die.

There's a jagged seam the width of a wagon to the right of us and the crumbling brick building tipping slowly toward an enormous hole to the left.

I don't want to die.

The floodgates are open. Which will hit us first—the *tanniyn*'s fire or the river's water?

I don't want to die.

Rowan raises his whip like he means to slash it at the *tanniyn*. I spin Quinn toward the wagon-sized crack to the right while behind us, footsteps stomp through the ruined building, coming closer by the second. I don't have time to wonder who it is because in front of us, a trio of the creatures lash their tails, sending a hail of debris onto our heads, and then cough an unending stream of fire straight toward us.

CHAPTER FIFTY-THREE

LOGAN

"Rachel!" I yell her name as the *tanniyn* spew fire at Rachel, Quinn, and Rowan.

Quinn and Rachel dive to the ground and slide down a hole beneath the unsteady building. Frankie shoulders his way through the building's door and throws himself toward the place where I last saw Quinn and Rachel.

James Rowan doesn't move fast enough to evade the *tanniyn*'s fire. It hits him, pushing him against the brick wall behind him. He screams—a wail of terrible anguish—as he is consumed. When the flames die, a charred, smoking heap is all that's left of the man who thought he could control the monsters beneath our feet and use them as weapons.

I sprint toward the building, frantically looking for any sign of Rachel, Frankie, and Quinn, my heart pounding, my mouth dry, but before I can get there, a wall of water as high as two horses stacked on top of each other explodes into the city.

The water rushes through the streets, banking off buildings

and splashing onto the second-floor balconies. I stumble over a crack in the ground and go down hard.

Where are my people? Where is *Rachel*?

Desperately, I get to my feet and run for the leaning brick building as the *tanniyn* shriek and bellow, clawing over one another to get out of the water's way. I skid toward the bottom of the grassy hill and see Nola trapped at the edge of the square, a crack on one side of her and a pile of debris on the other. Smithson is climbing over the debris pile, trying to get to her in time.

I reach the building as the wall of water bursts into the square, sweeping the beasts in front of it. They shriek, and then the water plunges down the holes that opened up to let the *tanniyn* out of their nests.

"Rachel! Quinn!" My breath tears through my chest in sobs as I pull myself onto the porch. Frankie, one hand wrapped around Rachel's wrist and the other around Quinn's while the two dangle over the gaping pit of emptiness that leads down to the *tanniyn's* nests, digs his heels into the ground and heaves himself backward.

Sprinting, I dive over the smoldering remains of James Rowan, slide on my stomach, and then slam my boots into the ground to stop myself. Wrapping my hands around Rachel's arm, I pull her out of the hole while Frankie does the same for Quinn. Then Frankie tosses Quinn at the single remaining stable pillar supporting the building's upper-level balcony and barks, "Hold your breath!"

Rachel and I run for the pillar as well, and drag in a deep breath as the water slams into us. It's like being hit by a stone wall. Rachel spins away from the pillar, caught in the current. I snatch her tunic with one hand and wrap the other around the pillar. The force of the water tears at me, and my grip begins to falter while gallons of water pour over my head until I'm convinced I'll never take another breath.

I try to hold fast to Rachel and to the pillar, but I know I can't keep my grip much longer. I have to make a choice. It's the easiest decision I've ever made. No worst case scenarios. No contingencies or backup plans. Just the one best case scenario that has been the foundation of every decision I've made in the last few months—keep Rachel safe.

Using the last of my strength, I shove Rachel toward the pillar so that she can wrap her arms around it. She latches on, and I try to recover my grip, but it's too late. The vicious strength of the water is my undoing.

CHAPTER FIFTY-FOUR

LOGAN

The water flings me away from Rachel, but then something jerks me to a stop and holds me in place.

I twist my head and see Frankie, his face red with exertion, gripping the back of my tunic with one meaty hand while he hooks the other arm around the pillar.

My lungs are burning, aching for air, as the initial rush of water subsides, sinking into the long underground tunnels made by the *tanniyn* and leaving us to collapse, gasping and choking.

"Thank you," I say to Frankie. My voice is hoarse, my entire body shaking as I gather Rachel into my arms and hold her like I never mean to let go.

Frankie glares at me and then includes Rachel and Quinn as well. He raises one beefy finger and stabs it at us. "Don't you *ever* scare me like that again." His hand trembles. "I'm here to tell you that if I have to fish any of you out of sinkholes or keep your fool selves from drowning again, I will personally beat the sense right out of you. Are we clear?"

Rachel smiles at him. "I love you, too."

He tightens his lips, and his eyes glisten, and then he hauls all three of us into a hug. It's like being squeezed by an enormous bear. "Fool kids going and putting yourselves right smack in the worst possible places every time I turn around."

"Cozy," Willow says as she and Adam approach. Frankie lets go of us, turns on his heel, and drags Willow and Adam against his chest as well. I expect Willow to give him grief, but she tolerates it.

"Where are Nola and Smithson?" Frankie asks after he's done giving Adam and Willow the same lecture he just gave us. I reluctantly let go of Rachel and take stock of our surroundings.

Outside, the sounds of battle are unmistakable. Clashing swords. Shouted orders. The Rowansmark army doesn't realize it's lost its leader.

"Adam, see if you can find something that will work as a white flag and fly it from one of the turrets," I say.

As Adam hurries to do my bidding, I search the square for signs of Nola and Smithson. The river's new path takes it right through the square and down the multiple tunnels created by the *tanniyn*. The current is strong, and the water looks deep. A few of the *tanniyn* still flop around in the water, trying desperately to gouge their claws into the cobblestones and drag themselves out of the water's flow, but it's too strong. Too high. Too powerful, even for them.

I last saw Nola trapped between a pile of debris and a crack in the ground, with Smithson trying desperately to reach her. With Rachel, Frankie, Quinn, and Willow on my heels, I hurry past *tanniyn* corpses and crumbled piles of brick until I reach that spot.

They're gone.

I spin on my heel, a slow circle to survey the entire square, and then I see them. Smithson is lying on his back at the edge of the water's flow, his eyes staring at nothing, while Nola is hunched over his body, sobbing.

"Oh no." Rachel runs past me and flings herself onto the ground beside Smithson. I'm right behind her.

"He saved me," Nola sobs. "He picked me up and threw me onto the grass so I could climb the hill and be safe from the water, but that meant he couldn't get out of the way in time."

Rachel lays her head on Smithson's chest, tears shining on her cheeks, and I swallow hard past the lump of grief in my throat. "He saved me, too. I was about to fall into a crack, and he grabbed me. He was a good friend. I'll miss him."

I want to say more—I *should* say more for the boy who chose to follow me, even after he lost Sylph. For the boy who quietly fought at my side, and who sacrificed himself to save his friends—but I can't speak past the ache of loss. I hope he's with Sylph again. That he's found a measure of peace he couldn't find on this earth.

"I'll help Nola," Frankie says quietly. "Seems to me we have one more enemy who needs to be dealt with." He nods toward the gate, and I realize the sounds of combat have ceased. Up on the wall, Adam is waving a white flag of surrender.

The Commander has won his battle. Now he needs to lose the war.

CHAPTER FIFTY-FIVE

RACHEL

"One last thing to finish," I say, and take Logan's hand.

He pulls me against him, wiping the tears from my cheeks. "One last thing."

Movement catches my eye, and I see Marcus walking with unsteady steps around the edges of the square.

"First, though, there's someone you need to meet," I say. Logan doesn't argue as I pull him with me.

We climb around the glistening, scaly corpses of the *tanniyn* to reach Marcus just as he stops beside the ruins of the stage. He sees me and hurries forward.

"Sons? Mine? Saved?" Worry trembles through his voice.

Maybe it's because the pain of losing Smithson is fresh, maybe it's because for all of the horrible things Ian did, he made the ultimate sacrifice to redeem himself in the end, but tears slip down my face again as I say, "Ian saved us. He sacrificed himself and died a hero. I'm sorry, Marcus."

He raises shaking hands toward his chest.

"But Logan was saved. He's right here." I grab Logan's arm and pull him closer.

Marcus takes three steps toward him and throws his arms around his son.

"Logan." One word, but the joy on his face tells the entire story.

Slowly, Logan raises an arm and awkwardly pats his father's back. Behind me, Willow, Quinn, Nola, and Frankie join us.

"Love you. Love. Always. My son." Marcus leans his face against Logan's and mutters a stream of words that make no sense but somehow still sound like him telling his son how much he was missed.

Logan's arm falls to his side, and Marcus steps back, a shadow of worried hurt on his face.

"Marcus, we have to leave for a bit, but then we can come back for you so that you can spend some time with Logan," I say. "You two just need to get to know each other. You've known about him for his entire life. He's only known about you for a few weeks."

Reluctantly, Marcus moves back, tears shining in his eyes. I look toward Nola and Frankie. "Will you take care of him until we return?"

Nola nods.

"Wait." Logan steps forward and wraps his arms around his father. Marcus hums Julia's song as he holds his son for a long moment. When Logan lets go, Marcus is smiling, though tears are in his eyes. Logan smiles back, and beside me, Frankie sniffs.

"Are you crying?" Willow asks, her voice incredulous.

"Maybe." Frankie glares at her. "And that's another thing we won't be telling anyone."

"Ah, I see. We can't tell people you cry at family reunions and puke when you get a whiff of the sewer. You're really racking up the secrets, old man." She grins at him while Adam climbs down the wall and joins us. Then she looks at me. "You said you have one more thing you need to do. I hope that thing is killing the Commander, because if you don't do it, I will."

I wait for the hatred and anger that fueled me for so long to rush to the surface and claim me at the thought of heading out of the gates to kill the Commander. Instead, I feel nothing but resolve. This needs to be over. Not because it will make me feel better. Not because it will honor my father.

It needs to be over because the Commander can no longer be allowed to hurt others.

"How do you want to do this?" Logan asks. I anchor myself with one arm wrapped around him and one around Quinn while we follow Willow and Adam toward the gate. Frankie stays behind with Nola and Marcus. Quinn holds me for a moment, and then lets me go so that he can walk on his own.

"I figured I'd go up to him and stab him with my knife, but I can only use my left hand, so maybe somebody else should do the honors."

"You don't care if you aren't the one who kills him?" Logan asks, a frown digging in between his brows.

"It doesn't matter who kills him as long as he's dead, and we can move on," I say.

Quinn smiles at me, and I say, "So you burned down some government facilities, huh?"

He gives a one-shouldered shrug. "A few."

"That doesn't sound like you."

"I took a page out of your book this time." His smile widens. "I made sure the buildings were empty so no one would get hurt, but I figured destroying the armory, the barracks, and the labs would weaken Rowansmark and give them something other than Logan's arrival to focus on."

"Thank you for that. And for following Rachel," Logan says. "I'm grateful you were looking out for her."

Quinn smiles a little but says nothing as we reach the city's gate.

"How did you get caught inside Rowansmark? You never get caught," I say.

"I'm not invincible." He sounds slightly offended. "No one is."

"I'm counting on that," I say as we leave the gate and see the Commander, his troops standing at attention behind him, striding toward the entrance to the city. The Rowansmark army—those who survived the *tanniyn*'s arrival—are kneeling on the ground fifty yards away from the city's wall, their hands on their heads in surrender. The ground between the two armies is littered with bodies wearing uniforms from Rowansmark, Lankenshire, Schoensville, Hodenswald, Thorenburg, and Baalboden. No city-state involved in the ground battle survived the conflict without casualties.

Another line of bodies catches my eye, and horror washes over me as I see many of the ranking officers from Rowansmark,

Thorenburg, and Schoensville lying on the ground, their throats slashed.

So much for accepting an honorable surrender. Just one more reason why the Commander can't be allowed to live.

The anger I was waiting to feel blazes to life within me, but it's a steady, determined flame instead of the blistering fire of revenge. The Commander sees us, and his lips peel away from his teeth in a snarl.

I let go of Logan's arm and move to where Willow and Adam are standing, just outside the gate, their bodies blocking the entrance as if they alone can stop the Commander from taking over the city.

"I have something I need to say to him, but then it's going to get bloody," I say. "Cover me, because I can't do this by myself."

Willow inclines her head, and wraps her fingers around her bow.

"We do this together," Logan says as he walks up beside me. "For my mother, and Oliver, and your dad."

I meet his gaze and feel strong and certain for the first time in a very long time. No silence within me taking away the things that hurt me and spewing lies in their wake. No voices whispering that I'm guilty or broken. No burning need to rip the Commander to shreds. Just a resolute purpose driving me forward because I'm not a weapon, I'm a warrior, and the Commander is a threat that must be removed.

"For all of us," I say, and then we move away from the gate and toward the Commander.

"James Rowan is dead." Logan's voice rings with authority as we come to a stop a few yards from the Commander. "Most of the *tanniyn* are too."

A slow, cruel smile spreads across the Commander's face. "And you think that entitles you to claim Rowansmark?"

"No," Logan says. "I don't want the city."

The Commander's scar twitches. "Well then, boy, get out of my way."

"You can't have it, either," I say.

The Commander's laugh is vicious. "Look behind me. I have an entire army at my disposal, and you want to stand there telling me what I can and cannot have?" He steps closer to me. "I can have anything I'm strong enough to take. I thought I taught you that lesson when I killed the baker, but I can see that you need a refresher."

He draws his sword.

Logan does, too.

I pull my knife from its sheath and say, "You aren't strong enough to take me. I choose not to bend to your will. I choose not to break."

"I know how to break girls like you." He flings the words at me.

"And I know how to stop tyrants like you."

His smile is cruel. "Not if I stop you first."

He lunges for me, his sword arcing toward my neck with terrible swiftness.

I whip my arm up to block him just as Logan does the same. We stand, hip to hip, our arms crossed at the wrists as we keep the Commander's weapon arm in the air.

He glares, his scar twitching. I hold his gaze as Willow's arrow streaks past me to bury its tip between the Commander's eyes.

He stiffens, his spine arcing. Slowly, he falls to his knees, his sword spinning away from him, and then he tumbles forward to lie unmoving at my feet.

Several Baalboden guards step toward us, their weapons raised, but a harsh order from a ranking officer in a Hodenswald uniform stops them. We turn our backs on what's left of the Commander and walk away.

CHAPTER FIFTY-SIX

LOGAN

We buried Smithson beneath an oak tree at the eastern edge of the Wasteland. Nola put flowers on his grave, and I found words that I hoped would honor the kind of person he was. The kind of friend he was.

Connor and Jodi left their lookout post in the Wasteland and joined us, and then I sent them with Frankie, Nola, Adam, Willow, and Quinn back to Lankenshire with the armada, promising to join them in a month or two. I sent Marcus with them as well, because he was in no condition to live on his own, and because I can't turn my back on my father.

Oliver would've liked him.

The armada left on a brilliant summer morning, taking the surviving soldiers from the northern city-states with it. A few of the ranking officers have stayed behind to help Rowansmark rebuild and to help them choose a new leader. I spend four days working with them to get a plan in place, and then, satisfied that the worst case scenarios have been addressed, I leave them to the details.

I don't want to make any more decisions. I don't want to make any more plans.

I want quiet. The space to think and invent.

And I want Rachel.

Three hours after sunrise on the sixth day after the battle at Rowansmark, I hoist my travel pack over my shoulder and take Rachel's hand as we walk out of the gate and into the Wasteland.

My heart feels like it could float out of my chest. I'm going to do the one thing I haven't been able to do since all of this started: I'm going to spend time alone with Rachel.

Without looking over our shoulders. Without running for our lives. Without grieving over our latest loss.

Time spent talking. Kissing. Just breathing and belonging to the girl with the fiery hair, the fierce heart, and the smile that makes every logical thought fly out of my head.

The sky becomes a patchwork of blue and gold glimpsed between branches loosely intertwined above us as we leave Rowansmark behind.

"This is new," Rachel says, her smile suddenly shy as she looks at me. "No one chasing us. Nothing we have to do because if we fail, everything will be ruined. It's strange not having an agenda."

"Who says we don't have an agenda?" I wink at her.

She laughs. "Let me guess. You have a list of worst case scenarios we need to go over."

I spin her toward me and wrap my arms around her, pulling her close. "I look at you, and I see nothing but best case scenarios."

She smiles, and I feel like a prince.

"How about this?" Her voice is sly. "Worst Case Scenario: Logan doesn't kiss me right this second. Any idea how to solve that one?"

"I think I can handle that." I lean toward her, but she's still talking.

"Another Worst Case Scenario: Logan stops kissing me before the sun goes down. Now that would be a serious problem, don't you think?"

"Absolutely." I tangle my fingers in her hair and tilt her head back.

Her breath catches, a tiny gasp that makes me desperate for her. "Or maybe—"

"Are you—"

"—you could—"

"—going to keep talking—"

"—just kiss me already."

"Yes." I crush her to me and kiss her like I never need to come up for air. Like everything I ever need is right here in my arms.

She pulls back. "I love you, Logan."

"I love you, too. Always."

And then I kiss her until the sun goes down and the stars prick the sky and all I can hear is the way her heart pounds against mine. Until her breath and mine are tangled up and I can't tell where one of us begins and the other one ends. Until all I feel is the way we love each other.

This is all I want—all I'll ever want—Rachel, and starlight, and peace.

EPILOGUE

<u>RACHEL</u>

I can measure my life in befores and afters.

Before I saw Oliver die or realized that I loved Logan. Before I killed Melkin and became focused on revenge. Before I chose silence inside me instead of feeling the grief that consumed me after I lost my dad.

That girl—a girl without scars, without doubts, and without the ability to see that life isn't always black and white—is barely recognizable to me now.

Now, seven months after the battle at Rowansmark, I live in the afters. After the loss and the betrayal. After the fight to right the wrongs and save those who needed saving. After I let myself feel the grief and the healing.

I'm scarred, inside and out, but I'm also stronger. I've learned how to be a warrior. I've learned that hope rises out of the ashes if I let it.

And I've learned that loving myself and others takes more strength than any sword fight. Especially if the person you're trying to love is a boy stubbornly determined to invent a new steam-operated system of transit that will connect the city-states to one another now that we can safely outfit the trains with a sonic pulse that will keep away any lingering *tanniyn*.

"It's dinnertime," I say as I enter the warehouse and push past the pile of junk—Logan would call it scrap or parts or nectar of the gods—and find him standing inside the framework for a boxcar that is four times the size of a wagon. Blueprints are stacked neatly on a table to the left, and schematics for the track are drawn on the wall to the right.

"I'll be there in a bit," he says without looking at me.

I roll my eyes. "That's what you said about lunch. Five hours ago. And yet . . . here you are."

"I wonder if we need an ultrasonic signal on each individual car or just on the engine?" He gazes into space.

"I wonder if you're ever going to come out of your fancy Lankenshire warehouse and eat the meal I'm pretty sure I didn't burn. Marcus made honey cakes for dessert. Nola and Quinn are going to come over tonight to sit with him so we can have some time alone. Or maybe because they want time alone. Quinn won't tell me anything, of course, but I think he really likes her. So, time alone . . . what do you think we should—"

"I've got it!" He snaps his fingers and looks around wildly before snatching a piece of chalk from the floor and climbing out of the framework so he can draw on the wall. "The trains don't need to carry the signals. We can post them along the tracks themselves."

"I'm going to post *you* along the track if you don't leave this alone for a few hours and come enjoy the sunset with me. We have things to talk about. The triumvirate is going to send me on my first courier mission next week. To Brooksworth. Of course, I have to take Cassidy I-Know-Everything Vaughn with me as my mentor, but still . . . Brooksworth!"

His hand flies across the flat gray wall as he draws yet another schematic, mumbling under his breath the way Marcus does when he's measuring ingredients for a new recipe he's experimenting with.

I guess if dinner and a romantic view of the sunset are going to happen tonight, I'll have to do something drastic.

"Think of it, Rachel!" He pushes chalk-stained fingers through his hair as he gazes at his drawing. "We could visit any city-state in a matter of days. Faster than using horses, because we wouldn't have to stop and—*hey*."

I slide my arms around his waist from behind and run my hand up his chest until I can feel his heartbeat quickening beneath my palm. Standing on tiptoes, I press a kiss beneath his ear.

The chalk falls from his fingers and hits the floor.

"Tell me more," I say softly, my breath feathering against his skin.

"About what?" He sounds dazed.

My smile is smug as I step around to face him. "All the reasons why you can't eat dinner with me and take a walk in the sunset and maybe kiss me for a while."

He wraps his arms around me and hauls me against his chest. "There's nothing keeping me from any of that. Especially the kissing."

"I told you that Quinn and Nola are going to sit with Marcus tonight so we can have hours to ourselves."

He grins. "I think Quinn likes her."

I roll my eyes. "I told you that, too. And then I told you that the triumvirate approved my courier-in-training status, and I get to go to Brooksworth next week with Cassidy. I think they're sending Willow as one of our military escorts, though how she and Cassidy will survive a trip together without killing each other is anybody's guess."

His grin widens. "I'm proud of you."

"Are you sure? Because you said something about tracks. Ultrasonic pulses. Trains—"

"I was a fool." He kisses me and warmth spreads through me, lingering on my skin like sunshine. When he lifts his head, he says, "I love you more than trains, you know."

I laugh. "I know. But you have been pretty distracted since we moved into Lankenshire permanently."

He runs a hand up my neck and into my hair. Tipping my head back, he says, "Let me make that up to you."

His mouth hovers over mine for a moment, and then he's kissing me, and I'm holding on to him, and I don't know where he ends and I begin.

"I love you," he says.

I smile at the boy who thinks I'm beautiful, scars and all. Who fought to find me when I was lost and refused to let me disappear into my silence.

At the boy who is mine to have, to hold, and to keep on his toes.

"I love you, too," I say. "Always."

ACKNOWLEDGMENTS

First and foremost, thank you to Jesus for loving me and giving me hope.

A huge thanks as well to the following people:

To my husband, Clint, for supporting me, picking up the slack while I'm on deadline, and for being my biggest fan. I love you.

To Tyler, Jordan, Zach, and Johanna for understanding when I need to work, for being excited about my books, and for being the most awesome kids in the entire world.

To my parents and my sister for being fans of mine whether I ever write another book or not. And especially to Heather for reading and giving feedback, even if you do keep threatening me with orange Spree.

To my amazing editor, Kristin Rens, whose tireless belief in this trilogy and whose incredible insight have helped make me a better writer. I love doing books with you!

To my agent, Holly Root, for being always in my corner.

To my incredible writer bffs for talking me off ledges, cheering me on, and keeping me sane. M. G. Buehrlen, Jodi Meadows,

Myra McEntire, Rae Carson, Shannon Messenger, and Claire Legrand—you are so cupcake worthy.

To Julie Daly for keeping me organized.

To the outstanding team at Balzer + Bray who do so much to make my books shine. It takes a huge team effort to put a book into the world, and you are simply the best. I appreciate you all!

And finally to my readers, who've come to see me at events, who've emailed me to wail about the ending of *Deception*, and who've read and loved my books. It remains a constant delight to know that you love my characters as much as I do. Thank you for being epic.